THE
LIBERTY
SCARF

THE
LIBERTY
SCARF

Aimie K. Runyan

J'nell Ciesielski

Rachel McMillan

HARPER MUSE

Published by Harper Muse, an imprint of HarperCollins Focus LLC.

This book is a work of fiction. The characters, incidents, and dialogue are drawn from the authors' imagination and are not to be construed as real. Any resemblance to actual events or persons, living or dead, is entirely coincidental.

Any internet addresses (websites, blogs, etc.) in this book are offered as a resource. They are not intended in any way to be or imply an endorsement by HarperCollins Focus LLC, nor does HarperCollins Focus LLC vouch for the content of these sites for the life of this book.

Library of Congress Cataloging-in-Publication Data

Names: Ciesielski, J'nell, author. | Runyan, Aimie K., author. | McMillan, Rachel, author.
Title: The Liberty Scarf / J'nell Ciesielski, Aimie K. Runyan, Rachel McMillan.
Description: [Nashville] : Harper Muse, 2024. | Summary: "In the midst of a seemingly endless war, a scarf connects three women in the cold winter of 1917 . . . "—Provided by publisher.
Identifiers: LCCN 2024029395 (print) | LCCN 2024029396 (ebook) | ISBN 9781400244317 (TP) | ISBN 9781400244300 (epub) | ISBN 9781400244324 (audio download)
Subjects: LCGFT: War fiction. | Novels.
Classification: LCC PS3603.I33 L54 2024 (print) | LCC PS3603.I33 (ebook) | DDC 813/.6—dc23/eng/20240628
LC record available at https://lccn.loc.gov/2024029395
LC ebook record available at https://lccn.loc.gov/2024029396

Printed in the United States of America

24 25 26 27 28 LBC 5 4 3 2 1

PART ONE

No minute gone comes back again,
take heed and see ye do nothing in vain.

—from the Liberty of London clock

CHAPTER 1

Iris

London
December 1917

IF THERE WAS ANYTHING IRIS BRAXTON KNEW, IT WAS THE PULSE OF design. Her manager, however, hadn't exhibited the beat of life in the past decade.

"Mr. Fletcher, this is an ugly war we are fighting, but there is still beauty and hope to be found. The world is changing, and Liberty & Co. must adapt with it or else be trampled under the heel of progress."

"Changing." Mr. Fletcher fanned himself as if the very thought might send him into a faint. "I should hope not. When this war concludes, the nation will want security and normality. Values and ideas they are accustomed to seeing and understanding. The last thing we wish to do is upset them with unfamiliarity."

Iris recognized that they were heading for the same disagreement they'd had only last week, so she switched tactics.

"After experiencing nothing but mud and dirty uniforms for the past three years, I'm certain our Tommies will adore nothing more than coming home to slippers and a pipe offered by a pretty wife."

At this wholesome image of domesticity, Mr. Fletcher brightened. "Pretty wives, certainly."

"After so long a separation, women will be looking for ways to attract their husbands' notice, but rationing has made buying new frocks and shoes a frivolous expense. A new scarf, however—well, that can go with any outfit for a fraction of the cost." Encouraged at his nodding, Iris opened the leather portfolio containing her sketches. "A scarf filled with a brighter hope for tomorrow and designed with a famous Liberty print—"

"Not this again." He pinched the thin skin on top of his nose. "Miss Braxton, how many times must we go through this? We sell imported woolen shawls in modest shades of taupe, gray, cream, and black. The few shawls that do have splashes of color strictly follow the Aesthetic palette—"

"Which passed its prime with Queen Victoria," she muttered.

"—And were designed by men. We do not hire female designers."

"Right now, Liberty spends a sizable amount on freelance designers that come in, work a single project, collect their payment, and leave. They know nothing of the brand Mr. Liberty labored to build here, the legacy, the history. By using the talent we have in-house, we can cut costs while encouraging creativity among our own."

"By 'our own,' you mean yourself." Mr. Fletcher stared in a manner meant to intimidate.

A waste of his time, really. She stared back. "Yes."

"Miss Braxton, as I've told you before—"

"I'm a hard worker. I arrive before anyone else and I'm the

last one to leave. My paintings are turned in on time or before. I know every color in the recipe book and have created new additions. I have even found and corrected inconsistencies in the original sketches."

He held up his hand to stave off her list. "No one doubts your skill or work ethic. It is simply company policy."

"Mr. Liberty built his legacy around the exotic, the un-attainable made attainable, and luxury for buyers to surround themselves with, yet the attire presented here is lagging behind and quite frankly outdated from our changing times. What could be more luxurious than for a lady to step out of the drab-brown and tired patterns of her grandmother's generation and slip on a cobalt or cayenne-red silk in a design from this century to welcome home her soldier in celebration?" Iris pulled the first sketch from the leather folder. "As in this one. Fresh, bold lines. Geometric patterns. Daring strokes of color."

His eye didn't so much as twitch toward the sketches. "They must find other ways to celebrate, perhaps by purchasing a sig-nature Liberty oriental vase. Our Japanese folding screens are always popular." Snapping back the cuff of his pressed black sleeve, he checked his watch. "Ah. I see your lunch break is over."

With that, she was dismissed back to the workroom. The familiar scents of turpentine, oil, paper, and paint mixed with the voices of paint girls returning from lunch greeted her as she stepped into the space that had been her life for the past six years. It was a long rectangular room stretching the attic space of the store's Regent Street location. Peaked skylights drew in glorious lighting for sketching and painting while offering sto-len glimpses of heaven.

"Any luck?" Sara, one of the other paint girls and Iris's soon-to-be sister-in-law, settled onto her stool in front of the worktable they shared.

Iris shook her head as she dropped the portfolio on her side of the table and slipped on a paint smock.

Reaching into her skirt pocket, Sara pulled out a roll and tossed it to her. "You need to remember to eat."

"That's why I have you." Iris bit into the roll and chewed, her stomach sighing in gratitude. Yet no amount of baked dough was enough to tamp her frustration. "The world is changing, yet Liberty & Co. wants to stick its head in the sand and sell the same imported rugs and design gowns from last century. The motto has always been bold and daring, yet it's lumbering along like an elephant in a zoo. Still exotic, but a sight the crowds have seen. High time the elephant was set free."

"You move too fast for them. Give them time to catch up." Sara smiled in her kind way. "The company must find its feet again after the recent passing of Mr. Liberty, God rest him, but I hear his nephew and successor, Mr. Ivor Stewart-Liberty, is eager to bring in new ideas."

Iris brushed away crumbs from the unfinished design on her table. Another exhausted art nouveau design of curling vines that an unknown had sketched, and it was now her job to fill in with shades of mind-numbing green. The painted design would then be taken to Merton Abbey for block printing onto fabric used to cover a scroll-legged chair in some aristocrat's posh parlor.

"I don't want to spend the whole of my life painting another's designs," Iris said. "I want to create, to experiment, to capture possibilities. To be a part of these new ideas."

Tying on her smock, Sara pulled out her brushes and paint jars, clumping them into a corner. "A dreamer. That's what you are. A dreamer of beautiful things, which is why you will design me the most brilliant bridal gown that has ever graced a wedding."

"Only if you allow me to use all my cast-off scarf designs. They're of use for nothing else." After polishing off the roll Sara had brought her, Iris set about arranging her work tools one by one. The jars of paint in a straight line from darkest to lightest. Brushes standing vertical to her right. Pot of clean water and smear cloth to her left. An orderly space freed the mind of clutter and ushered in artistry.

Sara swirled her brush in water, loosening the stiff bristles. "How unique I will look twirling in a scarf skirt. The ends fluttering out like butterflies."

"Very bohemian."

"Should I add a chain belt that jingles when I walk? Arthur would never lose me. That man would lose the nose right off his face if it weren't attached. Last week he wrote me that his first sergeant threatened to chain his rifle to his belt because he was forever misplacing it."

"Mother used to threaten the same with his shoes."

They dissolved into giggles, which had the unfortunate outcome of drawing the stern eye of Mrs. Philmore, the floor matron. The woman marched over with flat black shoes smacking the wooden floor and stared them into silence through her small, round spectacles. "You are not paid to chinwag. Do that in your own time." Her glare slipped to the sketches peeking out of Iris's portfolio. "Along with your doodles."

"Yes, Mrs. Philmore," they replied in unison.

Sara made a face behind the woman's back as she marched to another girl who had forgotten to tie her smock strings. "Old toad."

"Her shoes are probably too tight. Cuts off any humor to the brain." Iris carefully slipped her sketches into the leather binder and tucked it under her table. Doodles. Ha! She couldn't wait until the day it was one of her creations being hand-painted in this very workshop with a color palette to banish all thought of dreary gray. Until such a revolutionary day, she would continue dreaming and sketching and refining her argument to Mr. Fletcher that she deserved to help further Liberty's appeal with freshness and a pulse for modernity.

At six o'clock sharp, the dismissal bell rang. Brushes were cleaned and stored next to unused paints while unfinished paintings were left to dry on the worktables. Iris tapped the edge of drying vines. With any luck, soon she might be given a floral design, the new Poppy and Daisy design perhaps. It was still blues and greens, but at least petals helped to break up all those twisting stems.

Donning her wool coat and warm knitted cap in a bright poppy red that was all the rage due to the popular poem "In Flanders Fields," Iris descended the stairs to the ground floor with all the other employees clocking out for the day. She punched out her time card, collected her paycheck, and left with Sara through the store's rear service entry into a back alley. Cold winter air tumbled between the buildings, biting their noses and cheeks. High above the city, the spherical barrage balloons bobbed like round soldiers on guard in hopes of deterring enemy planes from crashing into them or tangling in their wires. Another silent reminder of a war that had breached their once-peaceful shore.

"Nothing sweeter than payday," Sara said as they stepped around to Regent Street, where the Liberty Georgian-style storefront loomed over them in five stories of windows and gray sandstone. During the day, they reflected the sun like mirrors, but night doused them in blackness so as not to attract further attention from the German Gotha bombers. "Where shall we go? The English Ruff? The Black Hare? Their sticky toffee is divine."

Iris strolled by and lingered over the wares on display in the darkened windows, where each department had been allowed to arrange a window as it saw fit. The fabric window with rolls of material draping this way and that. The metalwork window with dozens of clocks, silver spoons, and Tudric tea sets. Interiors and furniture emphasizing Arts and Crafts style. All exquisite in craftsmanship. All the same designs for the past twenty years.

"They really should find a more appealing way to display wares," she said, winding her scarf snug around her neck. "There's a lack of cohesion among the departments."

Sara tugged her arm. "We've punched out. Time to think about anything other than the workplace. I'm starved. And freezing."

"You should eat your lunch next time." Iris quirked an eyebrow at her.

Sara quirked a blonde one right back. "As should you so I don't have to give you mine."

A man stepped out from the front doors and locked them behind him with a shiny brass key. Tall and thick about his middle-aged belly, he was dressed in fine wool with an expensive cut.

Iris's feet stumbled to a halt on the footpath. "Sara, look! It's Mr. Ivor Stewart-Liberty. Where is he going, do you suppose?"

"Likely somewhere too posh for us. I'm in need of the nearest chippie."

Checking his pocket watch, Mr. Stewart-Liberty turned right onto Great Marlborough Street.

Iris's instinct flared to life. "Let's follow him."

"Are you off the crumpet? I'd rather my employer not have me arrested for stalking."

"We're not stalking, merely walking in the same direction." She linked her arm through Sara's so she couldn't escape and walked toward Great Marlborough. "Do you know what it would mean to have him look at my sketches?"

"Correction. We wouldn't be simply arrested but thrown into the asylum for being upstarts thinking above our place in the pecking order."

Once on Great Marlborough, they followed at a discreet pace as he turned left down Argyll Street, where little eateries and pubs welcomed in evening guests on wafts of vinegar and beer.

"No one who achieved anything great did so by orderly pecking. There. He's gone into the Argyll Arms." Holding tight to Sara with one hand and gripping her portfolio in her other, Iris dashed across the street with a light of hope burning hot inside her. "And wouldn't you know? They serve fish and chips."

CHAPTER 2

❧

Rex

THE ARGYLL ARMS SERVED A DELICIOUS FISH AND CHIPS AND AN EVEN better beer, but tonight Captain Rex Conrad kept a clear head and ordered tea for his upcoming meeting with a potential client for his architectural firm of Messrs. Higg & Hill. Rex had been a patron in prewar times of many London pubs, and the Arms was a favorite with its original eighteenth-century mahogany paneling and Victorian booths with etched glass partitions. It was an architect's dream, but tonight he wasn't here to dream. Tonight was for business, which his friends took every opportunity to distract him from while they waited for the client to arrive.

"If you refuse to take the bet, you must spend the entire evening in the barracks polishing our boots while we're kicking up our heels at the Christmas dance. If the girl says no—"

"She won't say no." Rex leaned back in his chair with all the confidence of a man who rarely failed.

His friends, Captains Stan Holloway and Clive Windeatt of His Majesty's army, exchanged a knowing look. "Not even after she discovers you've a bum leg?"

"I can still manage a few turns around the dance floor without my cane." Shrapnel had torn Rex's left leg apart, but it wasn't enough to stop him. Most days.

"If you take the bet and she says no, you still miss the dance and must shine our boots," Stan continued, his one blue eye a stark contrast to the black patch covering his missing one. A souvenir from Ypres.

Clive grinned as he tipped back his pint of beer. "I like my toes nice and shiny, in case you were wondering."

Rex stirred his sugarless tea. Rationing knew where to hit hard. "You two drum up the most absurd bets. Like who could catch the bigger rat in the trenches, or who was willing to eat the last tin of pottage meat that had been sitting on the canteen shelf since the start of the war. At least this latest one won't leave me with indigestion."

"Does that mean you take the bet?" Stan leaned forward, eye shining with mischief.

Rex met it with a twinkling challenge of his own. "When have you known me to turn down the opportunity to charm a pretty girl?"

"Looks have nothing to do with this. You simply must ask the next unattached and unmarried woman who walks through the door to the dance."

"And she must say yes by the end of the night," Clive added.

Rex glanced around the establishment, which was mostly filled with shop workers enjoying their few hours of freedom before punching into the drudgery of work the following morning. They were the only three in uniform and drew quite a few stares from the other patrons, especially the girls in their dark skirts and white blouses fresh from behind the service counters. He inclined his head to the nearest table, setting off a girlish wave of titters.

Turning back to his mates, he nodded. "Done."

The door swung open, kicking Rex's pulse into action. Alas, no lady, but a well-heeled gentleman who was pointed to their table by one of the waiters. The man swerved between tables and stopped in front of them, doffing his hat.

"Good evening," he said. "My name is Ivor Stewart-Liberty. Richard Conrad, I believe?" His eyes flickered to the bars on Rex's collar. "Forgive me. Captain Conrad."

"Rex, please." Rex stood and shook his hand, then offered introductions. "Captains Holloway and Windeatt."

"A pleasure." Mr. Stewart-Liberty shook their hands. He skipped only a fraction of a beat when Clive offered his left, as his right had been blown off by a grenade, then took a seat. "Firstly, I must extend my gratitude for your service to our country. May the war be over before Christmas."

"It'll take a miracle to pull that off in the next two weeks, but cheers to that." Clive raised his pint in salute.

"I trust your tour is going smoothly."

The Wounded Warrior Tour of England. A grand idea thought up by some Parliament leader to showcase the brave Tommies injured in glorious battle for king and country in order to bump contributions to the war effort by touting them about the country. The fact was, the fighting men were exhausted and barely had a leg left to stand on. If reinforcements didn't arrive soon, there was every chance that Britain and her allies might lose the war. With a slew of medals between them and none too grotesquely damaged to scare civilians, Rex and two of his regiment mates were rounded up and shipped back to Blighty for a bit of rest and drum pounding.

"As well as can be expected," Rex said. "Nothing stirs up patriotism or promotes enlistment like parading around the glorious wounded."

"Liberty & Co. is at the military's service. We would like to contribute blankets and of course a generous donation."

"On behalf of His Majesty's forces, we thank you, sir."

"Yes, you see this is where we might be of service to one another." Placing his hat on the table, Mr. Stewart-Liberty leaned forward. The polite gentleman slipped into shrewd businessman. "The world is full of uncertainty, each day more so than the last. I want to bring reassurance to the people of Britain, particularly here in London, as a reminder of our deep roots that can never be broken. Much like her people. My uncle had an affinity for the Tudor style, that most genuinely English period of domestic architecture, and to honor him I should like to redesign our premises behind Regent Street to reflect those half-timbered marvels of the past."

"A splendid idea, sir. Messrs. Higg & Hill would be delighted to assist you in this project."

"That is precisely what they said when they offered me your name."

Ah, there it was. The point to Rex's confusion as to why he was sitting here with a client and not his superiors. "I don't know how my services can be of more help than Mr. Higg or Mr. Hill. I'm merely a junior architect when out of uniform."

"Your uniform is precisely the help I require. That, and you were rising through the ranks to become one of the firm's most brilliant architects before the war."

"A job I gladly look forward to returning to." The day couldn't come soon enough when he could finally trade in his officer's pistol for a pencil and scale ruler and leave the bloody business of war far behind him.

"I would like to ask you to come to my store and take measurements and create initial drafts for this Tudor project." The businessman's eyes lighted on Rex's insignia. "A man in uniform working to help build an English model of assurance and steadfastness is precisely the boost we both need. Customers will want to shop in a store that supports the Tommies and by which a percentage of proceeds will go to help in winning the war effort. A better way to pound the drum than supping with the blue bloods, eh?"

A few months away from the trenches had seemed like heaven to Rex, but night after night paraded out in front of aristocrats, with their glittering jewels and starched bow ties, was its own minefield of polite smiles and stiff dancing when all he really wanted to do was skip the formalities, collect the offered checks for the war effort, and sleep for the next decade. This man was offering him a chance to put his true skills to work. Not the bloody destruction of a rifle, but pencil to paper in lines and angles of creating something good.

Pushing aside his teacup, Rex leaned his forearms on the table. "Let me make certain I understand you, sir. You're hiring me to come to your store and take initial measurements in my uniform as a type of goodwill campaign."

"On behalf of your employers, Messrs. Higg & Hill, yes. Though I hope this will not interfere with your tour dates."

"Our tour consists of several legs between which we return to London for a few days. That should allow me plenty of time to devote to projects not in relation to the tour, which is scheduled for another month and a half."

"Excellent. I've already drawn up the contract for their services. Though this is not a pretentious campaign. These measurements will be the first steps toward a new blueprint for my store."

The door opened on a rush of frosty air. In breezed two women bundled against the cold. The fairer of the two huddled in her coat while the other, taller with dark hair spilling out from beneath a bright red cap, stood straight and cast her gaze about the room. When those dark eyes of directness landed on Rex, they nearly knocked him out of his chair. An unsettling reversal considering it was typically he who sent women's lashes to fluttering and blushes to flaming, yet here he was with every coherent thought stunned straight from his head.

Clive nudged him under the table. Why was he— Oh! The bet. The dance. The first girl through the door. This girl! Rex rubbed a hand over his mouth to smother his grin. This wasn't going to be quite so bad after all.

Her gaze moved on, then snapped back to Rex's table, though this time it settled upon his well-dressed gentleman visitor. The woman's gloved fingers curled around a satchel hanging from her shoulder. Her companion nudged her and pointed to a table where three other ladies sat waving in recognition.

"—So of course the project will need to be kept quiet for now," Mr. Stewart-Liberty continued. "It's not a good image for the store to be spending so much on expansion with a war on, but seeing a soldier involved in the blueprints will perhaps bring encouragement that the end is coming swiftly. Encouragement is precisely what we need to help ring in the Christmas spirit."

The woman and her friend settled at the table with the other ladies as a waiter scuttled over to take their order.

Rex tore his attention away and focused on the important matter at hand. "If my employers are in agreement, then so am I." A task like this could finally move him out of the junior pool.

"Wonderful! You may start tomorrow. Nine o'clock, shall we say?"

"I look forward to it." Rex stood and offered his hand. Mr. Stewart-Liberty shook it, then gathered his things and took the stairs labeled Private to the first floor, where private dining rooms were offered away from the bar crowd.

Having observed the entire exchange with more than simple curiosity, the woman left her table and headed in the direction of the stairs.

"She's getting away," Clive taunted, swirling his beer.

"Wish me luck, lads." Ignoring the throb in his leg that tended to come on at night, Rex moved around his table and cut her off.

She stepped back in surprise but quickly regained her composure. "Pardon me."

"No pardon necessary, miss, but I would be obliged if you'd allow me to buy you a drink." He offered his most dashing smile.

She didn't return it. "Has that line ever worked out?"

"I'm waiting to see."

"You'll be waiting for a while." She moved to go around him.

Not so easily thwarted, he moved with her. "A dance then."

Her dark eyes flickered to his cane. "Sorry, soldier. I don't dance."

"Don't let the cane fool you. Providence was forced to whittle down my abilities in order to give the other fellows a chance to keep up." He widened his smile. The melting one.

"I see a sense of humility has remained intact."

"Unlike most of my leg, you mean?"

Her expression paled to horror. "Oh no! I didn't mean—"

"It's quite all right. Lying in hospital, I decided to seek the humor in my situation rather than let the blue devils take me." He laughed, which had the desired effect of clearing the embarrassment from her lovely face. His doctors had told him that those seeking the silver lining in every situation often fared better than those who didn't, and so he'd taken the challenge to chase the silver at every opportunity. Well, what resembled chasing for a man with a bum leg.

The coolness thawed from her eyes as she adjusted the strap on her shoulder. "I believe you have rather a great deal of cheekiness to beat off any devils that may come to call. They don't stand a chance."

"Ah, but it's not the devils I wish to take a chance with."

"I take it by that suggestive waggle of your brow that you mean me."

"If you play your cards right." He didn't mean to waggle again, but habit was habit.

"Afraid I'm dealt out for the evening, but I'm sure any other lady here would be happy to deal you in for a dance or a drink."

"They're not as pretty as you."

She didn't blush or look away. She held his gaze with a steady one of her own that was more than intriguing. "Is this how it's done now? Dropping all pretense of subtlety?"

"War has a way of clearing the unnecessary from a man's objectives."

"Your objective being . . . ?"

"To get you to say yes and dance with me. And I know, you claim you don't dance, but that's because you haven't danced with me."

"You're persistent, soldier. I'll give you that, but I'm afraid—"

"Iris! Pardon me." Her fair friend, eyes wide in alarm, popped up next to her. "Mr. Stewart-Liberty is leaving."

"What?" Iris spun around as the man of the hour exited the pub. "Drat!" She bolted after him.

Behind Rex, Stan and Clive brayed with laughter. "I'll have my boots lined up for you!"

"Got a fresh can of polish with your name on it, Conrad. Never been used."

Never one to back down to a scratch against his pride, Rex grinned at them. "Merely a warm-up, lads." With a lofty salute in their direction, he hobbled after the girl doing her utmost to slip the hook.

Flurries dashed against his face as he stepped out into the cold night air. He looked up and down the street and spotted her chasing a taxi. She tripped, falling to the footpath as the automobile rounded the corner out of sight. Papers fluttered from her satchel into patches of snow and slush.

He hurried as quickly as his tormenting leg would allow. "Are you all right? Let me help you." He grasped her elbow and pulled her to her feet. His bum leg buckled, but he caught himself as a hiss of pain escaped through his teeth.

Concern lined her face. "Are you quite well, sir?"

He patted his leg. "Just a little souvenir from the Huns. Comes back to bite me after a long day." Out of military habit, he did a quick check for bashes or blood on her. "Are you hurt?"

"No, I—my sketches!" She grabbed at the papers scattered about, clutching them to her chest like precious jewels.

Bending down, he plucked a paper from the slush. Water melted down the pencil strokes and dripped off the corner in gray droplets. The delicate details were ruined, but enough remained of the basic lines for him to note the skill. "Will you be able to salvage these?"

"Perhaps some." Her crestfallen expression told him otherwise.

"They're lovely."

"Thank you. Not that he'll ever see them." She gestured to the corner the taxi had disappeared around.

"Mr. Stewart-Liberty? I didn't take him for an artist."

"He's not. He's the owner of Liberty & Co., though I presume you know that considering you were meeting with him when I arrived at the pub. I work in the paint department coloring designs for printing." She ruffled the pages, but their sogginess stuck them together. "I was hoping to show him a few of my own designs, but it seems my two left feet had other plans. One more reason I would make a terrible dance partner." She tried to smile, but her lips didn't appear to have the heart for it as she stared at her ruined work.

He understood all too well the pain and disappointment of a design gone wrong. Laboring hours night and day over a single project, perfecting each line, ticking each measurement, only to wad it up and toss it into the rubbish bin. Or worse: have his supervisor rip it apart and demand he start over. "Do you have more you can show him at the office?"

"The owner of Liberty & Co. does not simply come to the attic workspaces for tea each afternoon."

"Ah, so you followed him in the off-hours."

"I did not follow . . . Very well, I did, but I had no other choice. My direct superior isn't inclined to bother the important owner with the doodles of a mere paint girl."

"Why is it imperative he see these?" He nodded to the paper in his hand.

A recognizable spark lit her dark eyes. "Because the company needs a breath of fresh air. As does the world. This war has dragged us into misery and gloom, and when it's finally all over, we cannot go back to how we were. We must look to new possibilities. Excitement, color, boldness." The spark sputtered, sending a red glow to her cheeks. "Forgive me. My passion runs away with me sometimes."

"It's good to have things that light a fire within us." That was what he recognized. A kindred passion for the creative.

Creatives weren't given enough credence in a world consumed with rigidity and boxes to check off. "Perhaps I can help you. My company has recently been hired for a project by Mr. Stewart-Liberty, and it would give me great honor to show him your work."

She raised a single eyebrow that glistened with dotted snowflakes. "Your company? Is the war not demanding enough that you require a second occupation?"

"Believe it or not, I did not always wear the uniform. In my former life and one I hope to return to, I was—am—what you might consider a bit of a sketcher as well."

The eyebrow slanted down. "I've been working long enough to know there is no such thing as benevolent favors. What's the catch?"

"A dance with me."

"Right now?"

"Hardly." He laughed and stamped his feet to get the blood moving. "My toes are about to freeze standing out here. One dance with me at the Royal Troops Christmas Auxiliary on Christmas Eve next week at Banqueting House."

She glanced at the warped bundle of papers in her hand, indecision twisting her lips. "One dance?"

"Unless you're completely swept off your feet and keen for a second round."

"I'm confident enough to say that will not happen. Very well, Mr. . . . ?"

"Conrad. Captain Richard Conrad at your service." He offered a salute that looked less than smart with the soggy sketch in his hand.

"Iris Braxton. Very well, Captain Conrad. We have an agreement."

"There you are." The fair friend Iris had arrived with stood in front of the Argyll Arms. Pulling mittens on, she hurried toward them, with each step a deeper frown pulling at her mouth. "What's happened here?"

"In my haste to get Mr. Stewart-Liberty's attention, I slipped. Captain Conrad here was kind enough to come to my aid, though I'm afraid there's little to be done for my sketches." Iris flashed the soggy papers.

"Let's get home and see if we might hang these to dry next to the fire. Maybe a few can be salvaged."

Iris smiled without conviction, then made quick introductions. "Captain Conrad, this is my soon-to-be sister-in-law, Sara Penrod. Another paint girl."

"A pleasure to meet you, Miss Penrod." Instead of another failed salute, Rex offered a small bow. "Miss Braxton, I'll see you soon. Hopefully with a sketch to present."

"Might I take that one from you? Add it to my rubbish collection." Iris pointed to the sketch in his hand.

Reluctant to relinquish it, he held it close. "I'd like to keep it if you don't mind."

"It's ruined."

"A bit of blotting and it'll be a fine memento of our meeting." Whipping out his handkerchief, he pressed the wet sketch between the folds. It required more than a simple blotting, but he wasn't allowing this token out of his grasp for all the dances in the world. "Ladies, before we all freeze out here, I bid you a pleasant evening and look forward to our next meeting."

They said good night and walked away. Iris cast skeptical glances over her shoulder before offering a small smile as they turned off the street back to Regent. He opened the handkerchief, peering through the smeared pencil to her signature in the bottom corner. Iris Braxton. A smile tugged his lips. He wasn't going to have to polish boots after all.

CHAPTER 3

～

Iris

FERNS FOR NEW GROWTH. NO, TOO ART NOUVEAU. GEOMETRIC. TOO rigid. Teapots and Buckingham Palace. Too on the nose. Iris mentally sketched each design and then tossed it. Nothing that came to mind was the design she sought. The design that would astonish Mr. Stewart-Liberty into hiring her as the first female designer and bring a smile to the war-weary world's face.

"Are you listening?" Sara's paintbrush waved in front of Iris's face. "You're doing it again."

Iris snapped out of her reverie. Paint dripped from her own brush, creating splotches on the worktable. "I'm sorry. What were you saying?" She grabbed a towel and wiped up the paint mess.

Sara sighed and pointed at the clock at the far end of the room, where it ticked over the dozens of heads bent silently over their work. "It's after noon and you've barely grunted at me all morning. You've got that far-off and deep-within look, which means there's a pencil whirling in your brain. Have you come up with a new design to show Mr. Stewart-Liberty?"

"Everything I come up with is passé, overdone, boring, and

bland. Last night I dreamed of a silk scarf with multicolored sheep that came alive to eat octagon-shaped hedges. Livestock and geometry. That's where my inspiration has spiraled to." Iris tossed the dirty towel into the used bin behind her stool.

"Perhaps you should spend more time with that captain fellow. He's handsome enough for inspiration."

"Handsome?" That came out louder than Iris intended. She busied herself by straightening her paint pots and lowered her voice. "I hadn't noticed."

"Likely not, as you were too busy crying over your sketches, which I don't blame you for in the least, but let me reassure you that the gentleman was indeed handsome. And he went after you in the cold without a coat on." Sara smugly smiled as if that settled the man's suitability. She always was the romantic one with her Jane Austen–esque ideals of courtship. It was a miracle Arthur managed to stand a chance, preferring fishing to cotillions, and *Punch* magazine to poetry.

"How many gentlemen would offer to take your sketch to Mr. Stewart-Liberty? None, I'd wager. So kind of him to offer." Sara swirled her brush in the jar of water to clean blue paint from the bristles. "What surprises me more is that you agreed. You, the island of independence."

It was true. Iris came from a long line of people doing things on one's own through hard work and perseverance. Yet none of those qualities were beneficial in a situation like this. Quite honestly, she needed help getting her sketches seen, and her stubborn pride on the matter did not fall into the helpful category. So she had done something completely at odds with her character. She had swallowed her reflex refusal and buried it beneath gratitude.

Sara continued, too preoccupied to ramble on about Iris's self-imposed isolation. "Though I do wonder at his generosity to a complete stranger, considering his own work agreement with the store."

Iris had told Sara all about her conversation with Captain Conrad from the previous evening. All except one thing. "It wasn't entirely selfless generosity."

Sara stopped swirling and leaned forward, eyes wide in anticipation.

"I agreed to dance with him at the Royal Troops Christmas Auxiliary on Christmas Eve." Iris cringed.

Sara squealed. All eyes swiveled their way, including Mrs. Philmore's. Sara tapped her chest as if it had been a cough. "Pardon me."

"It's a business transaction. Nothing more."

"With dancing shoes."

"I tried to explain it was a rather poor deal considering I don't dance, but the man was incorrigible."

As was Sara. "Excellent. Just the sort of chap you need. One to break you out of your comforts and spend an evening with something more exhilarating than a sketchbook and a set of charcoals."

Giving up all pretense of working, Iris set aside her brush. "If I want to be taken seriously in this profession, I cannot spend my time at frivolous parties or worrying about the most fashionable way to style my hair." Without thought, she reached for a pencil and added curlicues to the sketch in front of her. Another designer's sketch, never her own. "Sometimes I wonder . . . if I really have what it takes. Do I stand a chance, or am I setting myself up as a fool?"

"'A person seeking their dream can never be a fool.'"

"Do not quote your grandmother's stitched pillow to me."

"I love that pillow and I've spotted you snuggled up with it a time or two."

"It's soft," Iris mumbled, shading in her additions.

"This war cannot last forever. A brave new world is coming, and when it does, you're the woman to meet it head on. Talent like yours will not go to waste. When opportunity finally comes to call, be ready to welcome it in with all the Braxton confidence that can charm a square into a circle."

"No geometry, please. I half expect a sheep to spring out of nowhere and start munching." Was it her or were the curlicues starting to resemble ram horns?

"I know what we should do! Tonight after work we'll visit Carnaby Street. I hear they have the most delightful Christmas window displays." Sara's brow puckered. "A shame they won't be lit thanks to those pesky German bombers, but perhaps something will catch your eye, and Bob's your uncle, no more sheep dreams."

"Miss Braxton." Mrs. Philmore marched between the work-tables and stopped at theirs. "As you seem incapable of performing your tasks for today, you can be our runner since Bernard has taken ill. Take the outgoing paintings to Merton Abbey. They must arrive before three o'clock this afternoon, so no dilly-dallying."

"Yes, Mrs. Philmore." Iris hid her smile beneath a quick bob of the head.

Liberty Print Works located in Merton Abbey had been the center of printing and dyeing of fabrics by hand for centuries. Liberty & Co. used them extensively for their textiles. Iris's father also happened to work there as head printer, and it had been through his influence and impeccable reputation that she had gotten a position at Liberty.

"Sorry. We'll have to do Carnaby Street another time," Iris said to Sara as she slipped off her apron. Merton Abbey was an hour's ride away by train and bus to southwest London.

Possibly more if part of the line wasn't running due to worker shortages.

Sara waved goodbye. "Say hello to your father for me."

Gathering her hat and coat, Iris hurried to the ground-floor reception and delivery office, where a bundle of painted sketches carefully stacked inside a leather messenger bag awaited her. Before the war, deliveries were made every Monday and Thursday by a delivery lorry, but petrol rations had reduced many businesses to the old methods of bicycle or foot.

Taking the leather bag from the harried clerk who was juggling three times the amount of work thanks to the holiday rush, Iris started for the worker exit that led to the back alley but quickly changed direction. It had been weeks since she'd dared to walk through the main lobby of the store, but hearing all the shopgirls exclaim over the seasonal decorations in the canteen, Iris simply couldn't help wanting to take a peek herself.

Stepping through the curtain that divided the no-nonsense worker areas from the storefront, Iris found herself in an exotic land of silks, woven carpets, and electric lights. The emporium was an enchanting cave of wonders that reflected Mr. Liberty's fascination for all things foreign and colorful. The rooms of the sprawling premises were swagged in oriental draperies, and antique sculptures with touches of Christmas greenery enveloped the air in scents of pine and fir. She drifted to the Japanese smoking room with its silk painted screens, through the Arab tearoom where customers sipped Chinese tea, and at last into the textile room where displays were festooned with fabrics of all color and design: heavy damask with Moorish prints, ikat muslin, and Egyptian cotton with hieroglyphics.

Iris passed her hand over a Tana Lawn with a pretty pink and green flora motif, then glanced around. Similar pretty patterns were draped over tabletops as grand dames of London society with their iron-gray curls and Victorian corsets decided which to add next to their wardrobe. Not a single lady under the age of fifty to be seen. Iris sighed over the lack of excitement around here. She didn't consider herself fashion-forward, but not even she would be caught dead wearing something of her granny's taste.

"Looks like a funeral shroud." She eyed a rack with black and gray scarves drooping down like sad flower petals. "Are these our only options? Outdated or drab? What woman wishes to dress as if she were dead every time she leaves the house?"

"I shouldn't mind for a touch of blue or red." A pair of brown eyes peered over the rack at her.

Iris jumped, catching one of the dead petals—er, scarves—on the messenger bag. The fringe tangled around one of the strap's metal rings.

"Allow me." Captain Conrad came around the rack, and with a few deft flicks, freed her from the scarf.

"Thank you." Iris smoothed the scarf back among its compatriots, then turned to him. "You have a habit of popping up."

"I like to take people unawares. Breezes past formal courtesies to a more genuine reaction."

"And what does my reaction tell you?"

"That you just got caught with your hand in the biscuit tin."

Iris lowered her voice. "I'm not supposed to be in here."

"Why not? Is it not your lovely paintings that adorn these very fabrics?"

"Yes, but I'm not a paying customer. And they're not *my* paintings. I merely color another's design."

"Their loss. Speaking of which, have you that new design for me? I must say, I'm eager to see what you come up with."

"It's only been eighteen hours. Hardly enough time for a proper sketch, much less an idea."

"What you need is a lightning idea. One that strikes quick."

"I'm afraid I'm not a lightning kind of girl. I prefer to take my time, soak in details, allow them to bubble around, then begin work with a sure vision."

"I'll have a white beard waiting that long."

"Wonderful things cannot be rushed."

"If I thought that, I wouldn't be so eager to dance with you where I know we'll have a wonderful time."

"Blatant flirting will not get you far with me, Captain." Though she was surprised at how much she was enjoying it.

"Then I shall consider changing tactics for our next meeting."

"As to meetings, is that why you're lurking among the textile racks? This project you have with the company?"

"Yes. I have an appointment with John Llewellyn to discuss further details, none of which I can spill no matter how you flutter your lashes at me."

"Keep your details and I'll keep my fluttering."

"Then at least allow me the pleasure of taking you to dinner tonight."

"I'm afraid I must decline." She hitched the bag strap higher on her shoulder. "I was just on my way to—"

"Miss Braxton. What on earth are you doing here?" Mr. Llewellyn, the store's director, appeared. His tight-lipped smile for the customers' benefit failed to hide the annoyed lines on his forehead as he stared at Iris as if she were a milkweed among his prized roses. His gaze shifted to the bag on her shoulder. "Are those the Merton prints?"

"Yes, sir. Bernard is out ill and Mrs. Philmore asked me to deliver them. I am on my way there now."

"The service entrance is best suited for work deliveries." Turning his attention to Captain Conrad, Mr. Llewellyn's expression smoothed into congenial politeness. "I do apologize, sir. Our holiday displays are difficult to resist, even for the employees. How may I assist you today?"

"No apology necessary. Miss Braxton is an acquaintance of mine who was happy to lend her opinion on a scarf choice for my mother." The good captain turned on that charming smile of his. "And I believe it is I who may assist you. Richard Conrad of Messrs. Higg & Hill."

"We've been expecting you, Captain. Please follow me and I'll show you to the meeting room where we can go over a few of the particulars for this project."

Before following Mr. Llewellyn, Captain Conrad turned back toward Iris. "Miss Braxton. I look forward to seeing you again, and thank you for your opinions on the scarves. They proved insightful."

Iris mumbled a hasty goodbye before backtracking her way to the service entrance and out into the cold, crisp air of December. She took a deep breath, chilling her lungs until they hurt. Icicles were more pleasant than the heat fusing her face. To be caught browsing, and with a man, she would be lucky not to have her pay docked.

"Enough of that." She secured the satchel strap on her shoulder. "The man has a job to do, as do I. Time to get on with it."

Except the man wouldn't leave her alone when she boarded the Underground. His suggestion of a lightning idea followed her as she got off in Chelsea and caught the bus to Battersea. Another bus took her to the far outskirts of London, where the gray buildings gave way to green grass and Captain Conrad's words bumped against her with each rut in the road. He was eager to see her sketches. Most people, besides her father and Sara, thought her sketches a nice way to pass the time before a husband came along and offered her real duties to complete her life. More important than his eagerness, Captain Conrad was going to show them to Mr. Stewart-Liberty. A once-in-a-lifetime opportunity and one she was terrified to squander.

In her mind, she sketched sheep, squares, diamonds, flowers, and ferns with such overwhelming concentration that she nearly missed her stop until the woman next to her elbowed her.

"This you, dearie? Liberty Print Works?"

Iris snapped to attention. "Oh yes! Thank you."

Gathering her satchel and small purse, she climbed off the bus and started down the street dotted with Arts and Crafts–style buildings. Textiles had been important to this area for hundreds of years, the Merton Abbey Mills established in the eighteenth century by Huguenot silk throwers. Sometime around the turn of the century, Liberty & Co. began operating the site for their own textiles. Beauty and history were crafted here, but it was much more than that to Iris. It was a home away from home. Here she had watched at her father's knee the creativity of color and thread weave to life. Here she had learned to appreciate the beauty of seeing the world around her and breathing it into existence on silk. Here her father had taught her to pull the shapes from her mind and interpret them into something unique that might change the world's view. Or at least give the world something to hope about.

The River Wandle chugged along with its flecks of ice as it churned the water mill with a soft slushing sound. In warmer months, she and her father would pinch off flower blossoms and toss them into the river for good luck. Coins were forbidden as they could clog the wheel. With no blossoms to be found, she plucked a dried leaf from the ground, spun around once, made her wish, and dropped the leaf into the river. It floated along, collecting ice chips before tumbling under the rotating wheel.

Swinging into the printing building, Iris scanned the rows of workers hand-blocking paint onto massive lengths of silk. In the center of it all stood her father, Jim Braxton, manager of Liberty Print Works. He'd started off as a stock boy and quickly worked his way up the ranks to printer, master printer, and at long last, manager.

"Hello, Papa." Iris kissed him on the cheek. "Beautiful pink there."

"Needs a touch more fuchsia." He trundled down a row and stopped next to a block printer. "Bit more fuchsia here, aye."

The printer nodded and added the appropriate paint to his palette before dipping his brush into the mix and spreading it over the large woodblock stamp. Lining the patterned stamp on the silk fabric, he pressed it down with a light tap from a leather-wrapped hammer.

Retying his waistband apron, Papa came back to Iris, eyeing the satchel. "What have you brought me? Prints? When did you become a delivery boy?"

"Since the regular one decided to get ill today." She handed over the bag. "Here you go. Another delightful selection of vines, florals, and acorns in a dizzying array of cream, brown, and green straight from the last century."

"Not everyone sees the rainbow as you and I do, my girl. Let's take it to my office and see the latest offerings."

The office was a mere ten yards away and within direct eyesight down the center aisle, but it took only five steps before her father swerved down a row to adjust a printing block. Another two steps and he winged off to sort confusion over a misplaced pattern. And half a row over, he called for more drops of ochre

and vermilion. Smiling and shaking her head, Iris wandered over
to the ceiling-high built-in shelves where all the patterns were
meticulously stored in numbered books. She took one down,
smoothing her hand over the worn leather cover with all the
reverence due a prayer book. Inside was a treasure trove of ideas,
longings, dreams, and art. She knew each one by heart, having
memorized them since the first day her father brought her here
as a little girl. She had sat quietly at his feet watching him hand-
block the patterns onto the fabric until the shelves caught her
eye. It was love at first sight and she knew right then it was her
destiny to fill a pattern book with her own designs.

Only her destiny was taking its sweet time in coming about.

"When can I start adding your designs to my collection?"
Papa peered over her shoulder, reaching down to point at a
print of buttercream flowers and moss-green oak leaves. "This
could use a pinch of harbor blue."

"Cerulean. Brings out the yellow of the cream."

"See? A natural."

"Not natural enough for Mr. Fletcher. He turned me down
again." She slid the book back onto the shelf.

"Don't be blaming him. The man has no taste that isn't dictated to him. He said no. You go back again and again until he
says yes. Show him your sketches."

She gave a dry laugh. "Yes, I could if they weren't all ruined
by a slush puddle."

"Oh, my darling girl. Sorry I am about that." He tapped her
under the chin with his work-worn finger. "Chin up. One day
something brilliant will come along and you won't be giving
two seconds' thought to those slush sketches. Just no more florals, eh? Reminds me too much of the grannies."

Iris laughed, a real one this time. "How about florals and
something else? We don't want to cut the grannies completely."

"Compromise. That's my girl thinking." Lifting the corner of his stained apron, he rubbed at a spot on the bookshelf. "Your mum's been asking if you're still alive for all the times you've come to visit lately."

"I'm sorry I've been a ghost. There's been more work to do with most of the men gone to the front, and trying to find time to sketch . . . I've been a horrible daughter. Tell Mum I'll come round soon." Grabbing a scrap of cloth that had been discarded from the cutting table, she dusted loose fibers from one of the design book's spines. Her hands, like her father's, were never idle for long. Their minds bustled with activity that released through their fingertips.

"It's Christmas she'll be expecting."

"Wild horses couldn't keep me away. Not with sticky toffee pudding on the menu." Her favorite, and none made it better than Mum.

"And the Christmas Eve service? She's already told the vicar you'll be there to pass out holly wreaths."

Iris's hand paused over a spine labeled "Wildgrass 1896." "Er, not Christmas Eve."

Papa's thick brow scrunched into a frown. "Surely the store won't have you working late that day."

"No, it's not the store." Avoiding his eye, she busied herself wiping nonexistent dust from a shelf corner. "I'm attending a dance."

"Are they still having those during a war? I didn't think there were enough lads left in London for a proper go."

"Oh, there are some. It's the Royal Troops Christmas Auxiliary." Saying it out loud caused a funny flip in her stomach. She couldn't possibly be looking forward to it. Must be from skipping lunch.

"Mr. Braxton," called one of the blockers.

Papa hurried to sort out the problem, which appeared to be a design overlapped during the stamping process. Iris couldn't hear what was being said, but by the relief on the blocker's face and the reassuring hand her father placed on his shoulder, she could tell all things were well. Papa knew every trick of the trade and one mistake wasn't about to throw him off. Or his temper. In fact, the only time she'd seen her father turn an alarming shade of crimson was when a worker lit his pipe too close to the fabric. A dangerous scenario for any workplace handling flammables.

Problem sorted, Papa weaved his way back to her and picked up the thread of topic again. "Soldiers. Well, that does put a shiny spin on things. A uniform turn your head, did he?"

"Nothing like that. Captain Richard Conrad is his name, and he was kind in offering his help when my sketches were destroyed. He's an architect by trade and is working on a project for the store. He offered to show one of my designs to Mr. Stewart-Liberty if I agreed to dance with him." There was that silly flipping again. Perhaps she should stop in the canteen for an apple before catching the bus back to London.

"Clever lad. I like him already. Stepping out with a soldier is about the only excuse your mum will allow for your absence on Christmas Eve, mind. She'll expect to see the ring all the earlier the next morn." He tried to keep a serious face, but the twinkle in his eye gave him away.

"Papa!" The heat rushing to Iris's cheeks most likely gave her away.

He continued as if not hearing her embarrassed objection. "Now for me, I wouldn't mind you holding off on an engagement. Lets me keep you as my wee girl for a bit longer."

"I'm not so wee anymore."

"Think that all you like, but a father has his rights to claim it so."

Iris shook her head. "It's one dance. Nothing more."

"Your mum and I were engaged at a dance. I need to meet this young man before you start ringing church bells."

She groaned. "*One* dance, Papa."

"They'll have chaperones, a major or general keeping an eye out for all things proper?"

"No generals, but I'm sure they'll bus in a pack of grannies."

At this he nodded. "Good. One granny chaperone is worth ten generals. Nothing gets past them."

Slinging the now-empty bag over her shoulder, she started down the aisle to the door. "I need to get back to the city before blackout begins. The sun is setting sooner and sooner these wintry days."

Papa followed her. "They don't have you working past sundown, do they? Too dangerous for you girls to be walking home with those German Gothas on the raid. I read in the paper a few weeks ago, a bomb was dropped right outside Bedford Hotel on Southampton Row. Less than two miles from the store."

They stepped outside into the late afternoon light: a hazy yellow that did little to thaw the frigid air.

Iris tucked her hands into the wool mittens Mum had knitted for her. A leftover pair with a crooked thumb that wasn't suitable to send in a care package to the Tommies. "We're being careful, Papa. I promise."

Papa stood in the doorway, shirtsleeves rolled to his elbows without a single hair quivering in the cold. The man was impervious to any sort of unpleasantness, weather or anything else threatening to cast a gloom. "And tell that Tommie I'm not above putting him in his place if he should go and step on your toes at the dance."

"Goodbye, Papa." Smiling, Iris kissed his scruffy cheek.

"I still have my old print-blocking hammer." He made a smacking noise against his palm. "You tell him."

Iris waved goodbye and headed toward the bus stop that would take her back to London and all its gray dreariness. On instinct, her mind whirled together greens as rich as grass, blues as bright as a country sky, and purples, reds, and pinks. Warmth and light and beauty. The colors swirled together, stretching into lines, circling around into different shapes. Not florals. Not practical colors. Something new.

Beep!

The bus barreled down the lane and stopped in front of her with grinding gears. The burgeoning image faded to dust beneath the bus's large black tires. Iris sighed and pulled out the bus fare from her change purse. Better luck next time.

CHAPTER 4

～

Rex

Christmas Eve 1917

REX CHECKED HIS WATCH AGAIN AS HE WAITED ON THE STEPS OF THE Royal United Services Institute. Half past five o'clock. His date was late. Not having seen her since that day in Liberty's show-room, he hadn't a chance to formalize plans with her for the dance and was forced to send a note to her place of employ-ment. Not the action of a gentleman in his opinion, but then, securing a pretty girl demanded that one remain limber. In the note he had expressed his desire to pick her up and escort her to the dance, but she had written that afternoon that she would simply meet him there. Quicker than to call around to her home address.

So there he stood in the softly falling snow, wilting corsage in hand, with no date to be seen. Had she changed her mind? A knot jerked in his stomach. He'd never been stood up before, but there was a first time for everything. What if she decided that being seen with a bum-legged man was too taxing on her goodwill? No. He quickly stamped his good foot on that notion. The girl he met didn't seem caught up on airs. She had her nose too far buried in a sketchbook.

The thought made him smile. He'd been caught with pencil marks on his nose more than once.

"I'm sorry!" A woman's voice called behind him.

He turned around and found Iris dashing across the street, waving at him. She leaped over a puddle, and he caught her hand as she landed on the footpath.

"Apologies." She gasped for air. Her cheeks were bright pink with exertion. "I had every intention of leaving work on time, but then a whole stack of designs had been misplaced. Then I tried to catch a taxi and none were to be found. Then I quickly realized after skidding across a thin patch of ice near Piccadilly that running was quite the wrong option to make up time. But here I am."

Wrapped up in a dark gray wool coat, red hat, and matching scarf, he could barely make her out against the darkened backdrop of the surrounding buildings whose lights had been extinguished for blackout. The red tip of her nose was more than enough to spur him to action.

"You are here at last and all is forgiven." He tucked her hand into the crook of his arm and made for the soft yellow light streaming from the building's entrance. "Your hand is like ice. Let's get you inside before you turn into an icicle."

"More like a snowman." She shook her head, sending fluffs of white in all directions.

"I've never seen a lovelier snowlady."

"Do you have a line for every occasion?" Her tone was teasing as they joined the slow-moving queue of injured soldiers on crutches and sporting bandages of all arrangements, the ladies at their sides making a show of not noticing the grievances.

"A man must be prepared for flattery at all times."

"If you are so well prepared, then how can it be genuine?"

Looking down at her, he flashed her a winning smile. "With you, how can it be anything but genuine?"

"Easy now, soldier. I've already agreed to a dance."

"One, yes, but I'm angling for two."

"Hence the flattery." A smile of her own peeked out.

"No, Miss Braxton. With you, flattery is completely unneeded when the truth is more than enough." It was refreshing to find a girl who didn't simper away from compliments, nor did she allow her vanity to thrive off them. But that didn't deter him from wanting to offer them anyway.

Stepping into the institute, which served as the connecting building to the Banqueting House, Rex couldn't help but marvel at the old stone and pillars surrounding them. Not original, as the Palace of Whitehall had been razed by fire in 1698 and this new structure built in its place, but enough history to spark his imagination from classical to Jacobean to Tudor architecture. All those styles melding seamlessly under one roof was quite astonishing.

Peeling off his overcoat and officer's cap, he handed them to the cloakroom attendant, then turned to help Iris out of her coat. Underneath all those warm, woolen layers was a gown of deep burgundy. Simple yet elegant, just like her, and all the more stunning for it.

Standing off to the side were his mates, Stan and Clive, with two girls giggling between them. Eyeing Iris, the men's expressions saddened with good humor as they stared down at their shoes. Shoes they had been forced to polish themselves. Rex gave them a mock salute, then ushered Iris away before those two thickheads decided to invite themselves over for introductions. They would let slip this whole evening had been balanced on a bet, and while it was true to begin with, he found he was very much looking forward to spending the evening in Iris's company.

"I brought this for you." He presented the slightly crushed corsage. "Pardon the rumpled petals. Had a devil of a time trying to shield it from the elements under my overcoat."

"It's beautiful. Such a lovely gesture, rumpled petals and all." She held out her wrist, allowing him to tie the corsage's ribbons. "A chrysanthemum."

"Is it? I've never been good with flowers. Though I do know what a rose is." He offered her his arm and escorted her through the crowd humming with excitement as a small orchestra began tuning their instruments from the next room. Strings and clarinet notes lilted over the murmuring voices.

"Roses are nearly impossible to find at this time of year," she said. "Chrysanthemums do quite well in the chilly air. They're always popular for the store's autumn designs. That's how I know about flowers, through the store's catalogs."

"Is that so? Tell me about these." He pointed to one of the many vases scattered about and overflowing with fluffy pink flowers and densely packed clusters of purple and white.

"Camellias and sweet william. Representing adoration and gallantry."

"And these?" He pointed to another vase filled with star-shaped purple flowers and long stems with red berries.

"Hellebore and winterberries. Serenity and . . . you'll never guess"—the corners of her mouth perked up—"winter."

He laughed at her cheekiness. "Whatever they represent, they certainly make a statement against the Corinthian-style columns. See how the petal layers mimic the acanthus leaves and scrolls on the elaborate capital?" He pointed to the top of the column. "Its function is as mediator between the column and the load bearing down on it by offering a broader area of support."

Following the flow of the crowd, they entered the Banqueting House. Originally part of the sprawling Palace of Whitehall, it was the only surviving component of what was once a royal residence. The chamber was long with seven bays of windows with a gallery ringing the upper half, where the general public was once allowed to view the monarch dine. Tonight the gallery was crowded with musicians tuning up for the first number. Four elaborate chandeliers hung suspended from the painted ceiling, casting warm light over the cream walls and white columns spaced between the windows that were draped in heavy black to block the light.

Iris's head twisted this way and that as awe settled over her face. A feeling he understood well as magnificent structures never failed to catch his breath. "I never realized columns had styles. It's difficult not to notice their ornateness when walking anywhere in London, but it never occurred to me there was a distinctness. It seems rather obvious now that you point it out."

"You have your flowers and I, my columns. These are Ionic, by the way." He indicated the eighteen scroll-topped columns surrounding the room.

"Does your knowledge extend only to columns?"

"My lady, I am a wellspring of architectural wisdom. Take, for example, this room. It is a single two-story double-cube Palladianism, meaning all proportions are mathematically related. These Ionic columns reach up to the ceiling painted by Rubens, commissioned by Charles I. He quite lost his head over the splendor."

"That is a terrible pun for a king beheaded."

"Perhaps, but did you know he was beheaded in this very building?" Delighted to show off his collection of archaic trivia,

Rex whisked her to the north end of the room before couples could begin claiming the corners for canoodling. "In 1649 Charles I stepped out a window onto the scaffold. The window would have been just on the other side of this wall. It's gone now, but it would have been the next window over from this one." He patted the glass, or rather the black cloth covering the glass that did little to dampen the coldness against his palm.

"The history these walls have seen. Makes you feel rather small and unimportant in the grand scheme of things." Her gaze tilted all around at the splendor. He sensed she had that rare ability to look past the obvious and the crowds and to see the bare bones and their depth of possibilities.

"You bring beauty to life. I would call that a great deal important."

Her gaze met his. "I want more than ornate beauty."

"What then?"

Iris shrugged. "I'm not sure yet."

The orchestra struck up a lively tune. The floor crowded with dancers while those less inclined to move about watched from the sidelines. Rex had never sat on the sidelines. Especially not when there was a pretty girl next to him.

"While you ruminate on your next venture, may I have this dance?" He held out his hand.

Her fingers hovered over his outstretched palm. "One dance, remember? Are you certain you wish it to be this one?"

The woman clearly had no idea who she was bargaining with. Her hesitancy did little to sway him. "I have every intention of impressing you so much with this dance that you will be bereft if we do not continue."

She winged up a dark eyebrow. "Bereft."

He clasped her fingers. "Utterly heartbroken because my

charming company and dazzling wit will sweep you off your feet even if my bum leg cannot."

He swept her onto the polished floor. Their shoes reflected among the dozens of other shined army shoes and satin pumps as couples spun around in rhythm to the music. Her steps were timid and she gripped his shoulder as if fearful he might leave her stranded.

"I have you, Miss Braxton." His arm came supportively around her.

Her dark eyes flashed wide. "Pardon?"

"Relax your death hold. This is supposed to be fun."

"Apologies. It's been some time since I've danced. Not that I was very good to begin with." Her fingers relaxed a fraction, but still with enough grip to bunch the back of his uniform.

"It's not about dancing well or even knowing the steps. It's about enjoyment." Doubt still flickered across her face. Change of tactics. If he couldn't persuade her, he would goad her into doing it herself. "Or if I want to lay it on thick, it's about giving us poor Tommies a warm, shining memory to take back with us to the front. With the mud and misery all around us in the trenches, it will be your face glowed by Christmas candlelight that gives us hope to carry on."

Brow puckering, she glanced up at the lighting. "There is no candlelight. The chandeliers have been installed with electricity."

"Do not ruin a glum soldier's sweet memory of our time together."

Her fingers loosened the back of his uniform. "Do these lines ever work on a girl?"

He peeked over her shoulder at the couples spinning around them. Men in their pressed uniforms, their powdered and pink partners gazing adoringly up at them. It was a common enough brag among the ranks that a woman couldn't resist a man in uniform. "Look around. You tell me."

"If I look around, I may lose count of the steps."

He swung her around in a circle and sang along to the orchestra. "'*You tell me that our dream of love is o'er.*'"

She stiffened at once in his arms. "I beg your pardon."

"Shhh. I'm trying to remember the words. '*How can I forget you when in dreams I see your smile?*'" He was no Enrico Caruso, but he could carry a tune as long as the instruments drowned out his pitchiness. With each chorus, Iris leaned a little farther into his arms and stopped muttering the steps under her breath. At some point she began to hum along.

"Do you hope to see your family for Christmas tomorrow?" she asked after a beat.

He shook his head. "Tomorrow they're having a big to-do at St. Bart's hospital for the soldiers convalescing. A few of us are going as part of the cheering-up committee." He dropped his voice. "Otherwise known as a distraction to keep the Sisters looking away when the chaps take a tipple."

"Rather devious subterfuge. On Christmas too."

"All the more reason to sneak in liquid cheer. Those nurses have them on a diet of warm milk and broth." He made a face. His tastebuds were still tainted from his own run-in with the wounded man's regimen. "Tell me how a man is expected to recover under such bland conditions."

Her head tilted, catching warm yellow light in her dark upswept hair. "I confess I do not like warm milk myself, so I cannot chastise you fully for offering alternative refreshments."

"That's the spirit."

"*Spirits*, I believe you mean to say." Mischief sparkled in her eyes.

He laughed, spinning her in time to the music. "Why,

Miss Braxton, there's more subversion in you than I originally thought. Can't tell you what a delight it is."

It was her turn to laugh, the smile lingering as they went round and round on the floor until the music lilted to a different beat. Her head cocked to the side. "This is a different song."

"So it is."

"You tricked me into more than once dance."

He neatly sidestepped a soldier on crutches and his partner who was content to twirl herself about. Fumes of spiked punch drifted in her wake. "I did no such thing. I merely continued our moment enjoying the music together. Is that such a crime?"

"Do you know, Captain Conrad," Iris said, "I believe you could persuade a bird to give up his feathers before he realized it. I hope you don't use that art for nefarious reasons."

"Only ever with the best of intentions. In this case, I simply wanted to spend more time with you."

"Why?" It wasn't hurled as an accusation or coyly fishing for a compliment. It was asked with simple and honest curiosity. "I was frostbitten when you met me in a pub, hardly a proper introduction. Then you had the audacity to ask me to a dance after I'd just fallen into a puddle. Certainly not a picture from a romance story."

"Which is precisely why I like you. I like the unexpected." It wasn't entirely a lie. True enough that a bet had put him in her path that night at the Argyll Arms, but he wasn't one bit sorry for it. Meeting her that way, the bet didn't entirely free his conscience. She wasn't like all the other simpering girls he'd met fluttering their lashes at him over tea. Miss Braxton had a mind of her own, she was resourceful, and she didn't shy away from ambition. It was wildly attractive. More impressively, she was creative. She wanted to transform the world, as he did, through meaningful design. Through things that were not simply for beauty, but held purpose.

"Speaking of unexpected," she said, "how was your meeting with Mr. Llewellyn after you caught me in the showroom the other week?"

"Well enough. I got the information I needed to begin, though the fellow was rather matter-of-fact about it. I've met dry toast with more personality." The store director had taken him on a tour all around the building, pointing out the various goods for sale, expounding on the forward thinking and British heritage that Liberty & Co. prided itself on. Rex had filled his notebook with ideas, but he'd yet to find the key that put them all together. Not that he had any say in the actual designing of the new facelift. That honor would go to the senior partners of his firm. Because he was a junior architect, his skills were assigned to measuring. Someday, though, he would be the one to sign his name to the blueprints.

She nodded, understanding of course about dried toast. "Mr. Llewellyn believes in efficiency, which is to his credit as the store director. Liberty & Co. runs as a well-oiled machine. Though I expect you're being asked to design a few new cogs for us."

"Am I?"

"You are an architect. I assume you've been asked to . . . architect something."

"Draft," he corrected. "And yes."

Her eyebrows lifted. "For . . . ?"

He bent low to her ear in an attempt of mystery but managed to be momentarily distracted by the lily scent of her hair. "A secret assignment."

She laughed. A good sign. He liked to see a lady laugh instead of restricting herself to modest blushes and serious talk. "Keep your secrets then. I'll discover them eventually."

"I daresay you will, though for now the old boy wants to keep mum. At least until after the war when building expenses won't be considered unpatriotic as every shilling now is counted toward the war effort."

"I suppose that's what we're both doing. Spinning castles in the sky in hopes of one day truly building them." She paused, brow wrinkling until it quickly smoothed into a spark of interest. "Could you at least give me hope that you are refurbishing the paint studio with a working furnace? That place is drafty as a tomb in January. One morning I came in and all my paints had frozen solid."

"I cannot promise a working furnace; that is far beyond my skills as a junior architect. But I will say this: the changes your boss has in mind are set to be nothing short of spectacular. I only hope I measure up to his expectations. That's an architectural joke."

"I shall remember not to paint you with broad strokes in the future. That's a painting joke."

The orchestra swung into an upbeat number. Rex took the first step. Pain twisted his knee. He grit his teeth to cover the clench of pain, but it obviously wasn't quick enough. Iris glanced at his leg, then back to his face, an expression of politeness smoothing the flash of concern.

"Might we sit this one out?" she asked. "My two left feet have quite exerted themselves."

Grateful for the excuse, they found an empty bench tucked between two windows where other scattered chairs were occupied by those content to watch rather than dance in the merriment.

"Does it pain you a great deal?" she asked quietly.

Rex straightened his leg out to relieve the tension cramping the muscles. "I can tolerate the inconvenience of a shredded leg most days, but it doesn't care much for being overtaxed." He laughed and gave her a wink. "I'll need to use my cane for the next few days, but I wasn't about to bring that dampener of spirits; otherwise you never would have danced with me."

"Nonsense. An extra limb might have improved my steps."

He grinned. The woman was full of delightful surprises. "Well, Miss Braxton, now that you've upheld your half of the bargain by dancing with me tonight, I am happily obliged to present your sketches to Mr. Stewart-Liberty. How are they coming along?"

"I've doodled everything from flower vines to frogs on lily pads and nothing has sparked."

"Sparked *yet*."

Her hands that had been demurely folded in her lap picked at her skirt. Dried ink shone faintly under the curve of her nails. "You're much more confident in my abilities than I am at the moment."

"All artists hit droughts from time to time. The important thing is to keep working through them. So you have to sketch a hundred frogs in the meantime; one day those frogs will morph into the grand design and all that croaking will have been worth it."

"It will be worth it if Mr. Stewart-Liberty likes it and agrees to print it."

"You can still sketch something beautiful without him ever seeing it." He flexed his foot and drew his leg in, rubbing the taut calf muscle.

She turned on the bench. Her knee brushed his—thankfully not the pained one. "Yes, but I want it to mean something. I want my work to give others hope. That this war is ugly, true, but there is goodness still to be found. That doors are opening and the big wide world is right outside if we can only step through the door and seize it." Only then did she realize her knee was propped against his. She jerked away and straightened on the bench, her hands once more falling still in her lap. "Apologies. My zeal runs away with me at the most inopportune times."

He felt every word targeted to the core of his own passion. "That zeal is what will get others excited. Don't apologize for it."

"Perhaps I should apologize for our initial meeting. I wasn't altogether thrilled for your interruption, but in hindsight, it perhaps wasn't the savviest of moves to accost my boss in a pub. You saved me from humiliation more than once, and I'm grateful to repay your kindness tonight. Though I hardly think dancing with me is considered a kindness to anyone. You got more than you bargained for when you made that deal with me."

Those words targeted something different entirely. Guilt. All the bets he'd made with the lads had been in good fun, never intending to hurt anyone nor compelling a need to explain. Yet Iris had opened herself to him, allowing him to see that a few drawings smeared by the snow weren't mere whimsies to be traded for a dance card. "About that deal. I must confess I wasn't entirely truthful when I—"

The orchestra blasted off a fanfare, drowning out his confession. He couldn't tell if he was relieved or dreading the moment when he was later forced to once more summon the courage to tell her about that bet.

A man wearing a major's shiny brass stepped to the center of the floor and called for quiet. The dancing couples quickly skirted to the edge of the space, giving him center spotlight. "Ladies and gentlemen, thank you all for joining us tonight for our Royal Troops Christmas Auxiliary." Whistles and clapping. "We were told this war would be over by Christmas, but here we are three years later . . ." Boos. "Ahem, three years later.

Though what is happening across the Channel is not particularly what we would wish for Christmas Eve, we will do our utmost to keep our brothers-in-arms in our prayers and hearts so that we may all be together again soon."

Shiny-faced corporals wove among the crowd handing out paper stars with a ribbon tied at the top.

"As a special treat," the major continued, "stars are being passed out so each of you may hang one on our Tannenbaum tree."

With more fanfare, a twelve-foot fir tree was carted into the hall on a red sleigh outfitted with wheels instead of runners. The crowd oohed and aahed at the garlands of silver bells and candles bedecking the fragrant green limbs, which filled the space with the scent of sap and wintry boughs. A far cry from the reeking mud and men in the trenches. Rex doubted he would ever remove that stench from his nostrils, but the heavenly scent of evergreen needles might do the trick. If only for the night.

"Come!" said the major, motioning the audience forward. "Come and place your stars upon the tree."

The crowd rushed to claim the best spots on the front of the tree.

Rex took one of the offered stars from a passing corporal's basket and stood. "Shall we place our stars?"

Iris beamed as she dangled her star from its red ribbon. "Certainly."

They slowly circled the tree as others clamored to put their stars front and center. It was worse than when the barracks' canteen served hot meat once a month. A man could get trampled in the line.

Rex blocked Iris from being run over by a lieutenant in a wheeled chair. "We'll be crushed to death if we strike for the most obvious spot."

"Then let's not be obvious." Wiggling her eyebrows, she moved around to the back of the tree where fewer people gathered, and she hung her star. Rex hung his next to hers, the pointy arms touching one another. "Every bit deserves a spot of beauty, even if we're the only ones who notice."

As she stepped away to examine more of the stars being placed, the back of Rex's starched uniform collar was yanked. Tugged around, he found himself face-to-face with Stan and Clive.

"Hello, Rex ol' boy." A grinning Clive clapped him on the shoulder with his one hand. "So she showed up, did she? We were getting worried there for a while watching you stand forlornly out front in the snow."

"She did indeed." Rex readjusted his collar. That was the good thing about starch. It never lost its shape when being pawed. "Not only did she show, but I spun her around the floor a few times. Hope there's no hard feelings about having to shine your own shoes tonight."

"A bet is a bet, and we'll take our losses like gentlemen."

"Still can't understand what made her say yes to a face like yours. She's too good-looking for you." Stan rubbed his hands eagerly together as his remaining eye took on a gleam. "Maybe I ought to ask her for a dance."

The rules of polite society dictated that a lady of good reputation never dance with the same man all evening. If war had taught Rex anything, it was that polite society could hang. "Ask your own date."

Stan's expression slumped as he jabbed a thumb over his shoulder to a short giggling blonde hanging off an officer's arm. "She left me for a colonel with both his eyes. Missing an ear, though. Lucky blighter. Can't hear her nagging now."

"You could have solved that issue and stuffed cotton in your ears," came a female voice behind them.

Rex spun around and found a smiling Iris. A smile that didn't quite crinkle the corners of her eyes.

Rather than ruminate on her cooled reservation, Rex gave in to polite introductions. "Miss Braxton, may I present Captains Holloway and Windeatt. Lads, Miss Braxton."

Pleasantries were murmured all around as Iris inquired after the work they were doing for the Wounded Warrior Tour and if they had families to visit for Christmas. After a few minutes, Stan and Clive excused themselves, leaving Rex and Iris standing alone behind the tree as the orchestra struck up a rendition of "The Holly and the Ivy."

She slowly crossed her arms and turned to him with a sharp eye. "Won a bet for you, did I?"

He had been prepared to confess as much earlier, but her abruptness caught him on the back foot. His starched collar began to choke. He raced to get the words out before they cut off for good. "I had every intention of telling you just before the tree came out. Yes, you were the first girl to come through the Argyll Arms door that night, and if you agreed to go to the dance with me tonight, then I wouldn't have to shine their shoes." She continued to stare at him. He hurried on, praying he could salvage his blunder. "It was a stupid thing to do, really. I deeply apologize for the fraudulent way in asking you, but I cannot say I'm sorry you said yes. I'm having a pip of a time with you. Truly."

She continued to stare without saying a word. With each silent second a new bead of sweat broke out on his forehead. Why was she not reacting? He wished she would do something, anything, to put him out of this excruciating misery of stillness, though he had to admit he liked her, and it would crush him not a little bit if she were to haul off and slap his face.

At long last her arms loosened as a devilish curl played on her mouth. "Then I suppose you'll have a pip of a time when you take me to see *The Pirates of Penzance* next week to secure your apology."

The pent-up breath of anxiety heaved from his lungs. "You mean you're not going to call me a cad or slap my face?"

She waved her hand as if the suggestion were a pesky fly. "Making a scene is for the melodramas. Besides, if there's any way to make a man repentant for what he's done, it's to force him to the opera." That devilish curl took full possession of her mouth. One he found tantalizing with temptation.

A temptation that if acted upon would most definitely brand him a cad. Which he was in the middle of proving he was not.

"Miss Braxton." He took her hand and pressed a loud kiss to the back of her knuckles. "I happily accept your terms."

CHAPTER 5

❦

Iris

"TWICE IN ONE WEEK. I'D SAY THAT MEANS SOMETHING." SARA lounged at the end of her bed watching Iris primp her hair in the cracked mirror for the hundredth time that evening. Their shared flat was hardly big enough for mice, but the rent was low and their view from the top floor overlooked Hyde Park—if one squinted through chimney stacks.

"A week and three days." Iris held up a flower to the curl over her ear, then tossed it down. No sense in gilding the lily.

"Pardon me." Slung over the footrail, Sara's stocking feet twitched with irritation. "A week and a half. The fact of the matter is that you were quite the gutsy Gertie to ask a man to the opera."

"I did not ask him. I demanded he make amends."

"He must have been a smooth dancer for you to want to see him again after the lies."

Iris fluffed the curls dangling elegantly at the nape of her neck. It had taken nearly two hours and several sizzled hairs to perfect them with the heated tongs. "It wasn't a lie per se—more of a setup. I don't believe he's the kind to lead a woman on for nefarious purposes. Unlike Arthur." Iris shot her soon-to-be sister-in-law a pointed look.

As per usual, Sara ignored it. "Arthur did lie about that little dog belonging to him when the leash tangled around my legs and he rushed to rescue me from falling into the pond. But it was awfully sweet just to meet me, don't you think?"

"He plotted for over a week, then paid a granny five quid to borrow that yipping mutt. If that's not the definition of scheming, I don't know what is."

"Still awfully sweet." Sara sighed dreamily, then shook herself into a sitting position. "My point is, men are not always brilliant in the way they choose to approach women, but if we waited around for lightning to strike them with cleverness, we might be waiting forever."

"Captain Conrad is clever. And kind, and humorous."

"Handsome."

Iris took a step back to examine her dress, but it was impossible to gain the whole image in the small mirror. At least her upper half sufficed. "Yes, that too, but there's his way of looking at the world and all its possibilities for beauty and hope that I once thought was a vision that belonged to me alone." Talking to him had made her feel seen, her ideas heard, and that they weren't nonsense floating around without purpose in her head. Not only that, but she found herself looking forward to their banter.

"The only vision he will be observing tonight is you." After swinging her legs off the bed, Sara padded across the cold floorboards and eyed her with a critical assessment. "That shade of amethyst is magical for your coloring. Like a jewel."

Iris smoothed a hand down the rich satin fabric, feeling quite the duchess. Or at the very least like one of the ladies who could afford to shop at Liberty. "Thank your sister for allowing me to borrow it. None of my clothes are fashionable for the opera. At least not sitting on the audience side of the curtain."

Years before, Gilbert and Sullivan produced comic operas that often lampooned the Aestheticism fashion that Liberty sold. In a publicity coup, Liberty offered to provide the fabrics for the operas, and the two had worked as amicable partners ever since. Iris had become good friends with the design department heads who sneaked her in to watch performances from the wings. She loved the backstage hustle and bustle but dreamed of the opportunity to observe the magic out front.

Sara adjusted the simple sash tied about Iris's waist. "She couldn't stuff herself into this frock with a tub of lard if she tried. Not after four children. She's happy to see it be put to good use again. It looks much nicer now that I removed all those bows. Fripperies drown you."

"Your talents as a seamstress are much appreciated." Iris glanced down and frowned at her bare hands. "Where did I put those gloves?"

"Here." Sara picked up the pristine white gloves from the top of the bureau and handed them to her. "Stop fussing. You look beautiful."

A bout of nerves flailed in Iris's stomach as she pulled on the gloves. The clock on the nightstand ticked three minutes past five o'clock. Three minutes past the time Captain Conrad was set to arrive. "What if he changed his mind? What if there's been an accident? What if he's been recalled to the front and had no time to send word?"

"Don't be silly. I'm certain—"

Knock, knock.

"That's him." Calm as could be, Sara sailed across the room and waited a beat for Iris to compose herself. When Iris gave the nod, Sara opened the door. "Good evening, Captain Conrad."

He stood there in a pressed uniform with shiny buttons, his soft brown hair combed back and his officer's cap tucked neatly under one arm, looking every inch the dashing soldier. With a cane.

"Oh dear! Please do not tell me this is a lingering effect from the Christmas dance?" The words flew out before Iris could corral them into a more proper greeting.

Rex's smile widened as if not the least bit taken aback by her dramatics. "Good evening, Miss Braxton. How lovely you look tonight." He tapped his cane lightly against the floor. "I'm sheepish to admit that our evening together did prove taxing, but as to my current predicament—well, I'm afraid I was cajoled into a jig a few days ago while doing a speech for the Wounded Warrior Tour in Liverpool. Found out rather quickly this old battered leg can no longer keep up with a skirling bagpipe. Oh! Pardon me. This battered limb. I seemed to have been in the trenches and hospitals for too long and forgotten the delicacy of speech."

"Have no fear of our fainting spells. We're ladies of a modern era. Besides, we hear worse on lunch break at the store." Iris slipped on her wool coat, which sadly did little to enhance her gown, but at least it was warm. "All set."

They rode the Underground to the West End theater district. The New Gaiety Theatre stood majestically on the corner with its dozens of windows—all blacked out—and domed roof. During peacetime, the surrounding blocks were lit with thousands of lights, sparkling with the promise of entertainment. It had been a long time since anything sparkled after dark. Odd how one took for granted the commonalities of life until one day they no longer existed.

"Clear night," Captain Conrad said as they crossed the street to join the other theater patrons entering the building. "Perfect for a Gotha raid."

Iris shortened her stride to not rush him as he leaned on his cane. "But the barrages are supposed to keep them from flying over."

"Where there's a will, there's a way, and the Hun have proved they're relentless."

She scanned the inky sky. A full moon rose above the London rooftops with stars prickling the darkness, but thankfully no sleek silhouettes droned overhead. She pulled her coat closer as a chill breeze ruffled the air. Hopefully no death machines would ever drone over their heads again. If this war would only end!

Inside the theater they entered a world a million miles away from war. A red carpet, gilded mirrors, dozens of chandeliers, potted palm trees, and a sweeping staircase leading up to the box seats. Iris craned her neck in every direction, taking in each sumptuous detail and rich trim. She knew luxury from working at Liberty, but theater opulence was something different entirely. An experience to be enjoyed by all, no matter the amount of change in their pockets.

Of course, once you entered the theater, the amount of change you carried did determine your seating arrangements. Sigh.

"This way." Rex gently took her elbow and guided her past the sweeping staircase that led to the elegant box seats to another less refined set of stairs that wound its way up to the nosebleed section, where the less affluent found themselves.

It was a good thing Iris wasn't afraid of heights as they tucked themselves into their row and gazed down, down, down at the stage where floodlights beamed against the red velvet curtain.

"Hope you don't mind the peanut gallery," Captain Conrad said as he tucked his cane next to his leg.

"I don't mind anything this side of the curtain. Most of the time I watch from behind the curtain because I'm friends with the costume mistress. This is positively thrilling. Do you come often?"

"We didn't have many theaters in Somersham where I grew up. Then when I moved to London to join the architect firm, I had little time for culture." He cast her a side-eye glance. "Oh, I know what you're thinking. These pretty captain bars must mean I come from a long line of grand lords, but you're wrong. I was all ready to enlist when my old employer from Somersham bought me a commission to go and do the village proud. I've been trying to live up to their expectations ever since."

"You are making them proud. Every man fighting, every woman rolling, is making our country proud. I'm not doing either, but maybe one day a nurse on leave will come into the store and purchase a printed scarf that she takes back to France with her. And on those cold days she can wrap it around her neck to stay warm while she nurses the wounded." Heat flushed her cheeks. "A silly dream of mine, but I can't help but consider it my own little contribution."

"It's not silly or little. Especially not when one day it will be your design that keeps them warm. Your scarves under the new roof I design. Now that's a dream."

She could picture it all. Dozens of displays dotting Liberty's showroom. Her scarves fanned out like little rainbows. Customers clamoring to buy one in each color and design. Her name proudly printed in the corner of each scarf: Iris Braxton, Designer.

He reached over and squeezed her hand, smiling at her as if he, too, saw the dream. Though she wore gloves, it proved a weak barrier to the warmth of his fingers. She allowed it to linger for but a moment, then slowly pulled away and tucked her hands in her lap. The house lights dimmed, but not quick enough to hide the smile curving her lips.

Any other night she might have been swept away by the

rollicking spectacle onstage with pirates, major-generals, romance, and sea shanties, but Iris's attention was more attuned to Captain Conrad's elbow propped on the armrest between them, mere inches from her own elbow. If she were to lean a hair to the right . . . but then her attention drifted to her skirt brushing his trouser leg. He didn't seem to notice in the least, his focus riveted on the sea battle raging onstage, yet she felt the near touch along the entire side of her body.

When intermission came, she sprang from her seat in desperate need for fresh air. They climbed out of their seats and stood on the balcony that looked down on the upper swells mingling on their own private mezzanine balcony and to the grand lobby below that.

"Enjoying the show?" Captain Conrad casually asked as if she had been paying attention.

"Very much so!" Too loud. Several heads turned their way. Iris lowered her voice. "Always adore a good sea shanty." Sea shanty?! She'd never been to the sea a day in her life.

"I had a thought about your sketch," he said, leaning against the railing. Fellow audience members crowded around, laughing and reenacting the pirate sword fights they had witnessed onstage. "In the show, Frederic and Mabel are to be separated but vow their faithfulness to one another. It's much like a current scene from King's Cross Station, wives and sweethearts waving off their men bound to duty. You could evoke two elements representing those who are parted. Perhaps feathers in hope of being reunited."

"Why a feather?"

"I read a poem about it once. Brontë or Wilde or someone. I always appreciated the imagery of it."

A low bass note reverberated in her ear. Was the orchestra warming up for the second act already?

"Air raid!" screeched an usher from the ground floor. "The Germans are coming! Everyone down! Get to the basement!"

Women screamed. Men shouted. Like a pack of animals, the crowd from every level poured out of the house in a stampede toward the basement doors. Ushers did their best to calmly direct people, but no one listened or cared. There was nothing orderly about survival.

"Come on." Captain Conrad grabbed Iris's hand and hauled her toward the stairs, using his body and cane to shield her from the panicked tide of humanity surging around them. "We don't stand a chance on this floor if we're hit."

He practically dragged her down the steps. She clung to his hand like a life preserver as her legs shook with each step.

Boom! Boom!

She ducked against the wall. The terrifying noise boomed in her heart, heaving it into her throat.

"Keep going, my girl." Captain Conrad peeled her off the wall and pushed her forward. "Those are our anti-aircraft guns shooting back."

"A-are you s-sure?"

"Yes." How could he remain so calm when they could have a bomb dropped on them at any second? In that moment she realized what a stalwart figure he must have been to his men. What he was to her.

He didn't slow down as they reached the bottom of the stairs, dragging her across the lobby and through the door leading to the basement, where they crammed in with hundreds of other theater-goers with precious little room to turn around, much less breathe. She'd been elbowed, shoved, had her toes stepped on, ribs poked, and arms twisted, but the pain numbed beneath the terror racing in her blood as the droning grew louder. Dust and dirt shook loose from the rafters and rained down. The hissing light bulbs sputtered. Shrieks and panicked cries filled the air as the deadly noise grew louder. Iris buried her face in Captain Conrad's chest and squeezed her eyes shut. He stood solid and unmoving as his arm came around her.

An explosion ripped overhead, tearing the world and sound apart.

Iris clamped her lips together to keep from whimpering.

"A little one." Captain Conrad's voice echoed in her ear. "About two miles away."

Two miles away! Surely not when it sounded like the gate of hell flung wide open.

Boom!

Her fingers dug into the front of his uniform.

"East. Seven or eight miles." He sounded entirely too calm for her frantic state of mind.

Boom!

"They're moving farther away. The worst is over, Miss Braxton." His arm loosened around her shoulders.

Unhooking her grip from him, she took a hesitant step back and lifted her head. Dust floated to her cheek. She swiped it away. "Under the circumstances, perhaps you should call me Iris."

"Rex." He dusted debris from his own head and grinned. Her insides calmed. If he wasn't scared, then she refused to be the one caught cowering.

"Ladies and gentlemen," an usher called from the doorway. "The danger has passed and our magnificent performers have demanded that the show go on to show those Boche what for!"

The crowd all around blinked as if coming into the sunlight after a stint underground, then rose together in one cheer.

"What do you say, Iris? Has there been enough excitement for one evening?" Rex asked as they came up from the basement into the main lobby, where a few people were making for the exit. The theater itself was still intact, though, with a new addition of dust.

"Certainly not," she primly replied. "Can't have the Hun believing they scare us so easily. After all, the show must go on."

The show did go on. The performers returned to the stage that much more animated and singing loud enough for the man on the moon to hear. Or rather, the kaiser all the way over in Germany. It was the most thrilling performance Iris had ever seen, and she joined in at the end as the Pirate King led the theater in a rousing rendition of "God Save the King." Afterward, Rex took her home.

"I apologize for crinkling the front of your uniform earlier," she said as they exited the Underground station and turned down the block to her flat. The streets were quiet without a single light to be found peeking out from behind darkened curtains. Thankfully there was no sign of German destruction here. "I'm afraid I allowed fear to get the better of me."

Rex's cane tapped in synchronization with his measured gait against the pavement. "The one who isn't fearful of an attack has either lost his marbles or has nothing to live for. A sensible man, or woman, accepts the fear and carries on despite."

"No doubt you've experienced much of this before. The bombings, I mean."

"More times than I care to count. That's how I got this bum leg. It was a clear night like this one, or it was before all the smoke choked it out. The Hun rained shells on us for hours, but our orders were to keep pressing forward. One of my men fell into a mudhole, so I reached in to get him. Shell exploded right in the hole. Killed him instantly. I took a fair hit of scorching shrapnel. It's what we call a Blighty, a guaranteed wound to send you home."

"An enviable wound then."

"Enviable and lucky for me, especially after tonight." Moonlight glowed across his face as he smiled down at her. "It's not every day I get to put my arm around a pretty girl."

She'd been embarrassed enough that evening. He would have to work harder if he wanted to make her blush. "Oh, with your charming approach in pubs? I wouldn't *bet* on that."

He winced. "Ouch!"

"*Afraid* I'm too on the nose?"

"Ouch again! Though I'll have you know this is the first time I've wanted to continue seeing the lady after said bet has been won." His shoulder grazed hers.

She leaned in, grazing his right back. Up ahead, her building came into view. "Supposed to make me feel special, is it?"

"What would you say if I were to tell you that you are special?"

"I'd ask if part of the basement roof fell on your head."

He stopped walking, hand braced on his cane. "I don't need a roof caving in to tell me what is clearly apparent—"

"Iris!" A figure dashed out of her building and raced down the footpath. Sara. She stumbled to a stop in front of Iris, breath heaving and hair flying all about. "Where have you been?"

"You know where I was. There was a bombing raid and we took shelter in the basement. That's why I'm so late." The singing and planes and flirting banter clouding Iris's mind wiped clean at the tears spilling down her friend's face. She grabbed Sara by the shoulders. "What's wrong? Are you all right? A bomb didn't hit here, did it?"

Sara shook her head as tears dripped off her chin. "No bombing here, but we just got word that Wandsworth was hit."

Wandsworth. Cold shock jolted through Iris. Mum and Papa.

CHAPTER 6

Iris

"YOU'RE FORTUNATE NOT TO HAVE BROKEN ANYTHING ELSE." IRIS stared down at her father in the hospital bed. Two nights ago, she had raced to Wandsworth to find half the block in flames. A German bomb had landed on the neighbor's house and taken out a corner of her parents' house. Right where Papa sat in his favorite chair after work.

His bed was not the only one occupied. The ward was lined with those injured from the raid, each little starched bed partitioned off with a thin curtain in an attempt at privacy.

"What's left to break, my girl?" Papa gestured to the bandages covering the entire left side of his body. "And what isn't broken is singed."

"Oh." Mum sobbed into her sopping wet hankie as she curled onto the chair next to his bed.

"Now, Mary. None of that," Papa soothed despite the scratches on his face being anything but soothing. "You've boo-hooed enough to fill the Thames. Carry on like you do, it's a wonder folks don't think I'm dead."

Mum sobbed harder.

Iris's insides felt as ravaged as dried bristles raked through turpentine. While she'd been out laughing at the opera with a handsome man, her parents had had bombs dropped on them. She hadn't given one thought to their well-being while she'd huddled safely in Rex's arms, and the guilt gnawed at her. "I should have left the opera straightaway to see if you both were all right."

Papa snorted. "Nonsense. You're young and meant to be out enjoying yourself despite what this war is trying to do to us. We're alive and breathing, so that's all the amount of luck we need."

Tears streaked down Mum's ruddy cheeks. "Do you call a broken arm and leg and burns all along your side lucky?"

Papa huffed. "First-degree burns, the doctor called it. Like a sunburn. Whatever that be."

True enough. An Englishman would first need to see the sun before having their skin toasted by it.

"In a few weeks he'll be right as rain. We have that to be thankful for." Now was not the time to fray at the seams. Papa had always been strong for Iris, and she would buck herself up for him. She turned a no-nonsense eye to her father. "As long as you rest."

Papa huffed and scratched at his bound leg. Restless as a spinning top, the man had never been still a day in his life. The nurse had already threatened to bind him to the bed when he tried to get up and go to work the morning after he was carried in on a stretcher. He was proving to be the most irritable of patients. "A child needs rest. I'm a grown man and a grown man gets on with it. I've a shipment of Tana Lawns coming in today, and three color blocks cracked yesterday—"

Mum's head snapped up, as did her spine whenever threatened with disorder. "Mr. Rodney has stepped in while you're out. There will be no talk of returning to work anytime soon."

"Rodney!" Face clouding over, Papa rustled the bedcovers. "The man doesn't know a paisley from a toile, and they think to replace me with him."

"You are not being replaced. This is a temporary position until you return." Mum dabbed her nose with the hankie and tucked it away. "You trained Rodney yourself, which means he has no doubt between a paisley and a toile, or a Tana Lawn and a linen. Right? Good. So there's to be no more talking about returning to work until the doctor says you're well enough."

"When did the doctor say that might be?" Iris asked.

"Three months." Mum rose from her seat and smoothed the bedcovers with brisk efficiency. "Three months of rest, a light regimen of exercise, fresh air, and no exerting himself."

"Don't know about the other bits, but fresh air won't be a problem, eh, Mary? Not with half the side of the house blown out." Papa's petulance disappeared with a crack of laughter.

"Is that a thing to be joking about, Jim?"

"My left side is entirely useless, Mary. If I don't find the humor somewhere, you might as well throw a tarp over the rest of me and toss me out with the rubbish."

"Keep this lip up and I will. Here, dear. Let me comb your hair. You look like a broom gone through the wash." Digging through the bag of personal items, Mum pulled out a comb and perched next to Papa on the bed. She slowly worked it through his tangled hair. "Harold and Burt said they managed to put up a few boards to keep the worst of the elements out, but it's the debris that got blown in from the explosion that's the worst of it. Take a week or more before it's moved out and the house livable again."

After seeing her parents safely to hospital after the bombing, Iris had returned to their house, the very one she had grown up in, to gather a few personal items to make the hospital stay more bearable for Mum and Papa. While there, she had taken inventory of the damage. Most of the house was intact, but the corner that had been hit would need to be entirely reconstructed. Furniture had been reduced to bits, pots and pans blasted from shelves, and everywhere dust and rocks. Next door, where the bomb had detonated, stood an empty lot where Mr. Johnson's home once stood. Many of the neighboring houses had blown-out windows and toppled trees, with several roofs on fire.

As long as she lived, Iris would never forget the overwhelming horror of that night and the blessed relief that she was not now standing over two caskets instead of a recovery bed.

She shook away the morose recollections and focused on what she did best: pushing forward. "When are you being released from hospital?"

"Two days."

"Two days, but the house isn't livable."

Papa shrugged as his eyes drifted closed under Mum's gentle combing ministrations. "There's no choice about it. We can't stay here longer than necessary, not when they be needing beds for the Tommies coming in."

Mum looked up and smiled at her. "We'll manage, love." Humming, she continued combing.

Manage. It's what they had always done. Aching muscles from work all day, they would manage. Scrimping to buy the children warm clothes for another winter, they would manage. Drainpipe leaking water all over the floor, they would manage. No meat left at the market, they would manage. They had always gotten by, but Iris was old enough now to be part of the solution and not another worry. But where could they stay until their house was livable again?

Iris excused herself to go refill the water pitcher and stepped out of the ward into the corridor smelling of bleach and iodine. Spotless windows lining the wall looked out to a private garden, where a handful of male patients braved the wintry cold in warm blankets as they shuffled slowly around the dead hedges. They all carried the same look—war exhaustion. Everyone in London had it, but these men were different. There was a bone weariness to them, a stare in their eyes that gazed a thousand feet out. These men had seen battle, and each of them had carried it home with them in the form of a missing arm or leg, or red marks scratching their faces. Or the invisible kind known only to their soul and mind.

"Another Christmas come and gone." Her whisper fogged the glass. "Yet here we are."

"Here *you* are."

Iris spun to find Rex behind her clutching a book, a deck of cards, and a small bouquet of flowers. Her gloom lifted. "What are you doing here?"

Dressed impeccably in a pressed uniform and shined shoes, he looked straight off a recruiting poster. The cane added a dash of adventure. "I didn't wish to intrude or presume upon your family's privacy, but I wanted to send along my best wishes for your father's recovery. Having been confined to a bed myself before, I know how easily boredom sets in and have brought a deck of cards and book on exotic birds to keep him busy. You did mention he likes reading about birds? The flowers are for your mother."

Charming, dashing, and considerate. He couldn't be sweeter if smothered in whipped cream and topped with a cherry. "How thoughtful of you."

The night of the bombing he had insisted on accompanying her and Sara to Wandsworth. As they had tried to sort up from down, he had called an ambulance, organized a bucket brigade to put out the flames as the firemen were stretched too thin putting out other fires all over town, and led a party in search of Mr. Johnson beneath the rubble. Fear had twisted Iris's memories of that night, snapping only a few of them into still frame. Her father stretched out in the street, pale as a sheet. Arm and leg at odd angles. Clothes burned from his side. Mum huddled next to him, cradling his head and sobbing as she wiped bits of wood from his hair. Silvery moonlight and burning flames clashing on shards of broken glass. Children crying. Water hissing as it splashed against the fire. And Rex as tall as a mountain, as swift as a current in the middle of it all. Her blood pounding, her ears straining for another pass of the German planes, her knees screaming from kneeling in rubble on the street, his presence settled a comfort around Iris. Becoming rather a habit of his.

"How is he today?" Rex asked.

Walking to the table with fresh jugs of water, Iris refilled her father's. "Restless. He's not accustomed to being cooped up. The doctor said if he doesn't take it easy, the bones will take that much longer to mend."

"It's difficult for a man who's used to being on his feet suddenly thrust into motionlessness."

Wasn't that the truth. "If it were only that, the situation may not be so hard to bear. The smoke choked up his lungs. The doctor wants him to get plenty of fresh air to help clear it out and get the lungs pumping healthily again." A new knot tied itself into the headache stringing around Iris's head. She absently rubbed at her temple. "Trying to find fresh air in London is a bit of a needle-in-a-haystack situation. Mum does her best in keeping his spirits up, but I know she's worried about the next couple of weeks. And more pressingly, what happens when he's released from hospital in a couple days. They can't return home until it's been cleaned up, and even then, my father's injuries will make moving around difficult. He needs a place to rest properly. And . . . oh dear. I've run on. My apologies. I didn't mean to drag you into familial problems."

"You're not dragging me into anything. I came voluntarily." He cheerfully grinned.

"Then you are a very good sport who brings much-needed cheer." She nodded to the gifts in his hands. "Come. Papa was most eager to see you again. He wants to ask where you got your cane. As he now has a broken leg, he believes he's entitled to one as well. Personally, I think he wants to annoy Mum with it by poking her when she's not looking." She turned back to the recovery ward.

"That is a good use of it. Wait before you go in." He caught her by the arm before she crossed the threshold and tugged her out of view of the patients. "I may have a solution for your dilemma. My godfather owns a small country estate in Cambridgeshire. I warn you, he's a bit of an eccentric and rents out his rooms to artists and musicians and the like, but the place is surrounded by clean country air, trees, a few farm animals the army has confiscated, and more cushions scattered about for lounging than you could count. Your family would be most welcome there while your father recuperates and their home is fixed."

She was already shaking her head before he could finish. "Captain Conrad—"

"Rex, remember?"

"Rex, your offer is very kind, but—"

"Go ahead. Think of a hundred polite reasons to turn down a perfectly good offer."

Drat. Most people were too well-mannered to demand

explanations. "Well, your uncle for one. I am sure he doesn't want strangers dropping in on him."

"He adores it. The stranger, the better." Rex casually leaned on his cane.

She tried again. "They aren't artists or musicians."

"Your father hand-blocks painted prints for Liberty. I would call him an artist."

"With rationing I'm sure your uncle does not wish to provide for more mouths."

He settled in further against his cane. "Uncle Harbo grows his own vegetables and fruit in a hothouse supplemented by trout from the nearby stream and eggs from his chickens."

"Surely the inconvenience of an invalid under his roof—"

"—will give him an unescapable ear to practice his poetry on. I do not envy your father that challenge. It's really quite horrible." He was full-on grinning by then.

And she was fresh out of reasoning. "You have an answer for everything, don't you?"

"As you always have an excuse to say no. Our routine, it seems, until I finally wear you down. Would it not be simpler to say yes than go through the rigmarole?"

"Allow you to win without a fight? Never."

His grin faded, his expression softening. "This is not a fight. Not even a misunderstanding or disagreement, pity or charity. Simply an offer from one friend to help another."

His sincerity pierced her rigid defenses, cracking her open to a foreign sentiment. The acceptance of help. A recurring habit when it came to him.

"Very well." She held up a finger in warning to his elated expression. "However, my parents will be the hard sell."

His effortless smile returned. "Good thing I've had practice charming you."

On impulse, she kissed his cheek. "Thank you, Rex." Good golly! Who was she today? Lack of sleep was getting to her.

He, on the other hand, had no qualms about enjoying her slip in discretion as the smugness in his eyes caught blaze. "A kiss! If I'd known such heaven awaited, I might—"

"Don't spoil the moment with another flattering soliloquy." She bit the inside of her cheek. Sparring with him was proving rather enjoyable. Not that she would admit to it.

"Charming and flattering. My, my. Shall I continue for witty and clever next?"

"Please don't. Your head will be too swollen to fit through the door, and I've enough explaining to my parents as it is." Turning on her heel before a smile got the better of her, she breezed into the ward.

CHAPTER 7

❧

Rex

CLEAN LINES. BOX SHAPES. NO FRILLS. REX SCRIBBLED OUT THE design, flipped the page, and started again. Gingerbread house. No. Scribbling, he started again. Pillars, lotus carvings, horseshoe arches. Too Indian in influence.

He rolled his pencil between his fingers. What did the new face of Liberty & Co. look like? From what roots did it grow? What did it stand for, and what did it all mean to the British people? He brushed the tip of his pencil over the paper. The barest of marks, but there was something there, a mingling of past and future . . .

Stan nudged his shoulder. "You're up."

Rex blinked and the town hall packed with an audience swam into view. They all looked expectantly at him.

Stan nudged him again. "Your speech."

"My . . . oh, my speech." Pocketing his notebook and pencil, Rex made his way to the podium and offered yet another rousing and patriotic speech to the Ladies Knitting Auxiliary of Woolgarston on behalf of the Wounded Warrior Tour, to which they had donated a generous amount that would go toward prosthetic limbs for many of the Tommies.

Afterward, he shook a great many glove-clad hand, chatted over tea and scones, and outmaneuvered a few mothers desperate to marry off their daughters. All in all, a typical event day on the tour. Yet his mind was sketching shades of black and charcoal, rough timber designs, and gable roofs. Sprigs of iris flowering in window boxes.

Taking a moment of fresh air outside, he joined his mates beneath the bare limbs of a mighty oak tree behind town hall. Wisps of clouds scuttled across the muddled blue-gray sky. Birds chirped and scratched the dirt under a row of nearby hedges.

"We've a few days before we need to be in Lincolnshire." Clive sat on a stone bench and tucked his hand under his arm for warmth. "I say we head to the nearest pub and don't come out until then. Best place to stay warm."

"One of the mothers inside offered to knit you all the left-handed gloves you could possibly need," Stan said, leaning against the tree.

"If I took her daughter off *her* hands." Clive shuddered. "I'll sign up for another post at the front before I hang myself with that noose. What about you, Rex? Care to join us at the pub, or did one of those muddling mums manage to hook you by the nose?"

Rex snapped a twig from the tree and squatted to draw in the dirt. "I'm off to visit my uncle for a few days."

Clive and Stan exchanged pointed looks. "Your uncle, is it? Surely not a comely bird whom you rushed to the rescue of, like Sir Lancelot?"

Iris's face floated before Rex. "Very well. You've pegged me." He quickly drew the outlines of a five-story building to distract himself from sketching her bold, dark eyes.

Stan laughed. "Richard Conrad, the man whom ladies throw their hearts at, has finally gone courting."

He'd taken out many a girl and shared many a laugh with them, but none he considered seriously courting. None lingered in his thoughts until Iris. But the term "courting" was too stuffy for her. Too docile and by the rules. She was a woman defiant of rules. "Courting may be overstepping the truth. Let's call it a gentle wooing."

"And is the lady amenable to said wooing?" Clive stretched his leg out and drew a sun over Rex's gabled roofs with his toe.

"She hasn't slapped my face or set the dogs on me, but I am hesitant to claim victory yet lest I scare her off. Though she is proving to be hardy."

"You mean she doesn't swoon at your feet."

Rex added a few diamond-paned windows. "No, she does not. The lady is intriguing." He topped off the roof with a small fluttering flag.

"Then don't let us keep you from her, Lancelot. We'll see you in Lincolnshire in four days."

Bidding his compatriots farewell, Rex took the next train out and arrived in Cambridgeshire by late afternoon. From the station he caught a ride with the postman, who was one of the few souls that trekked far enough out of town to Uncle Harbo's estate. It was a beautiful spot surrounded by rolling green hills, ancient thick woods, and a stream winding through the land like a blue ribbon. All-around peace.

"My dear nephew. You've returned already." His uncle answered the door in a gold velvet Turkish robe, a red tasseled nightcap, and leather slippers. Under one arm he carried a fat gray cat, and in his other hand a snifter of brandy.

"The country air is too tempting," Rex said, stepping inside. The entrance hall was a jungle of potted plants and trees interspersed with taxidermy in various stages of molting. A parting gift from an artist once in residence.

"Don't lie to me, dear boy. We both know perfectly well what tempts you." Uncle Harbo closed the door and took a long sip of his brandy. "She's out in the blue garden. Joffry!"

Joffry, his uncle's harried butler, scampered into the hall. He was splotched in pink paint. "Yes, sir?"

"Take my nephew's bag to the Shiitake room." Uncle Harbo gave Rex an apologetic frown. "I'm afraid Mr. Valeno has taken your usual Portabello. Claims he's allergic to the Amanita."

All the guest rooms were named after mushrooms. The gardens after colors. And the animals after—

"Heavens, has Timbuktu gotten out again?" Uncle Harbo gestured in irritation at the pink paint dripping all over the floor.

The animals were named after cities. Timbuktu was a Barnevelder rooster.

Joffry wiped a glob from his eye. "Yes, sir. Mr. Valeno wanted a single subject to sculpt. I told him none of the animals could be removed from the pen until the paint had dried, but he refused to listen."

Uncle Harbo sighed and sipped his drink. "Very well. Best not to disturb the art." He blinked at Rex over the rim of his brandy. "What are you still doing here? Go at once to Miss Braxton."

Handing over his travel items to the long-suffering Joffry, Rex trotted off to the blue garden and found Iris sitting on a metal bench sculpted to look like peacock feathers. Her rich, dark hair was wound in a loose knot atop her head. Dried leaves clung to the bottom of her dress, and a warm shawl was tied about her shoulders. The picture of country beauty.

"Good afternoon," he called. Was that his imagination, or

did her eyes light up when she saw him? No imagining his heart skipping over itself.

"Hello yourself." There was that smile he'd sketched on the train ride. Or tried to. An architect's skills would never pass muster for an artist's. "Not out banging the war fund drum?"

"Not for the next three days. I thought I might come by and see how you're faring." He stopped next to the bench and swept off his hat. "How is your father?"

"Driving Mum mad. She expected him to lie in bed all day and merely gaze out at the countryside. He hasn't spent one day inside yet. I think he would sleep in the gardens if it weren't so cold." She laughed and tugged her shawl closer. "I suppose this is the moment I swallow my pride and admit that your prescription of fresh air is the best medicine."

"I shall endeavor not to crow too loudly at my own wisdom."

"I appreciate the gentlemanly restraint." She scooted over and patted the bench next to her for him to sit. "Thank you, Rex. It truly has been amazing. Your uncle is very kind."

He settled next to her, keeping a respectable few inches between them, and settled his cap on his knee. "I'm honored to help in any way I can. How are you getting along?"

She gazed out at the open country spreading beyond the tangled weeds of the garden where the long grass swayed blue against the sun setting behind the gray clouds. "It's taking some getting used to the quiet. No motors trundling down the roads, no newsboys hawking papers, no pattering of thousands of feet on the footpaths. It's charming for a nice holiday, but part of me misses the city bustle."

"Where things are happening." He dropped his gaze to the blank notepad on her lap. "Unlike on the page there."

"Oh, this. This is my fine attempt at creating a design that will dazzle Mr. Fletcher and Mr. Stewart-Liberty into printing it on thousands of silk scarves for customers who will queue in the pouring rain to purchase one. See how well it's going?" She pressed a hand to the paper as if willing the image to appear. "Not to mention I promised to hand this sketch to you before you leave on the final leg of your tour."

"You put that much pressure on yourself, and no wonder it's a blank page. Good ideas come from soaking up inspiration around you." He gestured to the landscape before them. Untouched yet brimming with discovery beyond the next blade of grass. "Then meld that with the emotion inside you. What do you want people to feel when they put on your design?"

She stared quietly for a long moment, the pencil twitching in her fingers as if it itched to jot down what swirled in her mind. "I want them to feel beauty. An excitement for tomorrow. I want them to feel hope."

"Sketch that."

Her gaze moved to him, deep and probing. "How?"

"You're the artist. I'm nothing more than a lowly architect confined to straight lines and ninety-degree angles. Hardly the stuff dreams of hope are spun on."

She gently closed her notebook. "I don't agree with that. Liberty is a bit of a dream for most people who walk through the doors. It provides the safe comfort of the past while surrounded by enticements from all over the world. A heritage that encourages progress, which to me is the very essence of hope."

"Hope is a good theme to build upon."

"Is that the basis with which— Oh my!" A pink blob shot out from beneath the bench. It clucked several times, then disappeared into a dead hydrangea bush, leaving dribbles of paint in his wake. Iris blinked several times. "Was that a chicken? Why is it pink?"

Rex brushed dirt over the paint splotches with the toe of his shoe. He didn't need pink staining the bottom of his service shoes. He'd never hear the end of it back at the barracks. "My uncle claims painting them deters the army from confiscating them. It's completely harmless, just a bit of crushed petals, berries, and cooking oil. Not to mention, he considers them moving works of art. The chickens, not the army. The peacock, he said, was colorful enough without paint."

"The peacock and I have met. He growled and chased me our first morning here and stole a biscuit from Papa's hand. Mum threatened to cook him for dinner if he tried it again. The peacock, not my father."

"Perhaps you should make your design with the peacock. To commemorate your time of survival here."

She tapped her pencil against her chin. "You may be on to something there. Peacock feathers have been a part of Liberty's Hera design since the 1890s. The designer was obsessed with mythology and named it after the goddess Hera, whose sacred animal was that magnificent if not temperamental bird." Her eyes lit up with inspiration. "You should draw them around the store."

He laughed and stretched out his legs. "I really should teach you the differences between an engineer, artist, and architect. *Junior* architect, at that."

"It wouldn't make the slightest bit of difference. In my mind you are building it brick by brick from the sketches drawn by the sweat of your brow. Which should include a peacock feather or two." She mimicked him and stretched out her legs, leaning back against the metal bench. A highly irregular position for a lady to sit in, but he was glad she didn't feel the need to perch ramrod straight next to him. Her inclinations to defy societal expectations harmonized with his perfectly.

"I haven't started sweating yet," he said. Far off in the clump of birch trees, a nightjar began to summon the closing of day. Another hour and the world would darken under nightfall, and he would no longer have a proper excuse to sit outside with Iris, but for now he would soak in each minute. "In fact, there's barely more than a rough blueprint. The working layout—rooms, corridors, stairwells—must be put down first before the building's personality is even considered. That will be done by a senior architect. I take the measurements and run errands."

"They can't keep you a junior for long. Soon enough you'll be out of uniform and designing the buildings."

He shifted uncomfortably on the bench as the lightness left his chest and sank heavily into the letter burning in his pocket. There would be time enough to tell her tomorrow. For now he was content to sit at her side discussing hope and building, pretending the war could not touch them. At least not until the following week, when he was ordered to return to France.

CHAPTER 8

～

Iris

THE SUNRISE WAS GLORIOUS. THE SKY WAS STREAKED WITH ORANGE and pink and gold, gilding the view with glowing light that sparked off dew droplets like tiny diamonds clinging to the grass. An artist's dream to capture such beauty.

Iris ignored all of it as her head bent over her notebook, the pencil scribbling quickly in her hand. After a restless night, she had thrown off the bedcovers sometime around four in the morning and pulled out her notebook, as she often did to calm her mind. At first she had drawn uninspiring shapes. Anything to fill the page and not her head. The shapes morphed into trees and bushes, grasses and wide-open skies. Soon there was a chicken and a peacock. And a bench upon which two people sat. She'd started a new page. This one with disconnected bits bobbing about. Vines. Sunrays. A dance card. Feathers. A pair of eyes. If she'd had her colors, she would color those eyes a soft brown with dark lashes. A shade similar to her own, but much more mesmerizing. Her cheeks had warmed at that, and the only solution was to dress and go for a long walk. But the walk had ended far too soon, and she'd found herself in the blue garden sitting upon the same bench with her notebook open on her knees.

Then the sun broke the horizon and that dastardly peacock cried from somewhere in the garden. And suddenly her mind blazed. A few strokes here. A bit of shading there. Four feathers touching like a diamond in the center.

"You're up early."

Iris jumped at the sound of Rex's voice. Her pencil skidded across the page, creating a writhing line along the edge. Hmm, that was actually an interesting touch. Like a vine.

"Trouble sleeping," she said, drawing another squiggly line on the opposite side.

"The peace and quiet again?"

She added a few leaves to the vines, her fingers knowing precisely where to place them before her brain could give the order. "Yes, and a bit of something more."

"The peacock barking?" His shiny shoes slid into her peripheral view.

She tore her attention from the page to the man standing before her and nearly lost her breath. He was dressed in pressed civvies of charcoal gray and light blue with a book tucked under his arm. His soft brown hair was combed back with a tiny wisp that had escaped pomade brushing his forehead. She'd never seen him out of uniform before, but he proved himself handsome no matter the attire.

The sunrise was glorious, but his sudden appearance spilled light around her in a wholly different way. "Peacocks and feathers and suns and beauty and hope."

"No wonder you couldn't sleep."

"Come and look." Giddy to show him her work, she scooted over to make room for him on the bench. He sat and placed the book on his other side as she held out her notebook, pointing at the various designs. "A modern sun of clean, precise lines in each corner. Four peacock feathers forming a diamond in the center."

A smile tipped his mouth as he traced one of the feathers. "So you did work our little temperamental friend in."

"Yes, a nod to this place, but also to Liberty's Hera feather design." It had come together effortlessly. As if the designs she knew and worked with each day were simply waiting for their counterparts to create something new and unexpected.

"And these vines along the edges?"

"A happy accident just now that adds a subtle touch of the art nouveau. Touches of the old to represent heritage with bursts of modernity for a tomorrow. A bridging of the familiar past with hope for a new day."

He studied it for a long moment, his attention taking in each detail with the practiced eye of someone accustomed to letting nothing pass their assessment. It also gave her time to study his profile. She would need to add faint lines around the eyes she had drawn, *his* eyes. *Please, please don't flip back through the pages and find them.*

Thankfully he didn't flip the pages to find her schoolgirl doodles. Instead, he turned those thoughtful eyes on her, and more than just the sun warmed straight through her. "It's perfect. Everything you said you wanted it to be."

"It was as if my hand and heart took over instead of my head." She smoothed her hand over the page. The slight indentions from her pencil marks rippled beneath her palm. "You were right. About taking the inspirations around me and allowing them to come together on their own. I just needed to get out of my own way."

"The crux of creativity. Allowing the art to speak for itself."

A small cloud scuttled in to blot her sunshine warmth, casting its shadow of doubt. "Yes, but will it speak to Mr. Stewart-Liberty? Perhaps this is a bad idea after all."

His hand closed around hers. "Now is not the time to lose your nerve. Iris, the world needs fresh beauty, vision that sees past today, and optimism."

She resisted the desire to turn her hand over where her palm could press against his. "What if they don't like my version of those things?"

"Then they need their eyes examined. You want to offer hope to others. Don't forget to give some to yourself, and if there comes a day when you find the inspiration lacking, I offer you this." Releasing her hand, he opened the book to a page marked with a crumpled peacock feather. "'Hope is the thing with feathers that perches in the soul, and sings the tune without the words, and never stops at all.'" He held the book out to her. "Emily Dickinson. I found it while rummaging through my uncle's library last night. It's been driving me mad since I first attempted to quote it for you, and I finally managed to unearth its origin."

She took the book, slightly disappointed it wasn't his hand, and ran her finger over the poetess's name in faded ink at the bottom of the page. "I believe you claimed it was Brontë or Wilde."

He winced. "My poetry knowledge was always subpar to my other studies, but I hope this at least redeems me."

"You are fully pardoned as long as you deliver my sketch to Mr. Stewart-Liberty, though I should make a cleaner version. Rather unprofessional to turn in a proposal with smudges and erase marks."

His cheerful expression dipped behind the cloud that had previously shadowed her. Looking out past the low garden wall, the muscles in his throat twitched as if words were stuck there.

He'd never been at a loss for speech before, and the obvious struggle knotted Iris's belly.

"It will give me the greatest pleasure to deliver it before I ship out," he said quietly.

Iris's response, however, rang out like a cock's crow. "Ship out?"

"I've been recalled to the front."

"But your . . ." She looked at his leg then back to his face. "You said your injury was a Blighty. Guaranteed no more active service."

He smiled blandly, still staring out to the horizon. "The truth of the matter is that we're barely gaining inches on the battlefield and the army needs every man they can get. The Yanks are reportedly on their way, but that could be months from now, so the clubfooted and those with hunched backs, heart murmurs, and limping legs have all been called up. That includes me."

"But who will continue your tour?"

"There is no short supply of wounded soldiers able to bang the war drum in my stead."

"It's not fair. You and the other injured have earned the right to return home and stay there."

"War isn't fair. I'd like to say I'm surprised at being recalled, but I've seen enough in the trenches that being prepared for the unpredictable is part of the game."

Her thoughts tumbled one over the other. She had come to believe that his injury would prevent him from returning to the fight. That he was safe now. That they could continue their flirtation, dancing through the season and teasing one another. His coming departure was like another bomb dropping. She should have known they weren't in the clear. They were far from safe as long as war raged on.

"What will happen to your architectural designs for the store?" The question rang hollow in her ears, as if that was as big a concern as being shipped back to the front, but she couldn't bring herself to ask the bigger questions. *Will you be safe? Will you still think of me?*

"Put in storage. Passed along to another. Or simply forgotten. My part was less integral to their overall plan than to their appeal to the masses as the Tommy in his shiny uniform seen on the show floor. A symbol to attract customers."

"A symbol set to reimagine the entire store."

His smile turned genuine briefly, before slipping again. "There you go again forgetting I'm a *junior* in the firm. Besides, no changes will be made to the store until after the war."

The war. A blight on humanity that refused to be snuffed out. Was nearly four years not long enough for the insatiable appetite for death and destruction?

She pushed off the bench and stood, clutching the poetry book to her middle. "It was to all be over by Christmas."

"With me back in the fighting, maybe it will be."

"You speak so glibly."

He rose and stood next to her, brushing her shawl with his sleeve. "I've learned that having humor keeps one from dwelling on the gloom, and I won't allow gloom to creep into this morning standing here in the garden with you. You're much too lovely for that."

"Charmer."

"No. Simply charmed. By you." He lifted the peacock feather from between the pages and twirled it between his fingers. "I was hoping to find plumage a bit less crumpled to offer you. The bird was less than obliging."

The feather's blues and greens swirled together in a mesmerizing dance of elegance and splendor, but her eyes drew away in search of his. "Everything need not be perfect to be beautiful."

Holding her gaze, he tucked the crooked feather behind her ear. "May I write you?"

She nodded, once, then reached for his hand. He laced his fingers through hers, and they stood together watching the day break before them.

CHAPTER 9

❧

Rex and Iris

Southampton, England
15 January 1918

Dear Iris,

*I presented your sketch to Mr. Stewart-Liberty yesterday when I
met with him to explain that my services had been once more called
on by the army. I must admit he had me quite nervous at first with
his silence, and I may have rambled on a bit much, but overall I
believe his interest was piqued. Especially once I described your
marvelous design of marrying the old with the new. His eyes glinted
a bit at that, but I am sorry I was unable to ascertain a definitive
response for you. He did assure me of his consideration on the matter.*

*Apologies for the brevity of this note, but I wanted to dash off
a quick word before boarding the ship to France and not have you
think I failed to upkeep my side of the bargain.*

Respectfully,
Rex

~

22 January 1918

Dear Rex,

Not for a single moment did I doubt you following through on your word, and I extend an extraordinary thank-you for rambling on long enough to spark a glint in Mr. Stewart-Liberty's eye. My greatest fear was that he would rend it in two, crush it beneath his heel, and set a match to it. Or worse, laugh.

I regret to say that he has yet to declare a parade in my honor for my genius, but I shall save you bits of confetti when he does. Two days after you left, I returned to London and my job, where I could no longer afford days off for fear of another girl swooping in and taking my position. I now remain faithfully at my table painting designs and doing my best not to fall asleep at the blandness.

My parents send you their best. They remain at your uncle's estate as he has so graciously allowed them to stay for the next week until a new roof has been added to their house. I believe your uncle's extended generosity is because Papa carved a stamp from a block of wood and has begun to paint-stamp the guest hallway. I went to visit them yesterday on my day off and overheard them discussing a pattern of the solar system to be stamped in the larder. Mum grumbles about him needing to rest, but she has been spending more time in the red garden unearthing a collection of ceramic gnomes that were buried upside down. She has righted each of them and lined them up according to height. Do you suppose there is a great discrepancy in gnome height? It seems to me the shorter of the creatures compensate with taller hats.

It feels odd to say I hope this letter reaches you well in France, for what can be well there? Lacking in well circumstances, I hope

*your spirits are not downtrodden and that you are able to find
beauty in at least one small thing in your day.*

Sincerely,

Iris

*PS: I leave this drawing of the gnome lineup for your
inspection. Notice how the short one at the end preens by sporting
the pointiest of hats.*

⌒

28 January 1918

Dear Rex,

*I cannot contain my good news and had to write you
immediately though I posted a letter only days ago. Mr. Stewart-
Liberty called me into his office this very morning to say he is quite
impressed with my sketch. He asked a great many questions of my
inspiration and the reasoning behind each selected design, which I
was happy to oblige with further explanation. Most of all, he was
quite taken with the quote I looped among the vines. Did you notice,
I wonder? You never made mention of it, though you are the one to
credit for its inclusion. "Hope is the thing with feathers."*

*Twenty-five prints on scarves have been ordered for a test run.
If they sell well, a larger print run will be made. On silk! Oh, a
lovely silk scarf with my design on it! By the end of the week, I am
to present him a painted version of the sketch. I was thinking a blue
background, dark purple vines, light purple feathers, and sunrays of
red. What do you think of the combination?*

I hope you are safe and well and dry.

Most excitedly,

Iris

~

8 February 1918

Dear Iris,

After four days of being stranded by fog, we finally said goodbye to dear old England and made sail for France. I won't bore you with the details of travel to camp, but suffice to say I was quickly reminded of how much I detest mud. Fear not, I managed to haul myself from the muck and settle into a tent that has a rather ill-placed hole in the roof that drips snow into my boots overnight. I've taken to wearing the boots while I sleep as they keep my feet warmer. The only other thing I imagine that might keep my feet warm is dancing with you. Your stepping on my toes certainly kept the blood flowing.

Hold on a tic—a letter has come from you! Make yourself a cuppa while I open and read it.

Holy smokes! Iris, that is wonderful news! My heartiest of congratulations that I should say that I knew you would win him over all along. Your talent and vision are too spectacular to ignore. I like the color combination very much. It is rather reminiscent of color gardens we sat in not so long ago. I think of that time often.

Warmly,
Rex

PS: Please send me a final mockup of the sketch in color. I would very much like to see the quote among the vines and believe you placed it there as a secret for the two of us.

~

27 February 1918

Dear Rex,

    The first prints have arrived! It truly is like holding a dream in my hand, yet the best news is to come. Are you prepared? They sold out within five days! More have been ordered, a cotton and a silk version. I think it is lovely to offer customers the option as silk is not always practical. Papa caused quite the stir hobbling on a crutch into the printing mill and demanding he be the first to stamp the fabric. Mum, for once, did not put up a fight but held his crutch while he blocked. Did I tell you? Every other Sunday they join your uncle Harbo for tea in his garden. They are delighted to have returned home again a few weeks ago, but do so miss the country's fresh air and rainbow of chickens pecking about the grounds.

    The headlines tell us Russia has signed a peace treaty with the Central Powers. It's all anyone can speak of, and I must admit to a trembling within me of what this means. I pray you are safe and far from the fighting, and most importantly, that this war ends soon so we may walk again in the garden.

Warmest regards,

Iris

    PS: I have taken the peacock feather you gave me and turned it into a quill with which I pen these very words. I do so feel like a true Dickinson now.

~

12 June 1918

Dearest Iris,

My apologies for the lateness of this reply, but the post has become spotty at best where it can be months before a letter and then suddenly fifteen all at once. Makes a fellow feel quite behind the times. Yes, I still carry the Feathered Hope scarf with me, though no longer tied about my neck for warmth. These days it is stuffed in my pocket and brought out to mop the sweat from my brow. Not a delicate picture, I admit, but its use brings a smile to my face as I imagine you sitting there in the garden, which must be in full bloom by now.

Do not fret if you don't hear from me for a while. The post is slow, as you well know, and my commanding officer is threatening us with a very long march to a place with less refined trenches. If that is indeed possible, as these are possibly the worst accommodations the army could offer, though we keep our spirits high with a good sing each night. I once was prideful enough to boast the ability to carry a tune, but tins of pottage beef seem to have dried my throat and now my singing would likely drive the chaps straight out of the trench clenching their ears, so their safety must remain my priority.

Tunelessly yours,

Rex

16 September 1918

Rex,

You told me not to worry about your infrequent letters, but that is a preposterous request as I do worry. For fear of sounding like

*that nagging girl you left behind, I shall not weep or scold you but
instead tell you of the lovely flower delivery I received yesterday from
Uncle Harbo. He planted irises in the blue garden, dried them out
over the summer, and had them wrapped in a lovely blue ribbon for
me. They are so sweet, and I will cherish them as the months turn
cooler and color is drained from nature's palette.*

*I pray for your continued safety and hope that we might share
another dance soon under a flag of peace.*

Affectionately,
Iris

⌐

30 October 1918

Dearest Iris,

*Keep your chin up, dear girl, as you read my next lines. Our
next dance must be postponed for I won't be much of a partner with
only one leg. A Hun in Meuse-Argonne decided I was too charming
with both feet and sought a way to cut me down to size. He was polite
enough to take the one that was already mangled from a previous
encounter with one of his comrades. As you can see, he did not entirely
lop off my humor, which I stubbornly cling to as I stay in hospital
somewhere in France. The nurses are stern and kind, but none so
pretty as you. I have tried to draw your likeness, but my skills fall
woefully short. I wonder if you might oblige me with your own artist's
rendering. I should very much like to carry it next to your scarf.*

With affection,
Rex

⌐

4 December 1918

Dearest Rex,

    I will have you know that I am still reeling from worry since
you first wrote me of your injury, though your humor reassures
me that recovery in Paris is not entirely without its benefits. It's
important to keep up the exercises no matter how mundane they
seem. A bit of walking each day will help strengthen your muscles
as I do expect a proper dance this Christmas. With your one leg and
my two left feet, we shall make the perfect pair.

    It seems London has finally run dry of champagne from all
the Armistice celebrating. The store is busier than ever. Orders for
the Feathered Hope can barely keep up with the demand, and I
overheard one young woman yesterday comment that it was her
first purchase in four years that made her feel pretty. I had to duck
behind a counter before weeping right there on the showroom floor.
That and if Mr. Fletcher caught me again when I was supposed to
be sketching a new design for the spring collection, but I cannot help
slipping down from time to time just to admire the scarves folded
like little rainbows on the display table.

    You may know that Liberty has a store in Paris, La Maison
Liberty. I've been asked to venture there and speak with the
designers about a collaboration. Something to stitch together our
bond as allies. My passage is booked two weeks from now, and
I would very much like to see you while I am there. I hear Paris
has breathtaking gardens to inspire even the most mundane of
artists.

With much affection,

Iris

TELEGRAM

<u>Miss Iris Braxton</u>   16 Dec. 1918

68 Albion St.

London, England

Not in Paris stop in Strasbourg stop big
surprise for you stop come at once stop
Yours Rex

PART TWO

CHAPTER 1

~❦~

New England Telephone and Telegraph Central Offices
Portland, Maine
December 1917

GENEVIÈVE TUGGED AT THE COLLAR OF HER BLOUSE, URGING MORE
air to enter her windpipe, but she forced herself to stop, lest she
look nervous. The recruiters were stealthy in their observation
of all the ladies gathered in the massive edifice, each eager for
a chance to serve her country overseas. It wasn't the same as
firing artillery or spending weeks on end in murky trenches,
but operating the phone system was hugely beneficial to the
war effort.

General Pershing was convinced the new technology would
be the key to winning the war, and Geneviève was convinced he
was right. And as Geneviève knew well, telephone operations
were the province of women.

The makeshift recruitment bureau in the central office in
Portland was so crammed full of women, it was oppressively
warm despite the December temperatures out of doors. Though

the branch office of New England Telephone and Telegraph in Lewiston was usually bustling, Geneviève was so focused on her work that she could have imagined herself alone. And there was comfort in knowing a person could escape the hubbub at the end of a shift. It seemed there was no escaping people in Portland. Heaven knew those selected for service would be packed in like proverbial sardines more often than not, and Geneviève prayed she'd be able to manage it.

She'd hoped the Portland crowds wouldn't unsettle her, but the hope had been a foolish one. Somehow she managed well enough at home. The ramshackle home she shared in Lewiston with her parents was stuffed to bursting with her five younger brothers and sister. Papa had worked at the paper mill since they emigrated when Geneviève was six, and though they'd been a family of four when they arrived in America, the family increased in number so quickly that neither their house nor their father's wages could keep up with the demands placed on them. Perhaps it was because they were family, but it was much different to be nestled in an apartment with parents and siblings than to be jammed in a room with strangers.

"Tremblay, Geneviève," the recruiter called in a deadpan voice. The recruitment efforts had redoubled in the past months, and Geneviève didn't wonder that the uniformed man was beyond putting on a pleasant facade for the aspiring operators. Everyone in that office had been subject to more than their share of twelve-hour days, or even longer.

Geneviève rose and walked, as confidently as she could, to the open door where the officer, a Captain Callan, waited for her. The lines under his eyes were dark and deep, the sort that even the strongest coffee couldn't touch. The man needed three good consecutive nights' sleep. More precisely, he needed peace, which none of them would have until the war was over.

"I'll have to ask you to pronounce your name for me," he said once they were seated in the office. "I struggle with French, I'm afraid."

"Trom-blay," she offered, trying to extend some grace, remembering her own struggles wrapping her Quebecois tongue around certain English words when she was young. She'd had to completely disregard the spelling of the word *February* to learn how to pronounce it properly. "It's not as challenging as some names, I think. And most of my colleagues call me Jennie once we're acquainted." She disliked the American nickname as a rule, but Peter was right . . . it did make her more approachable to those Americans who didn't want the bother of learning even a few syllables of French.

"You'll find, Miss Tremblay, that serving as an operator in the military will be quite a different proposition than working for New England Telephone and Telegraph. We have to maintain the distinction of ranks, so there is a formality that you might not have experienced in the workplace heretofore."

"I would expect so," Geneviève replied. It wasn't as though working for NET&T had been a warm and welcoming environment. She would much prefer cold formality to open hostility. "I can understand the need to make sure the chain of command is clearly delineated."

The captain nodded his agreement. "Good. I'll come right to the point. The Signal Corps believes that it's easier to learn the running of a switchboard on the fly than it is to learn French. That you come to us more than proficient in both makes you an especially attractive candidate. That your English is on par with a native is the chocolate frosting on the buttered pound cake."

Geneviève couldn't conceal a smile of satisfaction, or a slight rumble in her stomach at the mention of food. She was forced to eat in the cafeteria at lunchtime while she was in Portland, so she ate sparsely to save money. Peter had warned her that none of the others brought food from home in these recruitment sessions, and anything that called attention to her might reflect badly. She did smuggle in an apple from home in her bag and ate it discreetly in the washroom, but that had been hours earlier. "I am very eager to serve, Captain."

"Delighted to hear it. Are your parents on board with you serving overseas?"

Geneviève tried not to blanch. Her mother had been in tears at the idea but had come around after a good deal of persuasion. "They'd be proud to see me in uniform, sir."

"Excellent. If it weren't for one letter, I'd have you signing the enlistment papers now. While all the rest of the NET&T staff wrote you glowing recommendations, your direct supervisor, a Miss Penny Johnson, questioned your work ethic and ambition. Claiming that you flaunt regulations about mealtimes and arrive late to your shift."

Geneviève clenched her jaw but managed to control her temper. "I hate to speak ill of a colleague, Captain, but Miss Johnson isn't to be believed. I have never been late to a shift and make it a point to return five minutes early from lunch break." *And to make sure she sees me do it too.*

"That seems to be corroborated by the rest of your colleagues. Which makes me curious as to why Miss Johnson would take it upon herself to fabricate stories about you."

"Miss Johnson is not exactly fond of those of us from Quebec. She tolerates our existence because the French-speaking population of Auburn and Lewiston requires that we retain a few bilingual staff members, but if it were up to her, she'd have us packed off before the shift was over. Back to Canada altogether if she had that sort of authority. And thank God she hasn't."

She sucked in a breath, knowing she'd said too much. Disrespecting a direct supervisor was no way to win the approval of a military man.

He let out a weary sigh. "I'm afraid I understand a bit of that. My grandfather came to Boston seventy years ago from County Cork and found that fewer doors were slammed in his face when he changed his name from Callaghan to Callan and worked to lessen his brogue. He always told us to play down our heritage, but there wasn't much hiding this." He removed a cap to expose a thatch of fiery-orange hair that was cropped close in accordance with army regulations.

Geneviève knitted her fingers in her lap. "It's a shame."

He cocked his head. "What do you mean precisely?"

"When we come to this country, we're all told to blend in. To make ourselves as 'American' as possible, whatever that means. The Quebecois are told not to speak French at home so we get used to speaking English all the time . . . yet in her moment of need, my French is precisely what makes me of greatest use to my country."

"Well put. If only the rest of the country saw things as you do, we'd be living in a much kinder place."

Geneviève smiled at the beleaguered captain. "If the world saw things my way, Captain Callan, we wouldn't be at war at all."

He slid a packet of paperwork across the desk. "Welcome to the Signal Corps, Miss Tremblay. You'll be good enough to fill out those forms before you leave? You're to report to Manhattan for training in two weeks for deployment in the new year. I'm afraid it won't be a very merry Christmas this year, but we can hope for happier tidings in the next."

On top of the stack of papers was a paper titled "Uniform and Required Supplies." It was a long list that included summer and winter uniforms, first aid and hygiene supplies, and a whole litany of personal items that the army deemed necessary for service. Captain Callan must have seen the color drain from Geneviève's face. "Will the supplies be a problem?"

"H-how much do you think all this will cost?" she managed to stammer.

He looked apologetic. "On the order of $300. Perhaps more. Officers are charged with buying their own uniforms and supplies. I suppose the higher-ups expected the same of you ladies."

Geneviève wanted to protest that she wasn't some gentleman soldier from a landed British family that one might read about in novels. That they considered the operators on par with officers was a heady compliment, but it wasn't one her pocketbook could permit her to accept. It was the lion's share of what she made in a year, and every penny of that money was needed for her family.

"The address on the sheet is where you will report in Manhattan, and they're quite good about issuing credit to those who cannot afford the kit straight out." He spoke as though taking on almost a year's salary in debt was as trifling a matter as picking up a paper from the newsstand on the way home.

Despite her financial concerns, Geneviève allowed Captain Callan to show her to an empty office to fill out her paperwork. She was grateful for the relative quiet, happy to finally be able to take a full breath. When she finished, she handed the paperwork to the clerk as she'd been directed to and slipped the uniform list in her satchel. She had no idea how she would raise a small fortune in two weeks, but she would have to try. She didn't want to fail in her commitment, but neither did she want to saddle herself with a mountain of debt to do it.

Her mother always told her to trust that the era of mira-
cles hadn't expired two millennia ago, and she had to trust that
there was just enough magic in the world for another.

⌁

The electric train rolled into Union Station in Lewiston after a
speedy eighty-minute ride from the city that felt interminable
to Geneviève. She was no closer to finding a solution to her
budgetary crisis than when she boarded the train in Portland
and had nearly an hour and a half to mull over how impossible
it was. She'd have to explain to the Signal Corps that, despite
how happy she'd be to serve, she couldn't possibly devote such
a princely sum to the endeavor. She wished she could afford to
be so magnanimous, but there were five other children at home
to feed, and Papa's wages from the paper mill just barely covered their basic needs. She wanted more than just a roof and
almost-adequate food for her brothers and sister. Her parents
too. They deserved good dresses and suits for Mass on Sundays,
library subscriptions, and access to a few of life's advantages.

They had left behind their beloved Canada for a better life,
and Geneviève saw no point to that sacrifice if they were just
going to scrape by. They could have done that back in Quebec
without leaving behind their grandparents and countless aunts,
uncles, and cousins.

The chill she felt in her spine as she left the station wasn't
just to do with the weather, though it certainly played a part.
There were years when winter was sluggish to start, but as Geneviève pulled her hand-me-down coat tight around her, she
regretted that this would not be one of them. She was so lost
in her reverie, she screeched in surprise when Peter grabbed
her by the crook of her arm as she turned onto the sidewalk
to make her way home. He was leaning against his black Ford

Model T Coupelet, his newly issued uniform coat buttoned up against the bracing cold and drizzling icy rain. He was bound for transport overseas in the next week, and he was so eager for his service, she wouldn't have been shocked to learn that he slept in his uniform.

He lifted her up and twirled her around when she approached him, then released her with a kiss on the lips, just short enough not to offend any onlookers. "I knew you'd knock 'em dead, Jennie. You're the best operator in the state of Maine."

The central office in Portland had been gracious enough to allow her a phone call when she was dismissed. As her parents didn't yet have phone service, Peter was the only person she could think to call. She had conveyed the news of her acceptance into the Signal Corps but hadn't expressed her worry about the expense of it. Given the disparate financial situations of their families, she found it uncomfortable to talk about such things. She knew that Peter himself had enough money squirreled away in his wallet to outfit himself without even dipping into his rainy-day fund. His parents were more comfortable still. She often thought about what it would be like to be free from the shackles of worry like that, but she steered her thoughts away, not wanting to tempt the demons of envy that she knew lurked within her.

She placed another decorous kiss on his cheek. "I didn't expect you to come for me. I figured you were terribly busy getting ready for next week."

Like Geneviève, he had worked at New England Telephone and Telegraph since they graduated high school six years before. They'd been chummy, if not exactly friends, all through school until he'd unexpectedly asked her to join him for a soda after work one day eight months before. A quick soda became dinner the next week. The following, he brought her home to meet his parents. And when it became clear that America was going to throw its oar in the war in Europe, the courtship accelerated faster than Geneviève could possibly have imagined. There wasn't a ring on her finger yet, but the promises were all but spoken.

Unlike Geneviève, who had begun her work as an operator and remained firmly in that post, Peter had been promoted often, and quickly too. He was smart and ambitious, which helped. He was male and had a father in the highest echelons of the administration, which helped even more. It was Peter's dream to transfer to the Portland office after the war and surpass even his own father in wealth and standing. Geneviève thought it would have been far easier for him to satisfy his ambitions if he'd chosen a girl from the right family, but Peter seemed determined to bring Geneviève along with him up the social and corporate ladders.

Truth be told, she wasn't sure *why* he'd set his cap at her. She was a pretty girl, but that hardly seemed reason enough for a bright young man like Peter. She hoped that part of him also valued her intelligence and resourcefulness, but she didn't press the issue. He was a good sort of man, kind and hardworking, and he would ensure that she and—even more importantly— her family would have a brighter future. Food and opportunity for her family tempted her far more than the jewels that might follow in time. It wasn't the only or even the central reason why she let the courtship proceed. But it was a solid enough reason to make even a lesser man seem suitable.

"Of course I came for you, silly goose! Let's get in the car before we freeze."

She didn't hesitate to comply, but she felt the secret lurch of dread she always experienced when he drove her home. The Tremblay house on the outskirts of Little Canada was, in reality,

an apartment in a tenement building. He was gracious enough
not to say anything, but she knew he pitied her whenever he
saw the bleak building where her family lived. And pity was an
emotion she couldn't abide, even from Peter.

But it would be silly to refuse the ride in such weather. She
couldn't use the old excuse of needing to stretch her legs, as
he'd just think she was dotty. As he pulled into traffic, she realized he was navigating toward the commercial center of town
instead of the neighborhood where she lived.

She looked quizzically in his direction, which elicited a
chuckle from him. "I thought we could celebrate. I hope you
don't mind." Just then, he parked the car in a lot near one of
the restaurants that he and his family enjoyed regularly. It was
a seafood place that, while not the most elegant eatery in the
state of Maine, was far beyond the means of Geneviève and her
family. She looked up at the neat white building that was bustling with customers, eager for their halibut fillets and lobster
tails.

She felt a prickling of heat at her cheeks. "I'm not really
dressed for going out." She wore a serviceable brown wool
dress of her mother's that had been made over twice. It passed
muster well enough at the office but was dowdy for such an
establishment.

"You'll be perfect, I promise." He reached over to pat her
knee reassuringly.

Peter escorted her out of the car and into the building where
she discovered that his parents were already waiting at a table
set with white starched linens and a bottle of champagne chilling on ice. Mr. and Mrs. Blake smiled and stood when they saw
the young couple, the men shaking hands and the ladies kissing
the air above each other's cheeks. The handshaking always baf-
fled Geneviève. Her father never would have shaken one of his

son's hands if he were physically capable of embracing him. But it was just another way in which the French Canadians differed from their American neighbors.

Henry and Mildred Blake were opposites in a way that would have been comical if they didn't terrify Geneviève out of her very shoes. Henry was the sort of rotund man that appeared jolly, and he liked to cultivate that image because it drew people in. Geneviève had learned, however, that any pretense at jolliness evaporated when he crossed the threshold of a boardroom. If a person valued their life and livelihood, they didn't underestimate Henry Blake's ruthlessness when his own interests were at stake. Peter's mother, in contrast, was a tall, lanky, pinch-faced woman who made no attempt to emulate her husband's jovial persona. But tonight, as she stood and kissed Geneviève's cheeks, she was on the lukewarm side of neutral, which was, all things considered, an improvement.

Mildred did cast an appraising eye on Geneviève's plain dress and pursed her lips so quickly it was nearly imperceptible to everyone except Geneviève herself, who had an unfortunate knack of noticing signs of disapproval in others. But the look on Mildred's face turned to resignation soon enough. Dresses could be changed.

Peter pulled a chair out for her. "We had to take you out to celebrate. You're a credit to NET&T and we're all so proud of you."

"Indeed we are, Jennie," Henry said with unusual warmness. "You're one of the best operators we have, and the Signal Corps will be lucky to have you."

Geneviève mustered a weak smile. "Thank you so much. I had no idea if I would pass all the trials they put us through, but I wanted to make sure I didn't embarrass myself or the company in the process."

Mildred's lips drew upward in an awkward attempt at a smile. "You obviously acquitted yourself very well, my dear."

"Indeed she did." Peter raised a glass to her. "You'll be the pride of Lewiston over there."

Henry shot Geneviève a wink. "Oh, I think Jennie will manage to leave a few accolades on the table for the young men in uniform."

"I'll do my best not to hog them all for myself, but no promises." Geneviève's little attempt at humor was met, to her relief, with hearty chuckles.

The waiter took their order, and she was glad when Henry ordered generously for the whole table. She felt a bit of guilt slip away; she wouldn't have to concern herself with the cost of the meal quite so much if she'd taken no part in ordering it.

"I think I should say something." Jennie looked wistfully as the waiter walked away. His exchanges with people that night would be far less fraught than the one she was about to have. "I was very excited about serving, but the cost of the uniform and supplies is simply too much. I simply can't afford to go."

Henry chuckled. "Oh, there's no need to worry about that, Jennie. As you can imagine, Peter researched the whole thing before he nudged you to apply. Mrs. Blake and I would like to cover that expense for you, and NET&T will make an official contribution as well. It's one small way for us to support the war effort."

"That's far too generous of you. I really can't accept it." Geneviève was unable to meet their eyes. She knew the sum was trivial to them, but she couldn't bear the idea of being so indebted to them, even considering the seriousness of Peter's suit.

"Fiddle-faddle." Mildred waved her hand dismissively. "Of

course you can. You're quite sensible not to want to go into debt for your kit, and there's no need for such a thing."

"Some of the operators' towns raised the money in a matter of an hour or two to have the honor of supporting one of their own in service." Peter patted her hand. He was more sensitive to Geneviève's reticence, even if he didn't fully understand it.

"That's true enough. We could have raised the money in the space of your train ride from Portland if we'd passed the hat at NET&T," Henry chimed in. "We just didn't feel it necessary since we're fortunate enough to be able to do it ourselves."

Geneviève wished they *had* passed the hat. It would have been easier to express gratitude to fifty or sixty people for their five dollars' worth of generosity than to be grateful to two people for the full amount. But they didn't want to stoop to asking for the money. And Geneviève suspected they didn't want to share the spotlight of wartime magnanimity.

"It's all settled," Peter declared without looking at Geneviève. "I'll take you to Manhattan for training and outfitting myself before I ship out."

Geneviève exhaled. It *was* a solution to a problem, one she'd prayed for the entire train ride home, but it still weighed as heavy in her gut as bad fish. Her thank-you was listless as it floated from her mouth, landing with a graceless thud on the ear.

"We're just so glad you were successful, my dear. It will be a grand way to improve your standing in the community and to gain some positive notoriety," Mildred said.

Geneviève blinked. "I wasn't aware that my standing in the community was in need of rehabilitation."

"That's not quite the way to put it," Henry interjected. "It's just that immigrant families, industrious as they are, don't mix in the same circles. If Peter is serious about a future with you, your role in society will change vastly. He's an ambitious young man and will need a wife who can support him in all his endeavors."

"I would think the industriousness of my people would be an asset in helping him reach his goals, don't you?" Geneviève kept her tone from growing confrontational, but only just.

Mildred folded her hands neatly in her lap and straightened, as if explaining something serious to a small child. "You must understand, my dear, that so much of climbing the corporate ladder has more to do with social connections and a strong public image than you realize. You might be the best telephone operator the whole Bell outfit has ever seen, but that won't help Peter rise in the ranks in management, now will it?"

People assume I am with him because I come from a poor family and I'm after his money. And they think less of me for it. Of course a girl like me couldn't appreciate his finer qualities. Poverty makes me blind to anything other than money. And being the poor wretch that I am, I couldn't possibly have the skills to be a proper helpmate to him. You gloss over how your own husband is the son of a Cornish immigrant, and that you're no Astor yourself. How convenient for you.

The bitter thoughts simmered in her brain like poison in a cauldron, and she took a rather hefty drink from her flute of champagne before choosing her words.

"And you think my wartime service will . . . somehow sway public opinion in my favor?"

"Precisely that." Henry donned the winning smile he used when he'd finally persuaded an adversary to agree to a bargain. "People might have wondered at Peter taking up with a girl from Little Canada. No one will think twice about Peter being charmed by a girl in uniform."

"Cheers to that." Peter raised his glass once more.

It had all fallen into place. Peter's family wanted her to serve so that she would be worthy of one day marrying into the Blake family. She considered that she ought to feel grateful that they had the largeness of spirit to think an immigrant girl could ever be fit to wed their son. But as she picked at the outrageous bounty of food before her, gratitude was an emotion she struggled to evoke within herself.

CHAPTER 2

～

London, England
Late February 1918

"ARE YOU SURE YOU WON'T JOIN ELSIE AND ME FOR SOME TEA AND A chat?" Flora offered on the train ride into London. Flora, with whom Geneviève had become fast friends during the crossing, was meeting up with an old chum from Chicago. Apparently Flora and Elsie had grown up together, but Elsie "married up" and was now ensconced in a posh flat in Mayfair, one of the most elegant districts in the city. Flora spoke of her friend with some affection but not much envy for the dashing new life she led in Mayfair. Or at least it had been dashing before the war had started. Flora loved Chicago and was ruthlessly practical. It was that quality that had attracted Geneviève to her almost immediately.

"Absolutely sure. You don't need a third wheel for your visit. You'll both have far more fun reminiscing without me." Geneviève gave her a reassuring smile. Flora was older than many of the girls, nearing thirty and never married, but endeared herself by avoiding the maternal affect some women would have been tempted to put on when surrounded by girls a decade younger.

"I don't think that's true, but I can understand not wanting to 'feel like a gooseberry,' as Elsie claims they say over here." Flora shook her head as if her friend delighted in making up stories about the ridiculous expressions the Brits used to fill the pages of her letters.

"I'll see you to your friend's place and wander around a bit. I'll collect you by eight so we can make it back by curfew."

"That would be kind of you. You'd think that being a city girl, I'd be used to navigating my way around steel and concrete well enough, but I get so turned around in these places."

Geneviève and Flora chatted companionably on the walk from their temporary London quarters to the posh neighborhood where Flora's friend lived. Geneviève waited on the sidewalk until Flora gained admittance to a stately looking town house by a dour-faced man in livery. Some of Geneviève's friends in Little Canada were in service to the wealthy families of Auburn and Lewiston, and they were all expected to dress neatly and soberly, but it seemed the British took things to a different level altogether when it came to the social hierarchy.

As she turned onto the street to enjoy a stroll in the hours she had to wait for Flora, she couldn't imagine that in some places her prospects for social mobility might actually be worse. The place of her birth would have dictated not just her start to life, but it might have dictated the entirety of its course. At least in America, despite all the animosity against her people, she had the chance to climb the ladder a few rungs. She had no delusions that any door would open to her if she were insistent enough in her knocking, but she did feel that improving her situation, even without Peter's influence, was possible.

Geneviève tried to shuffle off the thoughts that would begin to weigh her down like a layer of heavy snow on her shoulders. She wanted to drink in the sights of the charming old city while she had the chance. As she ambled, she could imagine her mother's delight in wandering the city streets as clearly as if she were walking beside her. Lewiston seemed so bleak and colorless after Maman's childhood in Montreal, and Geneviève always felt she rather regretted leaving home. Papa's upbringing had been more modest, coming from a family of timber workers outside the city, so he felt the mill life in Maine wasn't quite the step down in life that Maman did. But she'd sacrificed for love, as so many women did.

Regent Street was a marvel, and she admired the artful shop windows, though she hadn't the means to indulge in any shopping in the way some of the other girls had planned to. One would have thought they were on summer holiday instead of going off to war, but Geneviève couldn't find it within herself to criticize. It would be their last chance to have a bit of fun before reality set in, and it wasn't for her to deny them.

She paused in front of Liberty of London, the famous department store she'd heard some of the girls gushing over. Through the glass doors, she could see row after row of bottles and squat little pots containing soaps and face creams. There were some displays of clothes and handbags that looked elegant and poised—nothing too audacious given that the country was mired in war. But there was an opulence about the scarves in the window display that even the horrors of war couldn't subdue. It was the colors. Even though the brutality of trenches was uncomfortably close, it hadn't yet muted Liberty's colors.

Though she doubted there was a single item in the shop she could afford, she wandered in, offering the doorman a polite nod as she walked back to the display of scarves in the far cor-

ner. It cost nothing to look, and she figured it could be something she could chat about with the girls when they spoke about
their adventures in the big city later that night. It might help
her feel the sting of her circumstances a little less keenly.

There were deep greens that reminded her of the forests in
Canada, there were reds that Geneviève admired for their confidence in being so unabashedly . . . red. But there was a light
blue one with dark purple vines and lavender peacock feathers
that caught her eye. The red sunbursts in the corners were a
bold touch, but they, astoundingly enough, didn't overpower
the effect of the softer colors. She looked around, and seeing no
clerk in view, took the corner of the fabric between her thumb
and forefinger. Her hands were clean and shouldn't mark the
precious silk.

And she could take with her the memory of the buttery sen-
sation of the luscious fabric between her fingers. She hoped only
there wouldn't be a shopgirl to spoil the moment by chastising
her for touching the merchandise. Then again, Geneviève was
dressed in her uniform—a smart-looking suit of navy-blue wool
that she rather liked, despite the occasional itch at the neck.
Her topcoat was also army-issue and the best coat she'd ever
worn. For once, she looked like any other well-born woman
in the shop, and she wouldn't be subject to the same scrutiny
that she was in Maine. They had no reason to suspect she was
touching a garment that was likely worth a month of her pay.
She couldn't bear to look at the price tag to see how accurate
she was.

"That color would be fetching on you," a voice said behind
her. It was not the clipped accent of the shopgirls who were
trying their best to emulate their wealthy patrons and to avoid
betraying their humble origins. It was a man with an accent.
Not unlike her maman's, but more polished.

"Oh, thank you." Geneviève turned to look at him. He was tall and in uniform as well, though not in the Signal Corps. His uniform was that of an airman for the French *armée de l'air*, though she didn't know enough about the various insignia to discern his rank. "It's lovely, isn't it? It's incredible to think of such a beautiful thing existing when there is such brutishness in the world."

She immediately felt silly for sharing such a thought with a stranger, but if he thought she was dotty, he was kind enough to keep that assessment to himself.

His eyes widened a moment. "Oh, that's all terribly logical to my mind. If there wasn't such beauty in the world, what would all the fighting be for? Though the scarf itself is insignificant, perhaps, protecting the people who make such beautiful things is worth the risk and sacrifice."

Geneviève nodded. "Knowing that maybe makes it easier to face the worst. You're right about that."

The airman extended his hand. "Captain Maxime Auvray, at your service." She took in his considerable height, at least an inch or two over six feet. He had dark hair and eyes, and the sort of even features that were pleasing, if not handsome in a classical sense.

"Geneviève Tremblay, US Army Signal Corps Operator at yours." She accepted his hand. "Though everyone calls me Jennie."

"But your name is French?" he replied in French. "How are you serving with the Americans?"

"I'm Quebecois by birth but a Mainer since I was six," she explained.

"Ah, so you are one of Pershing's 'Hello Girls.' I've heard of this plan. It's a good one. I hate to speak ill of my own country-women, but they haven't the patience for serving customers that our American—and Canadian—compatriots have. It wouldn't matter if two generals were discussing a peace treaty or vital strategy, my darling sister would cut the line after ten minutes out of sheer boredom."

Geneviève giggled. "That sounds like the stories we heard in training."

"I don't doubt they're all true. But why do your fellow operators call you Jennie? Surely women of some education can manage the pronunciation?"

Geneviève cast her eyes downward a moment. "It just . . . makes things easier."

"Ah, I understand. I've been in England off and on for three years now and I've had a small taste of what it's like to feel different. Though the uniform helps to dissuade confrontation. I can only imagine a lifetime of feeling separate."

"Oh, it's not that bad," Geneviève said, trying to downplay the changes she'd made to fit in. "I was able to get work at the phone office, and it led me here. I should be grateful for that."

"And I am grateful for that as well, but I will not call you Jennie. You are Geneviève."

She smiled. "It's nice to hear it spoken properly. And how is it that a French pilot is stationed in London?"

"Training command. The Brits needed me here, so France lent me to them. Happens all the time. But my run of good luck to have a cushy training job has run its course, and I'll return to the front after my leave is up. I'll get a week at home before heading back. My first since the war broke out."

"You head back soon then?"

He nodded. "I'll make the crossing to France tomorrow morning. I came in looking for a gift for that *darling sister* I mentioned to you. Her sixteenth birthday is next week, and I had the good luck to get my leave just in time for it. I thought a remembrance from London would please her."

Geneviève looked at the goods, all too fine for her pocketbook. "To get such a gift at sixteen, I'd have expired from the shock of it. She'll be ecstatic."

"Perhaps you can help me to select one for her?"

His expression looked so hopeful, she couldn't help but agree. "What does she look like?"

Maxime pulled a picture from his billfold. She was a charming young girl with a glint of mischief in her eyes, not unlike her brother's. "This is Aurélie."

"She's lovely. Is her coloring like yours?" Geneviève asked, unable to fully discern from the black-and-white photo.

"Her skin doesn't tan so easily, and her eyes are perhaps a shade or two lighter than mine, but otherwise, yes."

She studied the scarves with great interest. If Maxime's sister were a grown woman, Geneviève would have selected one of the bold reds, but at sixteen, young Aurélie could wait for such a daring accessory. She deserved to cling to the last moments of her childhood, given it was a privilege denied to so many. In the end, Geneviève selected one with a geometric design that looked like the inside of a kaleidoscope that was primarily a feminine shade of pink but also boasted a rainbow of blues, greens, and yellows.

"I would choose this one. It's youthful but modern. And it will go with anything. Perfect for a girl who is dipping her toes in the waters of womanhood, I should think."

"And it has the virtue of being easy enough to pack away in my rucksack," he said with a wink. "Though I'll deny the whole thing if you ever tell her that such practical considerations figured into the purchase."

Geneviève smiled. The chances of her ever meeting Aurélie

were next to none, but she loved how adamant he was. He clearly thought the world of this capricious young girl. "I'm sure she'll love it. I'll leave you to your purchase."

She left Liberty, the spell the fabrics had cast over her broken by the intrusion of Captain Auvray. But she was happy to have experienced such beauty if only for a few fleeting moments. It filled her with a sense of hope, however fleeting it might have been with war looming at England's doorstep. The captain was right to believe that beauty helped remind them that there were things worth protecting in the face of war, and she carried those thoughts with her as she exited to the street.

Geneviève set off down Regent Street again, trying to lose herself in the beauty of the architecture. A few minutes later, she nearly jumped out of her skin when she felt an unexpected hand on her shoulder.

"You're fast." Maxime wasn't winded from catching up with her, but he wasn't far from it. "You didn't give me a chance to thank you."

"You chased after me for such a small thing?" It wasn't as though the favor had been any sort of hardship. She'd been glad for the excuse to spend more time in the scarf room considering all the vibrant colors and artful patterns.

"It wasn't a small thing. To be able to tell my sister that her gift was selected with such care will add to her delight. Given that so many of her formative years have been marred by war, I find myself often guilty of the sin of indulgence where she's concerned."

"You seem like a devoted brother. Few would take such pains for a gift for their sisters." *Nor such expense*, but Geneviève kept that last remark to herself.

"I know of a coffee shop that has actual, honest-to-goodness coffee available for ready money. I would love to take you for a cup before we have to return to our duties. As a thank-you for your help."

In normal times, coffee would have been a small kindness, proportionate for the service she'd rendered. After two weeks on the ship, it seemed an unthinkable extravagance, but one she couldn't bring herself to resist. "Is it far?" She didn't want to wander away from the Mayfair neighborhood where she'd have to collect Flora in the next few hours.

"Not at all, just two blocks that direction." He gestured down the road and she assented. There was still plenty of daylight left and crowds enough that she could seek help if he proved to be a cad.

The coffee shop was full of patrons, likely thrilled to find an establishment with coffee on hand to serve its guests. Geneviève nodded her assent and took her place at a small table. Maxime exchanged two ration cards and a few coins at the counter, and the waiter came quickly with two brimming cups of the hot brew.

Geneviève took a sip of the black nectar and closed her eyes in delight. Earthy, rich, wholesome. Just as coffee should be. "The coffee on the ship was dreadful. This is heaven."

Maxime took a sip and nodded his head appreciatively. "Far better than the glorified mud they serve at the front. Though nothing compares to the coffee from back home. Before . . ." He gestured his hand broadly.

"Everything tastes sweeter when served with a heaping spoonful of nostalgia. Especially these days. This could be the very coffee your maman made back at home in that cup and you'd swear it isn't the same. But it isn't the coffee that's changed. It's you."

"War changes us irrevocably," Maxime agreed. "And it isn't over yet."

"It's just beginning for me." She tried not to let the fear show in her voice, but a trace of it snuck through.

"May your service be far from the front lines and of short duration." He lifted his coffee cup as though it were a champagne flute.

Geneviève raised hers and clinked china against china. "And yours as well. If you've spent so much time at the front, it seems fitting that you have a respite."

"Better to keep going and have it over with. The faster we can end it, the more innocent lives spared. And in my book, they're all innocent. Some just more than others. My fellow airmen disagree with me on that point."

"I imagine that perspective makes it easier for them to fight," Geneviève said.

"I've found that soldiers want two things: a villain and something to go home to." Maxime's eyes drifted off for a moment. "I manage to do my part without making villains of the other side. Especially the men at the front. After all, their government has them believing their cause is as just as ours."

"What did you do before the war?" Geneviève set her cup down and crossed her hands.

"I was in the family business," he said. "My family has a vineyard in Bourgogne, just outside Avallon. A beautiful place full of lush green hills. It's the first thing I think of in the morning, and I dream of it at night."

"Even the name sounds idyllic," Geneviève mused, imagining rolling hills covered in vines and a stately house at the center of the operation.

"Not to boast, but it is. My great-grandfather founded the vineyard and I'm next in line."

"It's good to be proud of your heritage." She noted how he grew animated when he spoke of the vineyard. His family legacy wasn't a burden but a blessing.

"I'm sure you'd love the place." He paused, realizing he'd been forward, and his cheeks reddened a touch. "I just mean the setting is lovely. Restful. I'm counting down the minutes until I see it again."

"I'm sure you are," Geneviève said, her tone reassuring. "I can't say you'd like Lewiston quite so well. It's not exactly a charming village."

"Do you plan to stay there?" Maxime leaned forward slightly.

She shook her head. "Not forever. Peter, my . . . well, my boyfriend, wants to move to Portland in the next few years." It was the first time Peter had surfaced in her thoughts that afternoon, but she tried not to chastise herself for it. She was in a new place and was swept up in the glory of London for a few hours before the real work began. She had no delusions that she was constantly at the forefront of Peter's thoughts either.

"And you want to go with him?"

"If things go according to plan, yes. Peter will climb the ranks at NET&T, and we'll create a lovely life there."

"Do you like Portland?"

Geneviève paused, remembering how she felt in the crowded offices, but she brushed the thought aside. If she were Peter's wife, she wouldn't be stuck in stuffy rooms all day. She'd be mistress of a comfortable home and able to do more or less as she pleased. "I haven't spent much time there. It's nothing compared to London, of course, but it's a shining metropolis compared to Lewiston."

"That's good. A girl like you deserves to be in a place that will make her happy."

"You hardly know me," Geneviève protested.

"I think most people deserve to be in places that make them happy. I wouldn't put Kaiser Wilhelm high on that list, but you seem rather more deserving than a lot of others."

"You've formed a lot of opinions about me in a short time, Captain," Geneviève said.

"I'm a quick study of character. I've found lately that I have to be."

"I'm sorry to think about why that's true." She looked to the sky, which was beginning to grow ever so slightly dimmer as the afternoon began to cede way to evening. "I think I ought to head back toward Mayfair and collect my friend so we don't miss curfew."

Maxime looked at his watch. "You're probably right. Let me accompany you?"

She nodded, thinking it would be prudent to accept the company of someone far more familiar with the city. They were only a block from the coffee shop when an earsplitting wail split the afternoon air with all the delicacy of a woodman's axe.

"What is going on?" Geneviève asked in terror as Londoners scattered out of the streets.

"Air raid. We have to get below. Now." Maxime pulled her by the elbow down a flight of stairs leading below the street to the tube. Dozens of people were huddled on the platform. If it weren't for the crying babies and worried expressions on gaunt faces, one might have thought the evening's plays had just concluded in the West End and the masses were headed back home. She felt her collar grow tight with the heat radiating off the bodies of all the people crammed into the confined space. She willed herself to fill her lungs with air, but each breath was harder than the last. When this happened, it always felt as though her windpipe was swelling shut after a beesting.

Maxime noticed her labored breathing and placed his hands on her biceps. "Are you hurt?"

Geneviève shook her head. "Crowds," she wheezed, ashamed that her proclivity had to manifest itself at such an inopportune moment.

Maxime scanned the space and tugged her farther down the platform where fewer people had gathered. "Sit," he ordered when he found an area where no one else lingered. Geneviève obeyed, praying her uniform coat would be none the worse for sitting on the ground on a filthy tube platform. The concrete was frigid, but she found it soothing against her flesh, which felt on the point of boiling. She rested her head on her knees and focused on taking deep breaths. She could feel the warmth of his hand on her back, gently rubbing as she regained her equilibrium. After a few minutes, she was able to raise her head and feel like the air was flowing freely into her lungs again.

"Does this happen often?"

Geneviève shook her head. "I can't stand crowds indoors," she explained. "The tighter the quarters, the worse it is."

"How did you manage working in a busy switchboard room?" he asked, draping his arm around her shoulders. She accepted the gesture and rested her head against his chest. It was a forward gesture from a man she'd known less than an hour, but even in her state, she knew he was trying to keep her from a full-blown panic.

"It was hard at first, but easier once I got to know people. And it helps that everyone had a defined space. A mob like that"—she gestured to the crowd several yards away—"that's the worst. I don't know anyone, and no one has a specific place to be. The jostling, the heat . . . it's just . . ."

"Too much. I understand."

She patted his knee, trying to downplay her distress. "You must think I'm crazy."

"Not at all. We all have our little foibles. Though I suspect this is one you didn't precisely advertise to the recruitment officer." His tone was, mercifully, not critical. Simply matter-of-fact.

"I'll manage. Especially as I get to know the people I work with. Really." Geneviève spoke forcefully, as though Maxime had the power to send her home and it was up to her to stay his hand. But while he didn't wield such power, he might know the right ears to whisper into that could have the same result.

"Don't fret. I'm not going to betray you. I've seen grown enlisted men do basically the same thing at their first air raid. There is no training to prepare for such a thing. Every other time you go through this will be easier."

Geneviève took a moment to consider his words. "Thank you for that. It helps."

"Not at all. I've no doubt you'll cope as well as any of us can once you're at the front. Though I hope your duties keep you safe in Tours or one of the other offices far from the action."

"They're all doing the same work for the cause. If they need me at the central office, that's where I'll go."

"And if they need you in Berlin, you'll go there too, bayonet in hand," he said.

Her wordless reply was enough. Just outside there was a loud rumbling and crash. There were some shrieks from the crowd and Geneviève tensed. Maxime tightened his embrace, and she felt the tension ebbing away.

Another boom sounded and Maxime looked heavenward. "Well, that's my leave canceled. I'd hoped the worst of this was over, but it seems the Germans didn't run out of bombs during the blitz."

"More's the pity," Geneviève said.

At the sound of the third boom above their heads, the crowd grew hushed. Their initial shock had given way to silent horror as they awaited their chance to return to the surface to see whether their homes and loved ones had remained unscathed, or if they, too, were to join the millions of others who, after three long years of war, had suffered loss.

"When the sirens stop, I'll have to report to my commanding officer. Will you be all right to get back to Mayfair on your own?"

"Yes, I can manage." Geneviève's worry now shifted to Flora and the rest of the operators. Would those who were enjoying an afternoon of shopping or seeing the great sights of London know what to do? She sent up a silent prayer that they were all well and safe.

Maxime stood and offered her a hand up. "I don't suppose this Peter of yours would object to you exchanging a few letters with a friend from time to time? It would brighten things up at the front if you would."

"Of course I'd be happy to write you." She doubted that Peter would look on the exchange all that favorably, but she could hardly deny Maxime the small glimmer of companionship her letters would offer. He pulled a small notebook from his breast pocket and scribbled the instructions on how to direct mail to him.

"Promise me, whatever happens, you'll stay safe," he said, his voice low.

"I don't like making promises that I might not be able to keep. But I won't be careless or reckless if you promise the same."

He bent down and kissed the soft skin of her cheek. "My first letter will be to ask forgiveness for taking that liberty, but I confess I won't be sincere."

Geneviève managed a weak smile and watched as he made his way through the crowd and bounded up the stairs toward duty.

⁓

Two days later, the little hotel where they'd lodged in Southampton buzzed with the hum of twenty women preparing for their crossing to France. The front room was a maze of steamer trunks and hatboxes, and Geneviève found a bit of solace from the mayhem on the front porch, where she calmed herself with slow, even breaths. A uniformed man approached, parcel in hand, looking disgruntled at whatever errand he'd been sent on.

"I'm looking for a Miss Jean-veeve Tremblay?" He was Signal Corps as well and above the rank where he should have been sent as a courier. "I'm supposed to give her this package."

"You're in luck, that's me." Geneviève extended her hand to accept the parcel. He peered in at the din inside the small hotel and looked relieved that he wouldn't have to navigate that particular minefield.

Geneviève opened the parcel, emblazoned with the seal of Liberty of London. Nestled inside the box was the scarf she'd so admired. Purples, reds, and blues, all coming together in artful chaos. Tucked in with it was a note:

A little remembrance from your friend. I hope you'll wear it often and find beauty in it when things get hard. And they will get hard. I think this particular piece was more prescient than you realized. It's a new design from a young artist, I was told. The shopgirl called it "The Feathered Hope" and it was designed to uplift the spirit in these trying times. The script intermingled with the feathers should give you comfort in those trying times and is all the more appropriate for having been penned by one of your fellow countrywomen. As for me, I will find solace in the memories of the charming moments we spent together before the sirens called us back to reality.

With all my warmest regards,
Maxime

Geneviève pulled the scarf from the box and looked at the minuscule script that interlaced with the vines. *Hope is the thing with feathers.* Below the scarf was a page from a book of poetry with the complete text of Emily Dickinson's poem printed in delicate script.

"Hope" is the thing with feathers -
That perches in the soul -
And sings the tune without the words -
And never stops - at all -

And sweetest - in the Gale - is heard -
And sore must be the storm -
That could abash the little Bird
That kept so many warm -

I've heard it in the chillest land -
And on the strangest Sea -
Yet - never - in Extremity,
It asked a crumb - of me.

Geneviève held the scarf and the poem to her chest for just a moment. Such a gift she'd never received, even from Peter, and she was glad she didn't have to endure Maxime seeing her reaction to it himself. It was too bold a gesture, too lavish by half, but she couldn't bring herself to shove it all back into the messenger's hands and tell him to return it to the sender.

He'd wanted her to have this token of his esteem . . . and the less noble part of her was unable to resist having something so beautiful to call her own. She wasn't sure why a man she'd barely met, and whom she was unlikely ever to see again in person, would give such an extravagant gift, but her heart was tight in her chest at the thoughtfulness of it.

Beneath the scarf was also a blank book, bound in cordovan leather with a gold flourish on the front, but no title. She flipped it open to find all the pages were blank, save a note in Maxime's bold handwriting on the inside cover:

> *In dark times, remember to cling to hope.*
> *Use these pages in the times that try the soul,*
> *and have no doubt, they will.*
> *Look for the beauty and joy that still exist in the world,*
> *and hold on to them when all seems lost.*
>
> *With great affection,*
> *Maxime*

She heard the girls calling for her inside, so she tucked the sheet of yellowed paper with the poem and his letter in the breast pocket of her uniform coat and tied the scarf around her neck. It wasn't a sanctioned part of the uniform, but it would be a shield as they crossed the frigid channel and entered the fray.

CHAPTER 3

❧

7 March 1918

Dear Mademoiselle Tremblay,

Thank you for your letter last week. Though I cannot tell you where I am, suffice it to say, your words were a sorely needed comfort in a dark place. I hope you're adjusting well to your duties and that you find yourself welcomed and admired by your colleagues, as well you should be.

While my leave home was canceled, as I predicted, I was able to forward the scarf we chose at Liberty to Aurélie along with a letter in which I describe the stylish young American woman who helped in its selection. She now considers herself in possession of the chicest accessory in the entire region of Bourgogne. Maman says she has worn it daily since it arrived, which of course gives me immense pleasure. I hope it will make you smile as well, though you haven't had the chance to meet her yet. The two of you would charm each other, I am certain. She writes to tell me that after the war, she wants to move to London or New York to study design so that

she can become to the twentieth century what CF Worth was to the
nineteenth.

    I am afraid, my dear friend, we have created a monster.

Cordially,

Maxime

GENEVIÈVE TUCKED THE LETTER IN THE JOURNAL MAXIME HAD SENT. It was a Dickens novel compared to the two letters—short notes, really—that Peter had sent. She'd excused his short letters, knowing he was busy and not under ideal circumstances, yet Maxime had managed to find the time to draft a lovely letter, despite higher rank and more responsibility. But Peter didn't have Maxime's flair with words, and she felt she couldn't hold that against him. Despite this, she couldn't help but draft a more detailed letter to Maxime than her last to Peter had been.

12 March 1918

Dear Maxime,

    I'm adjusting well enough to life in the Signal Corps. I can't tell you where I am working, as you well know, but I am not yet near the front. I have been given leave to say that much, as I know it will ease your worry. How kind of you to worry at all about the girl you met in a shop and helped as she acted like a fool during an air raid when she should have been able to keep herself together. I can only hope I won't embarrass myself like this in the future when I am actively serving.

    The girls are friendly enough. No, that really isn't expressing it well . . . They are friendly in a way I haven't experienced

*at work or school. Although I wouldn't classify what I have
with the other women as friendships so much as collegial work
acquaintanceships, no one has complained once about my
"foreignness." No one pretends they can't understand me, though
I haven't spoken with an accent since I was eight years old. No
one tells me I smell like the tenement buildings, though I admit the
smell is hard to scrub off. No one here has taunted my "long and
complicated" name, though they do call me Jennie, which isn't as
terrible as it could be.*

*The girls seek me out for French lessons, which is gratifying,
and I have earned praise from Chief Operator Banker for my
swiftness at the board. While it's true many of the girls speak French
and many have experience at the switchboards, few are as proficient
at both as I am. I know it's immodest to say so, but I'm happy to see
my heritage as an advantage for once.*

*I hope things aren't too grueling for you wherever you are. I
think so often about what you said about why you entered the war.
For so many, it was about the glory and the honor. I think if more
men viewed things as you do, wars would be far less common.
Though if women were to run things, there wouldn't be any at all.
No mother ever wants to send her sons off to battle, no wife her
husband, and no sister her brothers. My own dear brother Jean
has announced his intentions to enlist, and I pray our maman can
persuade him to change his mind. There isn't glory or honor enough
in all the world to risk his life. I can only imagine how my mother's
heart will rend in half to have her two oldest children in harm's
way. But it's not for me to talk him out of volunteering. If I have
made the choice to serve, I cannot deny him the same, though I hope
he has made the choice as soberly as you have done.*

*With fond regards,
Geneviève*

Dear Geneviève,

It gives me great pleasure to know the other women have accepted you so willingly. It pains me that is among the first times you've felt that way. A woman with your intelligence and warmth should have a ready welcome wherever she goes, but as the current world situation shows us, the better parts of men's hearts are not always in command. I like to think that man is, at his core, more good than bad. Though I must confess to you, dear friend, that this war has provided me with ample reason to doubt.

I do not mean to imply that there are no men, or indeed women, without evil impulses. Clearly, we have seen enough evidence of that on the front page of every newspaper since Gutenberg invented his press. But rather, man has a fundamental desire to do good. The problem arises when his notion of what is good becomes corrupted by impure motives or sheer ignorance. That is our true adversary, make no mistake of it. Though I will say there is enough of it to be found on both sides of the trenches. Our own generals are not flawless men with the purest of motives, though in my heart I wish fervently that they were. I've seen senseless orders that lead to injury and death more times than any man should. I forgive any man an error in judgment, but I admit I am less forgiving when they're born of arrogance and pride. I've found that, in war and in peace, there is far too much of that to go around.

I will also admit that your being posted back from the front sets me at ease. Though I know you are not afraid to serve where you are needed, I hope it will not offend you that I am glad you are not directly in harm's way. I am sure every call you connect is just as vital as the ones at the front. For the sake of making sure I am not misunderstood, I mean that in full sincerity and without any trace of condescension or smugness. In my heart I believe it is folly

*to consider the work of a secretary in Washington any less vital
than the work of an infantryman at the front. We all fight the same
battles; some are just fortunate to be farther from the bullets.*

Warmly,
Maxime

⌣

Dear Maxime,

*Letters from home are scarce, given that the distance is far, and
Maman's time is so precious. Though the children are getting older,
the demands on her time are great, so I am glad to see your script in
the mail. Apart from the occasional line from Peter, assuring me he
is alive and well, I get no mail. I am human enough to feel the prick
of envy when the other girls get stacks of letters or parcels from home.
But they come from easier circumstances where there is time for letter
writing and money to send packages overseas.*

*Though I don't covet the care packages, really. Most of the
gifts are so delightfully off the mark. We want for soap and fresh
stockings, and perhaps some sweets that can withstand the long ship
ride from America. The mothers send cookies that have crumbled
into a mess and are stale beyond redemption, clothes that are a direct
violation of our dress code, and needlepoint kits we don't have the
time or energy to even think about. I think it hilarious that Dottie's
mother thought she'd have the time to finish—or even start—a rather
large tapestry of a horse by the seaside she'd sent. I know a few tricks
when it comes to embroidery, but I've never had the time to invest in
such a detailed project.*

*But it was sweet that Dottie's mother took the time to send it to
her. It was sweet that Dottie put the fabric, thread, and chart lovingly
in her trunk where it will sit untouched until she returns home.*

I hope fervently that she'll have the time very soon for such an undertaking. I can imagine she'll have long evenings at home with her parents in the sitting room, listening to the phonograph or the wireless, or just chatting about their day while she embroiders the palomino horse set against the azure seascape. Dottie isn't especially fond of horses and apparently doesn't swim, but she finds nothing odd about the gift at all. I find that charming too.

What I envy is the news from home and the reassurance that the world is going on back at home without me. And I dread that too. I have spent so much of my life trying to ensure that my siblings have all they need that I wonder how I will react on the day when I learn the family truly no longer needs me. When the older ones are married or working. When Papa's salary stretches enough to provide comfortably for the younger. Will I be relieved, or will I feel unmoored? I know many of the soldiers will feel the same way when they're sent home. They have a purpose now, grander than any they've known . . . How will they cope when they have to accept once again the routine monotony of selling shoes or driving a city bus? Those jobs are essential, yes, but they don't carry the same perception of valor. And for one, I think it's a shame they don't.

Warmly,
Geneviève

"A letter from your beau, Jennie?" Dottie asked, checking her lipstick and adjusting the collar of her uniform in the mirror in the room they shared with Flora and Patricia in the boardinghouse that the YWCA had secured for them near Reims. "Your smile tells me it's not from your mama back at home."

"No, not Maman or Peter. He sent a letter last week, so it's too soon for another. And Maman's letters take ages to get here," Geneviève replied, not taking her eyes from the note.

She and Maxime had exchanged four letters apiece by this

time, and his precise script evoked a flutter in her that her reasonable side could not suppress entirely. She was delighted to receive another postcard from Peter as well. She was filled with relief when she saw Peter's block printing ending on a hasty note: *All's well enough here. Stay safe. ~Peter Blake.* That he included his surname was curious to Geneviève, but she didn't devote too much consideration to the point. He was gearing up for battle and couldn't spare much time for correspondence.

She could no longer pretend that Maxime didn't think of her with fondness, but she was able to dismiss it without too much trouble. She would likely never set eyes on him again. They might remain pen friends for a time, but even that would likely fizzle out after the war came to its blessed end. Even if feelings grew a bit tender, there was no harm indulging them, so long as they stayed contained to the page. And she repeated this litany to herself when the occasional twinge of guilt gnawed at her gut. She was entitled to the little escape her correspondence with Maxime provided as a way of coping with the strains of duty. She was, after all, a soldier like any other.

"The captain?" Flora's head cocked to one side. Geneviève had confided in her friend about the airman who had so gallantly kept her from falling apart in the subway tunnel. Flora had thought it a kind enough thing until he'd sent the scarf.

"How does such a man not have a sweetheart to write to?" Flora asked. "And if he has one, why is he writing to you?"

"Because a man and a woman can be friends without being romantically attached," Geneviève said. Dottie snorted in derision, earning her a glare from Geneviève. "Very ladylike."

"Come on you two, or we'll be late." Flora opened the bedroom door with an impatient flourish.

The women had undergone a whirlwind orientation on the ground but were not detained long in the central offices in

Tours but sent along to the field offices a few miles back from the front. Their shift was due to start in a half hour, and they had to manage breakfast in the remaining minutes before their shift or spend the next four hours trying to ignore their hunger pangs.

"I hope they've managed something other than lumpy porridge," Patricia grumbled as they reached the doors of the mess hall. She was from a small town in Connecticut, and Geneviève deduced that her family was from easy circumstances.

"Your capacity for hope is astounding," Flora quipped. They'd had lumpy porridge every morning for three weeks altogether. None of them loved it, but Patricia seemed to suffer the poor food and rudimentary lodgings more than the rest.

"At least there was some brown sugar yesterday," Dottie, ever the optimist, supplied. "I thought it helped a lot."

Patricia sighed heavily, eliciting an eyeroll from the rest. Exasperating as she could be, she was a fine operator and a hard worker, so they tolerated her complaints with some forbearance.

Geneviève didn't offer up that the food was more plentiful than it had been for many of the years of her childhood. It wasn't until she started at NET&T that they had meat on the table with any sort of regularity. Her siblings shared beds far lumpier than the ones they had in the boardinghouses that the YWCA sourced for them. Such admonition wouldn't endear her to them, but there were times the effort it took her to bite her tongue was the stuff of Greek mythology.

She thought of the lumpy bed back at home and how her younger sister, Odette, was likely thrilled to have their bed and the closet-sized room they'd shared to herself. The four boys had a larger room to accommodate the two beds they had to share, and their parents had the smallest room of all. They claimed their growing children needed the space more than they did.

"You'll have to hide your scarf," Flora reminded her as they sat down to their twenty-seventh bowl of porridge in as many days, all grateful that the bowl of brown sugar had made a re-appearance. Geneviève herself would have been glad to have a few spoonfuls of maple syrup from back home to improve the flavor. "We have inspections today."

"Work satchels are a wonder." Geneviève held hers up. "I can divest myself of the offending garment in seconds."

It wasn't like Geneviève to flaunt the rules, but she did feel more confident when she wore the scarf. And it was such a lovely thing, she hated not to get the good out of it.

"You'll get caught one of these days," Flora warned. "Is it really worth a dressing down to wear an unsanctioned acces-sory?"

Geneviève paused. The truth was that the scarf would look ridiculous with most of her clothes back home. Her uniform was finer than anything in her wardrobe. As the navy suit didn't bear any permanent insignia, she considered the possibility that she could wear it after her service ended, but she wondered if it might elicit some stares from those who recognized it as her uniform.

Once she married Peter, all that might change. She imagined awkward shopping trips with his mother where they filled her closets with modest yet fashionable dresses and suits, appropri-ate for a fashionable young matron. But that seemed a million years away, and she wasn't entirely sure she could adequately explain how she'd come to own such an expensive garment.

The window to enjoy the scarf seemed narrow, and she was loath to leave it in her trunk. She looked to Flora and shrugged. She didn't feel like divulging all of her thoughts over breakfast. "I don't see that it's hurting anyone."

"Uniforms have an important purpose," Dottie chimed in, uncharacteristically serious. "They make us harder to tell apart.

Your scarf identifies you from five hundred yards away. It may seem benign to you, but it could be a liability down the line."

"Oh, how could that be?" Patricia said. "We look different enough from each other to be recognizable. That seems silly."

"From a distance, with hats on, you'd be surprised at how hard it would be to distinguish us. And Geneviève wearing the same accessory every day? It makes her an easier target for the enemy to track."

"For what purpose?" Patricia pressed.

"I can think of a dozen scenarios. To get codes from her. To find out strategy she's overheard on phone calls. But it's the scenarios I can't think of that worry me."

"Listen to Dottie," Flora said. "She's making sense. She's perhaps spending more time than is healthy reading up on military safety and protocol, but she speaks the truth."

Geneviève pulled the scarf from around her neck and placed it in her satchel. "Satisfied?"

"Very," Dottie and Flora said in imperfect unison.

Geneviève felt a pique of regret, as though tucking the scarf away in a satchel was tantamount to hanging Van Gogh's sunflowers in a privy, but she knew the girls' concerns were justified.

Compared to the modern offices in Lewiston, the offices they staffed near the front were primitive. The equipment was essentially the same, though the boards were designed to be portable, allowing movement from post to post as the front pushed forward. The office was the same sort of makeshift wooden structure as the men's barracks. Compared to the impressive marble masterpiece in New York that housed the AT&T headquarters, which had been designed to last centuries, the impermanence of their workplace was striking to Geneviève. But there was something reassuring in knowing their duties here wouldn't last forever.

That this war wouldn't go on forever.

They relieved the night shift, who looked grateful for the opportunity to grab a hot meal, even if it was porridge, and use the blackout curtains to their full advantage as they tried to get some sleep.

Geneviève took her usual station and found the quiet board lit up like the skyscrapers in New York almost as soon as she sat down.

But instead of placing calls from a housewife to the grocer to inquire after the quality of the pork chops, or connecting a farmer to his feed supplier, Geneviève connected generals to the top-ranking officers at the front, relaying orders in a complex series of constantly changing codes that the operators were expected to memorize and employ flawlessly. She was connecting those officers to their generals so they could plead for supplies for the beleaguered men in the trenches.

The work in Lewiston was essential to the efficient running of lives and businesses at home, but the work here was vital. And the weight of that knowledge was heavy on all their shoulders.

~

My dearest Geneviève,

We hope all is well with you in France. We can only dream of what it is like to see the old country and to meet the people who, if life had turned out differently, might have been our friends and neighbors. Or at least fellow countrymen, as I suspect our people came from the west, and I fear you are farther east than any of us would like. Ah, but such is a mother's worry; constant and unshakable. Adding to the knowledge that my precious girl is too close to harm's way, your brother Jean has enlisted and will be heading over to you before long. I know you will remember him in

*your prayers, along with your Peter and the rest of your family, who
will not fail to remember you in their own.*

*With all my love,
Maman*

Maman had stolen a few moments to herself to write more
than the usual "all is well, thinking of you" notes that Geneviève was accustomed to. She smiled as she imagined Maman
hunched over the kitchen table with her favorite silver-filigree
Waterman fountain pen, a precious wedding gift from her father that she valued beyond jewels, indulging in her prose by
the dim light of her kerosene lamp. Maman had been an avid
reader and more than a little skilled with words, but circumstances had pulled her away from the written word. Geneviève
couldn't remember the last time her mother had sat down with
a book or scribbled her thoughts in a notebook.

But it was for that reason that Geneviève had gone to work
for NET&T, so that Papa wouldn't have the mental burden of
being the sole breadwinner, so that the children would have all
their needs met—and a few luxuries besides—and so the weight
on Maman's shoulders would be less. She didn't want to see
Maman's eyes hollowed with fatigue at the end of the day. She
wanted her mother to know the joy of an hour or two of well-
earned leisure each day. She wanted her mother to have some
time that was her own to recapture some small part of the life
she'd sacrificed for her family.

But Jean's departure, while it would mean one less mouth to
feed, would be a blow to the family. The constant worry would
wear on them like pavement eating away at shoe leather with
each step they took. Sweet, pensive Jean was not meant for life
as a soldier. He was too much like their mother, a scholar and a

poet, not a warrior. Étienne might have had a better tempera-
ment for the army, resilient and energetic like their father, but he
was mercifully three years too young to be called up for service
and far too baby-faced to persuade a recruiter otherwise. Having
three of her chicks out of the nest under such conditions would
have been too much for Maman to bear. Geneviève just prayed
the war would end before any more of the Tremblay children
would be eligible to serve.

"Would you like to come with us into town and see if anything
is open?" Patricia knocked on the open doorframe and paused.
"It's such a nice day, we thought we'd take advantage of it."

"Yes, thank you." Geneviève stashed Maman's letter in her
box of stationery to rest with the three letters she'd received
from Peter and the considerable number she'd gotten from
Maxime. Maman's letter deserved a thoughtful reply, and a
walk into town might clear her mind enough to find the words
she'd need to commiserate with her mother while not adding
to her concern. In just a couple of short months, Geneviève had
seen enough to know that the war was nothing less than the
evil Maxime described, and nothing like the heroic quest Peter
had hoped it would be. They were quietly expected to visit the
injured men to raise their spirits when their schedules allowed.
Jean was likely enough to be conscripted, so he was better off
enlisting. He'd be treated better both by his fellow soldiers and
by the people back in Lewiston when he returned home.

If.

The awful word hung in the air, but Geneviève swatted it
away like the pestilential mosquito it was and stood to join the
girls on their half day. Dottie and Patricia chatted companionably about French clothes while Flora and Geneviève walked a
pace behind them.

"I'd offer you a penny for your thoughts, but all I have are these little centimes, and I'm saving them for a few postcards and stamps in town. Maybe some caramels if there are any to be had."

Geneviève smiled. Flora was the most sensible woman she knew, but her weakness was her sweet tooth. The little flaw made her more human in Geneviève's eyes and she loved her for it. "You can have them for free, as part of your Signal Corps benefits package. I got a letter from home. My brother has enlisted and will be over here soon. My mother makes a brave front, but I know she's worried sick about him. She's twisted up in knots about me and I'm not the one with a bayonet slung over my back."

"At least he'll have one to defend himself with. We can't do much with phone wires and headsets if things go badly."

"But he'll be called on to use that bayonet, and soon. And he'll have to live with that. Some boys might be able to move on, but I don't think Jean is one that will do his duty without collecting some brutal scars along the way. The kind you bear on your soul."

"I'm sure he's made of stern stuff. Plenty of our boys will make it through all right in the end."

"Will they really?" Geneviève asked. "You saw the boys in the hospital as well as I did. Even the ones who make it back with their health, their limbs, and God preserve me, their faces, will they be all right? Don't you think the memories of what they saw will haunt them? The memories of what they were ordered to do may torture their every breath as efficiently as mustard gas. I don't think any of them will be all right, Flora."

Flora's lips formed a thin line as she considered Geneviève's words. "Don't you think that doing their service to their country will be of some solace? Knowing that they did what they must to protect their loved ones and their country?"

"It might take the sting out of it, but when the ships dock

back in New York and Boston and wherever else, I worry they will be filled with the ghosts of living men."

"You're far too morose for such a lovely day," Patricia interjected. "It's the first fine day we've had in ages, and it just happened to fall on our half day. It seems a shame to waste it brooding."

"And it won't help anyone if you do," Flora said, for once taking sides with flighty Patricia.

"Perhaps you're right." Geneviève spoke the words but knew that the only purpose her acquiescence would serve would be to keep her brooding to herself instead of sharing her worry with her new friends. It was unfair to burden them with such things when they had their own loved ones to worry about. And moreover, they didn't know Jean one bit. To them, he was just one of the many boys in uniform doing as they were bid to help end the war.

If she were honest with Maman about her worries, it would just drive her into a pit of depression. If she wrote to Peter, he would laud it as the smartest decision a lad in his position could make. She found herself itching to write Maxime. He wouldn't discount her dread or play down the ever-growing stone of worry that filled her gut and weighed her down. He would have found the words that could somehow validate her feelings and comfort her all at once. Shouldn't it be Peter who inspired her to write long letters and bare her soul?

But Peter was simply a different sort of man. He was raised to climb the ladder at NET&T, with the importance of social perception ingrained in his psyche from the time he could crawl across his mother's perfectly waxed wooden floors. This didn't make him lesser than Maxime. It simply made him different. But the question that niggled her brain was whether she'd spend the rest of her life contemplating those differences and whether she'd come to regret her choices.

CHAPTER 4

~

Dear Mademoiselle Tremblay,

At the risk of becoming tedious, I have to thank you for the regularity of your letters. To see your script on the envelope lightens my spirits on the gloomiest of days, and you may trust there have been many of those. I cannot offer up details of what we have endured here, and I am not sure I would be able to fully recount it to you if I were at liberty to do so. The horrors of what we have seen are not fit for a lady's ears, though I imagine your circumstances in the Signal Corps have made you less delicate than most. Even so, I could not bear to add to the list of atrocities to which your post demands you must bear witness.

You are more than equal to your work, but if I were a more powerful man, I'd ensure that you were kept safe at home and far from harm's way. Not because you cannot serve, but because no one should ever have to. I was born to a family of staunch pacifists. The men in my family have been sent to any number of wars started by some Louis or Napoleon or other. The most recent was a Louis-Napoleon, for good measure. Despots, the lot of them. I had thought with the blessed and seemingly definitive end of the monarchy in

France, the warmongering might be at an end, but alas the new century has simply brought new reasons for rulers to force us to kill our brethren.

    But I will not fill the rest of these pages with doom and gloom. I'm in possession of some good news for once and hope you will feel the same. As my previous leave was canceled, I have been granted another, though too short to permit me the chance to return home. I was hoping I might be able to spend a few hours of my leave with you. I understand you will be busy with your work, but I am hoping that I might be able to take you for dinner or at least a stroll somewhere farther from harm's way. I don't say out of it, as it seems no such place has existed in the whole of Europe for the past four years.

    I understand if you don't wish to see me. We are merely correspondents who spent a difficult hour together in the London Underground, but if my company would be welcome, please respond as soon as may be.

Cordially,
Maxime

"COMING TO VISIT?" FLORA SCANNED THE LETTER, THOUGH SHE HAD to ask for clarification on some of the French terms. "Do you really want to see him? Do you think Peter would mind?"

Geneviève stood at the mirror, brushing her blonde hair into a shine. She worked quickly with her comb and pins to sweep it up under her uniform cap. *Of course he would, but no harm will come of it. I am mistress of myself and can enjoy an outing with a friend and act like the lady my mother taught me to be.* But she couldn't say this to Flora, who would call her out on the carpet for such a rationalization.

"Would he mind if I have dinner with a pen pal? I should

hope not. If he does, it might give me pause about the whole thing. I can't abide jealous men."

"No, there's nothing pleasant about a jealous oaf of a man, but you can't expect him to be pleased about some gallant officer sweeping in here and taking you out for a steak dinner. No man is that understanding."

"First of all, if he can procure a steak dinner, he's either a magician or in on the black market. While the latter would be terrible, the former would at least make for an amusing meal. I rather like card tricks. Second of all, he isn't sweeping in anywhere. He has leave and can't get all the way to Avallon in the short time he has."

"And you're the first person he thought of to spend his leave with?" Flora pressed.

"Well, I don't know if I'm the first. Perhaps he's written to a dozen other girls hoping to see them and I was simply the next name on the list. But thank you ever so much for the vote of confidence. Of course no man would want to spend time with me if he didn't have ill intentions."

"I'm just the suspicious sort," Flora replied. "I didn't mean anything by it. Not about you."

Geneviève set down her comb on the dresser with a firm *click* of metal against wood and turned to Flora. "I know you didn't, but it would be nice to think that he could be a friend."

"When was the last time you heard from Peter?" Flora asked.

"Two weeks. He can't say where he is, of course, but I don't think he's at the front. From the length of his letter, he's likely very busy."

"I'm sure he is. And he's serious about you. It would be a shame to throw it away on a wartime romance that might end before the ink on the armistice is dry."

"What armistice?" Geneviève said, gesturing for the door so they could leave for their shift. "Have you overheard something on a call that the rest of us would all love to hear?"

"No, but it can't be long in coming. The Germans are making a push, yes, but it's the desperate act of an army who's going all in at the end and hoping for a miracle. At this point, it's a waiting game, and with the US in the mix, the Allied countries have more firepower and soldiers at the ready than the Germans. Read the reports. The German army is reduced to little boys and old men."

"I hope you're right about the end being near," Geneviève said. "Truly, it's what we're all praying for. But as far as Maxime and I are concerned, I'm sure you're right. I will probably never see him again once his leave is over. We're just pen friends, and it will be nice to have a pleasant memory of a nice dinner in France to tell my grandchildren thirty-odd years from now."

"A nice dinner in France with a man who is not their grandfather," Flora reminded her. Geneviève fought the urge to glower at Flora, but she knew she spoke sense. All the same, she'd been lonesome and Peter had barely taken the time to write two sentences since she'd deployed . . . at his urging.

"Flora, you're the best girl in the world, and I know you care about me. I just can't see what harm it will do. Don't we spend our free days cheering up the lads in the infirmary? Don't we dance with the officers to keep up morale?"

"None of those men have sought us out in particular. This feels different," Flora reasoned.

"Trust me, Flora. I'm a steady girl. I won't lose my head for someone I can't have. He lives in France; I live in Maine. Once the war is over, the clock will strike midnight and the spell will be broken."

"If you say so, Cinderella, but I worry the memories of

dancing with Prince Charming will haunt you once you go back to scrubbing floors for your wicked stepmother, or connecting phone calls in a remote branch office as the case may be."

Geneviève opened her mouth to speak but shook her head in silent acquiescence. She didn't pretend that Maxime's motives might have been less innocent if the circumstances were different. But she knew, even if he had tender feelings for her, that she was a smart enough girl to withstand any advances he might make. She wasn't as sheltered as many of the other girls in the Corps. Living in a tenement building, she saw some of the more sordid aspects of life that a gentle-born girl would have been spared. And she was glad for it. She didn't long for Dottie's, and especially Patricia's, porcelain-doll-and-candy-floss innocence. She'd seen more of the underbelly of humanity than Flora, despite being several years her junior.

The fights between Monsieur and Madame Pollard across the hall had been legendary, and she came up with some of the most creative excuses for the bruises that she ought to have considered a career in novel writing. There had been Madame Lavoisier, whose children were in such a state of neglect that they'd been carted away by the authorities while she screamed from her window and then threw herself out of it while her children looked on. The worst had been kindly Céline upstairs. She spoiled the children in the building with sweets their parents couldn't afford and was always willing to keep a baby for an hour or two while their mother saw to the shopping. To make a living, she had gentlemen callers who paid for the privilege of the company. It was an open secret, and no one thought worse of her as she would never have dallied with the husbands in the building. All was well enough until one of her clients decided to wring out his frustration with a life that hadn't gone his way on her neck. The only solace was that she was so ill with the pox by then, his heinous act had spared her a few more months of suffering.

All this had taught Geneviève an important lesson: life was too short for regret. The war served only to reinforce that message.

Before she reported for her shift, she grabbed a scrap of paper and a pen from the parlor and scrawled a note to Maxime.

Would be delighted to have you visit. Looking forward to a lovely dinner and a stroll farther from harm's way if time will allow.

Warmly,
Geneviève

CHAPTER 5

June 1918

THE TRAIN ROLLED IN TO THE STATION AT REIMS, AND GENEVIÈVE watched as Maxime descended onto the platform. He was handsomer than she remembered, perhaps improved by the beauty of the words he'd sent her with such regularity. She watched his eyes scan the crowd looking for her. When their eyes locked, the tremble in her core threatened to unnerve her. She fought the impulse to hide until she mastered herself and stayed rooted to her spot.

Maxime bounded over to her and kissed her primly on the cheek, then ran a finger on her scarf. "I'm so delighted I get to see you wear it at least once. It suits you just as well as I knew it would."

"I'm so happy you're well." Geneviève perched on her tip-toes to return the kiss. "I can't imagine how hard it is for you. I've heard so many horrible things."

Maxime gestured for them to move off the platform and down to the sidewalk where they could enter town. "As bad as it is for me, it's ten times worse for the poor devils in the trenches. I didn't dream you'd have the chance to meet me here."

"I traded half days with Flora and Dottie. It seemed a shame for you to come here and only see you for an hour or two, so I managed to get the whole day." She tried to make it sound like it was only a minor inconvenience, but it had taken more than a little pleading to bring it about.

"How marvelous of you," Maxime said. "I just hope it won't run you too ragged to have to go so long without leave."

"Not at all. So much of what we do on our half days is less amusing than our work anyway. Laundry and errands. All of which is a challenge here." She wasn't sure how she'd fit in those tasks now that her leave was spent, but she couldn't find the room for worry just then.

"Too true. And the people who live here have been dealing with these challenges since the war broke out. And it will go on for years after it ends. But that's always the cost of war. The civilians suffer, no matter how righteous the cause."

He spoke with such conviction, Geneviève wondered if he hadn't missed a calling as a priest. No doubt his sermons would have inspired a congregation to greatness, or at least far deeper introspection. "What did you want to do with your time? I only have the one day, so we ought to make the best of it."

He looked thoughtful for a moment. "I arranged to borrow a jeep from a friend serving here," he said. "Would you object to going out for a drive in the country? It will be a nice escape from things, and we can drop in on an old friend of my family's. I'm absolutely certain the two of you will be quite taken with each other."

"That sounds lovely." *An old family friend. A perfectly respectable outing.* "We've been so deep in our work that I feel like I've barely seen the country."

"And so you haven't. Not as France deserves to be seen. But we'll do something about that today. A memory of France for you to take back home with you." He offered his arm and Geneviève accepted it. Soon they retrieved the keys to an army jeep from an American pilot from Wyoming, who had apparently been trained by Maxime and who was happy to pull strings to get him the use of a jeep for the day.

"Have you been here before?" Geneviève asked as he pulled the jeep onto the highway leading out of town with an ease of movement that implied familiarity. "Before the war?"

"Yes. Many times. You're in Champagne, my dear Geneviève, and while the wines they produce here are very different from the ones we produce in Bordeaux, there is much to learn. My father brought me to the region in my teens to visit the vineyards and learn from the vintners. Many winemakers like to stick with the way things have always been done, but Papa? He is a scholar at heart and wants to learn. We've taken trips to the wine country in Spain and Portugal as well. If we'd let him, he'd probably trade Aurélie for the chance to see Napa and Argentina." The grin on his face betrayed what seemed to be a long-standing family joke.

"Ha, if it were my family, there would be plenty of children left to spare, and the child traded wouldn't necessarily be opposed to the idea. Especially if the end result was living at a vineyard in Napa or Argentina."

Maxime laughed, the sort of easy, light laughter that contrasted painfully with the ironic chuckling elicited from the gallows humor in the trenches. "Perhaps my father could arrange to trade one of them, yes?"

"I'll get my papa on the line one of these days to ask. Young Étienne is a promising one. He'd do nicely."

"The youngest?"

"Fourth of six," Geneviève said.

"Six?" He peeled his eyes off the road to look at her for the first time since he'd turned the key. She realized Maxime didn't know much about her family because she'd been reticent to share too many of the details. He was the oldest of two children and had been raised in gentle circumstances. Quite the opposite of her own upbringing. She didn't feel shame about her family, but it would just serve to illustrate how different the two of them were.

"Yes. Me, Jean, Fabien, Étienne, Odette, and little André," she replied.

"No wonder they picked you for the Signal Corps. If you're able to rattle all that off without a thought, the codes must be nothing at all."

Geneviève laughed in turn. "If only that were true. I've had years to memorize them and a million associations to make with them. The codes have no context, which is what makes them work. My poor mother is forever calling us by the wrong names. I'm 'Odette-I-mean-Geneviève' more often than I am called by my own name."

"She must work hard. Minding so many children must be quite the chore."

"Indeed. And she has a good thirteen years or more of it ahead of her before André is out on his own. But my work at NET&T helped lighten the load a little. She's able to send out some of the laundry and doesn't have to count out every cent at the grocer's anymore."

"It's good of you to help so much. Many girls in your situation would have married to disentangle themselves from that responsibility."

"I've seen that happen, girls who leave Little Canada and live in a clean little bungalow with no more than two or three children. They love to come back and gloat to the rest of us who are still 'stuck.'"

Geneviève noticed a slight clench to his jaw. "That's unkind."

"The thing is, none of us begrudges their happiness and the improvement of their lot in life, but they act like staying is a moral failing. That's what stings. I know I can't live at home forever, but I don't plan to abandon my family when I marry."

"You'll send your parents the lion's share of your pin money until the end of their days, won't you?"

"Every cent I can spare. It only seems right."

"You're a rare woman, Mademoiselle Tremblay. If you don't mind my observation."

"I'm not sure I fully agree. For every girl who attaches herself to a boy whose family has been in New England since the *Mayflower* and finds herself in the center of domestic bliss, there are three of us who try to improve our families' situations. Marie has her mending, Nathalie makes baked goods out of her kitchen. I was just lucky to get the post at the phone office and bring in a regular paycheck."

"I think I would love to visit this Little Canada of yours. It seems like your people would be fascinating to know."

Geneviève looked at him, assessing. Was there irony in his voice or sincerity? She could hardly imagine this well-born man walking among her neighbors. She'd never seen him out of uniform, but she imagined he dressed well when he wasn't in service. Perhaps not in finery all the time, but his clothes would be of the highest quality and tailored to suit. In the eight months they'd dated before their enlistment, Peter could hardly stand to come into her neighborhood and avoided it when he could. Invitations were always issued in areas near where he lived, and drop-offs were usually made quickly. He was likely worried how his car would fare in such a rough neighborhood.

"We've arrived," he said after a few more minutes. They pulled into an empty parking area in front of an ivory-colored, half-timbered building overgrown with ivy and marked with a wooden sign that read *Cave à Champagne* carved in bold script.

"A champagne cellar?" Geneviève's eyes widened in surprise. Such a decadent outing seemed impossible so close to a war zone.

"It is. And also the home of a dear friend of my family. François Soulet has taught me almost as much about wine making as my own father. Almost. I am pleased to see the place is still here."

The pair exited the car and Maxime knocked on the heavy wooden door. There was no sign indicating if they were open or closed, and there was a long pause until Maxime knocked again, this time more forcefully. He looked to Geneviève. "François's hearing isn't what it once was."

Finally, there was a groan as the door opened and the voice of an old man grumbling before he was even visible. "We're not open. There's a war on, haven't you noticed?"

"We're acutely aware, François," Maxime said, his tone dry.

At the sound of Maxime's voice, the old man opened the door wide and pulled him into an embrace as he might have done his own prodigal son. He then held him at arm's length to examine him. "My God in heaven, that can't be Maxime Auvray. If I am dreaming, may I never wake. You're well, my boy?"

"As well as a man can be in such horrible times," Maxime said. François ushered them inside and showed them to a beautiful tasting room where patrons could sample the wines as they considered making a purchase. Maxime knew the space well, but François gave Geneviève a detailed tour, proudly showing off the finer attributes of the space that was languishing in wartime. Sometimes guests came to the tasting room for a bottle or two for a special occasion; others came to invest in several cases. Casual consumers and serious collectors alike had flocked to Soulet's, and Geneviève understood the appeal.

François turned to Geneviève and Maxime once they were comfortably seated. "Now, young man, don't tell me—this is your lovely bride and you're finally bringing her to meet me. I will have to chastise your father for not sending old François an invitation. God knows my old bones are weary for a long journey, but I would have made the trek for you."

"François Soulet, this is my *friend* Geneviève Tremblay. She comes to us from Quebec by way of Maine and is serving with the Americans. She has graciously decided to spare a precious day of her leave to spend with a friend, and I could think of no place better to take her than this very spot."

"Well, I am honored to be your host, given how precious your time is. Make yourselves comfortable while I go arrange for some refreshment, will you?"

The old man shuffled off, presumably toward a kitchen. Maxime's eyes trailed him until he disappeared from view. "I haven't seen François in close to six years, but he looks as though he's aged twenty. His wife, Hélène, passed away just before the war broke out and he's never been the same, according to Papa, who is a far better correspondent than I am."

"I found you a rather faithful correspondent," Geneviève replied. "Though your duties must make it a challenge."

Maxime smiled. "The friendship you and I have is new. I find it awkward to resume a connection once I drop it. If I have a flaw, it's that I dislike being reminded of my failures. Even the ones that are small and easily understood."

"So you have a problem forgiving yourself for being human, is that it?"

"That puts a very fine point on it, but you're probably not wrong."

A few moments later, François reemerged with a tray laden with bottles and glass flutes. A young woman, who appeared to be in her midtwenties, followed with a tray of thinly sliced bread, cheeses, some sliced meat, and fruit. It wasn't heaping, but it was a plentiful assortment.

"François, you can't possibly spare all that. Why, it must be a month's rations worth of cheese alone on that platter," Maxime protested as François and the young woman placed the trays on the gleaming bar.

"My boy, I would never stoop to the black market, but I have always been amenable to bartering with friends and neighbors long before the Germans started causing trouble. A bottle of champagne to help people forget the times in which we are living? It's worth more cheese than you might expect."

Maxime laughed. "Are you sure? Geneviève and I won't be able to enjoy ourselves if we think you'll be depriving yourself."

"He has a healthy reserve," the young lady answered for him. "And plenty of stock to trade with the neighboring farms."

"Thank you, Eloïse," François said, patting her shoulder before she slid back to the kitchens. "She's a good girl. She comes to me from the Reynaud farm. Quite a large family, and giving her employment in such lean times was a blessing to them. She always knows which farms have goods to barter and which families need our help. She helps keep our little village from suffering worse than many others."

"She sounds like a gem," Maxime said. "I'm glad she's come to you."

"She's been a great comfort these past few years," François agreed. "Though I hope she'll move on and start a family of her own when this whole mess is over. She deserves better than waiting on an old codger like me. Any idea when the Germans might finally grow wise and go back home?"

"I've not been made privy to the timing, but I'm doing my level best to convince them that moving eastward would be in their best interests."

"I'm sure you are. And your friend here? She is a nurse?"

Geneviève shook her head. "No, I run the telephones as part of the American Signal Corps." She explained her duties and how she and Maxime had come to meet, which seemed to delight François.

He opened up a bottle of champagne. "This is a *brut nature*," he proclaimed. "From 1904. Solid year, though nothing in my lifetime will compare to 1895. Try this one with some of the Gruyère-style cheese from the Polinard farm there."

The wine was extremely dry, no trace of sweetness to be found in any of its notes. It was earthy, with subtle notes of cinnamon and pear. It married harmoniously with the cheese, and Geneviève could have gratefully gorged herself on the lot of it.

"*Brut nature* is notoriously tricky," Maxime explained. "No sugar is added, so there is nothing to hide the flaws in the grapes."

"There will be plenty of *brut nature* in the coming years, given all the sugar shortages, whether the grapes merited the designation or not. I expect five years from now, many Frenchmen will uncork a bottle of champagne and decry that the miserable grapes weren't drowned in a vat of sugar water. But I'm sure your papa will have the same lamentations."

"I have pages full of them," Maxime said. "He's convinced 1915 will be the worst vintage Bordeaux has seen in a hundred years. The rain and rot were a blight on every farm in the region."

"Last year's vintage will not be one I serve with pride," François said, shaking his head morosely.

"I'm impressed you have a vintage at all," Maxime said. "It was all Papa could do the past few years to get anything bottled. All the able-bodied men are gone."

"Then we do as we have done in such cases before." François gestured to Geneviève. "Call upon the able-bodied women. If it weren't for the women in the village, my vineyard would be a loss, as would every farm in the whole region that is still standing. I can't help much with planting and harvesting, but I advise where I can."

"You know the terrain and the soil and have worked it for fifty years. I'm sure your knowledge is invaluable," Maxime said.

"Ah, well. It is good to have some knowledge to share. Now enough about that. Let's try the opposite end of the gamut, shall we? Try this *demi-sec* with some of the fruit. It's the sweetest one I make. There is one classification sweeter, but one might as well drink honey straight from the hive in my view."

He poured scant glasses of each, and Geneviève let the bubbles burst on her tongue. Though she could respect the complexity of the flavors in the drier wine, this sweeter offering was far more to her liking. Notes of chocolate, caramel, and honeysuckle made the fruit taste even sweeter. "This must be what heaven tastes like," she murmured, not realizing she spoke out loud.

"Fabulous vintage; 1907," François said. "One of my favorites. I am pleased you agree with me."

Geneviève smiled at the way he referred to the vintages as though they were old friends. And in a way, they were. Each bottle of wine was associated with a year's worth of memories, tragic and beautiful alike.

"It's the most amazing thing I've ever tasted, and I include my mother's maple pudding in that assessment. Though please don't tell her or I'll be forced to lie."

The men laughed heartily at her joke, and she was pleased to lighten their spirits. "*Mon ami*," Maxime said, "would you mind if we take a stroll in your vineyards? The weather is so fine, it seems a wonderful day to appreciate your handiwork."

"Flattery will get you everywhere, my boy," François said. "Enjoy yourselves." He gestured to the doors with a flourish and called for Eloïse to help him with the trays.

Maxime showed Geneviève through a back door that led to a vast expanse of vines, expertly trellised and growing heavy with fruit. The bees buzzed, unconcerned with the threat of artillery fire less than fifteen miles to the east of where they stood. Geneviève's stomach was properly full for the first time in two weeks and with food more palatable than tinned meat or the infamous lumpy porridge. Her head was just the slightest bit tingly from the two glasses of champagne too early in the day, but neither excessively nor unpleasantly so. It was just enough that as they walked, the meticulously cultivated rows of vines felt more like a fairyland than a simple farm far too close to enemy lines.

She wasn't sure what motivated her, but she took Maxime's hand in hers. She knew Peter would be displeased she'd done such a thing, but she was hard-pressed to believe he wouldn't look at the nurses and other servicewomen with longing. She couldn't be sure he wouldn't have a dalliance. It was a reality her mother had warned her of when he made plans to enlist. Maman had warned her that she must be prepared to forgive, even if he confessed to the worst. Compared to the scenarios her mother had painted for her, holding hands with an airman she might never see again felt reasonably innocent. And the truth was that she missed the comfort of a hand in hers. First it had been her mother's, then her younger siblings', then Peter's . . . and she'd missed that feeling of closeness. It was dangerous and impulsive, but she hoped the only heart she risked damaging was her own.

The justification at least sounded good in her head in the moment.

He squeezed her fingers ever so gently. "Papa asked François to come stay with the family when the war broke out, but he refused to leave this place. I wanted to check in on him, so thank you for indulging me."

"I feel like I'm the one who's been indulged. This place is beautiful beyond description, Maxime. I can understand why he wouldn't want to leave, though I can also understand why your family urged him to."

"One of the beautiful things worth fighting for," he said, referring to their discussion near the scarf display at Liberty. "And far too close to the fray."

"Everything is too close for my taste. Even Maman and Papa and the children back in Maine. I got a letter from home . . . Jean is officially enlisting and will be over soon." Geneviève had held that information close to her chest, not wanting to mar their perfect day, but she couldn't hold it in any longer.

Maxime's face lost a bit of its color. "I'll continue to hope that the war will end before he can see his way to the front."

"Your hopes will echo my own," she said. "I can't stand to think of him with a bayonet in his hand and standing in the trenches."

Maxime squeezed her hand. "He's young and strong. He'll stand a chance."

"I want to believe you," she said. "But it all feels so wrong. It's no way for a boy to come of age."

Maxime didn't respond; he just held firmly to her hand. It was all the affirmation she needed.

They wandered hand in hand for hours, speaking of everything and nothing until the sun grew heavy in the sky and Geneviève would have to return to her boardinghouse.

"Thank you for today," Geneviève said. "I can't imagine a better way to have spent a day."

Maxime's face clouded a moment, but the heaviness lifted just as quickly. "It's been one of the best days of my memory. Certainly since the war began."

Geneviève turned to Maxime, her hand still in his. She gestured with her free hand to the vineyard that sprawled before them. "This world of yours is enchanting."

"It can be. It can also be maddening and heartbreaking. Weather and vines can be capricious . . . but there is always a bit of enchantment to it."

"Despite all that, it still sounds wonderful."

He stopped abruptly "It is. I won't insult you by pretending it hasn't been a lovely life. If circumstances were different . . ."

"Maxime, I—" Geneviève began.

"You don't have to say anything, sweet Geneviève. You are a woman of your word, and you will be loyal to Peter because that is who you are. I don't think I'd care for you as I do if you were any less steadfast."

Geneviève gasped despite herself.

"I'm a cad for saying as much, but yes, I do care for you. All we've had is a chance encounter and some letters, but it's meant the world to me."

"I understand. I—"

"Please don't say anything you'll have to confess to Peter," Maxime said, gently placing a finger on her lips. "I don't want that on my already overburdened conscience. I just hope you won't hate me for saying it out loud. It gives me some peace to say it this once."

"I couldn't hate you, Maxime," Geneviève said, her voice heavy with unshed tears. "I don't think I'm capable of it."

"I'm glad for that too. It was foolish of me to come here and tempt us both with something we can't have, but I can't say I'm sorry."

Geneviève took his other hand and looked into his eyes. He caressed the side of her cheek with his finger and suppressed a sigh. Their eyes locked and Geneviève wished beyond reason that she were bold enough to reach up on her tiptoes and place her lips on his. But, as Maxime had said, she didn't want anything on her conscience that she would have to confess later.

"I should get you home. I've taken too much of your time already."

She wanted to protest but knew he was right.

The ride back to her boardinghouse was quiet, as their moments together faded into memory and guilt was allowed to seep into the corners like a faded photograph.

When he pulled up next to the house, he reached over and squeezed her hand. "I will keep writing to you as long as you wish it, but I understand if you feel our correspondence should end. I'd be dreadfully sorry for it, but I would understand."

"I don't know," she said truthfully. "I'll have to think about it."

"I understand." He tried to keep his tone neutral, but his voice was as dry as a husk.

She couldn't bear to utter the word "goodbye," so she hurried back to the house where duty waited, heavy as her sorrow.

CHAPTER 6

❧

September 1918

TWO HANDS CLASPED OVER HER EYES IN THE MESS HALL AFTER HER shift. Since they'd moved closer to the front, Geneviève and the other women were working until they were forced to rest by their superiors, so she was too tired to yelp in surprise at the contact.

"Guess who?" asked the disembodied voice, presumably the one attached to the hands. It was deep and male, the hands large and free of calluses.

"If it's Flora, you need to rest your voice. You've gone down two octaves," she joked, but her heart pounded with surprise as she recognized Peter's voice.

"Very funny." Peter released her eyes. He claimed the seat beside her and kissed her cheek. "Glad to see me?"

She wrapped her arms around him. "I hadn't heard from you in ages. I worried so much."

"Busy times, you know. Hard to find the time to write."

"Of course," she said, though she couldn't help but think of the dozens of letters that Maxime had managed to write during their months of correspondence. She couldn't help but think of how much she missed it as she wrestled with her conscience over whether or not to resume writing to him. And despite the exhausting hours, she'd sent at least a quick note to Peter and her parents every week.

"So what are you doing here?" Geneviève asked, unable to form a better query.

"Finally got moved to the front after too many months and miles away from the combat. I was beginning to worry the war would be over before I got to see any real action."

Geneviève's face turned solemn. "You'd have been lucky if that had been the case. I'm sure all the lads at the front would have been happy to serve behind the lines."

"They're welcome to a break," Peter said, not catching the biting tone of her comment. "My regiment is ready to do their part. Earn some medals. Get our names in the paper."

"Be careful how you wish for that." Geneviève knew how the families of the enlisted pored over the lists of killed and the missing as the papers were released. The cries of mothers and wives at the newsstand near her family's apartment were soul-shattering, and she heard them as clear as the bells of St. Mary's, even with the windows shut.

"Don't be a killjoy, Jennie. You and the other girls are having a grand time, aren't you?" Patricia and Dottie were having their breakfast while Geneviève had her supper. They'd drawn the short straw and gotten the night shift for the next two weeks. Flora and Geneviève had the day shift with several others from the company, but Flora had been waylaid with a call and would be late for her dinner.

"Not sure I'd classify it that way." Dottie always struggled to wake up for the night shift. She clutched a cup of black coffee in her hands, as precious as a grenade with a pulled pin. "Long hours and endless codes to memorize. I could think of more pleasant ways to spend my time."

"Oh, what would be more important than this? I can't imagine work more satisfying than what we're doing," Patricia purred in her smug way. After a beat, she startled as though she'd spoken a terrible sin. "Excepting motherhood, of course—there's nothing more important than that."

"Hear, hear." Peter patted Geneviève's knee and looked at her meaningfully. She felt blood rise in her cheeks and bile rise in her stomach at the implication. She scolded herself for such an unfeeling response after he'd been so loyal to her in the months he'd been away.

"I never said it wasn't important," countered Dottie. "Quite the opposite. I wouldn't make so light of it as to classify it as a 'grand time' or imply that it's just a diverting pastime."

"Well, at least you're away from the worst of it." Peter took on the jovial tone he employed when he wanted to change the subject.

"It's close enough when the artillery fires," Flora said, claiming a seat across from Peter. She carried a gas mask with her and gestured to it grandly as she sat with her tray. She was never without it, though some of the others took the risk of leaving theirs at the boardinghouse.

Geneviève introduced Flora to Peter, neither of whom seemed all that impressed with the other. Geneviève supposed Flora was too plain for Peter's liking and Peter too flippant for hers.

"Your regiment is in for a rude awakening, I hear," Flora prodded. "Months and months of training behind the line and no contact with the enemy yet."

"Fresh recruits to give the seasoned boys at the front a break," Peter offered curtly.

"A break? You think any of those boys are going to see R&R? No, this is the final push these next few months. No one is getting sent back behind the lines once they're sent up now. Not unless they're on a stretcher or in a body bag."

"That's not what I heard," Peter insisted.

"And you think you hear more than we do?" Dottie interjected, gesturing to Flora's Signal Corps pin as if to remind him who he was talking to. While Patricia had retained her social filter despite the lack of sleep and dubious quality of the food they endured, Dottie had not been as fortunate. Geneviève and Flora often commented that the friendship between Dottie and Patricia, once steadfast, grew more tenuous by the hour. Geneviève found that Dottie was more of a kindred spirit than she'd realized, and she was glad to find more common ground.

"Come now, let's not gang up on poor Peter, shall we? Or should I say Corporal Blake?" Patricia said, beaming at Peter.

"Do you have something stuck in your eye, Patricia?" Flora snapped. "The way you're batting your eyes at Peter here makes me wonder if you don't need the infirmary to make sure you're not coming down with conjunctivitis."

Patricia blanched. "I don't know what you mean, Flora."

"It means you were wanted on duty ten minutes ago and need to move that lace-ruffled rear of yours to the switchboard."

Patricia glared at her, furious that she'd dare to mention her underthings in front of Peter, and angrier still that she brought up the time when Patricia had hung out her clothes to dry and the rest of the operators had mocked the elaborate undershorts that Patricia's mother had insisted on "improving" from the original army issue before allowing her daughter overseas. Apparently Patricia's family was the sort where a girl couldn't go out in public without at least three yards of hand-crocheted lace on one's bloomers. While most of the others chose to let that particular idiosyncrasy drop, Flora didn't mind needling her with it when the mood struck. Patricia *had* looked rather self-satisfied when she'd hung out her altered undergarments next to the plain ones everyone else wore.

But to Patricia's credit, she didn't hang her bloomers publicly anymore. And Geneviève wouldn't have been surprised if Patricia hadn't made good use of a seam ripper in the evenings when the other girls went to sleep. Hopefully she'd salvaged the lace for use at a more appropriate time, but Geneviève wasn't bold enough to ask.

Dottie rushed off to join Patricia with an apologetic look backward at Geneviève and something of incertitude toward Peter.

"I need to be off," Peter said, rising. The buoyancy he had entered the mess hall with was long since gone. "Have to report for my assignment at the barracks, and I don't want bottom bunk again."

"Good luck." Geneviève kissed him awkwardly on the cheek. She watched as he strode off and rubbed her eyes with fatigue when he exited.

"So that's the famous Peter." Flora's tone was not one of glowing approval.

"One and the same." Geneviève tried to sound upbeat, but fatigue was weighing on her. Perhaps not just fatigue.

"He's the one you're promised to?"

Geneviève showed her bare hands. The only jewelry the women were permitted were wedding bands, and a blind eye was turned toward engagement rings. "It's more of an understanding."

Flora swallowed back a comment and said simply, "He's as handsome as you described, and if he takes care of you the way you deserve, he's a catch."

The *however* floated over their heads, as noxious as mustard gas.

⁓

"Of course, General. I can put you through at once," Geneviève said, though her hands trembled as she connected the call. It was now eleven thirty on a sticky July night, and she'd been on duty since six that morning. She caught Flora's eyes, which had widened when she heard the word *General.* Things were moving into place and the Allies would soon be making a final push. And from what Geneviève had gleaned from military strategy, the time was at hand. The German forces were tired and depleted. If the Allies could scare the Central Powers into believing they were hopelessly outgunned before they had the chance to regroup, there might be a prayer for surrender.

Geneviève connected General Richards to Major Harrison at the front, who was leading a battalion that had been log-jammed in place for weeks. Jean's battalion. The call dropped after just a minute or so, likely due to the poor condition of the field phone. Geneviève tried the major back, knowing she might have an easier time connecting herself rather than connecting the two parties. She fought to keep her hands from shaking. She couldn't think about Jean just yet.

"Major, this is Operator Tremblay. Was your communiqué with the general complete, or should I try to connect you again?"

"Don't bother, it will just drop," the major grumbled. He was clearly at a point of exhaustion beyond the reasonable bounds of human endurance. "Give him the codes 0763, 8489, 2402 under my name."

"Very good, Major. I'll relay the message to the general now." *And please keep my brother safe.* She couldn't voice the words, but she longed to desperately.

Geneviève disconnected from the major and connected to the general again, not needing to consult the codebooks the way poor Dottie had to. She simply hadn't the knack for memorization needed for the job, but she was fast in other regards and had admirable French compared to many of the other operators. Some of the codes were three letters and could be used to represent a letter, number, or single word. When a name needed to be spelled out, the codes could be long and cumbersome, but these codes were the easiest; they were four-digit codes that were meant to represent prefabricated sentences of high frequency:

```
8489: We need reinforcements.
2402: We need supplies.
0763: We have suffered heavy casualties.
```

She took just a moment to swallow back her fear and her unshed tears before reconnecting with the general.

"General, we apologize for the dropped call. The major wanted to convey the following message: 8489, 2402, 0763."

"He got the message out before the call dropped, Operator Tremblay." Geneviève started at the sound of her own surname, but the general was renowned for his skill at retaining such information. It was part of what made the men admire him—and truth be told, fear him in almost equal measure. "Let him know the message has been received, and we will do what we can."

Geneviève learned that was military speak for *we have no supplies and no men to send you. So very sorry about the artillery fire.* If Jean was alive, he was likely starving and possibly defenseless. It was all Geneviève could do to keep the contents of her stomach in place and the sobs at bay.

Geneviève rang the major again, who responded to the

general's reply with the frustration and colorful language she expected. She shared his frustrations but knew the general couldn't provide what he didn't have to give. Knowing that the German side was even more desperate gave her a small glimmer of hope, but it made her ache for the wretched conditions those young boys and old men were forced to contend with as well. None of them had welcomed this, on either side.

She took a few seconds to breathe and uttered a prayer of gratitude that she'd been able to maintain her composure. All it would have taken was a few moments to make her appear flighty and emotional. And it would have been a stain not only on her reputation but on that of all the operators. It had taken a vast amount of the great General Pershing's clout to convince Washington that women were needed at the switchboards, and she would not be the one to disabuse them of this notion.

The calls, all similar in nature, had come in at the speed and frequency of German bullets. Geneviève and Flora had worked through their lunch, pausing only when two of the men from the Signal Corps brought them sandwiches and cups of coffee and took over the switchboards, practically by force, for a quarter of an hour so they could eat and relieve themselves. So steady was the flow of phone calls that the second round of sandwiches and coffee at seven at night had caught them off guard. But even so, they made no motions to leave their posts for another four hours until Dottie arrived to take over for the night shift. She approached Flora to take over at her board, but she motioned her to take Geneviève's instead.

Most nights, Geneviève was loath to pass over her duties, knowing they were fielding the most important calls of the war, but she had to put her drive and her ego aside so that she didn't run the risk of making mistakes. She passed her headset to Dottie and mouthed, *"Where's Patricia?"* to her, to which she received a shrug. Flora waved her away, her signal that she would be fine until her replacement arrived.

As Geneviève stepped into the crisp air of early autumn, she felt the inevitable wave of extreme fatigue wash over her, like her life force was seeping from her bones, and her adrenaline ebbed. This was one of those nights when she wondered if she would be able to make it to her barracks without falling asleep on her feet before she reached the door. She never had but was always concerned that her luck would end and she'd wake up in a mud puddle halfway between the makeshift wooden building that housed the switchboards and the one a hundred yards away that housed the operators themselves.

She walked carefully on the rutted road in the scant light of the sliver moon, wishing she could have availed herself of an electric torch, but knowing it would be as dangerous as walking into no-man's-land in broad daylight wearing an American flag and a bull's-eye. She saw two shadowed figures to the right of the doorframe of the barracks she shared with the other operators. She squinted, hoping to discern if the lurkers were friend or foe. She approached with trepidation until she heard the unmistakable sound of Patricia's giggling.

It was followed soon by the familiar music of Peter's chortling and the telltale sounds of a couple loath to be parted from each other.

"Patricia, Flora is overdue to be relieved," Geneviève announced without preamble. "Get to your post at once."

Patricia emitted a noise somewhere between a gasp and a shriek and latched tighter onto Peter and his embrace.

"Jennie, we can explain—" Peter began.

"I'm sure it's all riveting, but I don't care to hear a word about it until Flora has been relieved of her duties for the night. The woman is about to fall asleep at the switchboard, or don't you care about that, Patricia? If you don't, I'll be happy to find your replacement."

"Of course," she said. "I just—"

"I will have a call in to Chief Operator Banker at 0700 hours if you don't start walking toward your switchboard in the next three seconds, Operator Rodgers. I won't say it again."

Patricia drew her mouth into a grim line and marched in the direction of her post.

"Come on, Jennie, you didn't have to be that way with Patty. She's a great girl."

"Right now, she's being a damned lousy operator. To leave another operator so long past her shift is a dereliction of duty."

"Jennie, I know what this is about. You're sore about Patty and me, and I don't blame you. These sorts of things just happen, especially when there is a war on."

"Listen, Corporal Blake, I don't care what you and Operator Rodgers have gotten up to in the two weeks since you got here. That's on your conscience, not mine. But what I will not tolerate is one of my own shirking her duties, no matter how *amusing* the diversion."

"You need to calm down, Jennie."

"In case you haven't noticed from your post half a country away from the front, we're at war, Corporal. A tired operator will make mistakes that can cost lives. If you don't understand that, you don't belong here. Now you get back to your barracks or wherever the hell you're supposed to be, or I'll have *you* before your CO in the morning."

Peter threw his hands up in the air in exasperation. "God, I never pegged you to be petty. My parents were right. No matter how pretty a girl is, no matter how much she studies how to act, she'll never really fit in with people who are their social superiors. That's why Patty happened, you know. She's got a real upbringing."

Geneviève only just managed to keep from shaking in rage. She'd let her fondness for him and the gratitude she felt for the opportunities she'd had at NET&T on his account blind her to his utter snobbery. She was a fool to think she mattered to him in any real way.

"Social superior? Do you hear yourself?"

His face turned to stone. "Loud and clear. Some things you just can't learn. And I suppose class is one of them."

Geneviève immediately thought of Maxime. How his good breeding and gentle manners exuded from his very pores. How conveniently Peter's father had forgotten he was the son of an immigrant grocer from Cornwall. Geneviève took three steps closer to Peter, her eyes narrowed to slits despite the gloom of night. He took a step back, visibly shaking.

"You might be right about that, Corporal Blake—no matter how hard one tries, there are certain things one can't change about their nature. Like no matter how hard you try to play the all-American hero, you will always be a coward. And I want you to remember one thing."

"What's that?" he asked, unable to keep the quavering from his voice.

Geneviève flicked in the direction of her Signal Corps pin and the stripes below it that she'd earned for meritorious service in the months she'd served. Though there was no real equivalent for the women of the Signal Corps in the hierarchy, an entry-level operator was roughly equivalent to a lieutenant. She would be a first lieutenant on her way to captain.

"*Here*, I outrank you. The next time I see you, you'll salute me and the rest of the operators like any other officers, and you won't speak until spoken to. Do I make myself plain?"

His response was to stand open-mouthed as she walked away.

She entered the solitude of her barracks, grateful that Flora would likely be a few more minutes before she returned. The fatigue that had so completely enveloped her before was now replaced with rage. It was true that she and Peter had never formalized their engagement. No doubt his parents had kept him from crossing the Rubicon in hopes that he would find someone more "suitable."

She wasn't angry with Peter. Not really. She was angry that Patricia had kept Flora waiting so long past her shift. She was intensely annoyed with herself for thinking that Peter was in any way trustworthy. Angry for being so naive that she thought his family might ever accept her as one of them.

More than anything, she was furious that she'd forced herself to tamp down the embers of her feelings for Maxime.

Maxime, who had never, despite the disparate circumstances of their families, made her feel inferior.

Maxime, who had exchanged beautiful letters with her in their darkest hours at the front.

Maxime, who had turned their two brief encounters into golden memories.

Maxime, who was truly the best man she'd ever known.

She removed her uniform and slipped into her long cotton nightgown, then pulled the Liberty scarf from her trunk, where it had been stowed for months. It would benefit from a careful pressing, but it was still a thing of beauty. She made sure the doors were all shut and the windows carefully covered before lighting a kerosene lamp as dimly as it would allow and pulling some sheets of paper and her trusty fountain pen from her satchel.

Dearest Maxime,

It is an endless source of wonder to me how, in the course of something joyous—like a birth—or something utterly horrific—like war—that we learn about what truly matters. Once upon a time, it mattered very much to me that I would leave Little Canada and find a way to provide for my family so that my sister and brothers would have advantages I never did. Once upon a time, I thought marriage to the right man from the right family was my ticket to a better life. It was my path to improving myself.

I have learned, through an all-too-literal baptism of fire, that I am made of far finer stuff than the families who judged me and my family. I have served my country with sober dignity, without seeking medals or glory. All I hope is for my superiors to see that I have done my job and done it well. I have learned that I am worthy just as I am. I still hope to help my family, for the younger ones deserve as many advantages as their American-born counterparts receive. I have learned, however, that I deserve to have a life of my own as well.

If your feelings are what they once were, I hope you'll write to me, but I will offer you the same kindness you offered and assure you that I will understand if you do not and will remember you only with great esteem.

With hope,
Geneviève

Geneviève pulled the scarf from her neck, and in the faint light of the kerosene lamp, read the words "Hope is the thing with feathers" inscribed in the vines on the edges of the scarf. The litany repeated like a prayer, and Geneviève recited it to herself over and over as she succumbed to the sleep of the betrayed.

CHAPTER 7

~

October 1918

"Do you think my hair looks all right?" Dottie asked. Owing to the rare night off, she'd taken more time in styling her chestnut mane, and though she'd be forced to wear her regulation cap, she'd wanted to put forth some effort. The women all wore their hair up and out of their faces most of the time, but the concert that evening was to be a rare treat.

Geneviève studied her. "It looks lovely. I like how the curl sweeps across your forehead. Very dashing."

"I think it looks sloppy that way," Patricia replied, waspish, though her churlishness was impolitic. Dottie had been her only ally in the barracks, and to lance insults would not do much to curry favor for Patricia with Dottie or anyone else.

Since Patricia had been caught in her embrace with Peter, the atmosphere in the women's barracks was strained by the most generous of assessments. The women all took sides, and most of them were with Geneviève, either by principled stance or out of deference to Geneviève's rank as supervising operator. For her part, Geneviève acted indifferently toward Patricia, only speaking to her to issue orders as her position required. Patricia replied only when it was a matter of keeping her job. Geneviève suspected that Patricia had been hoping for Geneviève to act jealous or spiteful that she'd broken up her relationship with Peter, and Geneviève's aloofness drove her mad.

And Geneviève was perfectly content to allow Patricia to seethe. Not only that, she was also fully willing to report Patricia to the Chief Operator for poor conduct as she'd threatened to do. If it came to it, she would request her transfer to another group or recommend that she be relieved of her duties. So Patricia was forced to be compliant, though she despised every moment of it.

Patricia's saving grace was that Geneviève was too professional to send her away on a whim. And she was not so foolish as to think another operator could be transferred to take Patricia's place if she were sent back from the front. Not without great difficulty, if it were possible at all. Geneviève had to think of the needs of her group first, and to be a woman short would mean longer hours for all of them. Patricia hadn't dared to be late to a shift ever since she'd been caught with Peter, for she knew it could have sent her before a disciplinary committee or even court-martialed.

It was her professionalism that kept Geneviève sane when she heard, several times over in the past few months, that Jean's regiment had sustained heavy artillery fire, though each time Jean managed to survive. It was her professionalism that kept her grounded when the reports from the French Air Force came back bleaker each week. Patricia had no idea how much she owed to Geneviève's professionalism, and how close she came to finding its limits on a daily basis.

"You look nice, Dottie." Flora shot a scorching look in Patricia's direction. Dottie had looked on the point of re-doing her hair after Patricia's comment, but Flora patted her arm. "Let's not be late. The men will be glad to see a pretty girl in high spirits, and they'll think your hair is the loveliest sight they've seen in months."

Patricia huffed and exited the barracks first, Dottie hard on her heels. Flora emitted an exhausted sigh before joining them. Given that the concert was a special occasion and no one would bother inspecting their uniforms on such a night, Geneviève grabbed the scarf Maxime had given her and tied it artfully around her neck before bounding to the jeep with the other girls.

The concert was designed to build morale for the troops as the hope of an armistice loomed near but seemingly out of reach. The operators had been issued a special invitation, and their male counterparts in the Signal Corps had insisted they accept it, arranging for adequate replacements for the four hours they'd be away from base. All were glad to have a short break from their duties, but the acrimony Patricia felt toward Geneviève was palpable in the confines of the small jeep.

A few minutes down the road, Flora noticed the scarf Geneviève had tucked away for so many months.

"A beautiful touch for a special occasion," Flora remarked as she ran her finger along the edge of the scarf.

"I thought we weren't supposed to make any unsanctioned changes to the uniform," Patricia said, glaring at Flora.

"She's off duty. How many times did you wear civilian clothes on your half day?" Flora retorted. Patricia huffed and turned her glare out the window to look, presumably, at the darkness that swirled outside as they drove along. Dottie looked as though she wanted to climb through the jeep window and hurl herself in front of oncoming traffic. Geneviève shot her a sympathetic look, knowing she was an innocent party in the whole affair.

But Flora's gesture was more than just a compliment of her pretty scarf. It was an apology. *I'm sorry I tried to persuade you that the Frenchman was a bad choice. Clearly the American you had lined up was no prize if he chose that twit over you.* Geneviève patted Flora's knee in wordless thanks.

They arrived at a sort of makeshift amphitheater where hundreds of soldiers were waiting for the band with enthusiasm that crackled like switchboard wires. As was their custom, the girls chatted with the men—they'd been told countless times that the mere presence of American women was a boon to morale—but they did so in a group for the sake of propriety. Before long, the band assembled—all servicemen from Allied troops—and they played a vast assortment of music, everything from Mozart and Puccini to "Let Me Call You Sweetheart" to the crowd favorite "Over There." Geneviève's heart sank when she thought of how much Peter had loved Cohan's music. "Give My Regards to Broadway" was a favorite of his, and he'd always promised that he'd take her to a show in New York on their honeymoon. Like so many of his promises, he'd failed to see them through, and now Patricia would be the recipient of those same pledges.

It should have stung worse than it did, and the reality that she mostly felt indifferent toward Peter made her feel some-how . . . worse. That she was disloyal for not having stronger feelings about the relationship being over. But as she'd come to know Patricia over their months of service together, she saw how the pairing made sense. Patricia would fit in well with Peter's parents in a way Geneviève never would. Patricia had closets full of clothes, appropriate for a socially ambitious young matron. Patricia would know which wives to befriend and which she could safely snub. How many friends would be just enough to be appreciable, and how few would make her appear selective without being snobbish.

She had skills Geneviève didn't have, and more importantly, they were skills she didn't care about cultivating.

But with her relationship with Peter at an end, she felt well and truly unmoored. Her future at NET&T was so tied up in Peter's family that she couldn't count on that when she returned. Certainly she could find work at another telephone company, but that would involve moving to a new state. Pennsylvania? New York? They seemed as foreign to her as the ground on which she stood, thousands of miles from where she was born. Would her family come with her, or would she simply send money home each week and hope for the best? Worse, any such job would be dependent on references she wasn't sure would sing her praises.

And of course, there was the question of Maxime.

There had been no response to her letter. She had no hopes that they could rekindle what might have been. But she wanted to hope that whatever future she carved out for herself would hold something of the magic she'd known when she walked the vineyard with Maxime.

The band had just launched into a stirring rendition of "I Want a Girl" when an earsplitting screech rent the night air. The orange hue that filled the sky was unmistakable to anyone who'd been within a hundred miles of the front: artillery fire, and a lot of it.

"Take cover!" Geneviève yelled to the girls. She worried, and not without cause, that they might be trampled in the haste to evade the German bombs, but the men ushered them to the relative safety of an abandoned trench. This was territory the Allied countries had conquered weeks ago, and the front had advanced considerably since then. But now the trench was back in use. Patricia and Dottie clung to each other, white-faced and terrified. Flora and Geneviève, a bit steadier under pressure, split their time between assessing the strength of the German attack and swiftly mumbling prayers that the trench wouldn't be their final resting place. For a moment the walls felt as if they were going to move in on her, and Geneviève's familiar dizziness set in.

Not here, not now. She swallowed hard and willed the world to come back into focus.

And if she kept her wits about her, she might be able to be of use. If she panicked, like she'd done with Maxime in the tube station, she'd just be in the way. She was capable of better. If she'd learned anything from her months of service, it was that she was stronger than she believed.

And certainly stronger than Peter had ever realized.

Geneviève shrieked as a man collided with her as he slid down into the trench. He held a violin in his right hand but gripped that arm with his left like it was the only thing keeping it attached. He stood, taking stock of the situation, grew pale, and crumpled into a heap. Geneviève had next to no formal medical training, but she knelt down by his side hoping she could help in some way. She gently pried the violin from his hands, though he mumbled in protest. His words were in French, and she realized his uniform was French like Maxime's rather than American.

"It's okay, I'm not going to steal your violin," she replied in French. His eyes flickered in surprise as he registered a woman was speaking to him, and in his native tongue too, despite being surrounded by American troops. "I want to look at your arm, and I can't do that if you're holding your instrument."

He loosened his grip and allowed her to remove the violin, which she gently placed by his left side. There was a long, angry gash on his right bicep, so bloody she could hardly make out how deep it went. She didn't see any shrapnel, though the light was dim, and she hoped that there was none hidden that would linger and cause the wound to fester. He would need a surgeon and dozens of stitches, Geneviève surmised, but she wasn't one and was incapable of the other.

And he would bleed to death before he got either if she didn't stop the bleeding. She looked up, assessing the trench and wondering what she might use for a tourniquet. She wasn't sure if she hoped to see a first aid kit magically appear before her, but of course, none did. She pulled the beautiful Liberty scarf from around her neck, tied it above the wound, and wrapped it tightly as she would have a gauze bandage. She wasn't sure how well silk would perform the office she required of it, but she had no other options at hand that wouldn't require her ripping her uniform to shreds.

After a few minutes, it looked as though his color had improved slightly. The snug bandaging likely lessened the throbbing pain to some degree. More importantly, his blood loss had slowed dramatically, and his body was better able to cope. "Are you going to be all right?" Geneviève asked.

"Thanks to you," he said. "Though my arm . . ."

"Don't think about it," she said. "You'll play again. Maybe not tomorrow, but you will."

"*Vous êtes un ange en bleu*," he murmured. An angel in blue. His eyes began to flicker. He had to sleep. To escape the pain until his mind was prepared for it. Geneviève kissed his forehead and regretfully touched the loose end of the beautiful scarf that had been given to her with such affection.

"This scarf was given to me by a very dear friend," she whispered to him as he drifted off. "And it will bring you hope. I think you need it more than I do right now, so take care of it, will you?"

He nodded, half asleep, looking pensive for a moment before his eyes shut again. Perhaps he was hoping for the use of his arm to be restored. Perhaps he was hoping just to survive his injuries. There was probably a universe of hopes and dreams within him that Geneviève would never know. A universe within each of the men and women who lost their lives to this infernal war. And if Geneviève could save a few more lives that night, it would be saving those hopes and dreams from being forever lost. She tucked his violin in his arms to keep it safe, then forged on farther down the trench, doing what she could until the barrage of artillery fire ceased and the light of dawn gave them reprieve.

CHAPTER 8

November 11, 1918

GENEVIÈVE FELT THE WORLD GROW FUZZY AS SHE TRIED TO FOCUS ON the switchboard before her. She had been on duty for fifteen hours, but the pull to answer the calls was too great. It was obvious that the Germans were on the point of surrender, and if they missed the call for the ceasefire, lives could be lost needlessly. Flora and Dottie had been at the boards nearly as long, though Patricia had claimed fatigue two hours earlier. It was nearing midmorning, and they'd all worked through the night.

The call came through at half past ten, when the general gloriously announced that "all hostilities will cease at eleven hundred hours."

For the next two hours, Geneviève's hands were a blur as she connected calls and relayed messages. These were the most vital communications she'd ferried in the course of her service. The armistice was tenuous and any action that could be interpreted as hostility could break it. The men in the trenches had to be informed so the process of peace could begin.

It wasn't until the relief operators—aided by Flora—nearly dragged Geneviève from her post that she was willing to go back to the barracks. She and Flora walked, arm in arm, as much to keep each other from falling in a ditch from exhaustion as joy that the war was coming to an end. The ceasefire was only the beginning of the end of the war. There would be a slow de-escalation and treaty negotiations that would last months—maybe even years.

"Oh my God, we might be home soon. Within weeks." Flora's voice was uncharacteristically dreamy as she envisioned sleeping in her own bed and having access to all the warm food and clean clothing a person could ever want. "Won't that be grand?"

"Of course." Geneviève found fertile ground for cultivating some enthusiasm. "The sooner all this bloodshed ends, the better."

Geneviève knew that she should have been brimming with joy, but she couldn't ignore the ache that was beginning to form in her midsection. Naturally she was relieved beyond measure. She might have a post for another few months. Maybe even a year or two if she was willing to go to Germany. Or she might be sent home next week.

Home, where there was no future with Peter.

Home, where she might not even have a future at NET&T.

Home.

Thousands of miles away from Maxime.

"I couldn't agree more," Flora replied. "The only comfort I have is knowing that this is meant to be the war to end all wars. Humanity has finally gotten this idiocy out of its system."

Geneviève tried to share in her optimism, but she found she could not. How many generations would it be before these horrors were forgotten and other petty squabbles between rich men and crowned heads led to the sons of common men being dragged off to war under the false pretenses of glory, duty, and honor? But Flora, under a veil of relief and exhaustion, looked so full of hope that Geneviève couldn't voice her doubts aloud. Let Flora have her dreams.

"What will you do now that it's all over?" Flora asked.

Geneviève wasn't a skilled enough actress to keep her expression neutral, and Flora was too perceptive not to notice.

"I wish I knew." Geneviève wasn't entirely successful at keeping the worry from her tone but managed not to sound as unmoored as she felt.

"No word?" Flora didn't have to elaborate. The lack of correspondence from Maxime had been weighing heavy over Geneviève's head for weeks, and Flora was the only one she'd confided in on the subject.

There had still been no letter in response to hers. She had sent two more, praying they would reach him. Any more seemed excessive. She had to give him the space to respond, and there was no use in clogging the overtaxed mail system with unwanted letters.

"No." The word sounded so heavy, final.

"You know he may be perfectly well. There could be a very logical reason why he hasn't responded. It may all be fine."

Geneviève forced a smile. Of course her friend was right.

It was entirely plausible the mail was so unreliable that her letters never got to him. Easily explained and entirely out of their hands.

It could also be that when he saw her name on the envelopes, he cast them aside. Perhaps their parting was so painful to him that he couldn't bear to read her letters. Perhaps he expected that they were filled with nothing more than idle pleasantries and friendly chatter, and he couldn't stand a pale imitation of the communication he wanted. She hated to think this was the case, but men under less extreme circumstances had acted more bizarrely than this.

Or the worst had happened. And that was too painful to consider.

But as long as she was in France—or at least nearby—she found room in her heart for hope. She'd beg to be kept on as long as there were operators overseas, and her reasoning would be valid. She was of more use to her family here, earning generous pay that she could send home. She was one of the best at the switchboard and she was well-liked by those who mattered. There was a chance.

"We should get some sleep," Flora urged. "We're both dead on our feet, and who knows what chaos tomorrow might bring."

"Chaos indeed." Geneviève changed into her nightgown, willingly discarding her uniform after far too many hours confined in a prison of wool. But her bed, which should have been as appealing as an oasis in the Sahara after the day she had, was somehow uninviting. She murmured an excuse to Flora and went to the sitting room of the boardinghouse with her little case of writing effects in hand.

Instead of writing letters, she poured her words for Maxime into her illicit diary. Geneviève was always careful to keep any details about her work from the pages, as even small tidbits could fill in gaps that enemy troops could use to their advantage. She kept her diary on her person at all times and hadn't breathed a word about it to anyone. It was her solace when her thoughts grew too heavy to bear alone.

But now, perhaps, the worry was over and the secrets in her diary, however small, would not cost lives.

She opened the leather tome and removed the Dickinson poem from where she'd tucked it for safekeeping. *Hope is the thing with feathers.* She'd thought the notion silly when she'd learned the poem in school. Now she imagined a fledgling baby bird, covered in down, looking proudly at its first crop of feathers. In times like these, hope seemed that fragile. A baby bird, still dependent on its mother for food, warmth, and protection. So easily dispatched. So easily destroyed.

But if luck was with them, hope could grow. Hope could flourish and sprout magnificent feathers and soar above the treetops, leaving the safety of the nest behind until it was time to roost once more.

She turned to the first blank page, of which there were becoming very few as she filled the book with her worries and her hopes.

Dearest Maxime,

    I do not know where you are or indeed if you are still with us, but I pray for you every night before I sleep. Every morning when I wake, my first thoughts are of you. And in the hours in between, memories of you float to the surface more often than I can count. I know you will never see these words, but I hope that deep in your soul you know that I wish you all the happiness in the world. I would gladly live a solitary life if you don't wish to continue with what might have been. The world won't be such a stranger to me if I could simply have the solace of knowing you are alive and safe in it.

    Emily was right. Hope IS the thing with feathers. And my wish is that yours is a mighty falcon or a soaring eagle pointed steadfastly in its course back to Avallon. I dream of it, you know. Is it strange to dream of a place I have never seen and will never know? But it seems like a paradise to me, the way you have described it. I imagine long walks, hand in hand with you, as we wind our way through the endless rows of vines that we cultivate with such love. That life is a dream. A wisp in the ether that will never fully materialize. But even as it floats, ephemeral, such a thing of beauty does lighten my soul when times are bleak.

Hope for me is still a lone feather, drifting on the wind. I have no idea where it will alight. But I have enough faith in myself to know I can find a new path once my time here has come to an end.

I cannot say I won't have regrets. Very few, really. But at least the time we spent together is not among them.

And the image of the life we might have shared will bring me joy, even if it's just a faded remnant of a dream.

With my love,
Geneviève

She closed the journal and kissed the cover, as was her nightly custom, and knew she would never open it again. If Maxime wasn't to be a part of her future, she had to create a new one from the ashes of a war-torn world, and that wouldn't happen if she dwelled too long on what might have been. But she could, as she told this paper-and-ink facsimile of Maxime, pull the dream, like a jewel from a case, and bask in its beauty from time to time.

And that would have to be enough.

PART THREE

CHAPTER 1

Tielt, Belgium
Before the War

CLARA JANSSENS TOLD PEOPLE THE REASON SHE DECIDED TO PURSUE
nursing was an unusual one: a painting by Flemish artist Pieter
Bruegel the Elder.

De Parable der Blinden.

The Blind Leading the Blind.

The painter's work was so deeply *humane*, Clara felt she was
not standing looking at swirls of oily brushstrokes but actually
inhabiting them. The first time she saw it, she wanted to help
the subjects of the painting. There had to be a better way than
holding to each other's shoulders, a human chain of reliance.
Every human was a story, and theirs was quite a story to be told.

Clara loved a story. Her mother told stories through the
rolling of dough and the distribution of flour. Recipes passed
down from generations, telling the story of her family in small
tweaks and adaptations.

Clara's father walked with stories clung to his collar, to the musty or fresh scent that stayed on his coat as he shrugged out of its bulk in the doorway. The people and places of Tielt and beyond. The legends of Belgium and even of the artist Bruegel.

When the sun sank behind the horizon, heralding the last light of summer, her father's stories changed to the sort that prickled the back of her neck, just as the smell of her mother's baking Desem bread told the story of the generations who had fed their loaves from the same starter.

Stories about Olivier le Daim, the Ghent barber known as "the Devil," found Clara tugging at her father's shirt cuff. Le Daim was born in Tielt, as was Clara, but made famous in the story *The Hunchback of Notre-Dame*. The court barber of Louis XI, his penchant for intrigue and violence helped him rise far beyond his means. It wasn't the violence of the story that thrilled Clara so much as a Ghent barber finding new adventures at court.

"Stories often outlive their owners and keepers, Clara," Father said. "So long as they are told and retold, they assume the role their teller needs them to play."

"Nonsense." Her mother had the same contempt for stories as she did her circumstance in life. "Your father goes around telling stories about places we've never seen and people we've never met. Meanwhile here we are!"

Perhaps because her mother never had much choice in the beginning or even ending of her own story, she had little time for Clara's father's tales, less so in the waning years of her short life.

But he found stories everywhere and encouraged Clara to find them too. She didn't have a lot of friends her age, and even though a tutor came to teach her a few times a week, her mother was adamant she needn't have any education beyond what was needed to tend house.

Still, Clara felt she learned more from time spent with her father, especially when they studied a book of Bruegel's paintings together. "And unusual stories make for the most interesting ones," her father said as Clara looked over the muted colors.

Clara thought everything about herself was unusual. Her height, for one, and her hair. When she chopped her chestnut locks upon reading a lady's journal on "Parisienne Boheme," her curls sighed over her forehead in a shape that was *almost* fashionable but not really. They, like Clara, knocked at the door of fashion and current trends but were, sadly, left out in the cold.

The church ladies' guild tea at Saint Peter approved of the itchy skirt and plain blouse. They did not, however, approve of the Parisienne Boheme hairstyle even as it suited her.

Clara was used to such disapproval now.

But Clara convinced herself that her deceased mother's opinion was not of any great consequence. She had always been more like her father.

The world was a story, he taught her, and Clara was desperate to turn its pages.

Especially since Maria Janssens long believed she was meant for more than what life had doled her: marriage to a builder who never had two francs to rub together but who worked hard. Who had calloused hands but a soft touch at the side of Clara's cheek whenever he came home from a long day. Her father had so much to say about the people he met along the way. And yet Clara's mother had little to offer but a sleek looking-over.

Nothing was ever good enough for her mother: the only woman in a family who needed to sell off their houses and wares, and who needed to sell her off in hopes she would at least find a man to feed her and keep a roof over her head. One less plate at the table. One more woman whose dreams were swept with the last crumbs from supper under a worn mat.

And then she grew ill and resentful of an unlived life slipping away from her. When she had a daughter, she determined her weakness would be snuffed out once and for all.

Clara tended to her mother as best she could. She took on the household chores and said goodbye to the tutor. The Bruegel book collected dust on the mantel even as the candlesticks and tabletops were brushed clean in her desire to impress her mother. As her mother's breathing slowed and her face washed white and translucent, she begged Clara to think about her future rationally. "Your father's stories. The paintings. They are fairy tales. You need to take care of him. You need to prepare to tend to a house and a family."

In their final moments, Clara felt guilty for having spent her formative years chasing after her father's company while tolerating her mother.

"I will do what I can to tend to you now," Clara promised, smoothing a cold compress to her mother's head. She saw to her mother's every need and reported to the doctor of her mother's progress. Or lack thereof.

And when her mother finally passed, she made good on her promise. She saw to her father's dinner and to the baking of the Desem bread.

But when war knocked on Belgium's door, Maria Janssens's daughter had a different map for her future. One that stretched beyond tending her mother and her deathbed promise.

"She told me I should stay with you and take care of you," Clara said to her father, who was determined she find the opportunity to go to nurses' training in Brussels.

"And you have. But you need to take care of others. Just as you did your mother when she needed you. Just as you did me."

When she was accepted for training, her heart soared. Father ensured she remembered a shawl once belonging to her mother as she packed.

"She told me not to leave you." Clara could not clear her throat of the tears at the train station.

"But by doing so, you are honoring me. I *want* you to go, Clara." He kissed her gently on both cheeks. "And I want you to take this with you."

Their book of Bruegel paintings. A hundred stories sewn into muted, complicated colors.

"You will see them in a different way when you are there. And you will remember to come home and tell me all about the new story you are making for yourself."

CHAPTER 2

Strasbourg, France
Before the War

OFF THE SQUARE OF THE PLACE DE LA CATHÉDRALE, WHERE STRAS-
bourg's belfries and buttresses and the tall columns of Notre-
Dame towered over the rows of half-timbered facades of the
Alsatian-style houses, stood one such gingerbread house with
a distinctive triangular roof at the very end of a long matching
row. Attached was a sort of lean-to aside which hung a dangling
sign pronouncing:

R. ALLAIRE, CORDONNIER

Roman Allaire, the younger cordonnier, did not hold a pin-
cer or a cobbler's hammer, but rather a violin bow. The instrument was as beautifully crafted as the leatherware his father
cobbled and was a present from a patron at the cathedral who
heard Roman play and decided, as did the priest, that he had
a rare gift.

R. Allaire, Cordonnier, was now well acquainted with his
violin, C. Boullangier.

Charles Boullangier, maker, was of an illustrious reputation of craftsman whose name was now furnished in gold interlay in the frog of the violin.

For several years, Roman was torn between the cobbling instruments and the violin. Did C. Boullangier ever feel the same divide between conviction and passion? Was Boullangier Senior willing to accept that his son was better suited to the curve of purfling and ribs on the body of the instrument and the tuning of the strings than whatever enterprise ran in the family line?

As for himself, Roman was the latest R. Allaire in a long line. Didn't the sign swinging outside announce as much? His father's dearest dreams hoped he would not be the last. But dreams could not be inherited as easily as a set of premiere cobbling tools. Roman may have been the most recent, but he was also the first Allaire to imagine something else.

While his mother could make satin out of a sow's ear or treat stains from damaged leather, Roman could barely press the needle to the leather in the first place. While his father had an almost preternatural ability to make out even a hidden foible in a shoe sole, Roman's talents were always more musically inclined. The same precision. The same ability. But in song rather than in stitches.

They were an indomitable team, his parents. Father would fix, Mother would tailor and make new. Roman was an outlier—a dissonant tone in an otherwise perfect harmony.

He got by on passable attempts of each of his parents' strengths, certain one day he would overtake the business—not out of a sense of passion but duty.

It was a point of discontent, then, when the church warden introduced Roman to a visiting tutor from Metz, M. Tobias Bloch. Bloch had heard Roman had a proficiency on the instrument and an ear that allowed him to sing the hymns on Sunday with perfect pitch. Roman was musical, M. Bloch had explained several times over the course of a few years to Roman's parents.

"With the best tutelage we could provide," his father refined. Not that the senior R. Allaire was invested in Roman's prospects as a violinist; rather, he would not have any guest in his house doubting his family's capacity to provide.

Men needed shoes and leather and soles and stitches in an intricate rhythm of craftsmanship and purpose to take them over the stones from the square to the shuttered, close-cloistered town houses sighing up every narrow street, which exhaled down to the ribboning Rhine splicing through it. Roman needed to find a different sort of artistry. He had not been provided an opportunity on the violin until M. Bloch's visit.

Roman's father—caught between a rock and the hard place of his pride—clearly saw little option other than to let his son thrive. But within reason.

"Yes, he can play at church."

Roman would play in a ditch if he could play.

Roman's talent under M. Bloch's supervision developed at an exceptional pace for a young man who did not start in early childhood as so many other violinists did, and the first mention of the illustrious Beaux-Art in Brussels burrowed deep.

Roman had never wanted his future prescribed in a composition of stitches. A Lembert or an Everting or a Connell Suture or a Cushing Stitch through the tender part of leather in a continuous, gentle tenacity as his father had taught was a nuanced and deft craft of the trade. Instead, he wanted the same even and ongoing lines interpreted not through the little diagrams above his father's work desk but above a music stand. With keys and signatures and jaunty eighth notes he could interpret merely by the pressure of his index fingers on his bow.

Eventually he wanted it so much he would risk his father's disappointment at the end of a lineage of trade. His mother, dreaming for him long before Roman could dream for himself, softened the blow.

"I will make him understand." She cupped Roman's face with her worn hands. "I will begin with *food.*" He knew her smile was an attempt to convince him.

Roman would leave in celebration of his new life and the mourning of his passing of the old one at once. And that meant the smell of Christmas in a mélange of savory and spice wrapped in his mother's *baeckeoffe*: an assortment of layered onions, potatoes, juniper berries, and herbs.

The traditional Alsatian dish was such a communal event that it required the baker down the street and his large oven for the bread, which freed up the kitchen for his mother to make the supplemental dishes. Roman knew his mother swiped at her perspiring brow with her worn handkerchief for *his* sake. An acknowledgment of his pursuing his musical dreams as potent to him as the lessons and carols of the first Sunday of Advent.

His mother had worked her magic with his father much as she had the pastried top of the baeckeoffe: with deft, folded precision. Still, Roman sensed his father would be placated only temporarily. He was the only son and he was choosing something else entirely. It made him more determined than ever to succeed. He'd prove himself not only on account of his own pride but also his father's.

Roman arrived at the train station with his talent and ambition shoved as tightly in his pockets as the anxiety he balled with the embroidered kerchief his mother had recently passed him, slightly damp with her farewell tears. "Your eyes. One brown. One blue. That is when I knew you would be different. That you would be extra special."

"That I would be teased by all of the other boys?" Roman winked and gave her a squeeze. "Thank you for believing in me, Maman. And for helping Father see this is what is right."

He knew his father's farewell would not be as warm. But he was pleased that it was not stern or resentful. His father shook his hand firmly. He was disappointed, but it was a start.

Roman's first letter home was written on his lap as the wheels chugged him farther than he had ever been from Strasbourg. In excited lines that smudged the ink with the slightest shake of a hand ready to run a scale, he scribbled his hope of replacing his father's disappointment with platitudes of realized dreams for music and perhaps even a first chair in a premier orchestra. He wrote of what he anticipated from the conservatory. Of how grateful he was for the foundation that set him on his way. How rare it was. How he hoped his father would understand. How he would write of what he would see in Brussels in hopes that his parents, who had never left their home country, would feel they were right there with him.

Roman clicked the violin case open and ran his index finger over the curves and lines of the instrument. A slight, soft strum of his finger pad over the E string drew the eyes of a few passengers.

He replaced the protective cloth over the curved and embellished wood of the instrument.

It might have been just perfect.

CHAPTER 3

~

1915

[BELGIUM HAD BEEN FORCED INTO WAR FROM ITS PREVI-
OUSLY NEUTRAL STATE BY A GERMAN ULTIMATUM. BEING
THE MOST DENSELY POPULATED COUNTRY IN THE WORLD,
BELGIUM WAS CAREFUL TO CHOOSE ITS CONSTELLATION IN
TIELT, DESPITE BEING CUT OFF FROM THE HOME FRONT AND
EXILED BY THE GERMAN MILITARY OCCUPATION.]

Father,

*I was relieved when the Boche chose Tielt as its Belgian
headquarters. Funny how we call the Germans a slang on the French
"slow-plate" or "thickhead." I suppose it is supposed to make them
less frightening. I hope you are not frightened of them, Father. Since
the moment I embarked on my adventure, hopefully now well-
known to you from my previous letters, I have been concerned about
your safety. They speak of zeppelins: great oblongs in the air that
rain down fire and blast destruction all around. But why would
they want to rain fire on the city they chose as their residence? I*

cannot assume they would for any reason. Especially not at the risk of their own countrymen. You are safer there even while I am far away from you.

You've long known I have needed a true friend. Long before the war began. That Pieter the tutor was not a replacement for another young woman my age and that the ladies in the church sewing circles were too old, and the ladies my age were too, well, married. You knew long before I cut my hair! As excited as I was to come here and as fulfilling as my work has been, I still felt alone. Even as I returned home for my short visits. The ones I always knew and loathed as they came to an end. Even as it looked like the mere months I anticipated being away turned into years and the visits home and with you more and more rare.

"Alone" is a scary word, I suppose. I never truly felt it until I opened my case and looked out the filmy window of my dormitory room, because it doesn't matter whether you are in a room of nurses raucous or rowdy or tugging your wool blanket up to your chin at lights out. Alone is just . . . well . . . alone. I suppose I never wrote of it before because I wanted to convince myself through you that my book of Bruegel paintings was enough. That I could honor Mama in the little moments by telling the girls of a tip or trick in the kitchen.

Alone can happen whether you're in a rush of people choosing their bunk beds in a palace-turned-hospital training center, or smoothing the creases of a starched collar on a new uniform, or raiding the supply cupboard for bandages or tape. Alone is in a rush of hundreds of soldiers at Ypres. Two years ago, yes, when I was at Ypres tending to the thousands of nameless and sometimes faceless Canadian soldiers, blinded by gas and pain and feeling as far away from you as I do now.

Still, no matter who I meet and what I experience, I have Mama's stern training melded into my brain just as I have the voice *of the matron who ran our training not with compassion but a far stronger virtue: expectation. As with Mama, I never wanted to disappoint her. I fold bedsheets properly, quartered and creased with Mama looking over me and the matron's voice in my head.*

When work is done, I have explored the many shades and colors on the palette of alone. Sometimes vibrant red or muted green, like the brushstrokes in my Bruegel book.

You told me my book of Bruegel paintings was a poor substitute for a breathing human. That brush and paint and contour were a poor replacement for a true friend. You were right, I admit. Though keeping it under my pillow every night, my heart sinks and relaxes a little bit. So similar to what I feel when I recall one of your stories. How your voice rises and falls.

I hope I can tell you stories as well as the ones I folded in my pocket when I left home.

As for our matron, I believe if I were to hear her given name straight out, for example, I would shudder deep down into my regulation cape or be strangled in its regulation collar and knot.

But Clara was not friendless for long. The camaraderie forged by the matron and her antics found many girls huddling together if only to commiserate. It wasn't long before Clara wrote her father again, this time about the girls she met and how they all survived the matron's stern—but fair—teachings in preparation for their part of the war.

Clara heard of the matron before she met her. She was, after all, the head of the nurses in the Belgian hospital and ran a tight ship. For all the hearsay that Matron was perfunctory to a fault and that she had a no-nonsense policy for tardiness, it wasn't until Clara was reprimanded for her inability to fold the corners of a bedsheet that Clara truly felt her presence.

She wasn't a tall woman, nor a particularly intimidating one in stature. And yet . . .

With trembling fingers, Clara made efficient work that finally pleased her.

With the matron's curt and accepting nod, Clara's shoulders raised and her lips pressed in a smile.

Some of the girls scowled when the matron showed Clara particular favor in those early days. Others recognized she was as they were: petrified.

"Attila the Hun!" Clara heard several times. Especially in regard to her perfunctory set of rules.

For Matron had a firm policy that a mere two moments of tardiness was punishable by the loss of two *hours* of spare time. Still, Clara knew she would risk far more than two moments' tardiness for a shared moment with the young woman who finally *said* something about the matron's firm fist.

"We're nurses!" she overheard the same young woman say, and with the defense, she felt the string bonding them tighten. "We should not be viewing this experience as a firing squad, but rather as an opportunity!"

The young woman who defended her was Annelise De Groot. Though with merely a week's seniority over Clara, Annelise seemed to know *everything*, not only of the world of bandages and nursing charts but beyond. She taught Clara how to speak to men in her care with warmth, suggesting compassion while never belying an invitation.

Most importantly, she steadied Clara through the barked instructions of orderlies who frantically rushed in from the front lines with stretchers bearing men in dire need not only of resuscitation but also perfunctorily pulled starched sheets over briefly empty cots—too briefly. Sometimes within the time of a bedding change, more wounded appeared. Sharp corners and crisp lines, however, were as important as their triage and care. A routine. A proficient detail.

The detail to which Clara could ensure a soldier's hypothetical comfort in training was a far cry from Annelise's natural talent at the same.

"Who are you trying to impress?" A young woman scowled at Clara.

"Don't be sour just because every time you make a bed, the sheet is so lopsided a patient is like to roll himself up in it like a cocoon and fall off the bed," Annelise retorted, winking at Clara.

They fell into a rhythm: Clara read in Annelise's eyes what she was feeling (it was often equally balanced trepidation and a little bit of exhilaration at this brand-new world). They were scared and excited at the same time and could hold long conversations with a glance at the matron's retreating figure or with the first sound of the morning bell.

It was that alchemy of emotions that shattered every last defense for Clara. Her vulnerability melted. Homesickness. Insecurity. The matron's orders demanding that she do a simple task again and again.

"Perhaps I was too hasty in thinking I could live up to this," Clara admitted one morning, tucking a haphazard curl from her overlong haircut that drew several harsh looks from the matron. "I could be at home seeing to my father."

"Perhaps." Annelise smoothed the collar rising above her pinned apron. "Or perhaps you just need to see what you're capable of."

Even though they wore the same regulation uniform, Annelise's suited her differently—from the peaked cap to the sleeve protectors that looked like starched, overstretched caterpillars on Clara's own form yet were a perfect accordion of fabric on her friend's.

It wasn't until they were preparing to board the lorries and tuck their training into their starched collars and the smoothed wimples atop their pulled-back hair that Clara noticed something slightly different about her new friend's collar.

A slight splash of color winking at the base of her neck interrupted her otherwise perfect uniform.

"Annelise . . ." Clara whispered before tilting her head in the direction of the slight indiscretion.

With aplomb, Clara patted the fabric, and magically she was a vision in ivory white.

"We all must have *something*, mustn't we, Clara?" Annelise nudged Clara's shoulder. "Something no one else needs to know. This isn't a *true* Liberty of London scarf. Do you know Liberty? It has the most beautiful fashions. I have only seen it in pictures, but I know I would love it there. This is as close as I could afford from my milk money before I came here! Besides, I like knowing I have a little secret and sometimes I open my collar just so." She unfastened a button. "And show the men. It makes them smile."

Clara supposed her *something* was in her regulation kit. A copy of Bruegel's paintings to blast a tiny bit of home against a theater of shells and gunfire.

Soon, all of the matron's teaching and all of Clara's wide-eyed optimism stitched a curtain ripped harshly open at the first view of war. With everything she *imagined* when words and sentences were painted to help her anticipate the experience, nothing could have prepared her. No training. No practice or acting a role as if there was a real patient on the empty bed affront her.

Hospitals and Casualty Caring stations dotted a haphazard and makeshift mess against the near trenches and no-man's-land of the war.

But when she shared a silent conversation with Annelise, it rang louder than any verbal exchange. For the first time in her life, she was not the odd girl, the tall girl, the girl with the bobbed hair. Annelise had her own eccentricities, as wide and varied as the patterns of the scarves she spoke of from a fashion catalog. The soldiers she tended, wounded and afraid, looked at her like an angel of mercy.

No matter how tired, no matter how cold or hungry, Clara never failed to send a weekly letter to her father.

Ypres, 1915

Father,

Do you remember the first time I saw De Parable der Blinden? Oh how I miss our sharing Bruegel together in my beautiful book. When I open its pages, it is almost as if you were there. Father Matthew spoke of the biblical parable from Matthew. Of the blind leading the blind . . . men linked in a chain of resilience.

When I think of that painting, I think of tutor Pieter, who rumbled to our house in his father's milk cart to teach me. He made the trip from Aarsele into Tielt and accepted your payment in fresh bread or root vegetables from the cellar. She never approved, did she?

And another:

We are stationed outside of Ypres and do not see much of the city proper, but what I have seen is more than Mother would have imagined for me. But even though she might be disappointed that I left you, I have not completely abandoned my domestic training.

I can nurse any ailment you have when I return. It will be a nice reprieve from the wounds and surgeries here. I am also learning more about fabrics and textiles. I have a friend, Annelise, who knows every last stitch and line and popular fabric. She can identify the latest fashions on the covers of La Petit Echo de la Mode or La Mode Pratique magazines. The world is opening so for me . . . and it is far larger than when Mama took me to Ghent and the broad Korte Steenstraat where she once bought me woolen mittens.

The Ypres letters were a stark contrast to those following. They were a calendar as time ticked too quickly by. The events were not merely of the dragging, unending war but also Clara's broadening world. *I am not the same girl I was when I left.* Unused to a close female friendship, Clara hung onto every one of her new friend Annelise's words, whether she spoke of a magazine or how best to engage with a soldier. They had the same rudimentary training, yes, but Clara learned some educations were innate.

Such as Annelise's wonderful rapport with the soldiers.

"Focus on their faces. Don't look anywhere else," she told Clara.

Clara sometimes found it difficult, such as when a face was badly burned or scarred from mustard gas. In these instances, if possible, she focused on their eyes. She kept her voice even and she talked to them about *anything.* While she was waiting for the doctor to triage and assess the situation, while the men were slowly rousing from morphine-induced sleep. She told her father's stories.

They held on to her voice. They looked up at her from stinging, tired eyes, and Clara was their tether to the world slowly slipping beneath them, but also their anchor to their families back home. One last breath of hope that even if their personal prognosis was slim, their words might live long enough to touch their wife or sweetheart or comfort their worrying mother.

Men were far more concerned, Clara soon learned, about those who were worrying *about* them in their hours of the valley of the shadow than their own fate. It only made the matron's honest evaluation of the intricacies of their job more transparent to Clara. No one wanted anyone to worry about them. Everyone wanted to be strong enough to withstand this absolutely unpredictable world. A world they were unprepared for.

The worst injuries were treated in makeshift tents on crimson fields. The dying were transported to cold, dank churches where the Holy Mother and all of the saints provided the last comfort to men whose mothers, wives, and sweethearts were nought but another rambled name from a parched, swollen tongue. Nought but a name and an affection in Clara's somewhat-steady hand. Hospitals and stations were transient. As was Clara.

But even as time slogged on and her duty on the front ended, the nightmare followed her to the hospital in Brussels. The Palais Royal de Bruxelles, repurposed as a hospital, was an interesting blend of starched linen, lined cots, grand chandeliers, and gilt-framed oil paintings rising from sheened, waxed parquet floors. By the time the first transferred shell-splattered, gas-asphyxiated men blindly looked up at her in the starched, bleached corridors, she was able to offer something she hadn't near the front: safety. The outside conditions were something else entirely with the Boche's severe occupation, curfews, and rations, but inside was a cocoon.

The nightly silence fell as harshly as the darkness. The deafening new quiet shrieking as loudly as the rippled shrill of artillery fire and just as unsettling as the moans and screams from the front.

Clara had little time to steal into Bruegel, so she turned the pages of her mind after a long day of pulling sheets from beds, taking temperatures, and consulting each round through a clipboard chart. Suddenly she had a gallery of soldiers propped on pillows or with their creased foreheads banded by cool washcloths.

Despite the ministrations, men were terrified. What was left of a soldier's right arm was a stump she cleaned as best she could, winding filmy gauze she pretended was chiffon even as it was stained yellow and brown. Another shouted so shrill and loud throughout the day and night with terrors jolting him from sleep, the noise resounded in Clara's ears long after she had returned to the nurses' quarters.

"When you finish your shift, choose someone who had a good day," Annelise advised. "That way you are not closing your eyes to tragedy but seeing something good. Positive. Hopeful."

It calmed her to see men slowly finding their way back to life.

Even as she continued to wrestle with what she wished she could unsee. That she could follow blindly like the men in Bruegel's painting did. All in a line. All without the nightmare of what she had witnessed in Ypres.

All silent and frozen in brushstrokes of paint and careful shading.

Well, *almost* silent. There was one man who sparked into conversation long after the other men were at least attempting to sleep. The slowly rising crescendos of snores. The restless turning from side to side, and yet *this* man.

The patient was eerily intense and, it seemed to Clara, almost anticipating her shadow brushing over his starched bedsheets.

She wasn't certain *how* he could cause her breath to lurch in her chest when he was flat on his back and recuperating, but still. It was something Clara was not soon to forget. The sudden chill when she was near him was as startling as the wind rustling the hospital tent flaps.

"That's Martin." One of the orderlies pointed out the man. "He seems to be convalescing well."

"Martin," Clara repeated. She would forever remember him.

"I would keep a distance from him as much as you can," Annelise said when Clara mentioned him later. "Rumor has it he should have been discharged days ago. But somehow . . . due to some influence . . ." The young woman raised her shoulders in lieu of finishing her sentence.

"Influence?"

"Who knows with these rich lads." Annelise smoothed her apron. "They buy commissions and they buy ranks and they buy their way into a bed when they should be blasting the Huns at the front."

"But he could be harmless!"

"Harmless?" Annelise shook her head. "Perhaps in so much as he won't taunt you at night or come to a violent end like Olivier le Daim, that devil barber your father told you about. But there are several ways to do harm."

Clara wanted to ask how but knew she would just sound like the innocent Tielt girl her friend assumed her to be. Besides, she sensed she was on the verge of a piece of Annelise's wisdom. Many times these were hidden in one of Annelise's stories.

Clara continued to inspect a patient's chart, but a moment later Annelise rejoined her and gently leaned in. "You'll soon notice the way he looks at us. The way that even if you meet his eye, he will move toward you within a moment. How he speaks cruelly to some of the older nurses but his tongue is all honey to the younger ones." Annelise adjusted her collar, ensuring her scarf was safe from view. "Use your instincts and keep yourself busy. The slightest interpretation of encouragement from his end and . . ."

"And what?" This time Clara wouldn't wait for a revelation of wisdom.

"And he'll try to shove you into the supply cupboard." Annelise's voice was plain. "Much as he tried to me."

⁓

Now, overly aware of Seth Martin, Clara noticed the smallest things about him even as she was careful not to make eye contact. She could be compassionate without extending an invitation, just as Annelise had taught her. He was always pale to the point of translucent. Clara wondered if this was his natural pallor or on account of his never leaving the hospital. The overhead electric lights met his face and neck with an almost electrically charged hue that startled her. And even without his iridescent pallor, Clara felt a palpable tension when he was near. As if he were reaching out to her. He loomed so large in her peripheral vision, given Annelise's warning, that she often stopped and turned, surprised that he wasn't right there next to her.

When she was in Ypres in her first nursing station, she was taught to be on guard. That she was only ever a step or breath away from danger. She developed a sixth sense even as she developed a strong outer layer. She would walk through each skirmish she faced with invisible armor. She would more than keep her wits about her.

⁓

"Turn a slow chapter. Don't rush the pace of a page." Her father's words steadied her even when he wasn't nearby.

One story she wanted to learn was Annelise's. She found

her friend endlessly fascinating. Unlike Clara, Annelise had a wonderful relationship with her mother, who encouraged her daughter to see as much of the world as she could and who believed Annelise might make whatever she wanted of said world.

Clara said, "So you would *design* and create what people would wear?"

"Of course! Silly goose, how did you think what you were wearing was made?"

Clara looked down at her service uniform. It was bland, if neatly ironed. Matron always wanted it to be a shining example. Clara treated her uniform as one might the most perfectly ornamented wedding dress. Annelise was willing to color outside of the lines of a painting book.

"Liberty in London is like an emporium. Have you ever been to London?"

Clara smiled. "The farthest I have ever been from my home is here."

"I have not been either. But I have a cousin who has been to Liberty of London. It is so lovely that they have postcards of its windows." She flourished the scarf at her neck. "She told me there are rows and rows of silk scarves. They have the most elaborate patterns, you see." Annelise's eyes were fireworks. "There are scarves designed especially for the store."

Clara tried to imagine a sort of art, but she found it hard to see anything but wool homespun blankets and bandages and the dust and heat or impenetrable cold of the changeable barometer, which shifted as quickly as the nearing artillery fire.

Still, she didn't have many friends, and so what was significant to the one she did have meant a great deal. "Liberty, you said?"

"Isn't it a beautiful name? The most beautiful place on earth."

"And here we are in hell," Clara countered.

"Which is why we should bring the most beautiful place on earth to us . . . at least *as* beautiful a place on earth as in our power." Annelise tucked her scarf underneath her collar, a swath of hidden art.

If Clara's father could toil and slog, bringing home stories for Clara with the same attention as he did his paycheck, she could treat the creased fold of a sheet and the careful crease of a pillow with the attention Bruegel had.

Granted, it was still hard to carve beauty from misery and noise and mud and despair and mustard gas that blasted the sight from young men and stole the last of their youth with the swift removal of their limbs and agency.

"So we will give them what beauty we can," Annelise insisted, smoothing her long fingers over a makeshift coverlet much as she would the finest down comforter at the Ritz Hotel.

"And yours is hidden under your collar?" Clara smiled at a splash of blue in an intricate pattern and only *just* behind her friend's regulation blouse.

"What can I say?" Annelise smiled. "You carry your art in a book from home. I carry my art close to my very skin."

CHAPTER 4

～

Brussels, Belgium
1918
Koninklijk Paleis van Brussel

Father,

*It seems another lifetime when I first arrived at Le Gard du
Midi. As long ago as when I began writing these letters to you.
Three years and I feel like days have melted into each other as in
the sticky canvas tents in the summers here when we all wait for
evening's chill. I have looked over each letter, and I can now scarcely
believe I was so green. I remember thinking that Antwerp was, to
that moment, my only point of reference. Brussels has always been
so much more than that. The buildings were so prepossessing that
when I strolled out from its broad entrance and turned my head
over my shoulder, it seemed to go on forever. Its columns? I felt I was
seeing something from books come to life. There was a large clock
that announced noon on the hour and the sun in its zenith spot.
Then, above, a grand statue of Nike rising from a triumphant arch!*

*Nike was the goddess of victory, and when I finally surveyed the
streetlamps and gardens stretching from the station on a manicured
path to what I hoped was the city, I felt I was turning the page.*

*Trams and buses and rumbly Renault cabs warred for the
right of way. Children wove around their mother's knees, and you
mightn't have known there was a war on at all save for the soldiers
in sharp uniforms and militant airs and the nurses already ivory
white in aprons and caps.*

*I suppose I ramble. But it is because I want you to see it all as if
you were here. Now I am far more familiar with it than my days in
training. Now I am far more appreciative given my time at the front
and on the battle lines.*

*I am quite busy now at the Palais-turned-hospital unit. But
also quite safe.*

*Vrijwaren. It is a word I say over to myself. Safe. I am much
safer here (as safe as one can be during a war) as you are much
safer in Tielt. A stroke of luck (if any action from our unwanted
guests can be seen as lucky) that the Germans chose our hometown
as their headquarters. Our earlier instincts that they wouldn't
want to blast their own with zeppelins have come to pass, thank
God. Though I fancy it is quite odd for you to walk to church or the
market and see them roaming about. One, then another. Perhaps
several at once like the ants that crowded Mother's cupboard come
April. It must startle you.*

*I will admit I still startle at the slightest clang of a fork against
a tray or a door accidentally slammed. I will not write a lot about
what I saw. I do not want to revisit it so deeply that I have to
fashion it into words. But the wounded I nursed are as much a part
of my story as anything before and everything that will stitch into
my recollections of this time after. This time that has stretched longer
than any of us could have anticipated, but has, still, disappeared as
quickly as the drop of a pin.*

WHAT HER FATHER DIDN'T KNOW, AND WHAT SHE TRIED THEN SHEEP-
ishly failed to include in a letter, was how despite Annelise's
friendship and her affinity toward the other nurses, doctors,
and orderlies, Clara wanted to truly look after someone. Beyond her father. Beyond her memories of her mother. A romantic nature was peering through. One that stirred when she
watched passionate farewells as she alighted from the Brussels
train station those years before. One drawn on the pale faces
of soldiers dictating one last bedside letter for her notation before their bleary eyes closed forever. One waylaid given she was
tucked away during her mother's long illness and believed she
was unusual. There were boys at church and her tutor, but she
always felt a little odd—and far safer studying the pictures in
her art book.

Still, when a handsome soldier winked at her while she attended to taking his temperature or a young doctor opened
the door as she balanced a water tray, Clara wanted this care to
serve a purpose beyond the war.

Clara wanted her story to have a chapter into which she
finally funneled all of the feelings that sparkled just under her
surface like Annelise's scarf under her regulation collar.

But it remained an unsent letter and an unsaid conversation
with Annelise. Near Christmas of 1917, the war that was supposed to be over three Christmases previously dragged onward.

Annelise and Clara smiled as holly branches, boughs, pine
cones, and ribbons adorned the opulent surroundings of the
castle. Even a Christmas tree found its way into the grand ballroom.

"This will be better than medicine for the men!" Annelise
said. "Well, for some of them, anyways."

Their chat in the corridor nearest the recovery wing was a
frequented spot for Seth Martin, who even now silently passed

by and looked them over. Annelise folded her arms over her chest.

"Merry Christmas, Clara," Martin said.

Clara was so off guard and so offset by her friend's reaction, she couldn't fashion a response.

When he was far from view, Annelise's entire body exhaled.

"Annelise . . ." Clara gently crooked her finger under her friend's elbow. "Did Seth Martin ever . . . ?"

"No. But he's the type who *would*." Annelise smoothed her collar and ensured the top button was fastened to hide her secret scarf. "Let's not speak of him anymore, eh? Let's keep their spirits up. The young men who *deserve* the holiday. Not the ones who skulk in the corners." Annelise had such an ease in weaving liquidly through the corridors as she did now with Clara in tow. "Did you hear we are to have a concert? That should raise morale! And I fancy a few handsome musicians in our hallways will be almost as sweet as my mother's *cougnou*."

Morale was raised when the staff learned there would soon be music from the Symphonie L'Armée.

This group consisted of soldiers, who were first and foremost classically trained musicians. Their presence was often required to follow those in battle on the front or to raise money for various war charities or to bolster the good cause in Brussels and beyond. For their Christmas concert, they chose not to be on the road but in the city that saw the start of their unique, but very appreciated, contribution to the war cause.

Clara used their upcoming appearance and first chamber concert as a means to entice the men to get well. To fight beyond the endless days of a schedule dragging through the rotation of meals and linen changes.

"You could pay ten francs and still not be able to afford to see this level of talent."

Clara and Annelise joined the excitement.

We have seen so much, she wrote her father. *And* heard *so much. Few people ever talk about the noise of war. It's loud and distressing. Grown men reduced to wails for their mothers, coughs and chokes and the rattle that hums as softly as a barrel drum just as a life slips away. So the prospect of hearing something lovely is stirring the corridors with anticipatory hope.*

The night of the concert, Clara ensured the men in her usual rounds were taken care of. Those in wheeled chairs were positioned in the great hall with care. Those unwell enough still in constant care.

When Clara first arrived, the Palais had been unlike anything she had experienced before, stretching out onto the rue Brederode. But now . . . she could see how day in and day out these men—many who would never return to the life they knew before—found it a prison.

Just as she was making her way to join Annelise, she overheard a soldier tell Seth Martin, "In some ways this is worse than the battlefield. At least in the fighting you knew you were doing *something*. Your mind didn't have time to catch up to what your trigger finger had done. Now we have all the time to stare at the ceiling and replay every horrid moment. At least in the fighting we were *in* it."

Clara walked on a little more somberly. She was happy that at least for an hour or so, this soldier's mind would be filled with music rather than gunfire.

∼

There were as many colors and shades to the music as there were brushstrokes of a Bruegel painting. Clara wasn't certain which strand to follow.

The small orchestra was animated. Especially, she noted,

a young man in the second row. He was a master at the violin, that was easy to see. But he didn't play with the same physical intensity as the others. He played . . . *feverishly.* His cheeks were flushed, which only accentuated the molasses hue of his hair, and his deep brown eyes were glazed.

She hadn't noticed she was leaning forward a little in the direction of his chair until Annelise tugged her back to earth.

"Fancy that one?" her friend said. Tonight her scarf peeked slightly from her starched collar in honor of the occasion.

"He fascinates me," Clara said. "He *feels* the music with his whole body."

There was a short interval after a rather long Brahms piece. Yet while the other musicians left, the man with the brown eyes remained in his seat. Perspiring. And not on account of stage lights.

Clara's instinct told her that this was more than the intensity of a musical movement.

"Where are you going?" Annelise asked.

But Clara was already halfway to the slightly raised platform that constituted the stage.

"It's all right," Clara whispered. For now, the young man was shaking. Trembling so much that she feared for his violin. She put her hands over his and gently guided the instrument away from him. Its case was at his feet, and it took but a moment to secure it before it fell completely from his hands. His limbs were gelatin. "I am a nurse. You're ill, aren't you?" His head was ducked toward his chin. "How fortunate you're here. In a hospital." Clara smoothed his hair from his forehead.

"I . . ."

"Save your voice." In one syllable she heard a rasp. Not to mention the rattle in his chest as he wheezed a breath. "I've got you now."

And she did. Literally. Catching him in the ensuing split second before he tumbled over.

Clara hoped he pulled through. Sicknesses that may have seemed routine during times of peace were exacerbated by the conditions and anxieties of war. She was, of course, daily learning at the hospital much as she did near the battlefield. While her education might never provide more than a rudimentary understanding of how men responded to devastation and why some lived and others died, she attempted to make patterns nonetheless. Perhaps like her mother's tried and failed attempts when she experimented with a new recipe or supplemented makeshift ingredients when the market ran low.

Men could slip away from seemingly commonplace illnesses merely because there was a disruption in the fabric of their lives.

Clara could only ensure they had something concrete to hold on to before their grasped fingers unfurled and let go.

Clara prayed it wouldn't be the same for this man—he of the molasses hair and violin. Just now, his long fingers didn't play over an instrument with deft precision. Rather, they wound in and out of intersection, haphazardly folded over his torso as he lay dormant. His hands, however, were not still. Clara would learn him by those hands. Some frenetic tapping perhaps speaking what his fevered brain could not.

And, as with so many soldiers before, as his eyelids shuddered, a calmness overtook him. "I brought your violin to visit you," she said two days after he had slipped into a delirious state. She sensed his eyes moving behind their closed lids. He was aware. Perhaps he could even hear her. "Shall I take it out of its case?"

The first thing she noticed when she clicked the instrument case open was the signature—embossed gold overlay embellishing the crafted hole underneath the strings. C. BOULLANGIER.

The soldier's name was R. Allaire. That much she knew from his chart as she recorded his temperature every day.

She ran the pad of her finger over the instrument's lines before turning her attention back to him.

He had a nice face. Very well, she finally admitted to herself, he had a *handsome* face. The type of face that made her want to fixate on it as she did her art book. There was a curve to his lip. A reason why she had noticed him the night of the concert that had drained the last of his energy. In addition, it was so easy to slide a chair next to him when Seth Martin was prowling the ward like an unexpected alley cat.

Seth had taken as long an interest in her as he had a long chain of influence that allowed him to stay at the hospital even as his unit was shipped off. The superficial shrapnel wound in his arm was long healed, but his father had influence enough to gild the pockets of those who kept this castle-turned-hospital in service. So he was deemed not quite fit for duty.

Seeing the men less fit than Seth being shoved into the fray, pale and thin, while he prowled the wards unsettled her. Seeing R. Allaire, whose pallor was whiter still given the dark color of his hair and lashes while Seth Martin joshed at her attention to him, was more unsettling still.

Seth Martin was well. R. Allaire was not.

The latter's collapse was a result of fluid-filled lungs. He had a rather advanced case of pneumonia. Serious but not dire. Untreated long enough that it held to him tightly and caused him to sleep for long unconscious hours in order to fight what had been building but had only now reared its ugly head in attack.

R. Allaire was a safe post. Especially in the evenings. A look at his chart with deep concentration and Martin was momentarily avoided (save for a quip about her hair or her eyes or the way her blouse fit in a way pleasing to him). Annelise began to call R. Allaire Clara's soldier. And Clara (with a fresh blush bloomed on each cheek) began to tell R. everything as if he were the first blank page of a journal. The snippets that did not find their way into her letters to her father. The odds and ends of her daily thoughts. Her memories. Her mother's recipes.

"He's not a soldier." Clara flushed, explaining her attention to Annelise. "Not so much as I can tell. He's a violinist."

It was promising to see that the violinist was so active even in his sleep. She could sense the wheels turning in his mind, which meant that the fever had not slowed his thought process. The longer he slept, the more he turned. The more his long fingers pulsed against the turned-down coverlets.

He's practicing. She smiled. Even in his sleep.

She wondered what symphony held a fevered patient so rapt.

CHAPTER 5

ROMAN ALLAIRE COULD NOT FULLY APPRECIATE THE PERFECTION OF his father's outsole stitch, but he did daily wonder at the bustle of a magnificent city. The elder Allaire told Roman that threads, lines, and leather up close would show the true intricate beauty unnoticed to an eye fixed solely on the footwear alone. The city where the Parc d'Egmont and the low-hanging branches surrounding its fountain stirred a kind of song. The outdoor concerts near the Jardin du Mont des Arts filled the whistling trees with a song new to him. When he frequented the markets that spilled into the streets stretching from the Grandplace, he found music in the corridors named for herbs and spices.

It was easy to become cloistered from the war and headlines, especially when Roman learned there was more than one way to serve the war effort.

It was his music theory professor who provided him with an option that opened a door away from the battlefield.

"It will be a bow in your hand, Allaire, not a firearm."

A symphonic orchestra for the Belgian army. The Symphonie L'Armée. A collective of the talented musicians amid the Belgian and French ranks.

Roman never could have dreamed that such a position existed. Nor such an officer . . . The same officer who had sternly allowed the presence of his violin now welcomed it, it seemed.

"A lot has changed," the officer said, perhaps in response to Roman's incredulous look. "This is not the war our ancestors fought. This is not a war of honor and dignity. Men facing each other armed and mounted in many situations. This is a war of hazardous gas and artillery fire. Of no-man's-land. Perhaps because no man . . ." He stopped. The pause was as emphatic as his words. "No *true* man, no *true* soldier, would accept this fate as civilized."

Roman wasn't certain he had experienced enough that would allow him a genuine decision as to what was civilized and what was not.

But Roman knew *music* was civilized. It was an equalizer. It was a pacifier. So when the officer's rant melted into a requisition, Roman was all ears.

They wanted men who were the most talented of their ranks and regiments to form a new type of armory: music. There was an allowance (that was the term the officer used) of small performances during "calm periods" at the front. *Calm periods,* Roman decided, clearly translated to "the firing squads will restrain their guns, and cannons won't blast each side to smithereens."

And, the officer continued, when they were not in the theater of war, there was a theater of peace. It needed *music.*

It needed *Roman.*

And his role, the officer emphasized, was just as important as those with guns slung over their shoulders. Socks sinking in their boots. Shrugging into the trenches. Bully beef tins and haversacks exposed to artillery and air.

Roman took the moment the officer gave him. A moment wherein he contemplated if he could look himself in the mirror or sleep at night (beyond the artillery and gunfire, beyond the arena at war).

But as he was deliberating, he thought of his father. A man as much as conscripted (even if by conscience rather than law) into the service of cobbling given the limitations of other trades and the legacy of his father before him.

And as he was deliberating, he thought of his mother, who was so adamant that he find a tutor, so adamant that his gift was not *ordinary*. Was not merely ascribed to him by a proud parent.

"You really think it might help?" Roman said after several moments in which he had become well acquainted with the scuffed floor.

"I really *believe* this is the role you are meant to play," the officer said. There was conviction in the officer's voice. It was natural, not a shudder or a tremble or a stutter in his voice.

Roman acquiesced. It was a far sight better than conscription and obligatory military service. He would cheer the soldiers. He would rally the troops. He would slice through the terror of war with a bow ready and willing. The same bow he used to saw through the evenings when the men were uncertain or on the occasions when they were a few cups in and almost tipsy . . .

Just tipsy enough for nostalgia. Just tipsy enough to remember and *want* to remember home. A few languorous chords of a sentimental song that recalled home. Home was a blessing and a curse. Too far to be a comfort, too near to give any comfort.

When battle was near, when the threat of the enemy was near, home was another wound sinking deep, deep down into one's consciousness.

But . . . at a weekend when there was a song or two and watered beer or wine in metal jugs clenched hard into whitened, grasping fingers and perspiring palms?

Home was a balm and the perfect melody to play across the strings of a violin.

◡

Now, Roman Allaire eased into waking much as the sun eased into rising. Without, of course, a sudden blast of rays nearly blinding him through closed eyelids.

There was neither a bow in his hand nor a firearm.

His arms registered heavy over the blankets and sheets coarse with what he assumed was starch. His mouth seemed stuffed with cotton. Where was he? *How* was he? The more lucid he became in stops and starts, the more conscious he was that he was not alone.

Still, over it all, over his ragged breath and the usual clamor of a "quiet" hospital ward, he heard a noise even more persistent than the snore of the bed adjacent.

Roman drifted in and out and yet the voice was still there. If he could only pry his eyes open to focus on the speaker.

Not yet.

His mind slowly colored in the moments that ticked to his being there. Or *almost* being there. In body if not wholly conscious.

He filled in the arches of the grand rail station and recalled how Brussels immediately set a different rhythm than Strasbourg with its carriages and automobiles warring for right of way. The cab finally dropped him past the iconic Mont des Arts and to the Rue de la Régence and the Conservatoire.

Was it his imagination, or did his fingers begin positioning the notes against an imaginary violin?

The nurse hadn't stopped talking. If Roman wasn't so blasted exhausted and if his lungs didn't very much feel like they were slowly filling with water, he might have laughed. A few times he tried to. But as it was, even the twitch of his mouth in a smile he could not control was painful. Sometimes he understood what she was saying when he looped close to consciousness. Other times, her voice was distant, as if in an echo chamber, and he gathered a word or two. Little breadcrumbs that almost trailed to a full sentence.

She spoke of food a lot. *Waterzooi.* An odd-sounding fish stew. She elaborated on its preparation and how what her mother never said in words, she showed in dishes. *"We had mussels and haddock and julienned carrots and whatever Mother had bought from the marketplace near the Cloth Hall."* Except she called it *Halletoren.* On another occasion, the voice broke through his feverish dream ("dream" was a strong word for flashes of disjointed images) as she was describing the process of rolling out dough.

"Of course, it would be very romantic to have pneumonia," she was saying, clearly unaware he had rustled and moved. "It sounds a lot better than saying *pleurisy* or *dropsy.* They don't sound like diseases; they sound like little bunnies in the Beatrix Potter books. I suppose you don't know those. She is a British writer of little stories for children. Peter has many bunny friends. Flopsy, Mopsy, and Cottontail. Pleurisy, Dropsy . . ."

It was oddly charming. Might have been more so if his throat wasn't on fire. He emitted a single dry-as-sand cough, then slowly peeled his eyes open to blink into the scalding light.

To that moment she had been a throaty alto voice that never *said* words so much as painted with them. There was a stop and a start to her bubbling enthusiasm. Despite his exhaustion and the very fact he felt as if a horse had trod on his skull, he recognized through this haze that her words were a gift. A small grace.

She was, for all intents and purposes, talking to a near

corpse one foot from a blank cedar coffin bound for a blank ivory-white cross.

But she *chose* her words carefully. And in *three* languages. Yes, she translated, not knowing whether he would understand her in slumber in Dutch, French, or German. At the brink of sleep and with the rapid pace of her words, sometimes he understood little. Sometimes, too, even without truly registering anything but her silhouette, he imagined her in as much detail as his blurred brain could muster.

Or English. She tried this a few times and failed so wonderfully that he was sure it was a dream.

Then she unfolded from her seat and rose to a height that was comparable to his not inconsiderable own.

"Sit, *Scheherazade*," Roman rasped, several moments after her long, lithe figure sprang up like a reed aside his bed.

Because if she stood any longer, he was like to go dizzy and fall into a fit again. Not on account of his illness but on account of how delightfully . . . unique she was. Her hair was a rich chestnut, but even under her pristine white cap, he could see it did not spill out onto her back. This was not just the proficiency of pins. No. There was a gap in the back of the train. Her hair was short. Perhaps cut just beyond its neckline. The front was in a small fringe that accentuated her high cheekbones and her round doe eyes.

"Scheherazade?" She looked at him quizzically.

"The tale of the thousand and one nights," he explained. "A woman charmed a king with more stories each night to save her life."

"Is my life in danger?" she asked.

"Never when I am around," Roman said without a beat and with a seriousness that belied the playful nature of their banter. "Though what danger I might present remains to be seen." He raised his arms and let them fall against the blanket turned down slightly with its military-precision creased tucks and curves.

"Scheherazade."

"I don't know if your naming rabbits or explaining the process of your mother's bread-making capability counts as life-saving caliber of story. But they clearly roused me from death's door."

"I am glad. I have your violin. From your personal effects. I didn't trust it with anyone. Because you spoke of it when you . . . when you were delirious, and I knew it must be the most important thing in the world to you."

"My violin." He let out a breath he hadn't realized he was holding. "Yes. It is very valuable to me."

She nodded. "It is with my own trunk and effects in the nurses' quarters."

"That is very kind of you." She had spoken in three languages. He wasn't sure which one to use to address her. "Mademoiselle."

"C. Boullangier," she said with a smile.

"Oh, so you looked inside."

"Only so that I could find any more identification in case I needed to notify your family." She studied him a moment. "But I think you are well enough to think about penning a letter to them yourself."

Roman nodded and was overtaken with a bit of a coughing fit. The nurse's cool hand was a balm on the back of his neck, and she gingerly lowered him back to his pillow. "Though maybe not today."

"No, not today." His voice drifted. "Good night, Scheherazade."

CHAPTER 6

SLOWLY, SURELY, ROMAN'S MEMORY RETURNED AND HIS MENTAL faculties sharpened enough to recall why he was where he was when so recently he had been performing. He had stretched the bow of C. Boullangier's irreplaceable instrument and crafted note after note. He remembered how the men around him became little other than blurred figures, cameos against a setting sun and flushed-pink sky. Yes. How he had not been his usual self for days. Ah yes. Then there was the dizziness and the feeling that black curtains were quickly shutting on what was left of his consciousness. Had his voice slurred? Had he stumbled? Or fallen completely? *No.* Roman would have recalled the latter.

No matter, it came back to him. He had been playing his violin. He had been happy and content before his forehead was dotted with perspiration that a wipe of his cotton shirt did little to absorb. He remembered feeling as if his chest was in a vise.

Perhaps he was a victim of music! Playing too passionately. And now at the mercy of this woman. She didn't so much weave stories with a seductive timbre like a sort of wimple-wearing

Scheherazade. Rather, she blasted them at him. It worked, though. After a long time in perceived darkness with barely the energy to roll over in his cot, Roman roused and woke. Truly woke. No more fluttering eyelids or thoughts that melded into each other, glued like torn leather in his father's trade.

Roman joined *living* again and was eager to match the voice in his ear—waking and sleeping—with a face.

Clara was overjoyed that her favorite patient was conscious, but she was also a tad flushed. As if she were caught off guard. Guilty for outpouring secrets while slowly recognizing she spent more time studying the curve of his jaw, tracing the outline of his lips, and wondering *how on earth a man could have such long lashes*—like curtains over his cheeks—than would be in any way professional. Seeing him animated for the first time in stunning sunlight that pierced through the window startled her.

But then he opened eyes of two remarkably different colors.

"Olivier le Daim!" she exclaimed aloud before smacking her hand over her mouth.

"The Ghent Barber?" the patient said hoarsely.

"Just a story my father taught me. I suppose I wasn't expecting . . ." Clara waved the rest of the sentence away with her hand.

How had she not noticed his eyes? She supposed it was because she had a tendency to frequent his bedside at night. To tuck his blanket up to his chin and to smooth the covers. And the night of his performance, the overlight and his feverish pallor just glazed them brown.

She was so studious in this pursuit that even Seth Martin remarked on it: "Tsk, tsk, Miss Janssens. You must not entertain favorites."

Ironic, Clara thought, considering the reason she sought out the patient's station was to avoid Seth Martin altogether.

And now? Surely there was something devilish at work here. His *eyes*. She had never seen human eyes of the like. One was a rich mahogany. Almost black at first until she truly focused. The other was an ethereal white-blue.

Her mother would have crossed herself. The village ladies would have ascribed a dozen different explanations for a man who looked so *unique*.

Two things. As per Annelise's instructions. Just *two* things about a man were the first two numbers to unlock a coded safe, or the first two ridges of a key clicking to turn and open a door.

Roman Allaire. *C. Boullangier.*

His name. R. for *Roman*. His violin.

"You sound like you're always on the verge of a fairy tale." Roman broke through her thoughts. "I half expect that the next words out of your mouth will be *Once upon a time*."

"I talk too much," Clara said coyly.

"No. It is rather that you are administering your own brand of medicine, I think. When you speak of your home, you are doing it so that we feel a little bit better, are you not?" He smiled at her. "Then I want to turn each page of the book that you seem to be reading from every time you stop and speak to one of us."

He was so much more now than a staid and static name on a chart. And a quick antidote to Seth Martin.

"Perhaps you think of a fairy tale because we are in a castle," Clara said.

Roman responded with a long answering look around the high ceilings and over the chandeliers prismed by window light.

"Perhaps." He shook his head a little, then raked his fingers through his matted hair. "I must be a sight." He scrubbed at his unshaven jaw. "I know so much about you," he said. "And you know so little about me. I'm Roman."

"I know. What a *novel* name."

He smiled tiredly at the pun about his name's translation in his language.

But it was his eyes that were truly the open book, and she turned the page from right to left.

She had never seen such color. The right one was a watery blue like the canal ribboning through Ghent, and the other brown: a rich mahogany brown that so often found its way into the muted pathos of Pieter Bruegel the Elder. Like the touches of the roofs and churches and tunics in the tableau *The Dutch Proverbs*.

"I'm Clara."

"Clara with the stories. Such *hope* in those stories, Clara. Made me miss my mother. Made me miss home. Ah—but perhaps not all sunshine stories for you. There. Just a shadow. So, I can assume you use your stories and recipes to beguile a sleeping stranger? Medicinally. But perhaps there is sadness. How could there not be? You are a nurse. In war. I . . . Pardon me." He reached for the water glass at his bedside table. "I am not used to using my voice."

"And you are my book without a cover. *Roman*."

"Without a cover?"

Clara nodded. "Only because there is little but that sheet covering you and your night shirt." Then she blushed to the ears. "I didn't—"

Roman laughed. "I should write a strongly worded letter to the hospital board. You see, my mother told me that folding . . . or *tucking* . . . one into bed was a delicate and intimate art. I think it's a term used in England. I like it. It makes me imagine being the closest and most secure."

"It is not my fault if you have tossed and turned."

"Have I?"

"Enough for now," Clara said. She did a quick survey of the room and, finding no Seth Martin, decided it was high time she retire for the night. These stolen moments with Roman Allaire were a nice reprieve from the chaos of the wounded rushed in to overtake the broken fairy tale of a castle.

Now that he was awake, she counted the moments until she could slide a chair over to his bedside, read his chart with an intensity that would waylay prying eyes, and focus on the way his mismatched eyes lit like candles in bubbling wax the moment she was near.

I have Roman and I have Annelise, she scribbled in her next letter to her father. *It is rather a pity he gets stronger every day. Not that I wish him ill, but it is not as it was before. Now, when the men get well, they are sent back into violence and gunfire.*

"You spend a lot of time with him." Annelise looked her friend over.

"He's my bit of color." Clara emphatically looked to her friend's collar, where the scarf was just hiding.

"Well, your *color* has mail to contribute to his *rainbow*," Annelise jested.

Clara tried her darndest to keep her eyes from the post marking as she made her way to Roman Allaire's cot.

A wife. A girlfriend.

"I bring you word from home."

"Why, thank you."

"I also brought your violin for a visit. C. Boullangier."

⌒

Roman was accustomed to Clara's visits now. He looked forward to them much as he did the letters from home.

What was more, Clara treated his violin in its royal blue velvet bed as she might a relic in church. There was a reverence and awe in her breathless request to touch the varnished sheen of the upper bout and bridge.

Clara cradled it like an infant.

Roman laughed. "You needn't be so scared around it. It is your friend. It is *my* friend. It is valuable, certainly. But it is still meant to be played."

She studied it closely. "When you were asleep for those many days, I tried to make sense of it."

"Perhaps I can teach you."

Clara leaned forward.

"This is the bow." Roman held up the instrument. "And at the end here? See right at the bottom. This is the frog."

"The frog?" She was delighted.

"It encloses the bottom like so and keeps the hair ribbon safe so that I can tighten it." He demonstrated.

"Frog." Her nose wrinkled as she repeated the word. "What a funny name."

But then she was distracted. She inspected the violin from the C. BOULLANGIER visible through the lazy, curved F hole to the scroll and neck and peg box, the bout and button and bridge.

Roman joined her inspection, patiently explaining every function to her.

She held out the instrument like it was the holy grail. "C. Boullangier must be a very important person."

"He is. He lived many years ago. He was from Mirecourt in Vosges. Near where I am from in Alsace-Lorraine. But he spent the last years of his life in London. In Soho."

"Soho." Clara tried it on for size. "I like it."

"Frith Street."

"Frith." That suited her even more.

She liked tasting words and he loved when she did so. Even though her mouth was all too distracting in the shapes her lips made in framing them. Still, he noticed an infinitesimal change when she heard the slightest movement or noise.

Her shoulders raised and her eyes stood at attention. Not quite seeing him. Not quite seeing *anything*.

He still slept for long spells at this point. When waking, he couldn't recall if it was one day or two before he heard her again.

This time when he blinked and slowly opened his eyes, she was not alone. A man was by her side.

"I must carefully monitor this patient," Clara said in a tone unfamiliar to Roman.

But, soon enough, Roman was lucid and Clara was chattering on as was her wont.

"You showed me your violin." She smiled when his now-clear eyes reached hers. "Now I will show you something precious to me."

It was a book of paintings by the Flemish artist Bruegel. They studied it together a moment. "I don't think I have ever seen a woman look at a painting like you do," Roman said.

"Hmm?"

"It's like I startled you from a dream."

"Oh." She smoothed her skirt self-consciously. "A memory, maybe. Not a dream."

There was a world in what she was seeing, and he merely had to follow the trail of her eyes to see it.

"This one is called *The Procession to Calvary*."

Roman had never seen a living soul look at a nonliving thing with such tender dedication. He was surprised and delighted when Clara grabbed his hand and led his finger over to a near-hidden part of the painting amid the throng of peasants and the eruption of color. There was the eponymous procession with Christ on the cross and the two thieves beside him hidden in a blast of activity.

The mess and the chaos. An eruption of peasants and soldiers going about their day.

Clara didn't look up from the painting when she began speaking again. "I like to think there is some grace in this. It is so messy. I have seen a lot. And I have not always understood what I have seen."

"I can only imagine," Roman said lowly. "I am prepared for the worst when my time comes."

Clara took a beat. "I would look at a *scene*. I would view the men in my care and the horrors they had seen and withstood through Bruegel. Sometimes it was the blind leading the blind. I don't mean to upset you, but there is a type of w-weapon that . . . that . . ."

"I know." Roman put his hand over hers. His trembled a little. Hers was clutched in a protective fist against her apron.

"And now we have something to share."

"We already had something to share," Roman said softly.

"C. Boullangier?"

"A mutual friend."

"You have your music and I have my art and my friend . . . my friend Annelise."

"I know her. About *this* high"—he held out a measuring finger—"and coaxes you to go to bed after your shift?"

Clara nodded. "She's a bit of an artistic eye herself. Any textiles, really. Their patterns and designs." She wound phantom fabric around her neck. "Beautiful and expensive scarves from a place called Liberty in Soho in London." She punctuated her action with a nod. "Just as Annelise talks about. Crimson and blue and ivory and all of the rainbow. With designs that we haven't ever seen before. Or so she says."

"Memorable. Just like you."

The conversations continued in a similar vein. Hers was a language of Bruegel while his was one of Brahms, and yet in the middle they met. Both far from home.

CHAPTER 7

CLARA KNEW SHE WAS CLOSE TO SAYING GOODBYE. JUST NOW ROMAN was leaving for another ward to complete his recovery, and his bed was needed for patients with far more pressing illnesses. In turn, Annelise was also being transferred when the wing for nearly recovered soldiers became understaffed.

Both moves troubled Clara, who held so tightly to the small world she had built here.

I can make stories with these people, Father.

Or so she had written in her last letter.

The knowledge that those closest to her would move on while she paroled the same regulation cots was a new type of grief. She had grieved when her mother died. She had grieved for her expectations and the relationship they never had. She had grieved, too, for her inability to resuscitate her mother near the end.

This was a different sort of an emotion whose colors and layers she was just beginning to learn. Much like the patterns Annelise spoke of when her cousin wrote with more postcards and designs from glamorous London.

"You are sweet on him," Annelise said after her final shift in their ward. They were alone in a soon-to-be-bustling corridor once the men well enough to sit in a cafeteria returned from breakfast. Still adhering to Matron's instructions, Clara concentrated on perfect creases and lines, on the ends of the starched bedsheets as tight and geometrical as the corners of an envelope. She had been at her station well before the gong for her shift started, and not merely because it would be her last morning intersection with Roman Allaire's routine.

"It is more than that." Clara surprised herself and her friend with her blunt honesty. "I've been sweet on many young men who come through the door." She stopped. "Like you seeing one of those beautiful scarves you like. Not every design is the same."

Annelise smoothed a coverlet and wrestled a flat pillow until it resembled softness.

"It is like I have known him forever and my life was just waiting to catch up to the moment we met."

Annelise laughed. "See? You're sweet on him."

"More than *sweet*." Clara exhaled. "I am *sweet* on the little bird that perches in the west window every morning." She shook out the wrinkles from a linen sheet before billowing and spreading it over a firm mattress. "This is something different."

"And his mail?"

"Annelise!"

"I saw a woman's name on the postage!"

"He was *almost* engaged to a girl. His family wants him to marry her. They were childhood friends. That is *quite* different than his entertaining feelings for another woman while . . ."

Annelise propped a pillow at the top of a metal headboard. "While what, Clara?"

Clara ignored the tease in her friend's question. "They're

moving him anyways. I was told today. He's almost well enough to leave. The rattle is out of his chest completely."

"Absence makes the heart grow fonder." Annelise, neatly folded washcloth clamped under her chin, took a quick breath. She mustn't have slept well the night before to be so taxed by a simple task. "And you can find a way to speak to him." Annelise's eyes were warm and her smile wide. She caught her friend's romantic moments with a butterfly net. "You must find some way to speak to him," she continued. "The matron's voice is still in your ear, but you can find a way to break just a rule or two."

"I suppose," Clara said after a moment. "Perhaps *you* . . ."

"Me?"

"You can be my *rule or two*! You . . ."

She shrugged off the rest of the sentence when she couldn't decide how best to describe Roman. Was he a friend or a man or a soldier or a fiddle player or the one balm that had somehow smoothed over the sting of his leaving?

A slight sound drew their attention.

Seth Martin.

"A rule or two?" Martin asked. "A rule of what?"

His eyes skimmed over Annelise but settled on Clara.

"You shouldn't be out of bed," Clara said to Seth. "Not in this chill. What are you doing wandering the wards?"

Clara flicked a glance at her friend. Annelise's spine was straightened, and she leaned slightly forward as if at any moment she might drive the man's weight back through the door or even through the plaster wall.

"You know better than to disturb nurses on duty, *monsieur*."

Martin *didn't* know better and all three knew it.

Somehow, though, it worked. Martin retreated at a slow backward pace in the direction he came, but not before his eyes lingered long over Clara. *Don't look, don't look*, she coaxed herself.

Still, she couldn't stop her eyes meeting his. The smirk on his face, the steel in his eyes. He left, yes, but not before training his eyes around the room and establishing his presence.

After Seth's departure, Clara recollected herself. "I can still communicate with Roman Allaire through *you*," Clara told Annelise. "You'll be taking more shifts in the outpatient ward, will you not?"

"Happier patients." Annelise's answering smile was tight. "But more Seth Martin." They both turned to where Seth's shadow had recently been.

"You mean he is finally . . ."

"On his way far, far away? Soon but not soon enough. I don't even want to address him as soldier, just as civilian. I . . ." Annelise stopped suddenly and took a few deep breaths. She seemed slightly uneven. Then she coughed.

"Are you all right?" Clara leaned forward and instinctively put the back of her hand to her friend's forehead.

"A little under the weather, is all." She coughed again and Clara heard a telltale rattle that startled her.

"You should go to bed."

Annelise recovered, albeit slowly, and patted the pockets on either side of her apron demonstratively. "Lots of room for letters." Her voice was a little hoarse. "I'll be a rather dainty packhorse." She loosened her collar a moment, and the flash of color from her hidden scarf drew the pink flush on her cheek. A deep contrast from her otherwise pale pallor.

"Annelise . . ."

"I am fine, Clara." She straightened her chin. "I have a mission, don't I? And so do you. Letters and small messages are a poor substitute to a grand romantic gesture. Here." She unfastened the collar of her regulation shirtwaist and removed her precious scarf. "For luck."

"I cannot take this."

"I don't have a beau to impress." She wound it around Clara's neck. "And you'll find your romantic moment. With Roman!"

"I'll keep it safe. I promise."

"I want you to do the opposite. Use it as a talisman! Or a good-luck charm and steal a moment with Roman."

"Maybe someday . . ."

Annelise held up a finger, then smothered a cough with a handkerchief. She collected herself. "I'll replace it. I won't have just a replica but the *real* thing someday."

"Right from Liberty of London." Clara finished her friend's thought. "A real Liberty of London scarf!"

"Precisely. Think of it as a trade. You have the scarf, and I require you to use it to confidently tell Roman how you feel! Or *show* him how you feel." Annelise winked. "Either or." She beamed a smile and whispered dramatically. "But preferably the latter. And for me? I'll have the satisfaction of knowing that my scarf was a good-luck charm and you got a small fairy-tale moment from it."

~

Clara's romantic moment startled Roman as much as herself. It was not planned out and happened precisely two days after her friend gave her the scarf. Indeed, she mightn't have gone through with it at all if she had noticed more telltale signs Annelise was ill. *Truly* ill. Her friend shrugged it off as a cold: "I'll do anything to get out of night patrol." But they both knew it was more than that. Just as Clara knew Annelise's gift of the Liberty scarf was not only a talisman or good-luck

charm but rather a benediction and perhaps a farewell. Just as
Clara knew Roman's remaining time at the Palais hospital was.

Contrary to her friend, Roman was on the mend. He moved
around the corridors as often as he could as per Clara's own
suggestion. A few times since he moved to his new ward on the
cusp of discharge, she spotted his tall, now recognizable frame
stride paces before her.

Clara unpinned her apron and removed her nurse's cap
while walking in the direction of her quarters and in anticipation of changing into her nightgown, bidding good night
to Annelise, and crawling into bed, hopeful that sleep would
meet her as quickly as her duties had worn her throughout the
day's shifts.

"Mademoiselle Janssens," Roman said from behind just as
she neared the common stairwell.

Clara turned and, with a sudden flush on her cheeks, looked
Roman over. "You are looking quite well," she blurted. "I meant
literally well. *Medically* well." She pushed a strand of hair from
her forehead.

"Why, thank you."

The deeper the blush heating her cheeks, the wider Roman's
ensuing smile.

Write your own story, Clara.

"These must be your final days here before you are discharged."

"Yes."

Her eyes flicked downward in the direction of the hidden
scarf beneath her collar. Without her apron, it was more exposed. She gasped when she noticed Roman following her
sightline.

"A happy and sad thought at once," she recovered.

"I was only *just* beginning to know you."

She touched his elbow and moved him from the middle of the hallway where several nurses were changing shifts at once. The slightest touch, and her neck tingled under the scarf and her fingers tingled over his cotton shirt. A *fairy-tale* moment. She could go back to her quarters and tell the friend so dear to her that she used the gifted scarf to have a cordial conversation with Roman *or—*

Or would soon become her favorite word in the English language.

Or was the start of a new chapter. One whose frantic pace she met as sure as C. Boullangier's strings would flurry over a quick-tempoed Vivaldi.

"Follow me." She tugged him away from the foot traffic and down a hall away from a main stairwell.

"Where are we going?"

"I'm acting on a rare whim!"

She was nervous. Excited. The faster she set the pace, her heart met it, and by the time she reached what was once a library given its extensive bookshelves and now a sort of makeshift supply closet for newly pressed linen, she had made up her mind.

"I am not your nurse anymore, Monsieur Allaire."

"Pity that," Roman said breathlessly.

"Which means what I am about to propose would not be a professional indiscretion but a personal one."

Roman raised an eyebrow. "Tell me more."

"Over the past several years every letter I have written to my father has been a variation of the same theme. Just as if C. Boullangier only plucked out the Minuet in G. Without variance except for commonplace things . . ."

"Like battles and near-death experiences?"

His lips teased a playful smile. She had difficulty drawing her gaze from them to his eyes.

"I have decided to kiss you." Clara tilted her chin upward.

"Do I have any say in the decision?" Roman's voice was coy.

"I suppose. I mean . . . yes. If it . . . if it is *amenable* to you."

Roman stepped closer to her. Soon his scent—a bit of bleached hospital sheets and the lemony soap in the lavatory—overtook the usual lye and turpentine permeating the storage area.

"I suppose it would be *very* amenable." His eyes were on her lips now. Clara bit them quickly. Roman noticed. "Is that a retreat?"

"N-no. I just haven't done anything like this before. But you're leaving and I want to live out a moment with you."

"In a supply cupboard?"

"Well, the cafeteria will be overwhelmed," Clara said rationally. "And the nurses' quarters are off-bounds."

"Very logical." He tilted toward her.

"Wait! We can't yet!"

"But *logically* . . ." he protested through a teasing smile.

"Not until I do this right. A fairy-tale moment." Clara made quick work of unfastening the buttons of her starched shirtwaist and tugging out Annelise's scarf, arranging it like a haphazard, lopsided flower under her chin. She warmed under his expectant stare. "Now I am appropriately *ornamented* for the occasion."

Roman lowered his mouth to just above hers.

The letters Clara took to dictation from waning soldiers so often spoke about their desire to look at the same moon as their beloved back home. The same stars. Now she realized both were a euphemism for a far more intimate detail: sharing *breath*.

It was happening, this brand-new chapter, and its promise sparked tingles up her arms and over her back. She swallowed and leaned in expectantly.

"I forgot," Roman said. "You are to kiss *me*. Not vice versa. That was not the proposition. Please. Ladies first."

She liked this playful Roman. The one that peered through in recovery but now was fully buoyant and alive as he healed.

"Very well. I hope I do this correctly."

"I am sure you will be just mag—"

She cut off the rest of his sentence with her mouth.

A first tentative kiss. It was soft and a little surprising. Her lips trembled a bit under his.

She fell back.

In this moment, with his standing so close and his breath so near as to tickle her just below the earlobe, she was writing her *romance*, and it was far more breathless and exciting than she imagined.

Her hand instinctively moved to her open collar and the loose knot of Annelise's scarf.

Not from Liberty of London, as she had been reminded. But truly elegant and special given its purpose here, was it not?

"My turn," Roman said. "I mean, *should* you accept the proposal."

Yes, she thought—her last thought before giving in to him and the moment entirely—*I have earned that scarf.*

Liberty indeed.

Her lips were pink, and her eyes were blue-white like snow that dusted the peaked rooftops of the cathedral back home in Strasbourg before melting into a kiss over the cobbles below. And Roman ran up and down mental romantic platitudes much as he did a sloppy scale before a Beethoven concerto.

"Your mouth is the most interesting thing about you,"

Roman said when they breathlessly stopped a moment. "I knew this from the moment I heard it form words. Endless words."

"I assume eventually this will become a compliment?" Clara's lips curved in a comma of a smile.

"Oh, it is. My mother always told me to give compliments more interesting than *you have such pretty eyes.*"

"But you do have such pretty eyes." Clara studied them intensely. "I've never seen the like in my life. I didn't know they were possible. Two different colors. Startling colors." She spoke in a daze. Almost as if inebriated. By *him.*

"And I didn't know it was possible for a cobbler's-son-turned-violinist to be swept into a storage closet by a pretty nurse. So."

When Clara's eyes met his, they glistened and searched and were even expectant.

This is all new to her. New to him too.

He respected that the bravery that found her through the door dissipated with the introduction of another new experience. She had drained her supply, it seemed, even amid the starched, neatly folded linen.

Her skin was soft to the touch of his knuckle on her cheek just like he imagined, and kissed with just the slightest heat due to their close confines and the reaction blushed on her face.

"A proposal to—" Roman said playfully.

She leaned closer. "I like these conversations of ours, Monsieur Allaire. The ones that don't need words."

Clara was drowning. There was no air. *Funny that,* some inkling at the back of her preoccupied mind thought to conjure.

If I don't breathe soon.

She drew back and gulped at air a few moments, and it felt in so many ways as if she were *alive* and truly breathing for the first time. She removed her hand from the side of his face to linger on his shoulder a moment. This conversation had been different from the ones previous. More intense. Not as sweet as the first tentative touch. A little desperate. A little bit of anticipating goodbye.

Stunned, Clara tripped back a step until he steadied her. "I don't know what came over me," Clara said. But only because she thought that seemed to be what women say. Yes. A permissible reaction to the fireworks that blasted through her and the small bombs that exploded in her belly and in her fingertips and claimed her throat entirely.

Roman blurted a laugh. "I do. It was the same thing that came over me."

"Common symptoms." Clara placed her palm on his chest . . . just over his heart.

"Common symptoms." This time he took a moment to catch his breath.

"Still recovering, I see. Perhaps you shouldn't be moved to a new ward after all."

"I am not sure I ever want to recover."

And he lowered his lips to hers again.

The sound of commotion in the hallway drew them apart and set them at attention.

"Shift is changing," Clara said.

"If we time it right, I can just meander with the throng and your personal and professional reputation will be rightly intact."

She nodded. Roman slowly opened the door and looked left and right. "Good night, Mademoiselle Janssens." His smile was a moonbeam. "Thank you for the proposition."

Clara waited until Roman was a safe distance away before she planned her own departure. And she almost got away with it. The whole night. She walked as if slightly levitated with a secret in her pocket and a story to tell her friend.

It might have been perfect if not for an appearance by Seth Martin draining the heat from her face. His eyes looked over her suspiciously before settling on her open collar and the state of her hair more slightly tousled given how Roman had loosened a few pins with his fingers.

"Out late, Nurse Janssens," Martin said. "Shouldn't you be tucked into bed?"

"Duty called." Clara looked left and right. She and Martin were the only occupants of the hallway.

"I could have sworn I just saw that Allaire fellow around. The musician whose bed you hovered over."

"I recall." Clara smoothed any reaction from her voice. "I mean, I recall Monsieur Allaire. Not any music or any bed. Now, if you'll excuse me, before I call an orderly on behalf of your crass manner and speech."

But Seth Martin grabbed her arm. "Is this a usual haunt for you?"

"The linen cupboard?" Clara remonstrated. "As any good nurse, I assure my patients' cots are well attended."

"I happen to know there's one much closer to your ward. And the nurses' quarters."

"This one has fresher sheets."

"Is that so?"

"Please let me bid you good night," Clara pleaded.

Thankfully a nurse who pursued the linen closet for its

intended purpose crossed in its direction and Clara made a fast getaway.

She cursed Seth Martin the closer her quarters came into view. Her heart still quickened. Her breath still caught, but now not in remembrance of stolen kisses but immediate fear.

By the time she reached Annelise's bedside, her anger was abated. She smoothed the comforter.

When her mother passed, there was little Clara could do to comfort her. When the men in her care passed, she knew they looked at her in hopes of finding another's face looking down on them in compassion.

"But you, my friend," Clara whispered. "You would *want* to see *me* and for me to assure you I had my fairy-tale moment."

Clara pressed her hand to the scarf, then retreated to perform her nightly routine. But she didn't remove the scarf from her neck. *No.* Not even moments later in bed. Now, instead of tucking it behind her collar and apron, she tucked it behind the collar of her starched nightdress so that its cool silky fabric warmed her collarbone and its slight floral scent took her back to a linen closet of all places.

Clara smiled herself to sleep.

CHAPTER 8

～

GIVEN ROMAN HAD KISSED MANY WORDS FROM CLARA'S MOUTH, HE found the ensuing silence unbearable. Granted, said silence was little more than an off-time grandfather clock, a change of orderly shifts, and the prepossessing feeling he was on borrowed time. Soon he and C. Boullangier would play their way beyond the palace walls.

Much sooner, he exhaled in relief as he realized his conversations with Clara were merely transposed from spoken word to print.

There was a new banter and intimacy after their sojourn in the linen closet. One *in writing*.

She had a way to keep talking to him. (Or as her friend Annelise would joke, talk *at* him.)

Roman,
Are you still a book without a cover? I will never tire of playing
with the meaning of your name. Roman. My novel. A story I want
to be told.

And a few hours later (and more anticipated than any meal tray):

>   *Roman, how is your frog? Dear C. Boullangier. See how I
>   know your violin?*
>
>   *It has not been many hours since I wrote you, but I had the
>   opportunity to sojourn into the sunshine today to accompany the
>   current matron to the apothecary.*
>
>   *Brussels is a world without color these days. The Koninklijk
>   Park is stripped of its trees, and it looks shivery and cold like it is
>   in its underthings. Every tree's knots and gnarls are exposed. The
>   little bandstand near the Bas Fond is empty and cold and could use
>   your fiddle and its tunes to warm it . . . Annelise is a wonderful
>   messenger, is she not? Else all of these thoughts would roll around
>   in my brain without reaching you. I do worry about her sometimes,
>   though. As someone so recently ill, you can see she is pale and has
>   developed a bit of a cough. We all work hard, but she works at such
>   a fevered energy. The same hours and shifts, but she puts in more
>   somehow just by virtue of being, well, Annelise.*

Unlike the soldiers pining for the first word from a wife or sweetheart, the responses found their way between them within a span of hours.

>   *Scheherazade,*
>
>   *There is a legend from my home, Alsace, that floats around
>   every Christmas by the fire. In it, King Dagobert, who lived many
>   centuries ago, was besotted with a beautiful young lady from
>   Kuttolsheim. She asked him to build a pipeline of white wine
>   directly from Strasbourg to her village. It was so successful an
>   enterprise that soon red wine made a similar journey. They spoke in
>   beautiful wine. I wish I could deliver such sweetness to you. You are*

quite to my . . . pardon my pun upon the *ahem* recollections of our recent activity . . . taste.

~

Dearest Roman,
    I have a double shift today since Annelise has been ill, and I regret to inform you I will not find a way to your ward. I know we are on borrowed time . . .

~

Dearest Clara,
    Imagine I am the Alsatian King Dagobert and this letter is the finest vintage of champagne. How I wish I had champagne to send to you. Something to toast brighter days.
    Except instead of a passage from hospital wing to hospital wing dug like a tunnel, we have Annelise's apron as a mailbox.
    Speaking of, I've noticed she looks about the color I suppose I was when we first met. I know you have been concerned about her of late. You and she have my thoughts and my prayers for her recovery.
    The ward is a bit like purgatory. I know I am about to be discharged and sent back to my little troupe, but the waiting and the in-between are difficult. For one, why couldn't I have been this lucid when you were my attending nurse? Then I wouldn't have slept or drifted through half of your stories.
    For another, why must I finish my convalescence so close to you and yet so far from a particular linen closet?

~

The messages Clara sent Roman stopped outright only when Annelise was not well enough to attend to her shifts. She was barely well enough to pepper Clara with every question she had about her rendezvous with Roman. "I almost underestimated you. You're the *perfect* home for my talisman." She nodded at the scarf just beneath Clara's collar.

"You sound tired. How are you? Truly? Are you being checked on often?"

"Probably faring better than you." Annelise tried to be animated, which just made Clara worry more. A pendulum swing from flirtatious banter and a kiss in a closet to Annelise whose sparkling personality was dulled.

"Not with that cough," Clara said lightly. "You pull me straight down to earth."

She smoothed her apron, settling at the side of her friend's bed, disrupting the creases and starch in uniform lines.

When Annelise didn't respond, Clara barreled ahead. "Maybe I want you to tell me that I am being rash," she said. "That I am being foolish. That I am compromising my professional reputation."

"You already did as much in a linen cupboard," Annelise said proudly. Her following laugh rattled her chest a little. "By writing letters to a soldier? You're boosting morale! Serving the troops. Or *troupe*. In his case."

"You should probably take Roman Allaire's bed," Clara said softly. "You sound much as he did when I first tended to him."

Annelise waved her hand. "And risk an even closer proximity to Seth Martin?"

Clara squinted to study the purple commas smudged underneath her friend's eyes. She wished her friend's translucent pallor wasn't the same hue as her mother's when the words and life and blood slowly drained like the light through the frosted winter window in her periphery.

"Annelise?"

Clara placed the back of her right hand to her friend's forehead. With the other, she found the pulse at her friend's wrist, deftly counting a few beats, startled by the faint, uneven rhythm.

She treated Annelise as she would any fevered soldier.

"You would tell me to remember two things about my patient." Clara wondered if her friend heard her behind fluttering eyelids. "But with you I have dozens. I have your wisdom and your eagerness for me to turn the next page of my life to a new chapter. I have your scarf around my neck and your awe at its beauty. I have your knowledge that it's a replica. A facsimile. Just like the paintings in my Bruegel book. I cannot see them in their frames in a gallery just like you cannot see Liberty in London. But we both have a little bit here."

When she was certain Annelise was asleep, she looked around a moment: women exhausted and snoring, limbs stretching from their blankets like trim branches on a lopsided tree.

Clara's mother's loss had been long in coming, an hourglass flipped and leaking sand, but Annelise faded fast. Perhaps Clara should have seen more signs and earlier, but the hospital wards were a study in contagion. Things bounced from one person to the next like a note-passing game in the schoolyard.

Still, in the last moments, Clara used every free moment to tend to her friend.

The more she sensed Annelise slipping—tepid water held to cracked lips, glazed eyes roaming over the frosted, murky windows and trying but never finding a place to settle—the more she realized that death was swift on the battlefield just as here. Annelise was no longer in the nurses' ward but in an isolated unit. There was little she had been able to do in Ypres, little she could have done with Roman had he the constitution. How much of death was a game of chance?

A name and a common interest. Just as Annelise taught her so long ago in hopes Clara would establish connections between herself and the soldiers they worked with.

"However competent I am as a nurse is because of you," Clara whispered.

She looked helplessly at her friend. The cold compress placed to Annelise's head was nearly heated almost as soon as administered. Tangled sheets bunched in Annelise's fists pulled tightly.

Clara had the phantom memory of her mother's rattled breathing in her ear. She anticipated her friend had passed even before the pulse she felt under her thumb was completely still.

She called for the nurse on duty and sat frozen as everything moved in slow motion. Frantic girls and a call for a doctor. The time of death logged and recorded. Another number to stack with the many on clipboards and logs.

Clara knew Annelise would want her to keep the scarf they surreptitiously tucked under their collars. A reminder of the joy of their collective excitement.

Moments later, the current matron slowly approached Clara in the corridor and cupped her elbow. "There were a few things in her personal effects addressed to you," she said gently. "In hopes you can send them to her family."

"O-of course."

"You can personalize it. A note. A card. A line. If it were my family, I would want them to know I had made such a friend."

If it were my mother, Clara thought, *I would hope she would want the same.*

Thereafter, all that remained of Annelise was a scarf tied around Clara's neck, a handkerchief, and a small address book she would return to her friend's family. But a few trinkets did little to represent her friend's buoyant joy. Did little to represent her friend's ability to create instant rapport while knowing precisely what the men in their wards needed.

Her ensuing shift was a blessing: keeping her mind occupied. She was gratefully working through a filmy daze wherein she practiced fashioning her feelings into a letter to Annelise's parents when she overheard the conversation of two nurses by the tea tray.

"It's unfair that Martin can stay forever and that handsome violinist cannot. I overheard him say he is leaving tomorrow."

"I will miss his smile. He's so polite."

"But always with the letters. Always writing letters. Talking about how he loves the violin."

"Seth Martin doesn't love anything but the music of his own voice."

"He must have a sweetheart," one said.

"A very *wordy* sweetheart," the other returned.

"Hopefully she'll find him wherever he ends up. It's near the end now. But men are still—"

The nurse didn't need to finish the sentence.

There was no greater villain than time, Clara thought. It crept and haunted like the legend of Olivier le Daim and trickled like the wine from the Alsatian tunnel Roman wrote about. *Yes.* When you begged time to pass, it sighed slowly. When you needed it to hurry—such as at the first smell of Clara's mother's baking bread or the promise of consulting Roman Allaire's medical chart—each fleck of sand in its hourglass timer was endless.

Clara made up time by a shortcut down the corridor where Roman's wordless conversations still buzzed against her lips. The pause between the bustle of meal service and the change of shift, and she supposed time was finally in her favor.

"Nurse Janssens."

The voice stalled her. Chilled her.

Slowly Clara turned until she was face-to-face with Seth Martin. Recalling his grip on her arm, she recoiled.

"How may I help you, Martin?"

"I see you are in the direction of the linen closet of such interest to you before."

Clara repurposed a bit of the bravery she found in the same storage room when giving Roman Allaire her proposal of the other evening. "I see you are still here while other men far more ill than you are back fighting," she retorted. "It must weigh on you." She clicked her tongue. "But you mustn't keep following me. No matter how bored and insignificant you are. If you'll excuse me—"

This time when he grabbed her, it was more intensely than before. Before Clara could verbally protest, stamp, or scream, he tugged her into the same space she had occupied with Roman.

Time was a villain again. It sped her heartbeat. It accelerated her deep gulps of breath. But it was endless all the same.

The slow trail of his right finger over her neckline, then down to her collar button. The endless weight of his left hand on her waist.

"I figure if you are willing to attend to one patient here, you might be willing to tend to another."

Time slowed completely. Until she was unaware of it. *Terrified of it.*

As terrified as in that second (*moment? hour?*) when he rammed his mouth against hers.

⌣

When Roman kissed her, it was a conversation. When Seth Martin kissed her, it was given not in proposition but forced demand. Could the same word hold meaning for both?

Clara squirmed. This was a chapter of her story she needed to reclaim before it was imprinted on her memory forever.

"You are a *cad*!" She wished it didn't come out in a tone as loud as a kitten's.

Clara felt around and above him for anything she could grab. Seth continued on her shirtwaist. He didn't undo the top buttons so much as pull. His occupation was enough of a slight distraction that she could fumble, shove away from him, and reach for the door. He lunged after her, but she was faster. And while she sensed his footprints behind her, she broadened the gap between them.

Flustered and wiping at a sting of tears, Clara sped until the side hallway was far behind her and the promise of more populated areas in her pursuit.

She rounded a corner. And, while looking over her shoulder to ascertain the distance between herself and Seth Martin, she collided with someone.

Not just someone. *Him.*

"R-Roman," Clara gasped.

He grabbed her elbows. "Watch where you're going, Scheherazade. You . . ." His teasing tone leveled when he took her in. "You are . . . What happened?"

She supposed given how his eyes brushed over her face and hair and down to her collar, he made a calculation in his mind.

"I need a moment," she said. *Time was on her side again.*

"What happened?" he repeated, his voice tight, his face dark as he surveyed her. He tightened his grip. Not enough to hurt her, but firm enough to keep her with him.

"I need to know that you're all right." He lowered his voice. There was commotion in the hallway now.

"It's late. You should go."

"I won't leave you like this."

"Monsieur Allaire," she said.

His eyes softened as did his voice when he next spoke. "I am leaving tomorrow. I was just on my way to see if I could arrange to say goodbye to you, and I find you in this state. Who upset you like this?"

"It doesn't matter. He didn't do as much as he wanted to."

"He—"

"When I was with you . . . I want you to know . . ." She wanted him to know she stepped out of her conventions and upbringing to share a moment.

"When you and I were together, you weren't *crying*, Clara."

She liked the way her given name sat in his voice even if the timbre of his voice was urgent.

"Please."

"We cannot say goodbye like this."

Clara sniffed. "We won't. I promise. I will find . . ."

Suddenly the parquet floors and broad windows suffocated her. The pressure of Roman's hands were clamped irons.

"Please let me go." She needed to breathe.

He did, of course. He gently disengaged. She thanked him softly and turned in the direction of the front doors. Away from the hall. Away from him.

She knew he watched her retreating figure, her name probably bottled just at the top of his throat.

At least she hoped it was. His was stuck in hers.

Clara walked briskly to the broad central doors and shoved them open.

She escaped the palace-turned-hospital and its echoing

corridors into a cool breeze of evening that swept up and stirred a few leaves by her stockinged feet.

"You should be inside, mademoiselle," an outside guard said. "It's late and you are not appropriately dressed."

"Just found it too close in there." She gave a wavering smile. "I'll only be a moment."

She gulped a deep breath. The same thrill of excitement that had seen her from the gigantic train station when she first alighted in Brussels was a pale comparison to what she felt now. Flat. As if she mightn't live up to the adventure Annelise had imagined for her.

The night was devastating. Especially if she took a moment to imagine what might have happened.

Her quick thinking was a small mercy, though. For Seth Martin was part of her story now and a memory she would have to take home with her.

Yes. And she was part of his. The realization crept up her arms and over her back like a spider slowly inching across its web.

She could never write this in a letter to her father. But if she did, she would tell him that it seemed so unfair. *I found my first friend and she died. I found my first kiss and sense of adventure with one man only for another man to view that as his equal right. I wonder if I can ever trust myself to be brave again.*

Clara measured the thrum of her heartbeat and that's when she noticed it was gone. A slight, familiar raise underneath her collar.

Annelise's scarf. Her *talisman.*

Clara dashed back inside and shakily traced her steps toward where she had just been. Nearing the door to the small closet, she bunched her hands at her sides, folded her fingertips into her palms until they hurt.

Exhausted and flustered and not too keen on lingering near where she had only minutes before railed against Seth Martin, she gave up her search.

She didn't fancy the nurses' quarters that evening. She took a slight detour and asked a young nurse—Margaret—if she might sleep in the small bedroom where the on-call matrons sometimes spent a night.

"Of course." She studied Clara intently. "You are still grieving your friend. You probably are tired of all of the questions and condolences." She squeezed Clara's shoulders.

Clara *was* tired of questions and condolences. And now she was tired of the million ways her brain tangled, wondering how she might have prevented an unwanted touch on her neck and her hair and her lips. Even as the most valuable thing in her possession was taken from her.

CHAPTER 9

~

THE CORRIDORS IN THE ECHOING PALACE WERE NOW SILENT AND still. Roman was all too aware of the sound his shoes made on the tile. A few dim lights spilled out, attendants posted and keeping watch, but they thankfully ignored him.

His own watch was short-lived.

He watched Clara return through the double doors she had exited. He had stayed far enough behind, of course, that she wouldn't notice as he traced her steps.

He stayed a distance behind her as she returned in the direction of the linen room, all too aware of how the dimmed lamps outlined her figure before him. Her shoulders were sunk a little even as she attempted to straighten her back.

Next he saw her through a slight light mellowing the doorway of a private nurse's room. Funny, he hadn't noticed this room before. Maybe because it drew little attention to itself. Perhaps it was kept beyond the usual cots in the usual corridors for exceptional circumstances. Clara *was* an exceptional circumstance. To him at least.

Roman waited until the dim light was augmented by a torch

she clearly found. Then, in a stream of lamplight, he slowly peeked his head in. She was clothed but sitting on the bed.

"You can't be here," Clara whispered.

Clara turned her face from him. Even as she raised her chin defiantly, her shoulders trembled. He wanted to take her in his arms. He stepped slightly forward.

"I already risked my reputation for a moment with you." Clara sniffed in the half darkness. "Would you risk my losing it altogether?"

"That's not why I am here."

"I came here to be alone."

"You will be alone. After I make sure you're all right."

Clara sighed as she slowly removed a few hairpins.

"I lost Annelise's scarf. After—" She put a hand up. "I went back everywhere. Perhaps a custodian swept it up or Martin took it himself. I was so preoccupied." She shook her head. Her voice wavered but there were no tears in her eyes. "That was all I had of her."

"I'll do another look after you're asleep."

"Probably won't matter. He took it. It wasn't all he tried to take."

Fully clothed, Clara made a fortress of her blankets and hastily hopped in.

"That cannot be comfortable," Roman surveyed.

Clara had made a complicated knot of herself in sheets and blankets. She didn't seem to care. "I wanted a life beyond what I wrote in my letters to my father. What I was never able to live for my mother. What I wanted Annelise to live. I was so brave and I was *burned*."

"But you were brave. And quite remarkably so." Roman searched for ways to calm her. To cheer her up. "When C.

Boullangier plays a sour note, I always get another try. You should give yourself another try, Clara."

She thought about it awhile. She looked calmer now, save for her eyes, which, on a turn, darted around the room or found uneasy focus toward a pointed spot.

"May I?" Roman asked, slowly approaching her bedside.

"May you what?"

He wasn't put off by her anger. Not after what almost befell her that night. He needed to assure her that she had armor. Right now the only armor he could give her was the safety of a routine as second nature to him as a scale over C. Boullangier's tuned strings.

"There's an art to getting into bed." He had meant it innocently enough, but seeing a flush on her own cheeks inspired one of his own.

"I thought you were a cobbler's son, not a hotelier," Clara said.

"Permission to approach?"

She hadn't doused the lamp yet, so the shadows danced over her cheekbones—cut like a knife. Still, her eyes were sad. "The reason I am in this mess is because someone saw you and I and thought he could take the liberty." Her fingers played over the tangled sheets. "So I very much got myself into that mess." Her voice was a tight wire. "I am not . . . the kind of girl . . ."

"Of course you are not, but you've made quite a mess of those coverlets and blankets."

"I needed to preserve my dignity from unexpected visitors."

"Ah."

Roman easily made out the shape of her long legs contoured by blankets. He took a small step forward. A cough ricocheted across the quiet ward, but he ignored it.

"May I approach?" he repeated.

"Roman . . . I lost her scarf and I had so little from my mother."

Assuming her silence as assent, he reached her bed and gently coaxed, "Move up a little."

Even his shadow set her on edge. Roman wanted to slaughter Seth Martin for how she shivered and recoiled from *him*. The last person who would ever hurt her.

"Lift your head."

"Roman . . ."

"Lift it."

Clara acquiesced. A few strands of her hair strayed. Some over her forehead and some trailing back to the pillow he gently removed.

"First you rotate the pillow," he explained, absently noticing how in her forced forward position her neck was long and swanlike. Rising over the laced collar of her nightdress. Roman flipped the pillow and beat it with his fist a few times. "Right here," he said. "Just in the middle."

Settling, her shoulders shrugged and shimmied down a bit even as her nervous hands grabbed for anything: the sheet, the coverlet, the mattress cover, the sparsely down-filled mattress itself.

"It's in the corners and creases." Roman's words explained just as his mother had taught. His hands made quick work. "To see to one's safety and to demonstrate one's love is to perform menial tasks."

"Love," Clara said softly.

"You sound like you're trying that word on for size." He pulled up several blankets to her chin, then smoothed the covers. "Don't be angry with me, Clara."

"I'm not angry with you." She blinked so a tear escaped and trailed from her right eye. "I'm angry with myself."

Roman wanted to end Seth Martin. But alas, there would be time for an end. Or six. Or fifty.

Watching her calmed him. She was agitated, but she would be fine.

"Seth Martin tried to accost me because he saw me with you," Clara said after a long silence.

"I see."

"Do you?"

"So you blame me?"

"Of course not!"

"Because I blame myself, Clara. That I should have been there even earlier."

"How would you have known?"

"I anticipate before most when a conductor will change a bar or a phrase. I want to be able to anticipate any sense about you."

"That's ridiculous. You can't predict everything."

"I predicted I would fall in love with you when I heard your incessant talking."

She didn't answer for a moment and Roman stared at his shoes, waiting.

"That's too much for tonight," Clara said quietly.

He looked up at her, but her face was downward and studying a piece of lint she picked from the regulation blanket. She yawned.

"Love is never too much. When you're feeling brave again . . . and you will . . . then I hope you will take my proposition."

Her ears visibly perked at the term that ignited a moment—many moments—between them.

"I'm listening."

"My proposition is that you will take all of the little moments we had together. In my language of C. Boullangier and yours in that artist you love. My proposition is that you think about that pesky *love* word that so easily finds its way to the tip of my tongue when you're near, and you allow yourself to accept that yes, your mother died. Yes, you left your grown father to help others. Yes, your lovely friend Annelise died as well. And yes, that skunk Martin skulked his way and tried and failed to overpower you. But you have so much bravery left. A new chapter."

"You see more for me than I do myself."

"Well, I was trained to anticipate a phrase. To look at a score and interpret every last note and spiral it into something wonderful. I have an education that made it so easy to study you."

"I suppose I . . ." Her sentence was swallowed by a yawn.

"You should go to sleep now."

"If I am conscious, nothing can happen," she said evasively. "So I should stay awake . . . forever." Perhaps she noticed his eyes on her cheekbone and over her chin and up to her forehead, swirling several brushstrokes. "You're staring at me." He painted her as he imagined Bruegel might do. In the contour and color of an intimate moment.

Clara opened and closed her mouth in quick succession. "I took a chance, Roman. I wanted to kiss you. Just as I wanted to *meet* you. Someone else saw, and I have to live with that guilt."

Roman scrubbed his hand over the back of his neck. "You mean when I passed out in the orchestra?"

"I mean *before* then. Someone *like* you. *Anyone* like you." A twitch that was almost a smile lifted her lip. "I began writing a romantic chapter in my head. But now you've seen me ugly and vulnerable."

"You tended me when I wasn't even awake," Roman countered.

He took a moment to inspect the door. It was slightly open and the scurry of a doctor visible through the crack in the direction of the east wing drew his attention. Roman folded his arms over his chest and watched her. There was a space between them now. Just as he sensed this might be their last shared moment. "You've made my time here an absolute—" Even if he could sift through all of the potentially right words, he doubted he could find one that would fit.

"Don't say goodbye. Not like this. If you say the words, I'll crumble."

"Very well. My turn to watch over you as you did me." He kept his voice light though his heart cracked at the clock turning on their last moments together.

"You'll stay?" Her eyes were half-closed.

"Just until you fall asleep." Roman moved slightly toward her and put his hand on her shoulder.

The final part of her conversation, the slight rise and fall of her breath. Perhaps the last he would ever hear from her given his rejoining the Symphonie L'Armée the next day.

"Tell me a story," she said drowsily.

"Once upon a time, there was a cobbler's son with mismatched eyes and an expensive violin. And even though he was separated from the girl he loved . . . yes loved . . . because love accelerates when you are away from what is familiar to you. And love chugs in at a faster pace when the world around it is falling apart. Love is best found when the world is falling apart. They found each other again. In a fairy-tale palace. Not a palace disguised as a hospital for sad, wounded men. One with chandeliers and buttresses and marble columns and motifs so easily filled with the opening bars of an overture.

And when they did, it was magical and as perfect as a perfectly designed scarf." He paused. *Was it too much?* But she quirked a smile, encouraged, and he continued. "And she learned how to love him back. Because it was *easy* when love was blind. She was used to different kinds of blindness just like the painting she loved."

"And she was brave," Clara whispered, half on the precipice of sleep.

"So brave," he agreed. "So brave that it didn't startle her at all when he said *I love you*. So brave that she wrote him all of the words that spilled so easily when she thought he was asleep."

She was asleep now. Looking small despite her height and breathing softly.

"Goodbye, Scheherazade," he said, closing the door gently behind him.

CHAPTER 10

⌒

ROMAN PROMISED TO WRITE CLARA, AND SO HE WOULD. STILL, HE wanted to fill a repository of stories that would break the ice after their parting. Truth be told, slogging through downpours and the hiccupped stops of the lorry bearing musicians through Belgium, on account of either torrential downpours or the threat of battle, occupied the parts of Roman's brain. He wanted to fashion a perfect letter for Clara and ignite the rapport that had flickered and died their last meeting.

For all of the soggy socks, mud-covered regulation boots, and frustration at the long waits and hours, Roman earned the attention of the men in the group partly because he was appointed concertmaster and partly because he was unafraid to supplement their rehearsals and allotted pieces with popular ditties of the day. Even American songs so new, popular, and completely at odds with the classical measure of their usual musical fare.

"After You've Gone and Left Me Crying," the men sang under their breath.

While Roman drew the words across his instrument, they settled in him.

"That is it exactly!" A man clapped his shoulder.

"You know precisely what I feel," another said.

Roman hadn't realized he was so on the edge of their common experience until that moment. They flocked to him. They *identified* with him.

"What was I before to you?" he finally asked of a man whose surname was Collins but whose given name was never, well, given him.

"A bit of a bookish sort obsessed with his violin." Collins smiled.

"If Ralph Vaughan Williams can give up composing to direct music for the British First Army, I can learn a few popular tunes!" Roman retorted.

But now he had a life separate from the bellows and the straight lines and the straight tucks of straight sheets and spit-shined boots.

Alongside his canvas kit and haversack and violin, he had the memory of a girl. His Scheherazade.

"Just ensure you don't do anything stupid like trade your life for it."

"No, sir."

The officer looked him over with watery gray eyes. "Because you seem as attached to that case as some men are to their wives and sweethearts."

"No, sir," Roman repeated. He was attached too.

His memory was tempered by *home*, and C. Boullangier reminded him of Clara. But also of home. How might she fancy the smell of sealing wax and varnish and the fastening of soles to shoes (soles that would have fared a far sight better than the boots forever drenched in muck and rain)?

On the weekends and through any rare pause in the fray, Roman acquiesced to the growing requests from soldiers and fellow musicians. His violin was often more a fiddle, adhering to the popular standards of the day. But every so often he was surprised at what would stir a thrill of nostalgia.

For one, Dvořák's "Songs My Mother Taught Me" had the power to still and silence even the most skeptical and protesting of the soldiers.

Clara loved to think in stories. Perhaps he could arrange her stories into song. He was far more aware of the importance of story now. How a few notes could link to memory.

The action took a while to reach from Brussels. The small cracks in the hard surfaces of anticipatory battle.

In these moments, their war was less uniformly prepared. Rehearsals. Venues. The Symphonie L'Armée moved into the wards of hospitals. As wartime hospitals were mostly appropriated palaces and castles and halls, the sound and space within each were ripe for Roman's taking. And while the audience was not dressed to the nines (rather, clad in ivory starched linen gowns and bandaged perhaps beyond recognition), they were more appreciative and more deserving than any listener known to Roman's formative years of practice and recital.

Occasionally, given the novelty of performers who traveled near violent action, the symphony was accustomed to staying near front lines, and while not directly in the line of fire, this was quite a different war from those Roman's ancestors had lived through. This was a war wherein cavalry and horse brigades and the cannons they trudged were outplayed by automatic warfare, machine guns, gas that blinded men by the dozens, and zeppelins raining fire from the sky.

Later, Roman would learn the last cavalry charge in Western Europe was hosted by the Belgian battlefields so familiar to the sound of his violin and so accustomed to the tempered weather. The dreary rain and sleet that made him conjure Clara standing over his cot with a clipboard over and over again in his mind.

Dear Clara,

If you had told me two years ago I would be playing the Royal Albert Hall and that C. Boullangier's singular tone would be appeasing the patrons of this grand old hall, I would have spat on my shoe.

(Pardon the crude saying. My father always thinks in shoes. Always spat in them too. For luck. For failure. Sometimes on a Sunday with no particular meaning.)

England is as changeable and as temperamental as I had read about, and yet there is something so elegant about it. I suppose it is because it spins its history into a constant fairy tale.

I always thought about fairy tales when you talked, Scheherazade. You could weave gold out of words and images. Now, this city of gray and damp tries to do the same. It succeeds, too, for the most part. Steeples stab clouds burdened with rain, and cobbles are slick with the last downpour before the sun brandishes a little bit of gold to catch the crisscrossed windows in the Tudor style. I wonder what Pieter Bruegel would make of it. How he might capture it on canvas.

My, but I never imagined I would sit in the Royal Albert Hall. The sound here is like a barrel: an opulent barrel, at that. With enough room to allow for a little bit of an echo and a little bit of reverberation. Let me explain: The hall is constructed so that the sound from the musicians will fill every last seat. From the outside, as it is situated in the posh surroundings of Knightsbridge and Kensington Gardens, it looks rather like a round layer cake. It is unlike any other hall I have seen before and certainly completely unique to anything I was accustomed to in Strasbourg. My education in Brussels, both as a conservatory student and then as a patient, taught me to quickly assess the potential of the acoustics of a venue or hall and to imagine the sound of my bow reaching a listener at the very back of the auditorium. Here the auditorium is much like the shape of a horseshoe—just like the American game. I suppose you haven't played horseshoes before. Say, then, a comma. Something that sweeps. A curve.

I have never felt farther from the war before and yet never so near.

I am not in the fighting, true.

Yet there is something here in the atmosphere. More than clouds and rain.

For the first time I am scared. I always told myself my role in this war was important. It was drilled into us as rigorously as any soldier's training. But now I see it, Clara. Men like me. And it is devastating. My hands shake in pieces my fingers as well as my heart had committed to memory.

But enough of this sadness. I want to tell you a story that bridges the distance between us.

Since I was in London, I decided to try to find the place Annelise spoke of—Liberty of London. I confess I only saw it from the outside as time did not permit me to explore inside and to admire things I would have purchased for you were I a man of the means required to purchase something from Liberty. Heavens, even from the exterior I could see that it would be a woman's dream. I peered through a window display that featured some rather beautiful scarves, just as you told me about. When the war ends, and all wars do, I will earn enough money to buy you your own scarf. As precious as Annelise's is, I know she would want you to have not a copy but an original.

There are many street buskers here who open their cases to welcome tossed coins. I would play C. Boullangier for hours and hours for anyone who asked if it meant securing that scarf for you.

So I will sign off, Scheherazade.

Best wishes from myself and C. Boullangier, who most especially wishes you were here to learn about the bout, bridge, and strings.

CHAPTER 11

ROMAN'S FATHER ONCE TOLD HIM THE GREATEST GIFT IN LIFE WAS THE ability to see beauty out of nothing. A mound of leather and a fractured sole were, to Roman's father, like clay to a sculptor. His father's special ability to imagine what could be fashioned out of nothing was what Roman now drew on to summon loveliness and art out of the dust and mud of war.

Roman wrote about the constant beauty of the calm periods at the front in his first letters to Clara.

> *The corps was created not only for the benefit of wartime charities abroad but to pair with vaudevilles and actors in each place we visit. So if there is a period (and it seems rare indeed) where the fighting is calm, then we perform. We act. We play.*

That was what they were there for, lugging their instruments as men lugged their rucksacks, shifting and hoisting them higher over their shoulders.

Anytime Roman moved his violin, he recalled how careful Clara was when she first discovered its worth. Even before, when she sensed the instrument was important to him and even before they had exchanged words.

When the bow crossed the strings over which his fingers hovered gently so that a vibrato spun.

There was ample opportunity for rehearsal. Or at least to talk and mime the movement of the instruments.

Hector Durand, their bandleader who was more than an accomplished soldier in his own right, was of the strong belief that anything could be an opportunity for cohesion and synchronicity.

One evening as Roman ran a silk cloth over his bow and looked to returning C. Boullangier to his case for the night, Durand inclined his chin and motioned him over.

"You should be a natural leader here thanks to your experience. I know that is a ragtag group of musicians in the middle of mud and rain, and likely as not, there are gnats in the beautiful hairs of your bow there. And likely as not, many of our rehearsals will be mimicking movements and a shadow of the sound we will imagine we are making. But . . ." Durand stopped a moment to choose his words carefully. "It will be just as important for us to *hear* ourselves as a unit in our imagination as it will be to finally play together."

Rehearsal was as seldom promised as peace.

The move from Brussels was slow and slower still amid a path of destruction. Sometimes the span of green and rolling hills and the sunlight kissing the path with a bit of gold made him forget.

Sometimes Roman felt—most certainly at the end of a long arduous day of measuring the time against the plodding of one foot in front of the other—that they were not moving at all.

Clara was still there, though. So long as he was in Belgium, no matter the encroaching distance, he felt close to her. As long as they shared a border, he could loop her name into sentences as he walked with the other lads.

Their journey was punctuated with small hiccups of change. Sometimes he shifted and bounced in the back of a lorry; other times their journey was reprieved by seats in a close (albeit stifling) train carriage. While it took them closer to the next performance, it took him farther from her.

So few musicians were chosen for the enterprise that it took Roman little time to befriend several. Hector Durand kept his distance, but he stood unwavering by his decision to appoint Roman concertmaster of their unorthodox crew. Indeed, it was easier to make friends of his fellow musicians than it was to befriend the army men in uniforms spilling in and out in a river of khaki at every train stop.

Roman met a patchwork quilt of men from the lowlands and from France *(Near Strasbourg? Just like me!).* And Belgium and Holland. He collected a repository of names: Louis and Jules and Claude and Alexandre and Antoine and Daan and Bram and Lars and Jan and Ruben.

When they played, they did so with a unified voice and no language barrier. When they talked, he thought of Clara . . .

"My Scheherazade," he had more than once described Clara. Vaguely. Roman soon learned it was a rite of passage to share a picture or cameo of a girl. Someone to play for. A muse. Or a letter stained with tears and flowery sentences that bordered on terrible poetry.

"Show us a picture then."

For one, Roman didn't have one, save in his mind. But he didn't want to diminish the connection he had with them by admitting as much.

"Why? It wouldn't do her justice."

"We haven't seen too many girls the last while, Allaire. We promise not to judge," Collins said.

Another orchestra mate, Timmins, chimed in. "We'll forgive her of nearly *any* imperfections."

"She *has* imperfections," Roman said resolutely. "Which means we can have *actual* conversations and I don't need to show you a Gibson Girl!"

"Fine, fine," Collins said. "Tell us about your actual conversations."

"She told me about the one *good* thing about her time at Ypres."

Ypres? His naming of the place was followed by a hushed reverence and men's voices falling over each other and ending in a truncated silence.

"The one good thing," Roman continued, "is she began to see the experience of war. What we are living for as a layered *symphony* of sorts. Men with different accents and languages all expressing the same thing. All experiencing the same loss. The same loneliness." Roman stopped. He chuckled and scratched at his chin. He reached for his violin case. "She found the language of music in conversations," he explained. "And that is something I found so *new*."

Roman's violin now out of its case, he prepared to play. It was easier to play a popular tune (this time "Let Me Call You Sweetheart") than to answer questions about someone he left behind.

He imagined her back in the palace-turned-hospital.

Hope is the thing with feathers. It was a poem he overheard Annelise reciting one evening when she did rounds of his ward.

Clara might say the end of the poem to new patients. Or use it as she introduced the opening act of a new entertainment on a quiet Saturday night in what was formerly a ballroom. Just as the war yawned to an end.

He imagined her as he languidly played a tune of lost love. He held the note a little longer than usual, not wanting the slight vibration to waver. He needed something surer. Whether or not he was guaranteed a perfect ending, his song would be.

Clara attended to listening and connecting the dots of each patient's recent experiences. It wasn't the same as when Roman was there, but she was perhaps even more attentive than before, given her guilt and loss at the way they parted. Perhaps, too, because she missed him.

She helped usher in a dose of medicine so different than what was prescribed for burns or wounds or difficulty sleeping. But she countered their moans and sighs with a belief that her scraping a chair over the floor tiles and lowering her voice against the broad, high columns of the palace-turned-hospital might help them find their way back to themselves.

To her patients, *memory* was the strongest balm. So she played the woman Roman imagined her to be. Stories outlived people and certainly bad memories.

"A friend of mine called me Scheherazade." Clara soon used this as her opening line to a new patient. It not only kept Roman front of mind; it stirred her into a world of stories she was comfortable in. She could turn pages and conjure words and images that would somehow stir the men in her care from the war blasting behind their closed eyelids to the men they were before war crossed their paths.

To the patients, curtains of night had been drawn back and starlight spattered in with the first lingering notes.

In this case Clara was a conductor. She took their memories

in stride while recalling her own. Especially those at Ypres. The bandages and general chaos dissipated when she recalled the first notes Roman played on his violin. The rattles of darkness and the bleak headlines melted into his smile.

"Miss, we heard music on the battlefield."

This observation was offered by a young, scrawny soldier whose uniform sighed over him in an indelicate and large yawn.

"Did you?" said Clara.

"We did." The soldier's name was Hans and he was about the size of the apprentice her father hired one summer.

"And was it wonderful?"

He expounded in great detail that Clara barely heard.

"A roaming band," he continued. "Music they play in those great halls."

Roman had once played in the great hall right here. She wondered if he was one of the musicians he heard.

A name. A background. Two or three pertinent facts.

Hans. Looks like Father's apprentice. Perhaps heard Roman play.

Annelise wasn't there anymore, but Clara treated each soldier as if she were.

~

The only way to survive the constant barrage of staccato and ricochet of gunfire was to repurpose it as a metronome.

For every cannon blast and for every shrill percussion of a rifle's bullet, Roman kept hope it would eventually finish. As all wars did. Even this one sometimes stopped and started, at least in terms of its noise. The shrill artillery of day often stopped, which was as startling as when it reverberated through him.

But silence, when it finally came, was as deafening as sound.

Roman's ears thrummed with the aftermath and his hands shook. He wasn't even near the action. Rather, on the sidelines.

Sometimes in a tent nearby. Sometimes in a lorry with his violin in his lap. He held as tightly to it as the men nearby held to their Enfield guns.

Yes, there was devastation. But every day when Roman roused after too little sleep and hoisted up his violin case, his strength diminished by too little food, he never faltered.

Some of the uniformed men, after a few too many sips of whatever passed for a drink, would question how Roman and his unique troupe were contributing to the war effort. But those men were few and far between. Most listeners held to each note. Roman knew how to read an audience now, much as his father knew how to read the sole and tread of a man's shoe. Here, however ragtag and mud-and-blood-spattered, the men were stirred as much by a unified sound as a unified silence. Eerie *nothingness* before the next shatter of cannon or percussion of gunfire. He knew how to hold to the way they leaned over and inward, drawn to the music by the tug of an invisible string. He knew how to sense when collective silence, save for a few coughs or cleared throats, was not an indication of displeasure but of awe.

Yes, the music and notation Roman and his compatriots shuffled in their rucksacks was what sustained them. Then, the stretch of their limbs as they positioned their instruments and just played.

Popular tunes were the ones the soldiers were drawn to as they wiped sweat from their brows and sank into an exhaustion so deep it crushed the day's tragedies underfoot with the first pulses of sound.

Loosened, lubricated tongues swallowed what they had seen and felt and heard.

In these moments, Roman could truly study them. See their faces and their movements and wonder as to their stories.

Sometimes the faces blurred into each other. But Roman sensed they looked at the reprieve as beginning a new paragraph of their stories and lives. Other times, given the exhaustion and hunger, Roman would transpose their faces into familiar ones. Ones whose names were easily ascribed and others drifting as through the halls of the Palais Royal hospital.

Dear Scheherazade,

It has been an age since I heard from you, and it makes me wonder if you are safe. If you are well. I often feel like I am a wandering nomad without a true sense of place or home.

A more permanent home, however, has been constructed for rambling players like myself. Soldiers who fight with our instruments and our talent rather than with bullets.

Our rehearsal halls are not the Royal Albert Hall or the Goldener Saal of the Musikverein in Vienna or even the grand halls of Strasbourg Minster back home.

Now we are in a tent. Well, a sort of tent. It reminds me of the nativity scenes under a tarp back home, and there we are attempting to tune our instruments against the chill and wind.

I feel like a musician, though. In ways, I feel very much like the man who first impressed you. Well, perhaps it wasn't me so much as my violin. Still. Perhaps you will read this and assume I am writing more to myself than you.

Théâtre de la Reine in Hoogstade is the first time we will have a set of performances in a place that resembles a theater. An actual theater, and not just a mud pit or a hospital tent. Thinking about it, I get the same rush of feeling that started in my fingertips at the first sight of your silhouette (Is that too romantic? Is there such a thing?). I could always tell when you were near. My grandfather once told me he knew it was my grandmother on the church organ even before he wandered in and saw the maker of all that sound in the big cathedral. The keys were the same. The player was not. That was you to me. There could have been a dozen shoes clacking on that old floor, but I would have known the rhythm of yours.

There. You've done it again. I pick up my pen after rehearsing but I was writing words even as I ran my bow over the strings. We were just rehearsing, and the signature reminds me of your name. Of you. Two syllables that could make up a whole world of a page.

I always get a little too sentimental at night. And, as I said, I am trying to sew back a connection I thought we had lost.

But, I suppose, now that I sit in hope that you might write me back . . . (that pesky thing with feathers) . . . that I should call you Scheherazade again in hopes we can re-seam what was torn apart.

It's dark now, and as happens every night, everything that seemed hopeful during the day has fallen behind a stark blanket.

So, I run over and over again in my mind (like a wheel) what might have separated us. Because it wasn't the war, Clara. A little thing like a war wouldn't be enough to change what we had into the last moments of our parting.

At least I hope not. So, I write this in faith. Perhaps a little bit to myself. As company. The company I miss leaning over my sickbed and talking about dishes from her hometown. No matter, I will see it finds a way to you. And then it will be up to you . . .

To weave a few stories back. Just like you did.

Just like when we met.

⌒

Dear Roman,

This is not the first letter I have written you, but God willing, it may be the first that reaches you. Not because of the war, no. It is quite easy to try to find you given that there are so few musicians even as you move from place to place.

Instead, because I am of the belief my writing you opens a casket of things I wanted to keep buried. Between you and me. And between me and Annelise.

Indeed, before sending this letter, I would often sit and fidget and loop my fingers around themselves before I flexed and prepared them for holding a pen. As I had in previous attempted letters.

Before my mother passed, I tended to her. I nursed her as best I could and I feel that I try to make up for her loss by caring for patients here. But while she was ill, I remember feeling guilty that I had not been as close to her as I was to my father. That the last months before she slipped away, I was not more aware of what she was teaching me.

When Annelise passed, I felt guilty about not spending more time with her as my thoughts were turned to you. Then there was Seth Martin. But he is a letter I write myself. I remember your gentle assurance that I had nothing to do with his advances. But I know I will be able to truly heal when I accept it myself.

I suppose I eased into it by telling myself that just because I wrote it did not mean I had to send it. So in a few stops and starts, I have unsent letters to you that read like diaries. When I wrote them, I imagined you lying in the cot where I first met you and you opened your astonishing eyes. I've missed our conversations.

I am doing well. The hospital has not changed much except that it is drained of you and Annelise. I was never as close to them. I've decided that since my world was so small in Tielt and I had so few friends that I could only handle a few at a time. Now I only really have one. You. And heaven knows where you are. So, going forward, I will continue to write you, and whether they reach you or not will be at the mercy of the mail service and not lain victim to my insecurities and a wastebasket.

CHAPTER 12

~

Near Souilly, Meuse, France
October 1918

IF ROMAN BLINKED THROUGH THE DIRT AND DUST, HE COULD IMAG-
ine the red seats of the Royal Albert Hall. The refinery of Liberty of London.

A brilliant red scarf in the window. A trade of a tin of bully
beef for sardines at Christmas, and in Roman's case, not only
the grace of his well-tuned violin but a postcard for Clara.

The nearer their troupe traveled to the front of the action,
the harder it was to fashion morale not only for the men they
played for but also for themselves.

The small villages dotting their trail to the next destination
were now still and silent. The windows drawn closed like shuttered eyelids. The streets a pent-up breath of boarded doors
and empty merchants unlikely to exhale so long as the enemy
encroached nearer.

Roman couldn't recall where they were, just that it unfolded
like so many other towns of the same layout. Cobbles below

and awnings stretched over shops, splashing color on the gray. Roman hadn't noticed Collins following him from their primitive lodgings. Here, as in so many towns, the central focus and the stop at the end of a main street's meandering sentence was a church. Roman slowed when they reached it. At first because he made to duck inside to the still and calm. Then because of the blasts of sound.

"Close," Collins said.

Roman kept calm as best he could. Even as the gunfire blasted nearer and nearer. He took deep breaths and stilled his shoulders. He proceeded much as he would facing the applause and bright lights of the Royal Albert Hall in London.

"How are you so calm, Allaire?"

"This is another type of performance."

"Or perhaps it's because you merely escaped death in Brussels, and you feel you are invincible," Collins joshed.

Roman tried to laugh in a spirit of camaraderie.

They stilled at the shriek of shells and thuds of cannon fire that had a moment ago seemed so distant. Roman white-knuckled the handle of his violin case. A sickening whir.

A blast.

Roman was tremulous.

"Perhaps not so invincible now," he said through clenched teeth.

Hoop is dat ding met veren.

Hope. Between the terror and Roman's realization that Collins was holding so tightly to his forearm that he might well cut off the circulation.

A shrill shriek of shells whistled against a gray, barren sky. A cacophony of voices bellowing and a split second before . . .

~

Dear Roman,

Far away as you might be, I can hear you in the grand hall of this grand ballroom in this grand palace. I can sense you and . . .

I am fortunate. I go to my corridor. I pretend to sleep the moment my head hits my pillow. I pretend enough that I almost believe it as the clock ticks away the routine of the day. Even when the matron is not here, her rules are as inevitable as the clock or the wounded men or the nurses flirting in the corridor.

But I am strong and I am healthy and I am determined. For Annelise's sake, if not my own.

I hope you are strong and healthy and determined too. Now, when I make my rounds at the hospital, I practice all of the things I will say when we are together again. How I will tell you each time I pull the coverlet up to my chin, I imagine your hand smoothing the sides of the blankets. How I will tell you the reason we parted as we did was because my story was interrupted.

Someday I will be brave and send you a love letter.

Someday I will sign it Scheherazade so you know I keep the name close (as close as Annelise's scarf) and with a secret smile.

When Roman gained enough reason to think beyond the ringing in his ear, he jutted forward, heartbeat thrumming. But with the slow unfurling of his faculties, the pain began, sharp and shooting. Like a hot iron striking against his forearm. He wanted to shout. He wanted to die. He slumped back down again.

His arm. His *right* arm, he surmised through haze. The strong one that held the bow of his violin. He wasn't lucid enough to blink through the layers of grime and shock to visually search for Collins. He tried to lift his neck, but it was an anvil. Tried again but his arm screamed with a searing jolt.

He hoped for sleep. He hoped to be knocked unconscious.

The pain blurred his vision so that when a figure appeared in his periphery, it was merely an outline. A shadow. He fought to keep his eyes open. Fought to respond.

Blinked the sting of smoke and perspiration until he could engage with the person before him. A woman. In blue.

The searing agony in his arm was more bearable as she tended to him.

He couldn't register all of her ministrations, but he felt it when his arm, already on screeching fire, was pulled tightly.

One more flash of blue before the world turned black.

CHAPTER 13

~

November 1918

Dear Roman,

I imagine you just as I first talked to you. When I wasn't even sure you could hear me. Perhaps that was why I felt so drawn to you. Because I didn't need you to understand. And I had no one else to listen.

I never told you, but I used you as a certainty of safety. It sounds rather horrid knowing you were suffering so. That you were in such discomfort.

Sometimes the sleeping soldiers. Sometimes the men under the influence of morphine or whatever medicine we have to attempt to take away the pain. I used you because Seth Martin (the very fact I can write his name means someday I will be rid of him) would look for me in my patrols. Like a leech.

War robs men of sleep and orientation. So they talk to you. And talk and talk. And you didn't. I sometimes felt I saved all of those moments listening to formulate an answer to a question I

*wasn't even aware was asked. I come from a family of stories, as
I told you at your bedside: My father and his need to impart every
word he collected on me. My mother, who would rather her stories be
beaten in dough and rolled out in flour.*

*Now I have more stories than I know what to do with. I could
write them into letters to you or scribble the thoughts of the men I
tend to into a diary. I would not betray their trust nor nighttime
ramblings. I could even impart what I see into my Bruegel book.
The Blind Leading the Blind.*

*I envy the blind men in the painting now. They have not seen
blood-soaked bandages or infections or the masks of agony on
mothers' faces as they visit their sons for the last time.*

⁓

Clara,

*We have moved out again today. It is raining something fierce,
and every time my foot sinks into the mud, I think about how
comfortable I was with you watching over me. Even before I knew
how much you would mean to me. My but my cobbler father would
do well to take a look at these army regulation soles!*

*Belgium is a beautiful country, and now when I roam it, I
think about how it draws me closer to you and to your family and
history. It is especially beautiful in autumn.*

And this country forever bears a mark of our advancement.

*You see, West Flanders is now a living testament to our
resiliency.*

*Oostkamp has been captured and it bodes well for
Flanders. But I am not here to tell you what you can read in the
newspapers.*

*Instead, if you were here with me, I would introduce you to the
horses from the cavalry. Noble beasts who seem to calm at the first
kiss of my bow to its strings.*

It calms them somehow.

I am not close with the other men in the orchestra. I am friendly and hopefully accommodating. But I would introduce them to you as well.

Isn't it funny to be at the apex of the world when it is in the process of spinning? Who knows how this will all look when it is over? Things change all the time, don't they? I got sick and I got well and in the space of these events I met you.

Perhaps we would know each other when we meet again. Or perhaps we would need to reintroduce ourselves.

For my part I would ensure you met this new Roman who was ready to turn the pages of his life. The Roman who was ready to accept you as more than the fairy tale he clung to while you so diligently found a way to keep our connection.

But you might be here soon.

I hope you are here soon . . .

October 1918

Dear Roman,

I am not sure if this letter will reach you as I am not sure where you are or, frankly, who you are. Your handwriting has changed. And your words about horses . . .

Are you truly content? Are you truly you?

I am no longer at the hospital that was a fairy-tale palace of Brussels. I returned home to my father.

My first thoughts of your recent letter were joy and then suspicion. Was that because of you or me? Granted, I hold everyone at arm's length now.

Partly because my mother died before I could tend to her. Before I had training.

Partly because Annelise became my first true friend and died much as my mother had before her.

Partly because the moment I opened up a part of myself to possibility and joy, a man stole not only my pursuit of them but my remaining thought of Annelise.

I wish you taught me how to move forward. You know how to measure things in a sure meter. And you were so patient when I determined to know the parts of a violin.

I worry now that I write these intimate thoughts to a stranger. Surely, it is not your hand. It's a cruel trick to play on someone who has fashioned a meeting in her mind. We'd be together again. We'd flick the match on our conversations before they burned through the night.

I maintain this letter is not written in the hand of the Roman I knew from the hospital ward. Still, wherever that Roman is, I want to find him. In letter or in person.

∽

Early November 1918
Strasbourg

Dear Clara,
   Writing has been difficult of late.
   I've been learning (or not) to play a hand of my own.

Roman's lips pulled upward at the irony of the sentence.

It took longer than he assumed to relay the story in pen and ink. She had not written him. Or, if she had, her words were on a lorry somewhere or perhaps crammed into some satchel bound in the direction of nowhere.

So, Roman stopped and restarted his sentences like a conductor unsatisfied with a rehearsed phrase. The longer the space of words between them, the easier it was to wonder if he had imagined her. Or perhaps augmented their relationship.

So, here I am, writing with a hand you will not recognize because it is not my usual. And here I am back where I began before I was on the adventure other men might wait a half dozen lifetimes for and never have. One with music. One with mud and blood and wreckage of human life. Danger. And one with love.

Yes, love. Not a word I have used too often before. One that feels safer to write than to say aloud.

I am back in my father's workshop failing with one workable arm much as I did with two.

C. Boullangier's case is a little scratched and a little banged up at the corners. But inside he is still my friend. Something so precious and refined. And he still fits perfectly in my arms, and someday when my right arm heals, I will be able to fix my bow in my hand and make a perfect sound. And I love this fiddle. This violin that made me realize that I loved . . .

Was it that you were so cautious and careful at determining that my violin was safe? Was it that you were so attentive in telling me story after story while I lay restless?

Sometimes I second-guess myself. I am a cobbler with a fiddle. I always supposed it would be wonderful to see myself and what I do through someone else's eyes.

And all I want to do now is see things through your eyes.

I spill a lot in these letters, don't I? I've had time, Clara, to take the moments we shared together and place them in sequence with my admiration for your beauty and my deference to your compassionate skill.

When I weigh them all (and bring my resuscitated heart into the equation), it seems difficult to imagine a life before you were in it, which makes it ever so hard to put my pen down and realize there

*is not necessarily a life with you ahead of me. I need to ensure there
is a life with you ahead of me.*

~

Dear Roman,

   *It is still not your handwriting. I should know. But you
sound . . . more like yourself?*

   *Perhaps I don't recognize your handwriting because it is what
Annelise used to speak of . . . the slight changes that could affect
someone in the midst of turmoil. She was a better nurse than I.*

   Or perhaps . . . someone has taken to writing for you.

   *No. I should not entertain these thoughts that spiral as fast as
I write them. I am no better than the young men back in hospital,
making up the outcomes before I could clear away the blood and say,
"See, this is a superficial wound."*

   *Though I suppose no wound is truly superficial. At least not to
the person wounded.*

   *And it made me think perhaps what I thought about you was
superficial. Insomuch as I left out a very integral part of why we
parted the way we did.*

   You see, the first night you kissed me, I floated.

   *A lot of people use war to reconcile the past. Or understand
their misgivings or tragedy. In my case the war became an
opportunity for me to live my story.*

   *In part I used the war to assuage my guilt. I wasn't able to save
my mother, Roman. So, I thought I could save others in penance to
her memory.*

   *I balanced Annelise's demise against the survival of others and
made out a morbid gamble of odds.*

   *Annelise would not have wanted her memory to linger there. She
would want me to imagine her life as beautiful and complicated as a
pattern on a scarf. My mother? Who knows what my mother expected.*

I am wise enough to recognize that I am more than what I have lost. Whether my mother or Annelise.

If this is Roman despite the changed handwriting, then let me assure you this: Some women will return home and commiserate over what was lost.

I know when I greeted my father, I did so with the intention of reassuring him (and you are included, Roman) of what I found.

⁓

November 1918
Tielt, Belgium

Clara surveyed her room. A small square. Did she even fit into its space anymore? Hadn't she stretched too wide?

Her worn, painted dresser scraped against floorboards in dire need of painting only to wedge against a wall in dire need of a gentle hand to paste up cracked plaster.

Clara reintroduced herself to a life of caring for her father and ensuring his security now that the Boche, whose mere presence in Tielt was a means of protection, were slowly trickling back to where they came from. To putting water to boil and sweeping out the front mat. To nodding politely over the neighborly women who wanted her opinions, or at least her experience, over tea. They seemed uncaring (at least in her company) of her hairstyle. In many ways, she felt as if her limbs were moving slowly through water. The motions were familiar, like clockwork, but her brain set a different pace and her memories were a metronome. His hand on her cheek, his lips over her breath, the way her heart set a pace at the tone of his voice. C. Boullangier. A frog, a string, a bow.

Time passed and war exhaled its final affront.

"You seem pensive, Clara," her father said. "You seem

sad." His wiry, thin fingers covered her hand one night at dinner.

He had complimented her earlier on how she was able to cook such a delicious meal out of so few ingredients. Clara had long since decided she would offer some morsels of war while keeping others tucked deep inside so as not to concern her father. She had also decided she would flourish what little they had with the same improvisational skills she had used at Ypres. The same she had used when the power flickered in the hospital at Brussels and she and Annelise did wonders with a few matches and a can or two of beans and sardines.

"How could I be sad when I am here with you?" She squeezed his hand right back.

"Because you will always be sad, my Clara. Sad so long as you do not turn your page."

"Father . . ."

But what else was there to say? Clara knew what it was like to be stuck on the end of a chapter when the artillery fire began in Ypres. Clara knew what it was like to be halfway through reading a soldier's letter aloud even as he slipped away before the final line.

~

When the telegram came, it was the precipice of a moment when Clara wondered if she would be better off shutting the door on Roman's chapter in her life completely Or, if she was brave enough to carve a little corner of her heart out for him. At times his name thrummed. At times a moment they shared or the possibility of a moment they lost stilled her.

Clara felt ill-prepared. Even after her mother passed, it didn't feel like this. She felt regret then. Guilt. Now she felt nothing but harrowing *loss*. Of her imagination. Of *hope* and its feathers. But then again, she had never lived through a war before. Never survived a war before. Never known its echoes rolling in with men wounded or lost forever before. Mightn't she just be treating this *unusually*? She was used to unusual.

As unusual as the headlines soon erupting Tielt. The headlines of truces. The headlines of bare shelves and encroaching winter and ultimate joy.

Then it came.

A telegram. She knew its sender in a few curt words.

MEET ME IN THE SQUARE

So the girl who stepped out of a Brussels train station to find her life told her father that she was going away again.

"Just for a while, Father." Clara repacked a case only recently unburdened of her clothes and accoutrements.

"It won't be a while," he said resolutely. "You've stepped into a new story." Still, she heard the smile in his voice. "Before, you told the stories I told you, and now you are living your own."

MEET ME IN THE SQUARE

She smiled and soon, alone, she revisited Roman—not in person as she hoped soon to do—but in words.

Dear Clara,

If you received my telegram, hopefully you will be on your way to me before this reaches you.

And when I see you, I will have the opportunity to tell you that you were not wrong.

I can assure we were not at odds. We were not two strangers passing. I think war wedges misunderstandings. We are so devoid of sleep, and yes, of hope, that our minds decide something must be on its way and positioned for an attack . . .

Clara smiled. *Yes.* War was as much her enemy as time. Yet time, these moments at least, seemed to be thawing in her favor, much as she hoped the train tracks would when she finally boarded the train to Strasbourg. To Roman . . .

Dearest Clara . . .

We had a few moments. But they were enough. They added up to enough to lead me to believe if we had more moments, they might inch toward memories and those memories might sew up into something more . . .

I am not sure as to the why and wherefore of connection.

Why I sensed you and why we shared stories and songs.

All I know is that when I finally find a way to play C. Boullangier again, I want your ears to be the first to recognize. Perhaps even admire?

It's easy to imagine.

Hope is the thing with feathers.

Now hope was the thing that would pull Clara out of her world.

Not just *pull* her. *Shove* her out of her world.

Clara's down pillow failed to cradle her in sleep.

The chickens pecking their hierarchy outside the frosty window the next morning failed to rouse her.

Blessedly, her father did not check in. Once Clara rolled over and heard the toll of the grandfather clock outside of her bedroom, she was shocked he hadn't.

She sighed, listening to the *tick-tick-tick* in its familiar metronome.

She instinctively placed her hand over her heart and wondered if its beat would find the rhythm. It was something Roman told her once about playing in a symphony hall and how each listener's heartbeat would synchronize with the time signature of the piece.

When she finally dressed and met her father in the drawing room, it was with a fresh perspective and determination.

"Are you all right, darling?"

"I *will* be, Father." Her smile didn't reach her eyes. "I was just thinking of how I will miss home."

But she wasn't sure if it was home anymore. It felt different somehow. A train chugging into a station for a momentary stop but no longer the final destination.

She wasn't at her final destination.

Her father knew it. Clara knew it.

She had to recalibrate. She had to imagine she was still under the arches of the Brussels train station, turning a new page.

And she knew she would find her way.

Dear Clara,

Ours is a tradition divided between the German and the French. I've always loved how we straddle a bridge of two worlds . . .

I've always enjoyed that my life was preternaturally determined to be complex. Interesting.

Beyond what my father imagined.

Well never mind that. Wherever you are, I wish you could see Strasbourg as I do. I keep trying to imagine it through your eyes, Scheherazade. You'd imagine a romance at the cathedral. You would stroll through the square hoping the open flames in each barrel were not merely a place to roast chestnuts but spin yarns.

You of all people would be attuned to the attention the ladies here take in their dress. This is a season of victory. Everything is pressed and paraded in Alsatian style.

There have been Christmas markets here for centuries. Dating back to the 1500s. The wine flows now at the holidays and with peace promised on the horizon much as it did in the time of Dagobert.

I never found Strasbourg to be anything particularly special before. I had never found anything to be particular special before.

This much was true. It was, instead, his home. As familiar as breathing or blood in his veins. A certainty with days formerly as certain as a winding clock like the one in the town square.

Any change I notice here is probably because I have changed, he scribbled.

Roman cursed. Five minutes with his bow and his violin and he could have spun her into the skies. As certain as the smell of spilled ink, he determined *she* was all that kept him from fully reintegrating into his life. His *new* life. One where his very weight needed to balance on a stick and his very sleep would be rattled by what he had seen.

Now he could barely fashion a letter given the errant usage of his dominant hand.

His mother clicked her tongue in attendance to him. His father muttered constantly and often in a monotone theme regarding his son's foolish and impetuous nature and how eager he was to leave when *wouldn't it have been better and caused less pain to stay and fashion army regulation boots?*

Still, Roman mentally balanced these dissonant moments with one of complete harmony. When he first stepped off the train, he was surprised not to see his mother but his father at the station waiting for him.

Roman spared no time in evading his father's outstretched hand in exchange for an embrace.

"I am surprised to see you!"

"I am just happy to see you," his father said gruffly.

They would say nothing more on the subject. But Roman knew with absolute certainty it was enough that he came home.

~

Roman set the letter aside as he had a half dozen times that morning and finally succumbed to his mother's not-so-subtle tap of the end of the broom directly under his bedroom.

The more Roman wrote, the less he trusted himself not to let his hand listen to his heart and begin to scrawl what his mind had not yet decided to write.

He took to helping his father and found that the delicate curve of a stitch and the refined movement of molding soles into leather was as easy as picking up his violin to revisit a difficult passage. It came so easily as if he hadn't injured his arm, as if he hadn't met a girl and found a life beyond his fairy-tale village, which now, under winter's hold, was everything said girl would love: latticed snowflakes against rambling, colorful houses, all leaning in together as if holding hands. All leaning in together as if to weather any storm. Any war.

One night he took to the unsent fragment of a letter again.

It looks a bit like a fairy tale, the city of mine. It feels like one too. All of the ladies have taken to mending and brushing off their aprons and long red skirts (known here as Kutt) and their large knot caps. My mother is no exception and will brew some magic of her own. The same fastidious and resourceful tips and tricks from some old wives' tale help my father when he is lost with a tricky sole, or

when a water stain on leather has befuddled him into a dither. And
I am a cobbler these days. A tenuous profession as I aid my father
and one that makes me think of Hans Christian Andersen. Wasn't
he always writing about shoes? Shoes that made a man more than he
was? Shoes—red shoes—that destroyed a ballerina's fleeting, prideful
beauty? No matter. My dearest wish is to play again.

There was always some manner of magic, an enchanted object in a fairy tale, wasn't there? Roman's mother, for instance, had seen to the stains on the scarf-turned-tourniquet. Suddenly the wrecked silk of the scarf from his *ange en bleu* revealed an intricate peacock pattern.

He learned its intricacies just as he acclimated as best he could to the streets and narrow cobbled alleyways of home even while Clara interrupted his thoughts.

She might notice the savory blended spices of cooking wafting from windows open despite the encroaching chill. With what little people had from fast-dwindling larders, they were in a constant state of celebration.

Clara might notice the church bells tolled a minor chord and perhaps would feel—as Roman now did—a little catch of something clean and as bright as the snow whispering delicate lace patterns on the dark stones.

No two snowflakes alike. No two wars alike either. The war Clara lived was different from the one Roman lived, and yet when each individual flake reached the ground, there was nothing to distinguish it from the others. Just a common experience in a common place.

One evening while his father was late in the workshop, Roman accepted a steaming cup of tea from his mother and in exchange leaned across the scratched and worn kitchen table and told everything he had omitted from his letters home. Of a girl. *Non.* A woman.

His mother sipped her tea. It was watered down a little and oversweet with the sugar she had added to compensate. "You must convince him that war has changed you. You must *tell* him."

"But it wasn't just the war," Roman continued.

"Of course not, Roman. It was because of *someone.*"

He knew she understood. Perhaps by the way her voice wrapped around the word *someone* and the way her lips tugged in a smile so subtle that he almost missed it altogether.

"This someone . . ."

But he couldn't finish what he began. *Someone* was too small a word in which to cram an entire person. As such, the sentence lingered like the fragments of letters in his bedroom.

"This someone," his mother repeated. Though he knew she didn't expect anything more from him then, a shared moment like a whisper or secret accompanied by a hand clasp over the table was met with a knowing look.

"Do you have something to say, Mother?" Roman chided.

"Your waste bin is like a bouquet of crumpled letters," his mother said as Roman rose to retire.

"I know."

"Perhaps take one of those letters out, Roman. Send it."

"Or you'll pinch my ear like you did as a child and make me clean my room?" Roman jested.

His mother twinkled. "Something like that."

"And what about Father?"

Roman collected the letters he received from Clara and folded them delicately. Then he slowly unfurled the rose paper crumples in the wastebasket. He wrote Clara about everything these days. Explained the workings of his father's shop. Then there was his mother's famous baeckeoffe recipe. Surely Clara would want to continue her mother's legacy by preparing it. Wouldn't she?

Yet unlike the letters he sent and the letters not answered, this was different.

Should he continue baring his soul to a stranger?

Hope was the thing with feathers, yes. But so long as editors hounded him, Roman's wastebasket was a veritable exhibition of words and feelings he failed to send.

In the end, it wasn't a letter that reunited Roman and Clara but a telegraph.

"This is a very sparsely worded message, Clara."

Clara's father was a soft-spoken man, save for when he was relating a story. As such, any raised decibel was much as a gong to those around them.

"I'm sorry, Father . . . were you expecting something?"

"A very sparsely worded message indeed." Her father shook his head. "Read this."

Clara took the message he passed.

"Oh!" she exhaled.

"*Oh*," her father exclaimed.

EPILOGUE

Iris

Strasbourg, France
Christmas Eve 1918

Bundled up against the wintry air nipping at her nose, Iris ordered another hot chocolate and settled into her chair at the small metal café table tucked to the side of Place Benjamin Zix located in the Petite France part of the ancient city. Not too long ago, the streets were crowded with occupying German soldiers, but today the place rang with the laughter of children skidding in the falling snow, notes of Alsatian songs played by musicians dotting each corner, and the smell of cloved gluhwein tingling the air. In the distance, cathedral bells reverberated from their high towers down through the winding buildings with a cheerfulness of the world once more turning in harmony as it had not in four long years.

"Hot chocolate." A young woman wearing a traditional Alsatian dress of a white blouse, black apron, and red skirt presented a steaming cup of deliciousness and set it on the table.

"Thank you," Iris said.

The waitress smiled and nodded, wobbling the most astonishing black knot of material perched atop her head.

"Might I trouble you for a few biscuits?" The woman's brow puckered. Iris searched her brain for the correct word from the French dictionary she'd purchased in Paris. *"Biscuit. Moelleux."*

"Un gateau," the woman said in a unique accent of German and French. One Iris had quickly learned upon her arrival late the night before was purely Alsace.

"Oui." At least one word Iris couldn't embarrass herself with.

"I will bring you *bredele*. A favorite here made with honey."

"Magnifique."

Accustomed to the language clumsiness of tourists, the waitress smiled and headed back inside the café, the trailing ends of her black knot drifting behind her.

Iris slowly stirred the provided little spoon in her cup, swirling around the soft fluffs of snow that drifted into the melting depths. All the seats inside were occupied as everyone was out today enjoying the Christmas markets, but she didn't mind sitting outside. In London she was too cooped up working from morning to night. France, on the other hand, had perfected the art of enjoying life. Perhaps more so now when life was no longer squashed under the Hun boot. Besides, sitting in the snow with hot chocolate reminded her of visiting her father when she was a girl. He always brought a thermos of tea, and on the days she tagged along, he packed one of hot chocolate for her. During his break, they would sit on the bank of the River Wandle and see who could drink faster without scalding their tongue.

Oh, Papa. She smiled and sipped her steaming chocolate. He'd returned to work much sooner than Mum liked, but she had confessed he was always underfoot at home and it was best to keep him occupied. It saddened her to leave them behind at Christmas, but she couldn't deny the thrill of leaving England for a new place for the first time. And to Paris! Never in her life did she dream to walk the Champs-Élysées or stroll beneath the Eiffel Tower. True, the city was still reeling from the war, but the citizens' zest was alive and well. And no one was more zestful than she when she stood outside La Maison Liberty in her crisp new suit of dove gray with her Feathered Hope scarf knotted about her neck. From a simple paint girl to the first female designer at Liberty to Parisian collaborator. She may have squelched a giggle before stepping through the door to her appointment with the head director of the French store.

"I've pictured you a thousand different ways in my memory, but none of them compares to seeing you again in person."

And suddenly there he was, standing next to her. Snow dusting his shoulders and hat, those brown eyes twinkling, and a smile that could melt a snowdrift.

"Rex!" Pushing from her chair, she grabbed his shoulders and smacked a kiss to both his cheeks.

He wobbled with a croak of surprise.

"Oh dear. I'm sorry." Iris gripped his arms to steady him.

"Don't apologize. A man back from war would give his good arm to be greeted so enthusiastically by a pretty bird. Or in my case, his good leg." He knocked his cane against his left leg. A wooden sound echoed back.

Her heart cracked a bit. She had sobbed into her pillow the day she'd gotten his letter explaining the loss of his leg, but she wasn't about to turn into that swollen-eyed girl today. He was alive, which was more than most young men their age could boast, and she would rejoice.

She gently squeezed his arms and stepped back as curious eyes lingered on their prolonged closeness. "You didn't say they gave you a prosthetic."

"Wanted to surprise you. Besides, I couldn't hop over all these cobblestones on one leg, so I made a nuisance of myself until the good doctors strapped ol' Woody on."

"You've named your fake leg?"

"People name their autos. Why can I not name my new leg?"

With a smile and shake of her head, she regained her seat

and indicated for him to take the one next to her. He eased himself down with a slight grimace and stuck his left leg straight out.

"Does it pain you much?" she asked as the waitress quietly slipped a plate of bredele onto the table and inquired if Rex would like coffee.

He politely shook his head no to the waitress, then leaned his cane against the table. "Only after a long day. Not to mention a few splinters when I went to rub at the phantom pains, but enough about me. I want to talk about—"

"Wait. Is your prosthetic the surprise that you so urgently requested me to Strasbourg for?"

"All in good time, my fair Iris. May I?" He pointed at the biscuits. At her nod, he selected the top one and took a bite. "Tell me how you took Liberty of Paris by storm."

Her fingers floated to the Feathered Hope scarf knotted about her neck, a lucky talisman as she had come to consider it. She never went anywhere without it. "It was a dream that I felt like an imposter entering, but they were so warm and welcoming. Not a rude or upturned nose in sight despite all the rumors you hear about the French. Their design manager gave me a tour of each department and the stockrooms, and had no fewer than thirty sketches to show me of what our collaboration design could be."

Nerves had nearly overwhelmed her, but she found when talking to the creatives that all of the doubts faded away. It was precisely where she was meant to be, bringing possibilities into a new era that didn't exist four years before. She had finally stepped into what her father called life's fulfilling purpose, and the future could not look any brighter.

"That's wonderful," he said, dusting off his fingers and reaching for another biscuit.

She grabbed one before he gobbled the whole plate's worth. "Yes, though we haven't come to a final decision about what the design may be. A blending of British and French symbols for certain." She took a bite. Delicious honey, butter, and sugar crumbled in her mouth. "I would love to incorporate something of those garments. The embroidery on the aprons is divine."

"That's the traditional dress of Alsace. Patriotic fervor has swept the region as they have officially been turned back over to French territory since being caught in a tug-of-war with the Rhineland for some time."

"All the more fitting." A design began to weave in her head. Threads of white and red, delicate flowers.

"Though perhaps in your new collection you might suggest pocket squares or handkerchiefs to go along with your scarves. Something for the gentlemen."

"I didn't think of that when I sent you the scarf. Of course you wouldn't want to tie a woman's scarf about your neck." She sipped her chocolate to wash down the lingering bits of biscuit crumbs. A skim of snow had melted across the top to cool the scalding brew into a more pleasing warm.

"Those trenches can be bitterly cold and your scarf saved my neck from freezing many a night. All the blokes were jealous. Though I have found a new use for it since it's too large to fold into my civilian pockets." He rolled up his trouser leg to reveal his wooden leg. It was quite basic in its functional shape tapering down to a stump, but he had made use of the canvas by drawing columns, rooflines, building facades, and other architectural wonders as adornment. He had even carved a ruler along the right side. There at the top, serving as a cushion between the wood and his raw knee, was her scarf. "Hope you approve."

Life's fulfillment without a doubt. "I can think of no finer use for it."

"Excellent, because I lack that bohemian flair to toss it jauntily about my neck and look fashionable." He pushed down his trouser leg and grabbed the last bredele.

"Is bohemian flair prohibited from architects?"

"From stolid English ones, yes, but that does not mean we are completely without flair. Come with me. It's time for the surprise." Selecting a few notes from his wallet, he placed them on the table. At Iris's protest, he merely grinned. "I need the practice of acting the gentleman again. Too long at war grinds a man's manners down to dust."

"You've always been a gentleman, even when making a bet just to get me to dance with you."

"A bet I do not regret in the least." Taking his cane, he stood and held out his hand to help her stand.

They strolled along the uneven streets, her hand tucked warmly in his elbow as she slowed her pace to match his. It was lovely not to rush and to simply enjoy the Christmas festivities and charming company. It was as if they had never parted, all those letters passing back and forth over the Channel allowing them an open intimacy often held back when face-to-face. Reading his words, she'd discovered the true heart of the man who had charmed his way into her life. A man who was kind, intelligent, and daringly optimistic, and who made her laugh. He also believed in her dreams as much as she had come to believe in his. A rarity in their entirely too sensible world.

"How old do you think some of these buildings are?" she asked as they passed white and brown structures that could have been snipped from olden fairy tales.

From the light fizzing in his eye, these were Rex's version of fairy tales. "There's been a settlement here since the Romans. Most of these buildings are a prime example of half-timber style from the sixteenth and seventeenth centuries, what we in

England know as Tudor. See the sloping roofs with the open lofts there? This district once belonged to the tanneries, and they would dry out the hides in those spaces."

"It's so strange to see a style we identify as Tudor, Henry VIII, War of the Roses, and all that to be uniquely our own. It wasn't, though, was it? Half-timbers were all over Europe."

"If it's a good design, everyone wishes to copy it. In France, they refer to it as *colombage*. Germany, *Fachwerk*."

They walked into a large rectangular plaza brimming with the mouthwatering scents of fried dough and sugared pastries, festive music, and lights twinkling between the fluff of falling snow. The open space was bordered by cafés and shops and the imposing Cathédrale Notre-Dame de Strasbourg in all its gothic towers and high arched windows. Details she'd never thought to take notice of until Rex swayed her interest; however, as lovely and ancient as the church was, it could not hold a candle to the source of merriment and delicious aromas already making her forget the hot chocolate and bredele. In the center of the plaza, dozens of booths and tables showcased a dazzling array of sweets, savories, wines, ciders, and beers. More booths overflowed with hand-carved toys, another with freshly cut evergreen wreaths. Freshly pressed soap cakes towered on a lace tablecloth, while intricately painted cuckoo clocks chimed and clucked with funny little birds popping out of their doors. Children chased one another with snowballs as a quartet played merry tunes that rang through the plaza with Christmas cheer.

Strolling down the center lane of booths, they stopped in front of a table piled with large wooden casks. Clove and cinnamon spiced the air.

"Have you had gluhwein?" Rex asked. Iris shook her head. "You're in for a treat."

He ordered two glasses. Tastebuds tingling in anticipation,

Iris watched the dark red liquid pour from the cask's spout into the glass. The seller topped each glass with an orange slice, then pushed them across the table.

"*Santé.*" Rex clinked his glass to hers.

"Cheers." She inhaled the warm spiced smell and took a sip. It hit her tongue and glided down her throat like ruby silk. "That's delicious!"

"And it'll help keep our toes warm in this snow." Draining their glasses, they set them on the table where the seller stood ready to wash them. After Iris tucked her hand into the crook of his arm, Rex steered her through the shopping crowd until they came to the north end of the plaza. He stopped and grinned up at the corner building before them. "Here's what I wanted to show you."

All the other structures were old in their own rights, but this here must have housed Methuselah. It was several stories high, with dark woodwork and carved figures, and a steeply pitched roof that set it apart from the creams and butters of the buildings surrounding it.

"Meet the most famous resident in Strasbourg, the Kammerzell House. It was built in the fifteenth century and is one of the most ornate and well-preserved structures of medieval architecture." He stared proudly as if his own hand had drawn the lines.

She couldn't blame him. The work was astonishing. "It's magnificent."

"It's seen a few changes over the centuries, but the best one was in 1904 when Léo Schnug painted frescoes inside, including one with a cat that he hallucinated about."

Iris laughed. "Well, inspiration comes from the most unlikely places."

"That's why I asked you to meet me here. In the place of

my inspiration. And to tell you my big news." Taking her hand from the crook of his elbow, he grasped it, kneading her fingers gently between his own. The icicles melted from her fingertips. "I've been promoted to senior architect at Messrs. Higg & Hill, and Liberty has requested me specifically to create the overall blueprints for the new look of the store. And this is it. Half-timber and whitewash. Taking the past and shaping it into the future." He squeezed her fingers. "Something I learned from you."

"I never instructed you on half-timber siding."

"No, it was more about bridging unique perspectives to make a whole. Heritage and adventure. Tradition with innovation. You've done it so artistically with Feathered Hope that it would be mad for me not to utilize the same brilliance in Liberty's construct. It's the face that shows the world what she's made of."

Overflowing with happiness, Iris laced her fingers between Rex's, holding tight. "This is wonderful! Many happy congratulations. I've no doubt you will create something remarkable to finally showcase your talent for all the world to recognize."

That gleam sparked in his eye, the one foretelling trouble. "You think I'm remarkable?"

She was entirely prepared for his sort of troublemaking. "I believe I was referring to your talent."

"As you seem to find it difficult to confess your true admiration for me, I shall tell you something."

"I wait with bated breath."

He took a step closer until their clasped hands brushed the front of his coat. His gaze never wavered from her face. "I found you remarkable the second you walked into the Argyll Arms and gazed about with the confidence of a queen."

"I was terrified with nothing to lose."

"Then outside when you fell in the snow, my heart fell a little as well. Taking that bet was the second best thing ever to happen to me."

The warmth from the gluhwein swirled through her limbs, but his words twirled in her blood until she was lightheaded. "What was the first?"

"It turning out to be you."

"After all this time, you still hope flowery words will make me swoon and sigh?" She was well on her way but wasn't about to tell him that. The man was positively incorrigible.

He inched closer. The back of her hand pressed against him. "You tell me."

Before she could respond, bells clacked all around as a group of children crowded around them. They shook hand-bells and sang a song that lilted this way and that like a rocking boat.

Her passable French did not rise to the challenge. "What are they saying?"

Rex squinted as if that helped his hearing. "Something about a tree. Or maybe a potato. My French is limited to order-ing food."

When a pole with a dangling bit of mistletoe was swung over their heads, the song's meaning became abruptly clear. The children's kissing noises solidified the understanding.

"Hate to disappoint them." He leaned over and pressed a kiss to her cheek, lingering a bit longer than polite.

The children rang their bells with whoops of glee and skipped off to the next unsuspecting couple.

"You missed." The feel of his lips tingling her cheek and heart racing, Iris gave into the perfect moment. She wrapped her arms around his neck and kissed him full on the mouth. She'd never kissed a man, but Rex made it quite delightful.

When she finally pulled away, her senses floated with spiced cloves and his fresh soap.

He looked quite like floating himself as he leaned his forehead to hers. "Just when I start to believe I understand you, you go and surprise me."

"Would it surprise you if I asked for you to formally call on me upon your return to London?"

Sighing, he straightened, though he didn't go too far if she desired to dart in for another kiss. "My dear Iris, if this relationship is to continue, you might allow me the dignity to declare my amorous attentions first from time to time. Iris? As I am in the middle of declaring myself to you, it would boost my ego greatly if you were to pay attention."

She was only half paying attention, for the other half was caught on a couple standing a short distance away staring up at the cathedral. They were both strikingly tall, he with a cane and she with unfashionably short hair that accentuated her straight shoulders. A woman stood with them, delight curving her face as she appeared in deep conversation with the couple, but Iris's exhilarated focus narrowed to the scarf being knotted about her neck by the tall woman.

"She's wearing my scarf."

Clara

Christmas Eve 1918

FOR A GIRL NOT SO LONG AGO SO ENAMORED BY A TRAIN STATION, Clara was aware her trip to Strasbourg would snatch her breath. Roman's hometown would soon be another pin she could stick into the map of her life. More still, the stop and start of his letters, the slow way he distributed breadcrumbs in a sure, subtle line, led her as gently into his world as surely as a tug of the blanket he pulled to her chin. For his sake (and her own), she was eager to see Alsace, to see the women in their ornate hats and carefully sewn costumes and to experience the first pent-up exhale of Christmas over the square he spoke of. To smell the garlands sighing from the thatched roofs and cozy houses hugging each other in rings around the cathedral. As eager to see it as she was him. As much as her throat caught with a strange somersault as the train tugged into Strasbourg, Clara was determined to keep her head. She steadied her feet as she alighted from the train, the steam and whistle still shrieking in her ear. Even as she adjusted her hat, smoothed her skirt, and picked up her bag and entered a world where she would find *Roman*. The man whose pages and history she could turn like a book. But still, there is a moment when one steps off a train in the dark that turns the ordinary ominous, and as Clara double-checked the address of the guest quarters she had procured, she shuddered.

It was more than the chill of winter now. It was the wonderful, harrowing moment hovering between old and new.

There's Bruegel light here, Clara decided. The way the light hovered, if melancholy, still centered on the men at the focal point of Bruegel's painting, much as it did here. The frozen ground melded with the frosty horizon. She only need focus on a focal point. Like the cross and crucifixion scene in a Bruegel painting spilling over peasants with a blur of color and light.

Snow sparkled around her.

What a sky. A mournful, beautiful sky that stabbed at her chest and tightened her throat. Her brain, however, compensated with words she would say to him:

It was hard enough to lose you.

Hoop is dat ding met veren.

Hope! That thing with feathers.

Hope quickened Clara's pulse.

Maybe Roman would fill in the lines left absent in his letters. Maybe he would replace the blanks on his ink-spattered pages . . . the words trailing into a dotted line. Maybe he would continue the conversation they had begun with their lips when she pulled herself out of her shell and him into the linen closet.

The pedestrian square was dashed with color—vibrant with gold bells and garlands and the smell of mulled wine and roasting chestnuts wafting from the licks of open flames in great barrels. Musicians spattered and aligned the perimeters, and the mournful tangle of a carol in a minor key under the grand shadow of a grand cathedral slowly rose like smoke from a barrel of chestnuts.

Clara took in the scene, swiveling on snow-smattered cobbles.

Northward a little she swerved *just* to the right of the church where she had been told to find tea and warmth and somewhere to place her bag.

But fate had another idea.

A figure against the din. One who stood out even in a woolen brown coat and with a woolen cap gobbling his molasses hair.

Her heart started at his sight. She studied him a moment. Roman Allaire seemed a little lost, and yet it took a few pressing moments for her to register that his arm was stiff, unmoving. That the long, expressive fingers on his long, expressive right hand clutched a walking stick steadying his slow gait.

Of course. She could curse herself. His handwriting looked odd because he wrote with the *opposite* hand.

Selfish, selfish, Clara. You dunce sow. His right arm. His right hand.

The hand that so confidently held his violin bow and made songs from horsehair and a funnily shaped hollow wooden body. Button. Bridge. Bout. Frog. Flopsy. Mopsy. Dropsy. Pleurisy.

She hoped he would play again. She hoped she would re-member to *breathe* again.

All the words her mind and mouth played with when Roman Allaire was near. The ones nestled in her heart when he inter-laced their fingers.

"Clara." Roman didn't get much beyond her name, though his glistening eyes said the rest.

Her lip trembled a little.

But before it could truly quiver, Roman set it all to right and lowered his mouth to hers. She felt the slight, tremulous uncertainty of his lips finishing their conversation and taking a new one in its stride.

There was, of course, the rather inconvenient need for him to balance his walking stick and the inconvenient need for breathing.

Finally, they disengaged.

"A gift." Roman finally found his voice.

Retrieved from his pocket and now offered in his outstretched hand was a delicate silk scarf. Rich in design and texture, its light blue background snagged the dying winter light and offset an intricate illustrated design.

"They call it art nouveau." There was pride in the clearly recited words. He had practiced for her. "Your friend—"

"Annelise," Clara finished. "She would love it."

Clara studied the ornate motif. Winding purple vines bordered four red sunrays in each corner. Then, purple feathers delicately creating a large diamond shape at the center. Her eyes prickled. How Annelise would love this moment. How Annelise would size up the design and know every intricate detail. How Clara might feel wearing it as she turned a new page in the story of the woman she became. War would always be sewn in her memories of tents in Ypres and the crisp, starched fold of bed corners while lye and bleach tickled her nostrils. But there was also a tapestry of Annelise's scarf and its design, Roman's music and the beauty Clara tried to carry with her through the corridor in letters to her father, the familiar scent of her mother's bread, letters capturing her first moments in Brussels, Roman's violin, and Annelise's scarf.

"I don't think I've ever seen anything quite so lovely in my life, Roman."

"Well, it wasn't always so beautiful." Roman shifted on his walking stick and gestured toward his stiff right arm. "A young angel of a woman all in blue was wearing it and sacrificed it for my poor arm."

With his mention of his arm, Clara gave herself permission to truly assess the damage. Her throat closed slightly at the awkward way it hung stiff and limp by his side. She said, "But it looks . . ."

"So new? So far from the blood-sodden mess it might have been when it was a tourniquet for my poor limb here?"

"Something like that," Clara said. "A cobbler's son with a penchant for beautiful scarves." She was embroidering a pattern on his forearm while surveying the scarf. The more she assessed the careful interlay of stitches and lines, the easier it was to see the whole of the full design.

All that he had done for *her*.

"My maman works wonders with shoes and fabrics. A stain is never forever, she taught me, with enough love and care to blot it."

"Your maman is a rare diamond to raise you so well," Clara said. "I will never forget how well you tucked me in that night."

Roman ducked his chin. "*De rien.* I suppose I have her to thank for my last letters. I kept wondering what she would say if she found them sitting on my desk."

"Letters?" Clara asked.

"Don't duck your head coyly, Clara. I know you received my letters."

"Letters? Oh no, dear sir. All I received were rather horrid attempts at sentences . . ."

He smothered her ellipses with a kiss.

Then he gently wound the scarf around Clara's neck, flourishing it with a little knot. Impressed with the symmetry, he unwound its story:

"My blue angel nurse had a little cap with a bit of a crisscross on it," he explained. "And a pin on her breast pocket so shiny, I am sure in my shock and confusion I . . . I followed its glare like a mesmerized cat." Roman laughed. "And she took the scarf right off her neck and wrapped it around my arm. A rather elegant tourniquet, wouldn't you say?" He looked down at his arm and the laughter faded. His arm was stiff and unnatural. "It might not be here . . ." His voice trailed a moment. "The scarf is from that shop—"

"Liberty," Clara said.

"Yes! Far away in London. The most beautiful place in the world. Isn't that what Annelise believed? Anyways, it is too pretty to have been a tourniquet. Still, it likely saved my life."

For a moment they stopped. Clara took in the scene. Half leaning against this man, half leaning on a walking stick in a magical moment of ivy and green. The musicians had moved to a happier carol. Clara touched the color at her neck and hoped, somewhere, Annelise appreciated the unexpected irony.

"I was so stubborn, Roman. I already played over a story in my mind and I wrote you in it." She gently ran her index finger over his injured forearm. "It kept me from having to *think* about you. If I thought too hard, I remembered. And if I remembered, it would be harder to lose you."

"Clara." Her name was soft in his voice. "Like the girl who had lost so much. Or at least *thought* she had lost so much. Like the little girl looking for a nutcracker in Tchaikovsky." The magic appeared only when she needed something, *anything*, to come to life. "Like the woman I met and brought a scarf home for."

He reached to touch the scarf wound around her neck, a bit of a rippling current like the Belgian river Meuse lapping the basin of the Seine. Liquid silk and so soft to touch. "*Met* is not quite the word," he supplicated. "Since I *listened* to you."

Clara shook her head. Pink flakes contoured each cheek. "Since I was so *certain*. Since I took the liberty of believing without complete proof."

Roman cut her off: "I think *liberty* is as lovely a word as *hope*."

❧

Their new story had truly begun. Now when their lips mingled, it was not with the rudimentary cadence of a piece sight-read for the first time—rather as if returning to a phrase. The more Roman fancied the rhythm of her touch over his hairline, his shoulder, and slowing over his collar, the more the heat punctured through his wool coat as if it were summer and not the icy chill of December. Fortunately, it didn't take long for him to calibrate his weight with one hand on his walking stick while the other looped over her waist. He enjoyed their collective unsteadiness. For every time he pursued her lips, she faltered. A fulcrum too easily pivoted at the slightest deepening of his kiss. *No matter*—if he toppled, so would she.

Roman painted her face with the intensity he was certain her artist Bruegel deployed to his brush. But as his eyes moved just over her cheekbone, they caught and stayed just beyond her shoulder. To a woman.

"Roman?" Clara tugged at his coat. "You look as if you've seen a ghost!"

Nothing other than this scenario would have drawn him from Clara's bright eyes and swollen lips. Even if said scenario led him to believe he was hallucinating. For there, haloed by lanterns and torches ribboning low light like a winding path, stood a woman from another life. Another time. Her silk Liberty scarf was not a tourniquet for his arm, rather around his beloved's neck and still lightly held by his fingers.

Roman blinked, but to no avail. The dream as so many others when he pressed his eyes closed. It was living now and playing out in colors of green and snow. Yet, as his peripheral vision cleared and the woman was his central focus, he saw her as clearly as the moment she leaned over his injured body. The moment after he paid his debt. After he noticed the muted throb that soon became a timpani in his arm. Her soothing voice and the concern glistening in his eyes were second nature to him now.

His *ange en bleu.*

Roman slowly disengaged from Clara. He let the silk of her scarf slip.

Later Clara would understand.

Later he would tell her everything.

Even as right now she looked up to him, cold and perplexed.

But for this moment the scarf he deftly wound around her neck belonged to the *fate* that not only brought him back to Clara but to the woman who had saved his life. His ability to imagine he would play C. Boullangier again. His means of drawing Clara close, much as he tried to just then.

Even as their timing was off.

"Roman—"

Roman gently placed a finger over lips, wishing he could kiss away the last of her sentence. He would find their rhythm again. But for now?

"Put a bookmark in that thought, Scheherazade."

Geneviève

Christmas 1918

THE SNOW SWIRLED AROUND THE SQUARE IN THE HEART OF STRAS-bourg. Not the relentless snow of Canada and Maine, but lazy light flakes that glistened merrily in the gaslight. Geneviève had welcomed her transfer to the charming city on the border between France and Germany with good cheer. Meanwhile, most of her group had been sent home in the first wave and were thrilled at the chance to return to their loved ones. Peter and Patricia were already back in Maine, as a letter from Maman had confirmed. Geneviève laughed at her mother's choice vocabulary when expressing her opinion about the situation and declared her daughter was well rid of such a louse, no matter how well off and well connected he was.

A handful of others from her group had been sent on to Paris to help field the cacophonous symphony of phone calls as the dignitaries arrived from all over the world to begin outlining the terms of peace, and they were delighted for the chance to get a taste of life in the city after the deprivations of Meuse. Geneviève was glad they would have the chance to explore the glorious city before returning to housework and child rearing in quiet corners of Nebraska or Wisconsin.

Geneviève was simply glad her petition had been granted to remain overseas in whatever capacity she was needed. Her days were busy, though not as hectic as they'd been in the last days of the war. She found that she missed the frenetic pace of it. It kept her mind from wandering to the dark corners where she knew no good would come of her lingering. No matter how seductive those thoughts were.

Ruminating over what her life would be like when she went back to Maine.

Dwelling on Peter's betrayal—though she understood, at least intellectually, that she was better off. It wouldn't make her family's lot easier when her paycheck would dry up.

And the constant worry of what fate had ever befallen Maxime. It was like a poorly healed bone whose ache never truly subsided. It might fade into background noise when she was busy, but just like a bone, it would flare up again with a change in the weather.

It was Christmas Eve, and she was no longer the supervising operator. A lovely woman, Gemma Schumacher, held the post in Strasbourg and had insisted she take Christmas Eve and Christmas Day off as a thank-you for her dedicated service since she came to the post. It wasn't quite the gift that Miss Schumacher thought it was, but she had to pretend to be grateful for the time off. In truth, it was only when she was on duty that she could feel somewhat at ease. Though the work was still demanding, it was infinitely better for her state of mind than time spent idle.

Her managerial duties no longer monopolized her time, and she found she missed it. She couldn't help but think of how much more efficiently NET&T would be run if she were at the helm instead of Penny Johnson. She wouldn't let favoritism get in the way of running an efficient office. She would have enjoyed that opportunity, but that future was fuzzy now, as if being erased from the list of her possible paths forward.

She'd not written to Maman about the fractured promise with Peter. She didn't want to add her matrimonial fate to her mother's list of concerns. Jean had been injured in the last weeks of the war and was returning home now. Whether or not he'd be fit to work when he recovered remained to be seen. The idea of her sweet, vibrant brother spending the rest of his life less than whole added to the ache she carried. She stalked the post for letters about his well-being with the same anxious prayers she had for Maxime.

She couldn't bear the thought of going back to her empty boardinghouse just then and being alone with her thoughts, so she wandered the streets of Strasbourg, bathed in the gentle glow of the gaslight. She meandered aimlessly, but her feet were drawn to the heart of town and the bustle of the final night of the Christmas market. She'd done no shopping for her family, with all the upheaval of her transfer, and thought little tokens of her love would be just as welcome early in the new year.

She found a lovely leather handbag for Maman that would last her for years, a good handmade pocketknife for Papa, and little trinkets for the children that would make them smile. She found a booth with leather-bound books and lingered a long while, running her finger along the spines of the tomes. Many were familiar, others new to her. When she saw the volume of Dickinson poetry, a gorgeous thing bound in oxblood leather with gold inlay, she held it to her chest a moment before offering the *bouquiniste* some coins.

This would be her gift to herself. She deserved that much.

She'd read the weathered page with "Hope Is the Thing with Feathers" so much that she was worried it would crumble to dust. She would be able to keep that copy safe, as a talisman and a memory of happier times, and could read this sturdy, bound copy as often as she liked. Or she could send it to Maxime. A reminder of the hope they'd shared for a few shining moments.

Her heart was lighter, having the comfort of those words

with her, and she allowed herself to imagine that now that the fighting was over, order would be restored, and she might be able to get letters through. And barring that, she might at least be able to find out what had happened to Maxime. She needed to know before she moved on to the next phase of her life, and there was nothing wrong with needing that solace.

She wandered past the stalls to the cathedral, a graceful building that stretched to the heavens. Imposing in the daytime and ethereal in its beauty after nightfall. She tried to appreciate the beauty of the frosty-hued evening, but as she saw newly reunited couples walking arm in arm toward the market stalls, she couldn't help but feel her heart clench in envy. It wasn't that she begrudged any happiness to these people who had been so long separated from their loved ones. It was just that she wanted it for herself as well.

At the cathedral she walked near a particularly amorous couple and recognized the colors and feather motif of the scarf at the woman's neck. Similar to the one Maxime had given her. She felt a pang, thinking of the beautiful token she'd lost, though she knew it was a small sacrifice in the grand scheme of things. Perhaps one day she'd save up the money to replace it, but that would be many years off. She decided to leave the cathedral square for the warmth of her room. Perhaps she'd walked far enough that sleep wouldn't be quite so elusive. She veered around the affectionate couple to cross back to the YWCA, when the man called out to her.

"Mon dieu, c'est l'ange en bleu qui m'a sauvé!" Geneviève heard a voice behind her as she neared the cathedral.

She turned to see a vaguely familiar face. The man she'd bandaged in the trenches near Meuse during the ill-fated concert. He stood arm in arm with a beautiful woman who wore the scarf Maxime had given Geneviève at her throat. It was becoming on her, and she looked resplendently happy in his presence. The knot of envy in her gut loosened to allow room for the warmth of recognition.

"Well, this is far more pleasant than our last encounter. How's the violin playing?" Geneviève felt the corners of her lips pull up in a genuine smile.

"Slowly, as I heal, but I'm confident the movement will continue to improve with time, though I will never be as I was." He turned to his companion and traced a finger along her scarf. "Clara, this lovely woman is the reason I stand before you today. Her quick thinking and this scarf saved my life."

The woman, who'd been looking slightly bemused by her beloved's exchange with an unknown woman, broke into a smile and took Geneviève in her arms in a warm embrace. No words had to be said; she was grateful to have her love back and Geneviève was thrilled for them. The violinist from the trenches was alive, and she'd helped bring that about. No matter what misgivings she might have felt about participating in the war, at least she could hold on to that.

They introduced themselves and chatted about their plans now that the war was over. Roman would settle with Clara in Strasbourg, and they looked all too happy about the prospect of that life. Clara wound the scarf around her finger as she spoke, and Geneviève felt her eyes transfixed on it. The scarf had saved the life of the man this woman loved and had been a great gesture from the man Geneviève could not bring herself to forget. There was something of magic in that.

Perhaps noticing her gaze, Clara looked down at the colorful swath of silk at her neck. "I should give this back to you. It's rightfully yours, and I hope it brings you much happiness. I can't thank you enough for the loan of it."

And for saving Roman's life. That part didn't need to be said. She knew she was one of the lucky ones.

"I think it has become more precious to you than it could ever be to me," Geneviève protested.

"I have all I need right here." The woman gestured to her wounded soldier. She took the scarf and wrapped it around Geneviève's neck with a wag of her finger to end the discussion.

Geneviève was about to protest when another voice, this one English, interjected.

"What a lovely scarf." A woman approached them, her arm tucked in the elbow of a soldier—British from the look of his uniform. Like so many men, his body had been broken by the war and a cane helped him compensate for the loss of a leg.

Geneviève's eyes flittered to the woman's throat and noticed she wore a scarf in the same design. If she were English, it would make sense . . . Liberty would have been a household name for her. Geneviève realized it was the couple she'd noticed not long before. Her eyes hadn't been playing tricks on her.

"You share good taste with the lovely man who bought it for me," Geneviève said, trying with some success to keep the emotion from her voice.

"Oh, thank you," she said, color rising in her cheeks.

"Don't be modest," her beau prodded. "She designed the scarf herself. The first woman to have a design in production at Liberty. And I suspect she'll make quite the name for herself."

"No doubt of that," Roman said. "She's remarkably talented."

"A painter with the soul of a poet," Geneviève supplied. "Hope got us all through some terrible times, and I thought of the words you chose many times when I thought it was lost."

"I'm so glad it helped you," the woman said. "I know designing it was solace for me."

"I can't thank you enough." The words were barely a whisper as they left Geneviève's lips. There was no way to express it to her in a way that would do it justice, so she wouldn't be made a fool in the attempt.

Geneviève felt herself shrink as the two couples became acquainted. They had been fortunate enough to come through the war, if not unscathed, at least together. It seemed this wasn't the life she was meant to have, but the fates hadn't even been kind enough to give her some closure.

She excused herself from the happy little group and decided to find solace in her room with a cup of tea and her new book before attending midnight Mass at the cathedral. The familiarity of the service and the joy of the celebration would give her some much-needed peace. Though she tried to will the tears away, there was no keeping them at bay any longer. She managed to walk with her vision blurred and chilled streaks of grief on her cheeks.

She was halfway across the square when she felt a hand on her shoulder. "Christmas Eve is no time for tears."

The voice. It couldn't be.

She wiped her face and turned, blinking.

Maxime.

Like the British soldier and Roman, he had made a sacrifice to the war. His arm was in a sling, and he was still healing from cuts and bruises, even this many weeks after the ceasefire.

She tried to be mindful of his injuries but couldn't resist flinging herself into his arms. He was alive. He was well.

"I'm so sorry, my darling girl. I just received your letters last week. I'd been in a hospital, and everything got misdirected. I came here as soon as I was able. I was worried I'd have to go to Maine and track you down there."

Geneviève pulled back. "Would you really?"

"My love, I would have even if you hadn't written. I would have begged you to come back with me. I would have offered that Peter the pick of any woman in Aquitaine that I could persuade to take him, if that's what it took. But while I was lying in the hospital, all I could think about was you. I want to spend my life with you, and I know that honor and duty are the only things keeping you from wanting the same, which is only right. But life is far too precious to marry for such reasons."

There was a merriment in his eyes that belied that he was eternally glad he wouldn't be subjecting another woman to such a fate. "Not anymore. He's not my Peter any longer."

He wrapped her in his arms. "And I can't feel sorry for it. I will spend the rest of my days trying to give you the life you deserve if you'll have me."

Geneviève melted in his arms, but after a few moments, the realities of her life came back to her. "I have dreamed of this for months, Maxime, but my sense of duty isn't just limited to Peter. My family depends on me. I can't leave them behind to live a comfortable life in Avallon while they struggle."

"Geneviève, I could never claim to love you and leave your family to their own defenses. Anything they need, anything they want, they will have. And we can bring them to us and go to see them as much as we can."

Geneviève lifted her face to his and allowed him the sweetest, softest kiss she'd ever known. "This will be the happiest Christmas I will ever have."

"I accept your challenge, my love. I plan to make each one merrier than the one before."

"A tall order, but I hope you succeed. It's hard to think of being happier than I am in this very moment."

"I know how you feel, but I'm convinced that our best days are still to come."

They walked, arm in arm, without any particular direction. They made plans to petition for a special license as soon as the *mairie* opened after the holiday and to have a proper wedding in Avallon once Geneviève was discharged from her duties. All seemed well in the world until they happened upon a young French woman in uniform—a nurse—sobbing quietly as she wandered. Geneviève recognized the tenor of her pain, having felt it herself only hours before. She wasn't dressed for the snow and looked oblivious to the dropping temperatures.

"You've had bad news," Geneviève said. It wasn't a question. And there were far too many women who would be spending that Christmas in grief instead of celebration.

The nurse nodded. "My fiancé didn't survive the last push at the Somme. I just got the telegram this night."

"Cruel to get such news on such a day," Maxime said, patting the woman companionably on the shoulder. Geneviève wanted to offer her some words of comfort, but given that she had been spared the same fate, any words she had to offer would have seemed trite. There was only one thing she could offer.

Geneviève removed the scarf from her neck and wrapped it around the woman's and tied it in a stylish knot. "I think you need this more than I do. It will bring you good luck. Better still, it brings hope."

"Th-thank you," she mumbled. The nurse looked down at the scarf, a bit bewildered, as if she wasn't able to fully process what she saw.

They walked with her until a group of frantic women—her fellow nurses—rushed to collect her and wrapped her in a woolen cloak and offered their thanks for looking after her.

"I hope she'll be well," Maxime said, his brow furrowed in concern.

"She'll be all right," Geneviève pronounced as they watched the women shrink in the distance, a flourish of color at the woman's neck still visible. Geneviève ached for her but saw the love and concern her sister nurses had for her. She wouldn't shoulder her grief alone. "If she can find room in her heart to hope, she'll find her way."

Authors' Notes

Aimie K. Runyan

The American government promised to have the troops home in time for Christmas in 1918. As happens so many times in the course of a war, those promises could not be kept. I was always intrigued at the idea of a collection of stories about the aftermath of the Great War and the battle-weary servicemen and servicewomen trying desperately to find their way back home after a conflict that would forever change the geopolitical climate and irrevocably alter the lives of all involved in the war, both at the front and at home. I was delighted when the opportunity presented itself to do just that.

Now that I'm ten or so books into my career (and I thank my lucky stars I'm able to say as much), I think it holds true that authors do have sentimental favorites in their backlist. One of my special darlings was my fourth book, *Girls on the Line*, my first and only other foray into WWI fiction. I was captivated by the story of women who broke all societal expectations to serve their country, effectively blazing the trail for the WACs and WAVEs of the next generation who received far greater fanfare for their meritorious service. The operators, better known as The Hello Girls, were a vital element in General Pershing's strategy to help win the war for the Allied forces.

The universe sent me a surge of good luck when I was researching the brave American telephone operators in the First World War, not the least of which was having the good fortune to meet Mark Hough, the bold young attorney who won the case for the so-called Hello Girls when the operators were denied their veterans' benefits after the war. When I penned the final words to *Girls on the Line*, I felt a sense of loss, having to leave Ruby, Margot, and Andrew behind, as I had so loved my time with them.

The character Margot, the French Canadian who had never received a warm welcome in the States, was the inspiration for Geneviève. I always wished I could more closely examine her story and give her the happy ending she deserved, but sadly I didn't have the word count to devote to a secondary character. While Ruby from *Girls on the Line* is a child of privilege whose opportunities and choices are almost without limit, Geneviève comes from far different circumstances as the oldest daughter of an immigrant family. Serving meant her family would be forced to sacrifice comforts and necessities her phone company paycheck provided them. Ruby's service, while noble and equally dangerous, is an individual sacrifice of her time and safety, and it presents no financial hardship to her family beyond a social inconvenience for her socially scheming mama.

To explore the other end of the social ladder in the context of the noble phone workers was a challenging and rewarding exercise.

J'NELL CIESIELSKI

The Tudor-style facade now recognized as the Liberty store was commissioned in 1924 and designed by father and son architects Edwin Thomas Hall and Edwin Stanley Hall. Timber from the two nineteenth-century Royal Navy battleships HMS *Impregnable* and HMS *Hindustan* were used to create the storefront. The original deck timbers were used for the interior floor and were cleaned every night by former Royal Navy personnel.

In 1952 Colleen Farr, a freelancer for the company, was invited to set up an in-house design studio. This was a turning point in the company's history, as up until that point Liberty used only freelance designers or bought prints from other companies to create their unique style. Her fresh talent brought new life to the traditional cotton fabrics and introduced new geometric and abstract prints. Her instrumental work, along with others, placed Liberty at the forefront of textile design in Britain, which soon became known the world over.

My apologies if I have placed the tradition of mistletoe in a time and place where it may or may not have been used. My Francophile collaborator, Aimie, informs me that French kissing traditions usually involve New Year's and cheese. As this scene toward the end did not involve the use of fromage, I decided, *what the heck,* and just went for it. Besides, any excuse (fact or fiction) to snog is a good one. As my other collaborator, Rachel, says, it's fiction, so we should be able to make up a few things.

RACHEL MCMILLAN

As a reader and passionate fan of historical fiction, I best love books that inspire me as a bridge to the past. I hope that just this whiff or sense of the time period will move people to read more about the remarkable events that inspired this story.

I am most interested in ordinary people being called to extraordinary things and finding community and forged family in the midst of tragedy, and I hope you find hope in Clara and Roman's story.

Do writers truly insert themselves in books? My constant pursuit of music is by now long familiar to repeat readers, but visual art is not something often explored in my stories. Pieter

Bruegel the Elder's marriage of religion and art are of a constant fascination to me. During the height of our endless Toronto pandemic lockdowns, I found solace in living in his all-too-humane paintings. Ones of connection but also of grace. I was waiting for a moment to express how I was creatively bolstered by him in dark, isolating moments.

In December 1917, the Quatour à Cordes de l'Armée Belge en Campagne and the Orchestre Symphonique de l'Armée de Capmagne were created, consisting of soldiers who happened to be amazing musicians. They went on tours abroad from France and the United Kingdom for the benefit of wartime charities but also provided morale for the troops.

The last cavalry charge in Western Europe at Burkel was a skirmish between Belgian and German forces in October 1918. The world forever shifted then and warfare would never be the same.

I absolutely leapt at the opportunity to appropriate the Palais de royal Bruxelles as a hospital given my love of exploring it when I am in Brussels. Queen Elisabeth of Bavaria did initiate said appropriation as a military hospital of the Red Cross in WWI, but I played a little fast and loose with the dates.

Acknowledgments

AIMIE K. RUNYAN

I express my eternal thanks to Kimberly Carlton, our steadfast editor, for her keen insight; my delightful coauthors, J'nell Ciesielski and Rachel MacMillan, for their camaraderie; and my unparalleled agent, Kevan Lyon, for bringing this contract about for all three of us.

J'NELL CIESIELSKI

Thank you to Liberty of London for having such amazing scarfs that served as the inspiration for this collection. They are truly works of art, as is the store, which has been through myriad changes to keep up with the whimsy of the ever-changing world and its wonders. Being able to step back in time and read about all these pieces being cobbled together into a masterful work of art was truly remarkable for this history researcher's heart.

A huge thanks to Aimie and Rachel for not getting tired of me and for saying yes to another story! Somehow we pulled it off and finally got to add some Christmas magic. A special thanks to Kim, our wonderful editor who believed in us enough to go another round, and to Kevan Lyon for stepping in to help navigate the waters. And we certainly couldn't have done it without the support and creativity from the rest of the fabulous Muse team.

I couldn't do this without my home team. Bryan, Miss S, and even Daisy—y'all are always there for me and believing in me when some days all I want to do is bang my head against the keyboard.

RACHEL MCMILLAN

I would like to thank our magnificent editor, Kim Carlton, for her genius eagle eye. I would also like to thank Karli Jackson, who is a story whisperer of the highest order. Many thanks to Becky Philpott for working her magic. Savannah Breedlove, thank you so much! Margaret Kercher, Kerri Potts, and the rest of the amazing Harper Muse team, thank you for the continued support. Thank you to Amanda Bostic for putting up with my loquacious rambles. Thank you to Kevan Lyon for championing this story on behalf of our trio!

I would like to thank my powerhouse team, J'nell Ciesielski and Aimie Runyan, for our daily chats. I feel I am such a part of your worlds and I feel privileged to create with two women I learn so much from both personally and professionally! I would especially like to thank Jiji cat for being my muse cat even from Colorado!

Kate Quinn talks me off so many ledges on our unending text chats. Thank you!

Annette Cann, please know anytime there is a whiff of music in anything I write, it has you behind it.

Sonja Spaetzel, thank you for always listening to my creative trials and triumphs.

With special thanks to my parents, Gerald and Kathleen McMillan, for their unending support. Thank you to my siblings for having children who have names that suit novels *so* well: to Jared and Tobin and Maisie, Ellie and Kieran Patrick (our K.P.!), to Leah and Ken Polonenko, and little Roman and Adelaide.

Discussion Questions

1. Iris is an artist in a time period when women had few creative outlets—especially commercial and financially lucrative ones. Who are some of your favorite women artists, whether in print, design, or canvas?

2. "Nothing stirs up patriotism or promotes enlistment like parading around the glorious wounded," Rex says at one point in the book. Do you feel that pageantry and military parades are a worthy expression of a cause, or do they capitalize on the suffering of soldiers? Do you read this particular statement as sincere or ironic?

3. "This war cannot last forever. A brave new world is coming, and when it does, you're the woman to meet it head on." Can you think of other points in history when a conflict, however tragic, allowed for social change?

4. Iris feels it is her destiny to create new designs for Liberty and a book of her own work, and yet she feels her destiny is a long time coming. Can you think of a moment in life when you couldn't wait for the future to hurry up? How did it turn out?

5. "Inspiration comes from the most unlikely places," Iris tells Rex when they visit the Kamerzell House in Strasbourg.

Has there been a moment when you were inspired to do or create something seemingly out of nowhere?

6. During World War I, women's service was often the province of those from the privileged classes. Was this surprising to you? What did Geneviève's service, as a working-class woman, mean for her family? Why is serving such an appealing prospect to her?

7. Maxime and Peter are radically different characters with disparate value systems and worldviews. How do you see this, specifically with regard to their relationships with Geneviève?

8. What do you think the scarf represents to Geneviève, and why is it so precious to her beyond being a simple keepsake from a friend? Does she feel like it will be something she can wear back home?

9. Clara discovers herself when she makes a true friend. Annelise brings herself out of her shell amid the devastating circumstances that introduce her to the horrors of nursing and war. Can you think of someone who has brought you out of your shell?

10. Roman sees the world through music, and Clara through the art of Bruegel. By the end of the story, Clara is more attuned to music and the beauty of Roman's violin, and Roman sees Clara much as a painter like Bruegel views canvas. If you were to see the world through an artistic lens, which one would you choose?

11. Roman and Clara's romance is very much grafted by their connection in defying expectations. Roman feels guilty he is not called to fulfill the family occupation, whereas Clara, unable to save her mother, wants to serve others as best she can. Can you think of a time when you followed a path that took a turn beyond what you felt was expected of you?

12. Clara grows up in a world of stories. While her father tells her stories in the more conventional sense of legends and history, her mother's stories are in a tradition of baking and housekeeping. Can you think of the function of storytelling in your own family history? Do you find that your traditions are of a tactile sort such as sewing or baking or in the oral tradition of narratives passed down through generations?

About the Authors

Internationally bestselling author AIMIE K. RUNYAN writes to celebrate unsung heroines. She has written six historical novels (and counting!) and is delving into the exciting world of contemporary women's fiction. She has been a finalist for the Colorado Book Award, a nominee for the Rocky Mountain Fiction Writers' Writer of the Year, and a Historical Novel Society's Editors' Choice selection. Aimie is active as a speaker and educator in the writing community in Colorado and beyond. She lives in the beautiful Rocky Mountains with her wonderful husband, two (usually) adorable children, two very sweet cats, and a pet dragon.

Visit her online at aimiekrunyan.com
Instagram: @bookishaimie
Facebook: @aimiekrunyan
X: @aimiekrunyan
TikTok: @aimiekrunyan

Photo by Bryan Ciesielski

Bestselling author J'NELL CIESIELSKI has a passion for heart-stopping adventure and sweeping love stories while weaving fresh takes into romances of times gone by. When not creating dashing heroes and daring heroines, she can be found dreaming of Scotland, indulging in chocolate of any kind, or watching old black-and-white movies. She is a member of the Tall Poppy Writers and lives in Virginia with her husband, daughter, and lazy beagle.

jnellciesielski.com
Instagram: @jnellciesielski
Facebook: @jnellciesielski
Pinterest: @jnellciesielski

Photo by Agnieszka Smyrska
Smyrska Photography

RACHEL MCMILLAN is the author of *The London Restoration, The Mozart Code,* the Herringford and Watts mysteries, the Van Buren and DeLuca mysteries, and the Three Quarter Time series of contemporary Viennese romances. She is also the author of *Dream, Plan, Go: A Travel Guide to Inspire Independent Adventure.* Rachel lives in Toronto, Canada.

Visit her online at rachelmcmillan.net
Instagram: @rachkmc
Facebook: @rachkmc1
X: @rachkmc
Pinterest: @rachkmc

For more from the authors, don't miss *The Castle Keepers*!

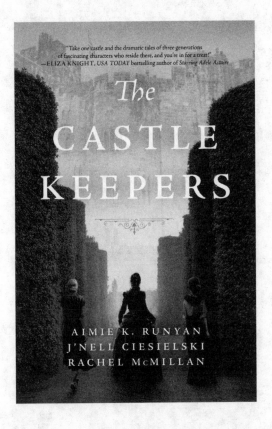

AVAILABLE IN PRINT, E-BOOK, AND DOWNLOADABLE AUDIO